a novel

Constellation

JENNIFER LOCKLEAR

Constellation
by
Jennifer Locklear

Published by Locklear Books
http://www.locklearbooks.com
info@locklearbooks.com.

Enchanted Publications

PUBLICATIONS
www.enchantedpublications.com
enchantedpublications@gmail.com.

Library of Congress Control Number: 2017914840

First Edition: October 2017
ISBN 0997860707

Dedication

For Morgan,
With all my love.
AJ

Constellation: A grouping of stars that make an imaginary picture in the sky.

chapter One

UPON WAKING, I became aware of the cotton sheets brushing against my naked skin. The sensation was so foreign and so tantalizing that it distracted me from the realization I'd fallen asleep in someone else's bed.

I lay on my side, facing the edge of the mattress with my back to the window. I lifted my eyelids and glanced into the reflection of the bedroom through a mirrored closet door. The reflected venetian blinds glimmered with brilliant pinpoints of sunlight.

It was impossible to ignore the radiant specks. I attempted to make sense of the randomness, searching for patterns and trying to detect images among the scattered fragments. In the midst of all the incandescence, I was surprised when my mind connected the individual dots and found the basic outline of a human form. Once discovered, the head, limbs and torso were visible.

The morning light that filtered into the room provided warmth and the air in the space was thick. Hours earlier, when everything was enveloped by darkness, we'd been rendered breathless by our erotic exertions. The lack of fresh oxygen in the room proved the entire thing wasn't a dream.

While recalling the encounter, I detected the weight of another body nearby. My gaze shifted across the mirror once again, this time coming to rest on the reflection of the beautiful man who was wide-awake behind me.

Jack sat behind me holding his tablet, his focus on the screen. He'd awoken before me but hadn't strayed far. His dark, wavy hair stuck out in odd shapes all over his head and he remained shirtless. The sun illuminated his toned, muscular chest in a brilliant display of fine masculinity. His olive complexion was entrancing and in complete contrast to my own pale appearance.

My consideration returned to the mirrored closet to inventory myself. In distinction to Jack, I appeared chaotic. My dark blond hair, which was long and fine, fanned about my pillow in tangled disarray. All traces of cosmetics, applied and maintained the day before, were gone, and I could see more than a few freckles in my reflection. My green eyes were almost as pale as my skin. And my body was more uncovered by the sheets than not.

Warmth pulsed through me as I remembered the tight grip of Jack's hands on my waist, positioning me in the center of the bed before moving his body over mine.

I beheld him once more, and my heart expanded upon seeing him. I willed him to turn toward me, but he didn't. I waited and yet his focus remained elsewhere. After a time, mild discouragement spread through me, its oppressive weight settling within my body. Attempting to combat the anxiety, I rolled over to face the window, and him.

I perceived the slightest hesitation of his fingers against the screen, the smallest brush of his long eyelashes against his cheek as he blinked, and the softest hint of an exhalation as more air escaped into the already stuffy room. I prepared to smile just as soon as he turned his eyes and settled their brownish depths on me.

But he didn't acknowledge me.

And I continued to wait, stubbornly insisting he initiate the morning ritual in whatever new reality we'd shaped for ourselves over the course of the night.

I can't recall how long I waited for him. It was long enough for me to become drowsy and allow my eyes to close. Perhaps it was a subtle act of defiance for when Jack decided he was ready to address me.

Suits him right.

I dozed long enough to distinguish a small passage of time upon reawakening. And there he was, still riveted to his tablet. And there I was, still laying on my side, waiting for his greeting.

Jack and I had worked together for close to a year, but had never socialized outside office functions. He'd competed against many other qualified candidates for his position and had agreed to relocate his family from Baltimore when offered the job. His marriage had fallen apart after he started at the company, and his wife had retreated to Maryland, presumably to return to a life she preferred. For reasons I couldn't comprehend she went alone, leaving Jack to look after their child. There was speculation at the office about the demise of his marriage, but no one had the nerve to discuss it with him. Myself included.

So much had changed in just one day. There was a great deal to consider, including how very little I knew of Jack Evans.

I looked back to the human shaped constellation on the window blinds. I'd drifted off long enough that the sunlight had shifted, and with interest I realized the head and shoulders of my discovery had vanished from sight, the outline demonstrating my increasing sense of invisibility.

I stretched my legs and my foot bumped into a solid form resting in the corner of the bed. The lump pushed back in response, and I realized it was the cat I'd been introduced to the night before. Jack must have let her in at some point. By the force of the shove back, there was little doubt I was messing with the cat's routine by occupying her side of the bed. I wasn't invisible after all. And I wasn't the only one feeling uneasy about the morning's events.

Provoked by the cat's assertiveness, I decided enough was enough. I was going to have to be the one to break the ice, and opened my mouth to speak, not even sure what words would come tumbling out. My rising voice was quelled, however, as a rapid series of knocks at the bedroom door broke the exasperating silence.

The noise startled me and I froze, knowing who was on the other side. It wasn't my place to lead the moment. It was his, and for the first time since I'd opened my eyes that Saturday morning, Jack turned his attention to something other than his tablet.

"Yes?" he answered with authority, although his voice held a tone of deep affection.

"It's me." The child's muffled response came from the other side of the door.

I remained immobile, convinced the slightest movement would reveal my existence to the little girl in a way neither I nor her father wanted.

"Do you need something? Are you all right?" he asked with a tone that somehow translated to an order for his seven-year-old daughter not to enter the room.

"Can I play the Wii?" The hope in his daughter's voice indicated she knew a golden opportunity when she heard one.

"Sure. Go ahead. I'll be out in a little bit."

"Okay!" Her already retreating footsteps and voice echoed from farther down the hallway. She wasn't going to risk missing a moment of bliss, and I was envious of her fearlessness.

With his daughter up and temporarily distracted, Jack placed his tablet on the bedside table and pushed the covers back.

Already unsure and vulnerable because of my state of undress, my dismay amplified when the blankets unveiled his body. At some point, perhaps whenever he let the cat into the room, he'd taken the opportunity to pull on a pair of light blue boxer briefs. The fact that he was somewhat clothed while I was naked under the sheets undid what little courage I'd gathered.

Perplexed, I watched him as he rose from the bed and walked around it. He disappeared from my line of sight, and I listened as he passed my side of the bed. He entered the adjoining en suite through an area he'd converted to his office after his wife moved out of the house. It was information I'd learned the evening before during my tour of his home.

He has to know I'm awake.

The sounds of his bare feet padding on the floor of the bathroom echoed before the door closed. The muffled resonances of water flowing into the sink drifted into the bedroom along with the familiar sounds of someone brushing his teeth. I pulled the covers up to cover my own mouth.

When Jack emerged from his bathroom, I heard the sliding of a closet door in the adjacent space, followed by the gentle clinking of hangers as he selected an outfit for the day. I couldn't stop myself from thinking how the closet across from my side of the bed must have been hers, and I wondered if I would be bold enough to look inside. It was in this moment, after sleeping with her ex-husband, that I first thought it important to know if it was empty.

My agitation increased along with my curiosity, but the rustling sound his pants made as he pulled them over his legs provided a welcome distraction. Moments later, he reemerged into my line of sight, dressed in slacks and a long sleeve shirt.

Jack paused at my corner of the bed, and I convinced myself he would say something—anything—to me. Despite my mounting confusion over the course of the morning, my heart swelled as a slow, relaxed smile began to spread across his features. He held the expression of contentment while anxiety emerged on mine.

He reached down toward my foot. I held my breath, remembering how the sensation of his fingers stroking my hair at midnight had ignited our mutual desire. Instead of touching me, however, he petted the damn cat, which squeaked her approval while I frowned and began to fume.

Wrong pussy, pal.

My patience was evaporating, but I continued to watch him in silence, knowing anything said or done in that particular moment would disrupt his entire household. Jack's lack of acknowledgment was undoing me. I wanted to yell. I wanted to cry. I wanted to throw something, but instead I remained frozen by shock.

I coached myself to calm down, and as I tried to listen to my own advice, Jack ceased petting the cat. He moved to sit on the opposite corner of the bed with his back to me. Jack leaned forward to pull open a drawer of the dresser sitting across from him and grabbed something. His misguided focus took hold once again and I watched in total frustration as he held his socks out to his side and studied them. He soon changed his mind, putting the socks back into the drawer and selecting a more satisfying pair.

As he bent forward to put them on, he didn't utter a sound.

Not a hum. Not a whistle. Not a breath. Nothing.

The task done, he stood back up and strode toward the bedroom door. I was angry but yet enthralled. Jack's confident posture and his graceful movements were the very things that caught my attention in the first place, and I couldn't help but admire them.

He opened the door, walked into the hall and closed it. He didn't even pause long enough to see that the door had drifted open, leaving a small but distinct gap between it and the doorjamb.

As a result, I was able to catch a glimpse of the hallway. If Jack's daughter happened to bound by, she would be able to see a confounded and naked stranger in her father's bed. The possibility should have compelled me to get up, but my bafflement held me in place.

As I began to weigh my few available options, I peered at the window, distracted from my dilemma. The sunlight had changed once more. In fleeting moments like these, it astounded me how quickly the earth spun through space.

My sunlit human companion had disappeared in the span of just a few minutes, and the relocated spots of light had already created an innovative image in its place. The new constellation was in the shape of a cat.

"Son of a bitch." I shook my head and sighed, accepting my humiliating defeat.

Spurred into action, I pushed back the covers, swung my legs over the edge of the bed and scooped my discarded shirt from the floor. I also made sure to avoid my own reflection in his ex-wife's mirrored closet door while seeking refuge. Holding the wrinkled garment against my body, I raced into the master bathroom and took great care to close and lock the door behind me.

It wasn't the notion of Jack's ex-wife I was desperate to avoid.

Simply put, I was the last thing I wanted to look at.

chapter Two

SHUT AWAY inside Jack's private bathroom, I untangled my blouse, thrust my arms into the sleeves and pulled it over my shoulders. My fingers trembled as I buttoned up the front of my blouse, and I pulled the hem as far down as it would go, consumed by discomfort.

I looked down to make sure my body was covered and found my head too heavy to lift back up. My long hair fell forward, draping my face, and my eyes welled up as I stared at my feet. I didn't know how to escape Jack's home without a confrontation of some kind.

I was determined not to cry until I was all alone and took some deep breaths to keep the tears from spilling out. I welcomed the relief when the effort only took a few moments. My plan was simple — gather up the rest of my clothes, get dressed and get the hell out of Jack's house. I raised my head and opened the bathroom door.

I stomped back into the bedroom with determination and found my things. With the exception of my panties, which I pulled back on, I threw the rest of my clothes onto the bed. Upon reaching for my skirt, I froze in mid-grab. Jack stood in the bedroom doorway, holding a bath towel. True to the morning's form, he didn't speak a word and his sudden appearance stunned me.

Jack looked uncertain, even hurt, and clenched the towel in his hands.

It was the first sign of nervousness I'd ever seen in him, but I did my best to keep it to myself. I clutched my skirt while my bra, garter belt, stockings and shoes remained unclaimed on his duvet.

"Do you need to be somewhere?" Jack's baritone voice was calm, but quiet. He closed the bedroom door behind him and then held still, as though preparing for an onslaught.

I narrowed my eyes at him. "No." My answer was technically true, but the word felt like a lie as it escaped my lips.

Jack studied me and then softened his expression as he spoke. "Good. I'd like to make you breakfast."

There was no mistaking the gesture. His offer was genuine, sweet and unexpected. It confused the hell out of me, and the strength of my glare withered with a few surprised blinks. The sudden shift in my emotional state was so powerful I looked away.

From the corner of my eye, I noticed Jack tilt his head. The action compelled me to look at him once again.

As we both regained our stances, he continued, "To be honest, what I'd love to do is bring you breakfast in bed, but ..."

Jack looked over his shoulder, toward the door. In another room, the sounds of a child playing a video game carried down the hall. When he turned back to me, he shrugged and offered a tight grin.

My foot tapped as I considered if this was a line of bullshit, but it was a useless endeavor. From the times I'd observed Jack and his daughter together, it was clear he was a devoted father. He was a man who took his responsibility as a parent seriously. My anger dissipated. Whatever we thought would happen the evening before, the consideration of holding an "About Last Night" discussion hadn't occurred to either of us. If it had, I would have gone home before things went too far.

My shoulders relaxed in the face of Jack's predicament. "Your daughter. Of course. I understand."

"Will you stay? For breakfast?"

The insistence I glimpsed within his dark brown eyes surprised me. "What about your daughter? I don't want to cause trouble."

"Don't worry about her. It's fine."

"Aren't you worried about her reaction to me?"

"No. Not at all."

I arched a suspicious brow.

"I'm not worried because she'll be fine. If we don't make a big deal about this, she won't think twice about it."

"Aren't you worried about what she might say to her mother?"

My mind raced to cover all the bases and the words were out of my mouth before I realized their potential sting.

Jack's mouth set into a hard line.

I had struck a raw nerve and despite my earlier frustrations, I felt terrible over my lack of consideration. I held my breath.

"That won't be an issue. I'll speak to her mother before she'll have a chance to," he said with a tone of terseness that didn't surprise me.

I counted to three before moving forward with the conversation. "Sorry, Jack. I don't want to complicate things for you. I can be careful. Discreet."

He sighed and shook his head. "I know that. Don't worry about any of this. We'll all be fine."

I nodded and he approached me.

Jack held the towel out, his dark eyes insistent. "Please stay for breakfast. I'll cook and inform my daughter we have a houseguest. You can take a shower or a bath, whichever you prefer. Take your time. Join us when you're ready. Share a meal with us, and then we'll go from there," he said with a voice thick with kindness.

Jack was a master at closing deals, and I was an easy sell. After the incredible, unexpected night we'd spent together, I was frantic at the thought of all our progress unraveling in the light of day. It wasn't usually in me to acquiesce, but Jack Evans was not your usual man.

"A shower and a meal would be nice," I confessed.

He smiled with more than a hint of shyness. "Great. I'll let you get started."

I accepted the proffered towel as he leaned forward and kissed my forehead. My body tingled under the sensual touch of his lips.

"Take your time," he repeated in a whisper, his warm mouth against my skin.

The words were still deliciously caressing my face as he retreated from the room.

chapter Three

FOR THE second time that morning, I wandered into Jack's bathroom in a stupor. My head spun as I tried to reconcile the aloof man I woke up to with the one who just offered me breakfast. His behavior this morning and the evening before, for that matter, was not what I was accustomed to from Jack Evans.

Bringing myself back to reality, I glanced between the large Jacuzzi tub and the impressive walk-in shower. I was so tired and emotional that making a simple choice between the two options proved difficult. The thought of a bubble bath was tempting, but one look around the man's bathroom told me the essential soaps would be difficult to come by. The tub would take a while to fill and much longer to enjoy. With Jack's daughter moving about, time wasn't on my side. So I peered into the stone tiled space and decided the chrome, square, rainfall shower head would suffice.

After turning on the water, steam drifted through the room. I inhaled in anticipation and the all-consuming eagerness to surrender myself to the moment surprised me. I removed my shirt and panties and dropped them to the bathroom floor.

I adored hot showers and smiled as I remembered how an irate former lover informed me that my showers were hot enough to boil a lobster. Early in my love life, I realized my preference for such showers ensured I would take them alone. That was fine with me, and this particular morning was no exception. I needed a few minutes to collect myself.

After testing the temperature with my fingers, I stepped into the shower and immersed myself under the rhythmic pulse of water. I moaned as my skin absorbed the heat, noting but not caring how the sound approximated that of my orgasms the night before. The shower was that damn good.

As if to entice me further, the subtle scent of Jack's soap drifted up from the shower. With delight, I picked up the round white bar, cupping it with both hands, and held it underneath my nose. After taking a deep whiff of its honeyed fragrance, I guided it along my body, to explore as much of my skin as possible. Soon, the essence of that gorgeous man surrounded me and I was aroused once more.

In that glorious moment of total privacy, there was one thought I could not deny. Sex with Jack had been surreal, yet magnificent. As I washed with his soap, I grew intoxicated by the combination of the vivid memory of our connected bodies and the lingering sense of his touch inside the most intimate part of my being. Although the overall effect was heady, an uncharacteristic calmness swept through me.

I relaxed my muscles, closed my eyes and let my head droop until my chin brushed the top of my chest. Then despite my better judgment, I thought less about the sex and more about the man.

What had taken place the night before was all so complicated, and yet it wasn't. There was no doubt my mind would be spinning for some time. The morning before, I would've never guessed we'd end up as lovers by the end of the day. Now, there was no way for me to know if we would remain lovers once I left his house.

The thought of losing whatever this was between us weighed heavy on my mind. I shook my head and sighed, pushing the debilitating consideration as far away as possible. Easier said than done. I fell into a trance, playing through several potential scenarios of what could develop once I left the sanctuary of Jack's bedroom. My fears ran unchecked, and I hid inside the shower until the water turned cold, forcing me to give up my temporary haven.

chapter Four

AS I emerged from the bathroom, a series of rapid knocks, once again, sounded on the bedroom door. Figuring that Jack had already mentioned the houseguest to his daughter, I decided to take the risk.

"Yes?" At best, my voice was timid and I flinched at the sound of it.

"Can I come in?" Heide asked.

I was clad in just my towel and still dripping from the shower, but I answered in a most unexpected way.

"Um. Sure. Hold on a sec though."

"Okay."

I patted my skin dry and pulled most of my clothes back on before turning my attention to the bed. Jack's stubborn cat still occupied the corner as I threw the blankets over my side. It was a desperate attempt to make it appear as though the only person to have slept there was her father. Lacking the time to bother with my stockings and garter belt, I stashed them underneath a pillow.

Satisfied with the appearance of both the bed and myself, I said, "Come in."

Before I finished speaking the words, the door flew wide open and stopped just short of hitting the wall. I was unprepared for the energetic blond-haired girl who crawled into the room on her hands and knees, and sported her father's huge grin.

"Hi," she greeted me while performing a somersault.

"Hello." My tone was cautious as Jack's cat scampered from the bed and bolted into the hallway.

"I want to hang out here for some reason," she announced after popping back up on her feet.

"Ah," was my less than clever response.

"It's a quiet space. I can read in here." She was searching for a valid reason to linger in her father's room, so I decided not to point out the fact she wasn't carrying a book.

"I'm hungry. Are you hungry for breakfast?" Heide stopped moving and tilted her head to the side, much like her father did earlier in the morning.

I nodded. "I think your dad is making breakfast. At least that's what he told me."

"He was, but now he's on the phone. With Craig."

I paused, allowing myself to imagine Jack's phone conversation with Creepy Craig.

"Oh," I muttered.

"Yeah. He's going to be a while." I grinned at her quick and accurate assessment of the situation.

"My name is Heide," she told me.

"That's a great name. Much better than mine."

"What's yours?"

"Kathleen."

"Hmm." Heide's response was noncommittal and I adored it. It was an avoidance tactic Jack had used on several occasions at the office.

"What do you make for breakfast?"

I shrugged and frowned. "I'm not good at making breakfast," I admitted. "I just pick something up at Dutch Bros."

Heide scratched her head. "What's that?"

"It's a coffee place."

"Oh." Heide furrowed her brow in confusion. "You don't go to Starbucks?"

"No," I confessed and shook my head. "I don't like Starbucks."

"My dad loves Starbucks. We go there." She looked out the door and down the hallway before making a confession of her own. "But I don't like it either."

I did my best to stifle a laugh before saying, "You should ask him to take you to Dutch Bros."

Heide thought about this before responding, "Okay."

Jack's voice interrupted our banter. "All right, Craig. Listen, I have some breakfast to cook. We can finish this discussion on Monday."

Heide and I glanced at one another in mutual understanding while Jack finished up his phone call.

"Have a good weekend, Craig. Bye."

"Never mind. My dad can get us breakfast now. Bye." Heide bounded out as quickly as she had somersaulted in.

As soon as Heide disappeared, my thoughts drifted to Jack's conversation with Creepy Craig. Craig had never had the balls to call me on a Saturday morning over anything. Robert would have—

Oh shit!

"Damn it!" I dashed around Jack's bed. Picking up his tablet, I was dismayed by the time on the display screen. Robert was expecting me for breakfast and I'd forgotten about him. But it was far too late. Robert would be pissed by now. He'd demand an explanation and there was no way he could know I'd spent the night with Jack. It would make things worse between us. The thought would infuriate Robert, which meant I would need to ask Jack for his silence even though he had just told me he would inform Heide's mother of our situation.

I remained rooted to the spot, pondering what to do next. Unsure and nervous, my stomach twisted into knots so tight that I was sure eating anything would prove impossible. I was overtaken by a compulsion to freshen my breath, and given a task by my useless and dazed brain, I turned on my heel and went in search of Listerine.

A few minutes later, I squared my shoulders and entered the hall, more or less ready to see what else the Evans house had to offer me.

I managed to walk all of three steps before Heide jumped out in front of me from the doorway located next to her father's bedroom. I stopped in my tracks to avoid running into her.

"I just read Can It Rain Cats and Dogs?" she announced with enthusiasm. "It can't really. But it can rain fishes and frogs," she concluded before bolting back into her room.

chapter  Five

WHEN I entered the kitchen, Jack was busy at the stove. He smiled and pointed to the chrome Keurig gourmet coffee maker on the counter. One glance at the machine, and I understood I was out of my element when it came to Jack's cooking skills. Here was a shining example of how he was an actual adult while I was still trying to find my own place at the grown-ups' table.

"I started some coffee for us. I assume that's what you're drinking in those windmill cups. Starbucks okay?"

Ugh.

"That's fine," I fibbed, not wanting to insult my sexy host. "Thank you."

With caution, I took a seat at the breakfast bar and watched Jack assemble and prepare several ingredients by the stove: olive oil, mushrooms, onion, green pepper, ham, egg whites and rye bread.

"I'm making omelets. Heide has a soccer game later this morning so I need to fuel her up."

Despite my certainty I wouldn't be able to eat a thing, Jack's choice of breakfast was perfect. "Sounds good."

"I hope Denver omelet is all right. It's her favorite and I need her to eat."

"Perfect. Thanks."

"I make a sandwich out of it to make it more appealing to Heide, but it's healthier than it looks." Jack winked and I all but combusted, watching the man in action.

Each movement he made was effortless and self-assured, and as he worked with the various ingredients, his forearms held a newfound fascination for me. No one had ever made breakfast more alluring.

My mouth salivated, but I wasn't sure if it was because of the aroma of the food or the man cooking it. "I can't wait to try it," I managed to utter.

As Jack poured our coffee, a rush of discomfort invaded my heart. I was still confused about his earlier behavior in the bedroom and feeling guilty about my reaction to it. The pained look on his face when he brought me a towel was now seared in my memory. Probably forever. Several minutes later, he was preparing me fresh coffee (albeit Starbucks) and a nutritious, homemade meal. I was at a loss. I didn't know what to say.

"Cream? Sugar?" Jack's continued good manners interrupted my brooding.

"Cream is fine. No sugar," I answered, knowing I needed to say so much more. I waited until Jack set the cup in front of me and then made eye contact.

"I'm sorry," I began. "I'm a bit of a mess this morning."

His gaze roamed over my face and hair, and he broke out into a spectacular smile, exposing his dimples. Jack's brown eyes were as soft and warm as his voice. "I didn't notice."

Jack's comment told me one thing. He'd misunderstood me. Before I could correct him, however, he went back to cooking. I rolled my eyes in frustration, sensitive to the fact that I was wearing no cosmetics. My hair was dry but untamed, and I was also wearing yesterday's clothing.

Sure, Jack. Sure you didn't notice.

Irritated, I sat back and sipped my coffee, savoring the warmth but not the taste.

A random laugh emitted from his daughter's bedroom, prompting me to change the subject.

"How does Heide like soccer?"

His back to me, Jack kept his attention focused on his cooking. "Well enough. She has a lot of fun. She's no all-star, but I enjoy watching her out on the field." There was a hint of laughter in his answer.

I smiled. "She found me and introduced herself while you were on the phone with Craig."

Jack glanced at me but didn't appear concerned. "Oh? How did that go?"

"Fine, I think. She knocked on the door, and I made sure things were decent before I let her in."

Jack nodded, then focused on the stove. "Good."

My brow furrowed at his one word response. Did Jack mean it was good that Heide and I had hit it off without a hitch? Or was it good that I had hidden evidence of my sleeping in his bed? A small part of me wanted to ask for clarification, but the larger part of me was terrified of Jack's answer.

"What did Craig want?"

Jack shrugged, but with his back to me I couldn't read his expression. "The usual."

"How did he manage to get your number?" I was legitimately curious.

"A few have asked for it. He was one of them. Little did I know what trouble I was asking for there."

That was an understatement. "You're nice. I don't give out my number."

Jack turned. "Not even to Robert?"

At the mention of Robert's name, my mood sunk even lower.

"He's the exception to the rule," I mumbled, taking another sip and looking away from the sensual chef at work.

After a few moments of silence, Jack prepared a plate and set it down in front of me.

I glimpsed up at him in surprise. "Don't you want Heide to eat first?"

He shook his head. "The game isn't for a couple of hours yet. These days, enjoying breakfast with other adults is a rarity."

Jack retreated from the breakfast bar and opened the silverware drawer.

"Are you sure?" I asked as he offered me a knife and fork.

He gestured to my plate with a nod. "It will give us a few minutes of quiet time."

As Jack prepared his own food, I sliced my sandwich into smaller sections and took my first bite. "Oh. Wow," I uttered, my mouth still full. "This is delicious."

Jack sat down next to me, satisfied and unsurprised by my reaction. His confidence in the kitchen was evident. "Thank you. I'm glad you like it."

I wiped my lips with a napkin before speaking again. "You need to teach me how to cook."

What did I just say?

I paused, sheepish. "Sorry. That was presumptuous of me."

"Not at all," he answered, primed to take his first bite. "You don't cook?"

"Not much," I said with embarrassment. "It's just me. I'm too lazy to cook for just me."

"Didn't you ever cook for Robert?"

My hand dropped down in reflex, and my unused fork clattered against my plate. My face tightened as my anxiety crept up another notch.

Jack paused before mumbling. "Sorry. I was just trying to make small talk."

I inhaled and sat up straight, my posture rigid. The tone of my voice was chilled as I responded. "Do you really want to talk about me and Robert?"

"Sorry," he repeated, his expression softening along with his voice. Perhaps he was apologizing for more than just the mention of Robert, but as touchy as the moment was, I decided not to pursue that theory.

We finished our meal in relative silence, each of us unable to find a way past our most recent exchange. A perfect demonstration of how little we knew each other. As soon as Jack finished his breakfast, he returned to the stove to prepare his daughter's meal.

He was the one to break the ice and did so with a surprising declaration. "I was going to ask if you'd like to come to Heide's game, but I don't know if that's something you'd want to do."

I was awestruck. Minutes earlier, I'd planned my escape, certain I needed to avoid an argument. Instead, he was treating me so nice. My defenses lowered once again. "That's sweet of you to ask, but I suspect that my showing up to a little league game in yesterday's work clothes would send the rumor mill into overdrive. No need to ruin your unblemished reputation in this burg. Besides, knowing my luck I'd run into one of Robert's friends and neither of us wants that."

Jack turned and studied me. I held his gaze, communicating that my remarks were serious.

"Maybe another time, then."

As far as Jack was concerned, he hoped we would have another morning date. I wasn't sure what to think about the possibility, but appreciated the sentiment.

"Maybe," I replied.

Jack moved back to the breakfast bar and me. He paused across from me, placed his hands on the countertop and leaned forward. I noticed how his chest muscles hardened against the fabric of his shirt, and I couldn't look away as he addressed the elephant in the room.

"Was everything all right this morning?"

I should have brought my eyes up to his, but I was too fascinated by his chest. "What do you mean?"

"It seemed like you were upset. Or in a hurry. Or both."

I shook my head, perhaps with too much adamancy. "Things are fine."

I looked up and noticed his expression tighten. He didn't believe me, but after my appalling behavior throughout the morning, the last thing I wanted to do was complain about rudeness. More than anything, I yearned for the comfort of his arms around me, but knew the time for that had come and gone.

"I should get going," I blurted. "Let you and Heide get on with your weekend."

"You don't have to rush."

Why are you so nice to me?

"Your shower was great, but I think I'd like to go home and get changed."

"I was hoping we could talk about things," he pressed.

I set my elbow upon the countertop and placed my chin into the palm of my hand. I needed to know what Jack had to say, whether it was going to crush me or not. The anxiety of the entire morning blossomed into full-blown fear. I was too scared to say anything, so I waited.

Patience, Kathleen. Strength, Kathleen.

Jack seemed to weigh his next words.

"Perhaps it's too soon for either of us to know what's happening here," he began. "I don't want you burdened by obligation. What I do want to say is, I don't pursue casual sex. I've never been good at that."

I remained still.

"I've always liked you, Kathleen. Right from the moment we met."

I nodded, but offered nothing more.

"Even if this doesn't work out for us, I know we'll still have to work with one another, and I'd hate to lose that connection."

His words filled me with tremendous relief. I tilted my head to meet his eyes as my own welled up in response to him.

"I like you, too, Jack. Last night was amazing, but it might be a good idea to take off the rest of the weekend. We both should let our emotions settle and then think."

"Last night was more than amazing," Jack stated with conviction. "But I don't have an adequate word to describe it yet. Give me time."

He smiled, and my cheeks reddened in reciprocation. He seized the opportunity.

"Are you sure I can't see you tomorrow? We could meet somewhere. Come Monday, we're back at the office, and then we'll be busy with other things. The next thing you know, a whole week will have gone by with nothing to show for it."

I considered Jack's request and was tempted, but knew I had other business to attend to. With reluctance, I shook my head.

"I'll need to deal with Robert first. I've missed something by being here this morning. I'm going to get an earful as it is."

"All right."

I wanted to show good intentions and good will so I tried to lighten the moment with a suggestion. "May I have access to your phone number? You let Craig have it. You may as well let me."

He grinned. "Of course."

Satisfied this was the best moment to make my exit from Jack's house, I stood up and wandered into the living room to retrieve my purse. He followed behind me. I pulled out my phone and was dismayed to see a message on my screen. I had four missed calls and just as many voice messages waiting for my attention. I didn't have to look to see who'd been attempting to get a hold of me. Robert was nothing if not persistent.

I could deal with only one man at a time, so I removed the alerts from my display, opened my contacts and handed the phone to Jack. Once he finished keying in his number, he handed it back to me, brushing his fingertips against mine and sending a shiver of excitement throughout my entire body.

"I'll go get my phone," he offered.

"No need," I replied, shaking my head for no discernible reason. I uttered my response without consideration, more like a reflex than a conscious choice, but the words were out of my mouth. There was no taking them back. I averted my eyes to the wall to keep my composure intact. My nerves were raw and my grip on my emotions was tenuous at best. When I spoke again my voice was lower and the words were heavy as they left me. "I'll text you when I get home so you know I made it there."

Jack sighed, but nodded. He knew me well enough from the office to know that once I said something, I was stubborn enough to hold my ground. "Do you promise?"

"Yes."

Jack exhaled with resignation and turned toward the front door. I didn't know whether I wanted to leave his house or not, but I wasn't sure what else to do. I followed his lead, but did so with a measured pace.

Jack grasped the knob, but then turned and positioned himself between me and the door.

I paused and looked up into his brown eyes, waiting to see what he would say to me in farewell.

His eyes fascinated me, but now that I could study them without trepidation, I was enthralled. Their almond shape complemented the dark color and while they expressed warmth and kindness, no matter what the circumstances, there was no mistaking the telltale tinge of sadness.

His face was smooth with no noticeable scars or blemishes, and although his features were soft, he exuded a great deal of character and complexity in his expressions. His nose was long, but neither narrow nor broad — just perfect. Despite his dark hair, eyes and complexion, his lips were a rosy pink, and I longed to trace them with my fingertip as I stared at them.

He blinked and his gaze shifted from my face, downward. As he lifted his free hand, my breath hitched in my throat. He traced the V-neck of my blouse with the pad of his finger delicately skimming my chest. My skin tingled underneath his light touch, and my nipples reacted to his close proximity, begging for him to reclaim them once more.

His eyes were riveted to the exposed skin of my upper body and after an eternity he whispered, "Like porcelain. I wish I could have enjoyed your body more in the light."

I watched his Adam's apple as he swallowed. My mind was devoid of coherency. I couldn't react, and it didn't matter what I would have said to him because Jack's hand released the handle just as his other grasped me. He pushed my blouse aside to reveal my bra and leaned in, bowing his head and pressing his lips to the top of my uncovered breast.

I arched my back toward his eager mouth, and his arm slid around my waist. His grip tightened as he pulled me closer. Jack's breath was warm, and as his mouth traveled along the inner curve of my breast, the cautious flick of his tongue on my skin produced a corresponding warm ache between my legs.

I plunged my hands into his hair and pulled his head upward. Jack didn't hesitate as he covered my mouth with his. I opened to him and moaned when our tongues reunited. It had been hours since our last kiss, and the experience of touching Jack was still so new. The thrill of his lips on mine evoked nothing short of an earth-shattering response in me.

I forgot everything that was complicated about our situation and enjoyed the blissful reconnection of our mouths. Time barely moved, and yet, I grew excited with each passing second. I pressed my body against Jack's, hungry for him. I was grateful that my skirt was just loose enough to cooperate with my deepest desires.

All too soon, he retreated. His eyes met mine once more as he pulled my blouse back into place. When Jack opened his mouth to speak, his voice was calm and thoughtful despite the unmistakable desire in his expression.

"Thank you for last night, Kathleen."

chapter

AROUSED AND confused after those last moments at Jack's house, I navigated the streets of my hometown of Bend, Oregon, grateful that I knew them well enough to function on autopilot. I paused at a stoplight and shook my head in an effort to clear it, taking a few moments to reorient myself to my surroundings.

Bend was located in high desert country, on the east side of the Cascade mountain range. Its proximity to the mountains made it a mecca for outdoor enthusiasts, and it was an easy getaway from the Pacific Northwest's metropolitan areas. I knew transplants from Portland, Seattle, Boise, even San Francisco, and although these newer residents longed to be away from urban life, they didn't want to sacrifice their cosmopolitan habits. Bend was known just as much for its gourmet food and impressive selection of microbrews as it was for its gorgeous setting.

And my father had seen it all coming at the opportune moment. The first decision he had made upon being named CEO by my retiring grandfather was to relocate the headquarters of the family business, Aurora Advertising, from the heart of Portland to the heart of Oregon. The choice was risky and caused my grandfather concern, but the unorthodox gamble paid off. My father had been in charge of the agency since I was in preschool, and even though I had been born in Portland, my childhood memories of the Rose City were of visits there to see my grandparents.

Although I was now in my mid-thirties, my father showed no signs of slowing down in his work, but it was understood that in another five or ten years he would be ready for retirement himself. So now he was working hard to ensure that I could lead the successful firm into its third generation.

I pulled my car into my parking space at the condominium complex I called home, gathered my belongings and made my exit from the vehicle. I moved with purpose, determined to get from my car to my apartment without running into any of my neighbors while in a state of morning-after dishevelment. I didn't need word getting back to Robert.

Somehow, I managed to make it inside undetected and laughed with exhausted giddiness as I collapsed on my sofa. I sat for a few minutes, trying to relax in my own home, but found it difficult. There was nothing else to do but yield to the understanding that something fundamental had changed in my life since I'd left the condo the morning before.

Fatigue began to overwhelm my senses, so I decided to reward myself with a bubble bath just as soon as I completed one final chore. I pulled out my phone and opened a new text message conversation, pausing as I figured out where to begin. I formed my opening sentence and typed as the rest of my words tumbled out. "I'm home. Hope things go well at Heide's game. Thanks again for breakfast and the evening that led up to it. I'll see you Monday."

I sent it off before I could reconsider a single syllable. I set the phone down, stood up and stretched my arms over my head as I turned to make my way to the bathroom. Before I made it to the hallway, my phone issued a ping.

The man is far too good with his fingers.

Turning on my heel, I marched with purpose back to the coffee table and retrieved my phone. Sure enough, there was a message from Jack Evans. "I'm glad I have your number now. Thank you. It's too bad I have to wait until Monday. Tomorrow is going to be a long day."

I was tempted to answer back with a flirtatious comment. Instead I set the phone down and began undressing as I walked away. By the time I reached my bedroom, the only thing I had on was a smile.

The bubble bath was wonderful and helped me set the agenda for the rest of my weekend.

After luxuriating in my oversized tub, I indulged in a self-spa treatment, donned my favorite pajamas, selected a book or two to place on my bedside table, turned the television on for a bit of company and settled into my king-sized bed.

Then, my phone rang from its place in the living room and my muscles tensed.

It was Robert. There was a certain impatient tone that radiated from my cell phone when it was him. I was never surprised to see his name on the illuminated display, demanding my immediate attention. I wanted to pretend it hadn't rung, but things were bad between us. I needed to eat crow and make the peace.

With a grimace, I jogged to the living room and answered the call.

"Hello." I braced for Robert's response by pressing my feet to the floor.

"Hi." There was a long pause.

"How's it going?" I responded, still defiant and feisty after my time with Jack.

"Where were you this morning?" Robert's voice was tight, controlled. I abandoned my stalling methods.

"I'm sorry." There was no way I was going to be honest about my whereabouts, so an apology seemed as good a place as any to begin.

"Hmm." I hated when Robert didn't offer his thoughts. I hated trying to guess which land mine to avoid, so I resorted to some version of the truth.

"I didn't sleep much last night. Then I wasn't well this morning." My voice was quiet and nervous, and it pissed me off that I worried so much about this conversation and his opinion.

"I called you," Robert huffed. "I left messages."

I rubbed my temple as I answered. If things were going to blow up with Robert, this was the moment it would happen. The shorter my remarks, the better.

"I just picked up my phone and discovered that a few minutes ago."

There was no response. I couldn't even hear Robert breathing on the other end of the call. Rather than allowing the silence to drag on, I moved the phone call along with the sincere hope that perhaps it would be over with soon.

"To be honest, I don't feel up to anything. I was just about to go back to bed."

"What's wrong?" Robert still sounded pissed, but there was a slight shift in his tone. It was a signal I knew well—it meant he'd decided not to pick a fight with me after all, but in a tone that indicated his intention to dominate the conversation.

I stuck to my chosen scheme of evasion, realizing Robert wasn't interested in me and my goings on. He was only concerned about how much I'd affected his morning.

"I'm tired. I just need to rest."

After a few uncomfortable beats of silence, Robert spoke again.

"You coming over tomorrow?"

Fuck no.

"No," I said. "I'll see you on Monday. I'll be better by then."

"I hope so."

I sighed before I uttered my next words. I needed things to be calm when I did see him again. "I'm sorry I missed breakfast. I didn't expect … The whole thing just slipped my mind."

"Okay," Robert acquiesced, satisfied that I hadn't ignored him on purpose.

There was, however, another long pause as he waited for me to say something else. What on earth that was supposed to be was lost on me. My patience with this awkward conversation was waning, and I decided it was time to end it.

"I'm going to go lay down again. I'll talk to you later."

"See you," Robert answered.

"Bye," I responded and hung up before he could stop me from doing so. A huge weight lifted from my shoulders as I realized I now had the rest of the weekend to myself.

I carried my phone back to the bedroom. Phone calls with Robert were terrible. It was easier to have a conversation with him in person because at least there were distractions to seize upon during the inevitable lull in discussion. But on a call, there was nothing but his words and mine to focus on, and the severe disconnect between us was never more evident than when we were connected to each other's phones.

I fucking hated phones and began to glare at mine as I fought the urge to fling it out the window.

But then I remembered Jack's text.

I opened his message up once again and re-read it several times. Each time that I did, a rare moment of serenity overtook me. I even considered calling Jack. The idea was so tempting it proved almost impossible to resist. I even began dialing him, but then opted out.

I was now as excited for Monday as Jack appeared to be, and it was the anticipation of being near Jack again that would get me through having to deal with Robert in person.

I set the phone down and returned to my lounging, the call with Robert set aside and forgotten.

My thoughts about Jack were so much more pleasant.

chapter

Seven

"**HEY K**-Dog!" My favorite barista at Dutch Bros. greeted me as dance music blared in the background. It was Monday morning, but I tended to forget that when I arrived for my routine dose of caffeine. No matter the time of day, the place had a party atmosphere and it put in me a good mood.

"Hey yourself." This had been our standard exchange for months.

"How was the weekend?"

It was one hell of a loaded question. I smiled as the poor young man making my coffee moved about his station, oblivious to the potential answer.

"It was good," I replied. "Yours?"

"No complaints. No complaints." He returned my grin as he strolled to the drive-through window and handed me my beverage. I set it in my cup holder before handing over my payment. It was a sign of trust I appreciated from Dutch Bros., even if my potential theft was only worth a couple of bucks. I added an extra dollar and the barista tried to hand it back to me. I refused with a smile and pointed to the almost overflowing tip jar.

"Did you change your hair?" the twentysomething man asked me as he pushed the dollar into the jar.

I shook my head and was surprised when he kept studying me.

He fixated on my blouse, which I had to admit showed more cleavage than usual for a work morning. From his vantage point at the elevated drive-through window, the barista had a prime position for a good eyeful.

"I like your shirt," he offered.

I glanced in his direction in mild surprise and raised an eyebrow.

"The color I mean," he stumbled over his words as he rubbed the back of his neck. "I like the color of your shirt. It's ah … nice."

I decided it was best to let him off the hook. After all, I couldn't remember the last time a college man had flirted with me.

"Thank you. Have a good day."

"You, too." He waved as he dashed back to his station.

I returned his wave and drove off toward work in good spirits and laughing.

God, I love Dutch Bros.

After stowing my belongings in my office, I grabbed my coffee cup and wandered toward the front of the office where Tracie, the receptionist was. She and I had made a habit of touching base each morning, and I was more desperate than ever to embrace the normal routine.

I strolled through the maze of cubicles and found it unusually empty for a Monday morning. As I rounded the corner before reaching Tracie's workstation, I glimpsed Jack's office. The butterflies in my stomach punctuated the anticipation of seeing him once again. The light in his office was turned off, which wasn't a surprise. Jack drove Heide to school in the mornings and arrived at work after I did.

I inhaled to settle my nerves and approached Tracie's desk.

She was involved in a phone call, so I set my coffee cup down on the ledge that divided the reception area and her personal workspace. She looked up and waved good morning while she listened to the person on the other end of the line. A white coffee cup sat on her desk, ignored while she tended to her duties.

Tracie enjoyed her Starbucks, too, and as I stared at the all too familiar logo I thought about Jack Evans and his mouth roaming over my body.

When she transferred the call, I giggled while she exhaled. Whether it was from her reaction to the caller or because I needed to release pent up tension from my body, I wasn't sure.

"Good morning," she greeted me.

"And to you," I answered. "How was your weekend?"

"Good. I went dancing Saturday night. I kept an eye open but didn't see you. Did you go out?"

"No. I stayed home. I needed a weekend in."

"What time did you get out of here Friday night?"

Friday night. I'd opted to work late and Jack had the same idea. My body tingled with desire as I recalled how Jack had noticed my office light still on and wandered in to say hello. He'd leaned against the wall next to my door and tucked his hands into his pockets. By doing so, Jack had drawn my eye to his hips, and not for the first time. I'd admired the pose since I'd first witnessed it during his introductory staff meeting.

Realizing Tracie was waiting for an answer, I pulled myself from my reverie.

"Not too late. Seven or seven thirty, I think."

In fact, the time had been 7:18, but I didn't want to say so to her. I knew the time because I'd glanced at the clock after Jack asked me to dinner. I couldn't say why I made note of the time, but now I knew I'd never forget that moment for the rest of my life.

Tracie and I soon fell into our regular chitchat, and I lingered at her desk longer than usual. I welcomed the distraction of hearing about her weekend. Tracie's carefree and energetic manner made me smile and her vitality filled my spirit. My mood lightened with each passing moment.

I heard the approach of familiar footsteps and steeled myself. When Jack appeared around the corner, my heart actually fluttered. He was tall without towering over those next to him, and his build was strong without appearing too muscular. His appearance was conservative to the unobserving eye, but each item of his clothing was contemporary.

Today, he was dressed in navy trousers with a matching blazer and a blue and white checked shirt. He cared about his outward appearance, but he didn't intend to draw attention to it. As he reached the side of Tracie's desk, I noticed the top two buttons of his shirt were open. I was riveted to the sight of his skin where the column of his neck met his chest and thought about his touch just before I left his house. I yearned to reciprocate the favor with urgency.

"Good morning, ladies." Jack held up his coffee cup in greeting, and I smiled when I saw that he carried a Dutch Bros. cup in his hand.

"Good morning, Jack," I answered, praying that my giddiness was well hidden. I pointed toward his beverage. "No Starbucks today?"

He shook his head. "My daughter suggested to me that I've been missing out by sticking to that routine."

Tracie laughed. "Your daughter said that?"

He grinned in my direction. Heide must have told him about our conversation in his bedroom. His expression, however, gave nothing away to Tracie.

I was flattered and emboldened. "Switching coffee places on a Monday morning is pretty daring," I flirted.

Jack shrugged and winked in my direction. "Oh. I haven't committed to switching coffee places. Just trying something different."

He turned and began to saunter toward his office, and just like that my good mood was obliterated. I assumed Jack was referring to more than the goddamned coffee.

I beg your fucking pardon?

Rage infiltrated every fiber of my body, but somehow I managed to hang on to my self-control long enough to walk away from Tracie's desk and back to my office. By the time I swept through the doorway and slammed the door I no longer cared if the entire building heard it.

chapter Eight

I SPENT the morning pissed off over Jack's comment. I couldn't help it. Despite telling myself multiple times to forget about the whole thing, I fumed in my office.

I attempted to occupy myself with work, but then something would distract me and bring back the stinging memory of his words. When my office phone would ring, I would check the display, hoping and dreading I'd see Jack's name on the screen. I was annoyed that I was eager to hear from him, although I wasn't sure how I would have answered his call.

I became more irritated when I'd check my e-mail as soon as a message notification flashed on my computer monitor. I wanted to see his name, even though I was inclined to reply in shouty caps.

The hours passed by and neither happened. No call. No e-mail. Nothing. With a frown I realized the treatment was not unlike the morning I woke up in his bed.

I pushed back from my keyboard, sat back in my office chair and attempted to chase away my frustrations and settle my emotions. I tried to process my weekend with logic.

Jack was interested in me on a deeper level. He'd wanted to serve me breakfast in bed and when that didn't work out, he'd asked me to stay anyhow. He'd invited me to Heide's game. He'd expressed his attraction to me as well as an interest in seeing me again. And when he'd made that comment about Dutch Bros. earlier this morning, he'd winked at me. He had been flirty and open-minded about trying new things.

And what had I done?

I'd blown a gasket and locked myself inside my office. Then I'd spent the morning acting almost manic as I waited for him to initiate first contact.

I'd long suspected Robert had fucked me up. Now I had proof.

To make matters worse, we were both scheduled to attend the same meeting this afternoon. We were working together on the upcoming annual client lunch in Portland the agency hosted for some of the firm's longtime and loyal customers. Over the years, it had also proved to be an excellent means for recruiting new accounts. By bringing the senior management team out into the field, the event was a rare opportunity to meet with urban clients on their home turf rather than attempting to lure prospects down to Bend.

It was one of the signature events for our firm, and Jack and I were part of the planning committee while Robert served as our project manager. The thought of sitting in a confined meeting room with these two men, today in particular, was unnerving. I could think of nothing more complicated and awkward than the upcoming meeting later in the day.

Wanting to make sure I made my best impression at this meeting, I fell into a work routine of sorts. By lunchtime, I needed a break from the office to calm my stress once and for all. I left, taking a route that wouldn't take me by either man's office, and opted for a nearby Chinese restaurant to indulge in some hot tea and teriyaki chicken.

Soon after I received my appetizer, Jack arrived looking as fresh and polished as when he'd strolled into the office carrying that fucking Dutch Bros. cup. He hadn't even removed his blazer, as many of the other men would have done over the course of the workday. Maybe that was an East Coast thing.

He noticed me just as soon as he sat down at his table but didn't join me. Once he placed his order, he seemed resigned to stay at his chosen table.

I shifted most of my attention away from Jack, but I caught him staring at me in my peripheral vision. I'd brought some work along to review, vindicated that I now had the opportunity to pay minimal attention to him for a few minutes.

My lunch arrived and I continued working while eating. If I stopped, it was possible Jack would try talking to me again, and it wasn't what I wanted. With such an important meeting less than an hour away, I didn't want the sexy side of Jack Evans to distract me.

I attempted to take a bite of my chicken while reading over my documents and some of the sauce dripped. While the material of my blouse was spared, the hot teriyaki landed on the top of my right breast. As soon as it made contact with my delicate skin, the instinct to avoid being scalded kicked in. I grabbed a napkin and dabbed my breast while holding my shirt away from my body.

With my blouse pulled away from my chest, I glanced in his direction, and my worst fears were confirmed. He was watching my debacle, and when he made eye contact with me, he didn't look away. I was appalled. He rediscovered his confidence.

He gathered up his things and sat down in my booth across from me.

I was stunned and still holding out my shirt.

"It seems ridiculous not to sit together."

I pulled my shirt back into place and set my napkin down on the table. "My food is already here."

"So?"

"Yours isn't ready yet. We're staggered."

Jack smiled, and I wondered if he found that quirk in my personality silly or attractive.

He winked. "I won't mention it to the boss if you take a few extra minutes at lunch today." He was toying with me. "If you like, we can make a meeting out of it. Make an honest man out of me."

I remained silent. After the morning's events, I wasn't sure I wanted Jack to flirt with me.

Jack tried another approach. "Did it hurt?" he asked with genuine concern.

"Huh?" My answer was less than intelligent.

"Did the sauce burn you?" he sounded apprehensive, and stared at my breast as though re-familiarizing himself with my body.

A shiver of desire radiated through me. "No," I managed to say. "I'm all right."

"Good."

"I'm not sure this conversation is appropriate?"

"Probably not," he agreed. "Let's move on to something else."

"Okay."

"Can we see each other again sometime this week?"

"I'm not sure that's appropriate either."

"Is that a no?"

I wondered the same thing. Was I even capable of saying no to Jack after our passionate night together? I wanted so much to hold this connection, to strengthen our bond and to grow our mutual attraction. But then I remembered how hurt I was after waking up in his bed and being ignored. And how his comment from earlier in the morning stung.

"I can't answer that now," I admitted while biting the inside of my lip.

Jack accepted this and didn't show any emotion from my potential rejection.

I took notice of this with a great deal of interest as he transitioned our conversation once more.

"There is something I've wanted to ask you." He hesitated, furrowing his brow. "But there never seems to be an appropriate way to do it."

"Sounds interesting."

"Not sure if you'll think so, but it's interesting to me."

I allowed the smallest amount of hope to settle inside my chest as I cut to the chase. "What do you want to know?"

Jack fidgeted in his booth before asking the question. "How old are you?"

I smiled and suppressed the urge to burst out into laughter.

"What?" Jack asked but didn't sound defensive. Perhaps he just wanted to know what was so amusing.

"My age? That's it?"

He straightened his already rigid posture. "Some people are sensitive about that."

Are you kidding me? After you ignored me in bed and insulted me at the office? This is the thing you're worried will upset me?

"I suppose," I answered with a subdued tone.

"Not you?"

"Not so far."

Jack waited, but quickly reached for his glass of water. I put him out of his misery.

"I'm thirty-six."

Jack nodded as he set the glass back down. His eyes telegraphed mild surprise as though he wasn't expecting that number.

I was younger than Jack, but now that he'd asked the question, I wanted to hear a number from him, too. We had to start somewhere.

"And you? Are you sensitive about your age?"

He mumbled an evasive answer. "I wasn't even married at thirty-six."

"Neither am I."

Jack laughed. "That's good to know."

He inhaled, revealing his answer on the exhale. "Forty-eight."

I knew the look on my face showed my surprise. "Seriously?"

He nodded and shrugged, but didn't break eye contact.

I surveyed his features, something I'd done many times before, but now I looked for something new to discover. Something that would confirm his claim. I had assumed he was in his forties, but now appreciated that he took more care with his appearance and his health than I'd given him credit for. With the exception of an occasional strand of silver in his hair and the rugged lines that caressed his eyes, his features were toned and smooth.

"Well, you are good-looking." I wasn't ashamed to tell him so. "But damn. I thought maybe you were closer to my age."

He tilted his head in surprise. "Even though I'm a divorced man with a seven-year-old daughter?"

I shook my head. "I have friends I grew up with who are on their second marriages and have kids in high school now. That's not much of a barometer."

As he considered my words, the first hints of self-consciousness broke through his carefully maintained exterior. "Maybe I should have told you. Before."

Was he worried I'd think he was too old for me? This revelation was unanticipated. And adorable.

"It wouldn't have made a difference to me," I reassured him. "The outcome would've been the same. Unless, maybe I'm too young for you?"

He shook his head with vigor. "No. I asked because I realized I didn't have a clue. Honestly, I'm relieved."

Another surprising admission.

"You are?"

"I thought you were younger."

I mulled this over for a few seconds before answering. "I can see that. I'm kind of juvenile for my age."

"That's not what I meant."

It took me a moment to realize what Jack meant, and I thanked him for the compliment.

"I spoke to Allison yesterday."

Changing the subject seemed to be a specialty of his, and I decided to pay more attention to that. As I pondered his latest statement, I discovered I didn't recognize the name at all.

"Who?"

Jack's face mirrored my own confusion. "Heide's mother. My ex-wife."

We were not yet done with the awkward portion of our impromptu lunch date.

I grimaced. "I'm sorry. I only met her the one time at your welcome reception."

Jack waved his hand. "She called to speak with Heide, and I thought about how right you were that Allison shouldn't hear about you from our daughter."

"What did you say?" I asked, unable to restrain my curiosity.

"I didn't go into detail, but I told her enough."

This answer, of course, told me nothing. I wanted to press for more details, but the last thing I wanted during the lunchtime rush at a Chinese restaurant was to talk about how he described our sexual encounter to his ex-wife.

I opted for a slight shift in the conversation. "Allison is in Baltimore?"

Jack nodded while playing with a discarded sugar packet.

"Why did she leave?" The question was out before I had a chance to reconsider, and Jack's brown eyes bore into mine with an expression I couldn't define.

"What do you know?" His voice was quieter. Cautious.

"I don't know anything." It was an honest answer, although Jack's sudden change in mood put me on edge.

"But you suspect plenty?"

His remark was offensive and laced with intensity. I struggled to maintain my composure. "No."

Jack's food arrived and the silence between us began to build. The raw nerve I'd glimpsed in his bedroom the last time I mentioned Allison was now on full display. I was straying into unwelcome, dangerous territory, and although he'd been the one to bring up her name today, I understood he was not in an emotionally secure position to discuss the disintegration of his marriage.

"Never mind," I said, hopeful that my tone of voice conveyed my sincerity. "It's none of my business."

Jack was silent and focused on stirring the food around his plate. After several moments, he leaned back into his seat. "She said I was more in love with my career than I was with her."

While one part of me celebrated a breakthrough in our communication, a more insistent part knew there was more to the story.

"Were you?"

Jack answered without hesitation, his tone unapologetic. "My career is important. My family benefits if my career is successful."

"That doesn't answer the question."

Jack shrugged and there was more silence between us.

As I waited to hear what he would say next, a sudden thought occurred to me. One that filled me with sadness and fear.

"Does that mean you'll leave this job, too? If the opportunity presents itself?"

"Depends on the opportunity."

"And where would that leave us?"

He blinked and brought his eyes back to mine for the first time in minutes. "Us?"

I couldn't blame him for the astonishment in his tone. I was dumbfounded by my reaction, too. Three evenings before we'd slept together on a whim. And although Jack appeared interested in seeing me again, I had rebuffed him.

"Perhaps, yet another reason I should hold you at bay, Mr. Evans." My response was terser than I anticipated.

His reaction was similar. "Don't call me that."

The silence thickened between us as we each rearranged the food on our plates without taking a bite. Our server passed by our table twice before stopping to check on the quality of our lunch. Once we both confirmed nothing was wrong with the food, she kept her distance.

"It's not a bad thing," I rambled, desperate to strike a truce before our scheduled meeting. "People take new jobs and move to new places all the time. Sometimes I wonder about whether or not I should have done that."

Jack looked up and studied my face before he chuckled. "You speak like you've lived your entire life."

You have no idea.

"In some ways I have," I admitted. "I've made my career commitment to my father. I couldn't leave my life just like that. Things are far too complicated now. I think people who take those kinds of chances are brave. But I'm just not one of them." I added the final sentence as an afterthought.

"Yes, you are," Jack whispered, which drew my complete attention. His eyes were soft and welcoming once again. "Brave, I mean."

Was he was trying to make amends for our awkward conversation? Now, he was the one entering dangerous territory without even knowing it. I decided to let him off the hook.

"You don't know me well enough to say that."

chapter Nine

I REMAINED with Jack until he was done with his lunch. I didn't know what to say to him, and yet I couldn't seem to detach myself from the situation. I was trying to relax and get a read on him at the same time.

Afterward, Jack and I walked back to the office together. He was on my left, with his head bent and his hands in his pockets. We strolled in the afternoon sunshine, neither one of us in a hurry to head back indoors. We were quiet, yet somehow the silence had become comfortable, even enjoyable.

I glanced a time or two at his handsome profile, acknowledging how fascinated I'd been by him for the better part of a year. His face was the type I was inclined to trust. Intelligence brimmed inside his dark eyes, and his relaxed manner often put my own racing mind at ease. There was something else in his expression that I'd glimpsed on occasion. I would have been hard pressed to describe it as sadness or anger or stress. It was something that made Jack mysterious and complex to me.

And who was I kidding? It also made him fucking irresistible.

I kept thinking I should say something to him. But didn't want to ruin the first moment of contentment between us since the weekend. There was no sense in pushing forward with uncomfortable conversation.

As we approached the side entrance to the building, Jack picked up his pace and reached for the door handle. He held it open for me and smiled as I walked through. I turned to thank him and considered pushing him against the wall just inside the door and kissing him hard while I greedily grabbed his ass.

Our respective offices were located to the left of the entryway, but he turned right. "I'll see you soon," he said.

"Will do." I doubted he heard my response.

I took a deep breath and rubbed my forehead. In truth, I didn't mind his hasty retreat. After a morning spent with frenzied thoughts of Jack, I needed to get my head back in the game and focus on our impending meeting with Robert. I'd dug myself a nice hole by forgetting our plans on Saturday morning. I would have to pull off a stellar performance to tamp down his bad mood.

I returned to my office, dreading the encounter with Robert and hopeful that Jack's presence would be enough to help me survive it.

Tracie offered to help me set up for the meeting, but I declined. I was intent on preparing for anything Robert might throw in my direction.

When I entered the conference room, I flipped on the lights and closed the door. I set my papers down on the oblong table and glanced at the large window on the opposite wall. The heavy floor-length curtains were drawn together and the green barrier of fabric was claustrophobic. I strolled around the table, pulled them open and allowed the sunshine to brighten the imposing space. For extra measure, I slid open a window to let in some fresh air. The relaxing and sweet high desert scents of springtime filtered into the room.

I took the long way back around the table, completing a full orbit of the meeting space. I pulled one of the light brown plush chairs away from the table and took my seat in front of my work. As I sorted my various notes into a manageable order, the door clicked open.

My body tensed and I angled my chair in the direction of the doorway.

Jack entered the room and I smiled with tremendous relief.

"Long time, no see," I joked.

"Too long for me," he teased back.

I grinned and shook my head as I returned to my work. Jack chose to sit in a chair across from mine on the other side of the table. To his credit, he opted not to distract me from the task at hand. He set about organizing his own notes as soon as he settled into his seat. The comfortable silence we achieved on the walk back from the Chinese restaurant returned, and I was grateful.

Despite the events of the weekend, I was happy to be teamed with Jack on this event. In the months since he joined the firm, Jack had developed a reputation as a solid and capable manager. He was still learning the lay of the land and its particularities, but he never appeared uncertain about how to proceed with any assignment he received. I knew without checking in with him that he'd completed all the tasks Robert would quiz him about.

Just as we both finished rifling through our various notes, I heard Robert greet Tracie as he marched by her desk. He entered the conference room, closing the door behind him without a backward glance. Dressed in khakis and a dark red polo shirt, it was clear he'd spent the morning multitasking his appointments during a round of golf. The color of his shirt complemented his fair skin and hair, which was now more gray than blond, and although Robert had his vices, his body had been well maintained by his love of the outdoors.

As Robert made his way toward me to assume his usual seat, he nodded to the man sitting across from us. "Afternoon, Jack."

I turned my head in Robert's direction, tilting it upward. If Jack offered a response, I never heard a word. Robert paused by my chair and with one swift motion pinned me into my seat with an uncharacteristic embrace from behind. Trapped by his strong arms, he then pressed his lips to my temple.

My back hit the chair, but I couldn't tell if it was from the pressure of Robert's invasive action or my instinct to retreat from it. His lips were firm and rested on my skin for just a heartbeat or two, but it was long enough for me to inhale the nicotine on his breath and my stomach knotted. When he pulled away and took his own seat, I was frozen by humiliation and revulsion. My forehead was moist from his touch and it took all my willpower not to wipe my face in utter disgust.

"Good afternoon, Kathleen." Robert's stern greeting broke through my haze of shock and I turned my head with deliberate slowness and met his pale green eyes. "I hope you're all better. I missed you at breakfast on Saturday."

Robert's attention turned to Jack. "How about you, Jack? How was your weekend?"

I risked a glance at Jack as fear radiated through my veins. His face was more or less composed, but his eyes were remote and cold. There was no denying the tension in the conference room.

Jack's answer was subdued and short. "Good. Just what I needed." Rather than ask about Robert's weekend, Jack changed subjects. "Good round of golf this morning?"

Robert beamed, either unaware or unwilling to acknowledge his disruption. "Yes. First time I've been out since last summer. Met up with Charlie Franklin out at Widgi Creek. Have I introduced him to you yet?"

Jack shook his head. "No."

"Do you golf?"

"I used to, back in college. But it's been a while." Jack attempted to lighten the mood, but I was unable to play along.

Robert didn't skip a beat. "Bend is one of the best places to golf in the whole state. One of the reasons I wanted to move here. Kathleen used to go out with me." Robert looked back to me and I winced. "Remember that?" His question held an unmistakable icy tone.

"Hmm." I wasn't willing to provide any more acknowledgements.

Robert's eyes narrowed for an instant before returning his attention to Jack. He grinned. "I'll take you out there one of these days. Lots of business to be done on the links. Gotta take advantage of the great climate we have here."

Robert continued speaking about his outing with Charlie Franklin, and as he went on I found it impossible to look at him. I was still recovering from the unexpected greeting, although my shock had dissolved into anger. If my eyes locked onto his, I was going to snap.

I decided to take my lead from Jack and watched him instead. I waited until his brown eyes drifted back in my direction. Jack watched with a solemn expression as I wiped the slimy residual from Robert's kiss with my fingers. I then crossed my arms and wiped my contaminated fingers on the underside of my sleeve. The expression on Jack's features transformed into concern, and I pulled my arms even tighter against my body.

Robert had blindsided me, and I was stupid for being outwitted by him yet again. Everything that had taken place since he walked through the door had put me at a severe disadvantage.

Jack looked unsettled by Robert's aggressiveness, and dread crept into my thoughts and my body. Perhaps it was because I was still so unsure about Jack. I would have preferred to remain on equal footing.

I didn't want him to understand certain things about my life so soon, if ever. I wasn't ready for it. I wanted to keep the same things hidden from Jack that I did from the others in my life. The fact that he'd observed such a power play moment between Robert and me firsthand was the worst-case scenario come true.

Jack Evans was a man capable of riling intense stirrings in me. He broke through my heavy defenses just by uttering a word or offering me a wandering look. No one had ever left me as raw and translucent as he did. He troubled and confused me, and in doing so, made me understand just how numb to my own life I'd become. And I didn't have the first clue how to process this avalanche of enlightenment.

As we progressed through the meeting, our professional exteriors attempted to compensate for the awkwardness in the room. Robert conducted his business affairs with tailored efficiency, and Jack and I were prepared for his scrutiny. While the tasks had been completed and reported back to Robert, he couldn't seem to resist poking me in other ways.

"You'll come to the house in Portland after the event," he announced in front of our colleague. "We'll have an evening together. It'll make up for this weekend."

"I can't," I said without pausing to think of his reaction. Robert's eyes flashed with irritation, but I pressed on. "I'm coming home as soon as the event is over. I'm meeting Sarah for dinner to talk about the fundraiser for the hospital foundation. I'll barely have time to make it back from Portland."

Robert paused and, because I knew him so well, I understood he was considering how he would address my second rejection of the week.

"Speaking of Portland," he began, "there will be any number of female clients there, Jack. It should be a good place to display some of that East Coast charm of yours. Who knows? Maybe you'll end up back in the dating game."

Jack was in the middle of jotting notes and paused. His composure remained intact, while I clenched my hands in controlled anger. Jack raised his arm and glanced at his watch.

"I'm sorry to cut this short," he announced, "but I need to pick up my daughter from school."

"Not at all." Robert slapped his palm against the conference room table. "It sounds like you two have things under control. We're good to go."

With that, we both began to gather our notes. As I collected my things, I considered how Jack avoided addressing Robert's suggestion. The evasion was a trait I would keep in mind moving forward.

Jack made his way to the conference room door and I followed, seeking escape. When Jack pulled the door open and stepped out into the reception area, Robert halted my escape.

"Hold on, Kathleen. I need more of your time."

chapter Ten

"**CLOSE THE** door." Robert sounded grave. His command gave me pause, but I complied when he added the rarely used please.

"Take a seat," he instructed as soon as the conference room door clicked shut.

Doing so would put in me in closer proximity to him, which I was reluctant to do. Despite my misgivings, I sat down. I waited in motionless silence and attempted to avoid his gaze.

When he spoke, he emphasized each word with a stern jab of his finger. "Call Sarah. Cancel your meeting. Spend the evening in Portland with your family."

"No." The word was out of my mouth before he could even draw another breath.

Despite my verbal boldness, my eyes were locked on his immense hands. They were twice the size of mine and, even under the friendliest of conditions, they never failed to intimidate me.

"No?" Robert was getting angrier, but waited for me to make eye contact before continuing. "What do you expect me to say to Courtney?"

The mention of the woman's name turned my oxygen into acid. "I don't care," I huffed. "Tell her whatever you want."

"She was offended when you didn't show up on Saturday. She spent all day Friday getting the house ready."

I couldn't quite bring myself to roll my eyes, although it would have been safer than my response. "You mean the housekeeper spent all day getting the house ready while your wife went to the spa."

Robert's foot kicked the underside of the conference room table, and I flinched in surprise. "Watch it, Kathleen. You're crossing the line."

Embarrassed by my reflexive display of nervousness, I snapped in return, "Your current wife is nothing to me. I have no obligation to her."

"What the hell has gotten into you, anyway?"

You mean besides Jack Evans?

As the immature thought flashed through my mind, I was unable to hide the accompanying smirk.

"What's so funny?" he demanded.

The smirk receded. "Nothing."

"Bullshit. You blow me off with no explanation or consideration. You thinking about the past again?"

I glared at him in total amazement. "Don't even fucking go there, Robert."

"You need to grow up."

His remark hit home like a wasp's sting and reminded me of my breakfast with Jack over the weekend. I'd stood in Jack's kitchen and compared his status as an adult with my own. It was one thing for me to think these things about myself. It was quite another for Robert to confront me with it. My anger flared.

"You want to go grab the kitchen sink and drag that in here, too?"

"You need to let it all go."

"I have," I spat. "You're the one bringing up the past. Doesn't matter if we're talking about twenty-five years ago or last weekend. That's all you."

"I'm your father, Kathleen." He made the declaration as though the mere fact was enough to merit my respect. It didn't. Not by a long shot.

"I know that. Believe me, I know that, although I try not to think about it."

"You need to pull yourself together. I don't know what triggered this, but you need to get your head back on straight."

"Stop talking to me like I'm fifteen."

"Stop acting like you're fifteen."

Our communication had never been good, but this scene had deteriorated to the point where I no longer cared to listen. And for the first time in my life, I realized I didn't have to.

"Do you have anything work related to discuss with me?"

Robert stopped at my question and abruptly sat back in his chair. "No. Do you?"

"No."

His face projected calm, but his eyes seethed with anger. "Anything else?"

"How about this? Don't you ever touch me in the office again. Let's see if you can master that first."

I stood up and exited the conference room while Robert continued to sit in stunned silence. I knew if he rose from that chair before I made it through the door, another one of our blowouts would ensue. I was banking on the fact that he wouldn't be dumb enough to go ballistic in front of his staff.

I returned to my office immediately. I sank into my chair with relief and began to plot my next escape. Lost in thought, I vaguely registered the fast footsteps approaching my open doorway, but I looked up when my intruder offered a bright, happy greeting.

"Hello, Kathleen! How was your day?" Jack's daughter stood just outside my office door, smiling. She was dressed in black shorts and a red and white soccer jersey with the word Fury emblazoned across the front.

She was also standing out in the hallway where any number of employees could overhear our conversation. Sleeping with Jack wasn't something I was ashamed of, but I was desperate to keep this news hidden for the time being. Besides the fact that it was no one else's business, I couldn't have Robert hear about it via the office rumor mill.

Talk about fury.

I stood up, waved Heide inside and closed the door. She took a seat in front of my desk without further prodding.

"My day was …" I paused as I considered how to sum it up so a seven-year-old could understand. "It was interesting," I said. "How about yours?"

"Well." She looked up to peer up at my ceiling. "It wasn't great, but it was okay."

While Heide was evasive, she was more articulate than I in the moment, and I was reminded of how much I enjoyed speaking with her.

"Did anything bad happen?" I asked, now interested to hear more. Any number of school playground scenarios began to flash through my mind, and I was concerned this relative newcomer to Oregon might be experiencing trouble with her peers.

Her attention returned to me. "No." She glanced over my shoulder and pointed to my desktop computer. "Do you have Minecraft?"

I shook my head. "No, but I've heard of it."

"You should try Minecraft. It's pretty good."

"I take it your dad lets you play Minecraft."

"Sometimes. If I get all my work done, but I'd like to play more. The next time you're at my house, I'll show you how."

I didn't know how to answer that, so I didn't.

"What's your favorite thing about it?" I ventured.

Heide looked back up to the ceiling while she pondered her answer. "I love to create things. There's nothing in your way to create stuff. It's like Legos, because your guy is all blocks. You can make whatever you want—no monsters or some monsters or the right amount of monsters or you can go hardcore with monsters. And if you get hit by one, you die."

I smiled. Heide was self-assured and smart. I almost forgot I was talking to a second grader. "Isn't that a little scary?"

"I've seen videos that are scary, but they're funny at the same time."

Her focus drifted away from the ceiling and back to me once again. "Like the Creeper. No one meant to create it. Someone was just trying to make a pig and shebam! He made a Creeper."

Heide sat, waiting for me to respond. I was at a loss for words, however, which prompted her to elaborate. "Creepers don't have hands, just like pigs don't have hands."

"That does sound strange."

"That's not the only thing that will scare you."

"What else would scare me?"

"The deadly Herobrine," Heide whispered for dramatic effect.

"Is he the bad guy?"

She nodded with excitement. "I don't know the story, but he can type in words backward and if you try to read it, he's asking you things like if you can see him or if you like him. That's scary. I don't know why he's evil, but I'll look it up on my tablet and let you know what I find out."

I blinked and stared at the closed door again, a thought occurring to me. I turned back to Heide.

"Does your dad know where you are?"

She shrugged just as there was a light knock on my door.

"That's him," she informed me.

I stood up from my desk and made my way over to open it.

"That's how he knocks." She remained sitting in my office, swinging her legs in the air just above the floor.

I pulled open the door, and Jack's attention went straight to his daughter.

She looked over her shoulder. "We were just having a nice conversation and you interrupted," she said, chiding her father, but her tone carried a level of affection that was absent in my relationship with Robert. My stomach tightened in an all too familiar spasm of awkwardness.

Jack raised his eyebrows in surprise.

If this interaction had been between my father and me, I would have been in trouble for being a smart ass — not that it ever stopped me. I waited for Jack's reaction with great interest.

"You wandered off without letting me know where you were going. We talked about this, remember?"

She lowered her head and nodded. "I know."

A small ripple of anxiety shot through me, along with a sudden urge of protectiveness. "She just got here a minute ago," I explained. "I was just going to make sure you knew she was with me."

Then I whispered, "I hope you're not too upset."

Jack's kind eyes met mine. "Of course not." He offered a slight smile before addressing Heide once again, "We should let Kathleen get back to work. And you need to think about getting your homework done before soccer practice."

Heide stood up from her chair and looked at me. "Are you coming over for dinner?"

Jack's expression morphed into amused surprise as did my own. Heide waited for an answer.

"Uh. Well. That's so nice of you to invite me over, Heide."

I glanced from her to her father, and when our eyes met once again, he said, "I'd be happy to have you. If you're up to it."

His words sounded innocent, but my body tingled in anticipation from his suggestive phrasing. I cleared my throat and rubbed the back of my neck while I thought about how to answer him. The day had been excruciating from the moment I stepped into the office, and although my argument with Robert had been the worst part of it, Jack had also contributed to the stress of the day.

"You were nice enough to share lunch with me, so I think I should let you and Heide spend some time together this evening."

Her chipper voice reminded me we were not alone. "We'll have to finish talking about Minecraft later then."

"Sounds good," I responded. "I look forward to hearing more about Herobrine."

Heide waved good-bye, and she made her way back toward her father's office.

With his daughter no longer in our company, Jack surprised me yet again. "Did things go all right in there after I left?"

I crossed my arms as I leaned against the doorframe. There was a crease on his forehead that I longed to smooth away, but I kept my hands locked on my arms.

"We're good to go for the event." I was guarded, but wanted to offer him reassurance. "No worries."

He glanced around our surroundings before speaking again. "I've been thinking about you. Can I call you tonight?"

I was surprised by the question and my cheeks began to blush. "Um. Sure. I guess."

"Good. Heide's bedtime is nine. Give me until around nine thirty?"

"Okay."

His eyes roamed over my face with great consideration. "Go home and relax. I'll speak with you soon."

chapter  Eleven

I TOOK Jack's advice. I bought a bottle of wine on the way home and indulged in a couple of glasses that evening. I settled into my room and prepared to speak with him from the comfort of my own bed. I wasn't sure what might happen during our conversation, but I was calm about it. I had faith that Jack wasn't about to make my day any worse.

My phone rang on time.

"How are you doing?" His initial greeting was pleasant and relaxed.

I smiled as I settled back against my stack of pillows. "Fine. Tired," I confessed. "It was a long day."

"I'm worried about you."

"You are?" Worry for my well-being wasn't something I was used to from others. The revelation almost made me worry for him.

"Yes. I'm uncomfortable about what happened today."

"Which part?"

Jack chuckled a little. "Don't joke, Kathleen."

He'd misunderstood me and I considered correcting him, but then he took a shaky breath.

"I don't know what to think about how Robert treated you," he began. "I saw your face. It disturbed you. And I worry I'll upset you more by telling you this."

I bit my lip and wondered if I could have a meaningful conversation with this man about the events of the afternoon without it dissolving into an argument. It was important to me that Jack and I ended this phone call on good terms.

"I'm sorry you saw that." I hoped succinct honesty would be the best policy.

"Don't apologize for something you didn't do. It was just ... I don't know how to describe it." Jack's voice drifted away into uncertainty.

"You wouldn't treat Heide like that." I made the conclusion with confidence.

His response was swift and strong. "You're right. I wouldn't." Jack had taken a calculated risk voicing his true opinion. After all, we weren't just talking about my father, we were talking about Jack's boss.

I gathered my thoughts for a few moments and waited for Jack to speak again. I wanted him to dictate what direction our conversation would take.

"It didn't seem affectionate. Or proper," he added.

I couldn't deny it, and I wouldn't insult Jack by insisting otherwise. "That's because it wasn't," I replied. "It was territorial."

Jack's bluntness was surprising, but I had to admit it was good to speak about Robert with such openness. It wasn't something I'd been encouraged to do.

Jack cleared his throat. "I should have gone to HR as soon as I left the room. I'm pissed at myself that I left you in there with him. I didn't want to do that. I shouldn't have done that."

I took a deep sigh. This was where we were apt to disagree, but I was determined to be as candid as possible.

"I appreciate that, but I do have to take some responsibility here. I'm not innocent in what happened today. He wouldn't have done that without provocation."

Jack's silence stretched out on the phone, and I felt compelled to add one more truth. "We don't have a typical father-daughter bond. At least I'm pretty sure of that."

"It's a lot to take in, Kathleen. I'm appalled and confused about what I saw in that room."

"I'm not going to make excuses for him or defend him. I'm also not ready to tell you a lot about him. He's my father and we have substantial problems. We fight. A lot. But this is the first time a personal argument reared its head at the office. What you saw was awkward and it embarrassed me, but it's not typical of him. I just need you to understand that. It was an aberration."

"It was wrong of me to leave you alone with him," he repeated. "I guess I was still trying to process what happened at lunch. I'm not sure what to think about that either. I thought we connected Friday night."

"We definitely did."

Now, I was trying to lighten the mood, but Jack was determined. Focused.

"You were upset with me Saturday morning. And today."

A complexity of emotion overtook me from the vulnerability in Jack's voice. A part of me was thrilled to shift focus back to our sex lives, while another part was remorseful over my poor behavior. I enjoyed my night with Jack and couldn't stand the thought of hurting him again with additional experimentation. In that moment, I was the immature girl Robert had accused me of being a few hours earlier. If I was going to remain romantically interested in Jack, I first had to gain a certain amount of self-control.

"I just need a couple of days."

"You said that on Saturday when I asked to call you," he challenged.

"I know." It was as close as I would come to admitting I was stalling.

"I still want to see you."

"I know that now. I realized that when Heide invited me over for dinner tonight."

"You didn't believe me on Saturday?" Jack sounded surprised.

"No. I mean, I did. I'm just tired. A bit confused, I guess." It was an insufficient answer and we both knew it. This time, Jack was patient while I figured out what to say next.

"I didn't see Friday coming. I don't know what's happening between us." My voice dropped to a near whisper. "Or what to expect now."

"Have dinner with me tomorrow, and we'll talk about it." Jack's voice sounded hopeful.

Still I hesitated. "I don't know, Jack."

"Why not?"

"I'll want more from you than dinner. I already do." There. It was out there. I still wanted Jack Evans. So much. But before Jack could respond, I rambled on, "Maybe it's just best to wait until the Portland event is over. Robert is complicating the whole thing. I need stuff to settle down with him first. I've offended him more than I've offended you. I'm on more stable ground with you, and I just need to calm him down before I can focus on anything else."

"Please don't think you've offended me. Not even for a moment."

Jack's words held such power and lifted a heavy burden from me. I was startled by the sudden lightness. Until the weight lifted from my shoulders, I wasn't aware of its existence. I thanked him for saying so, and our conversation fell into another small but comfortable lull.

"How long have you been fighting with your father?" His question should have put me on the defensive, but it didn't.

I thought long and hard before answering, "Always." It was the first time I'd said as much out loud. "I don't know anything else."

"Have you ever tried family therapy?"

I shook my head as I answered. "That's pointless. Even if I was still interested in trying to change the status quo, he never sees anything wrong in what he's doing."

"That's no way to live."

"Thankfully, we don't live forever."

Jack didn't respond and after a few moments, I became concerned.

"Maybe now I've offended you?"

"I don't know anything about the rest of your life. I only know what I saw today. I need to remember it's not my place to make judgments. But if I ever see anything like that again, I won't walk away like I did this afternoon."

I couldn't believe what he'd said — words I was used to hearing in movies or reading in books — but the practical side of me set my swelling emotions aside.

"You don't want to risk your job over this. I can handle Robert."

"Fuck the job. I don't care if he is your father or my boss. I won't tolerate you being treated that way." His passion now was in stark contrast to his ex-wife's claim that he loved his career more than he loved her. I was astonished. His words didn't make sense, but their effect on my smoldering libido was immediate and urgent.

I dared to change the subject. "So you still like me?"

"Very much."

"Can I tell you something?"

"Please do."

"I can't stop thinking about Friday night." My voice was bold, but my stomach was a flutter of nerves.

"Go on." His voice held the same husky tone from a few evenings before. He was daring me, and I was more than happy to play this game.

"I've been thinking about it so much I'm uncomfortable. Physically. If you want to know the truth, I may have to do something about it this evening if I'm going to get a decent night's rest."

"I'm not opposed to phone sex." As usual, Jack was cool under pressure.

"Are you serious?" There was no point in hiding my astonishment.

"It's not ideal, but it's better than nothing."

"I've never tried it." Another confession from me, but there was nothing to worry about. I wanted to explore this with him.

"Where are you now?" he asked. "Are you in bed?"

"Yes."

"Are the sheets over you?"

"Yes."

"Pull them down."

I didn't so much pull them down as kick them away with my feet.

"What are you wearing?" he inquired.

I glanced down to give him an accurate description. "A night shirt."

"A tee shirt?"

"No." I wrinkled my nose as I elaborated. "Silk. Blue."

"You have a fondness for lingerie. You were wearing some last weekend, too."

"It's an indulgence," I said.

"Pull your shirt up," he demanded.

I complied.

"Did you do it?"

"Yes."

"Are you wearing panties?"

"No."

Jack's rough sigh deliciously tickled my ear.

"Do you want to touch yourself?"

I smiled in anticipation. "I'd rather have you do it."

"So would I," he said. "Are you sure you want to do this?"

"I was going to anyway. You may as well keep me company."

"Are your legs open?"

"Not yet."

"Open them for me."

I obeyed. "Are you going to do this with me?"

"Not this time. If I was there with you in your bed tonight, I'd devote all my efforts to you."

I was apprehensive and a smidge disappointed. "You want me to do this alone?"

"We'll see. What I want most of all is for you to let go of went wrong today, so if I were there, you'd be focused on my touch."

My hand began to drift downward. "Tell me, Jack. Tell me what I should think about."

"I'd want us to try something new together. Something we didn't do on Friday night."

"What?" I pleaded with him to tell me.

"Where are your fingers, Kathleen?"

"Lower."

"Tell me."

"Moving through my hair," I said with a touch of shyness.

"Not low enough. Move farther down."

There was no denying the moaning gasp that escaped my mouth when my fingers made contact.

"I want you wet."

"I've been wet since Friday."

"If I were there my mouth would be where your fingers are now." Jack's voice had deepened, his tone possessive.

I escalated the speed of my circular movements, and I panted in response both to the sensation and to Jack's voice.

"You don't know how much I want to taste you. One night, I hope you'll let me."

His daring suggestion heightened my arousal. I was frenzied and had reached the point of no return. I needed to forget about the miseries of the day and allow Jack's words to seduce me into sweet oblivion.

"Tell me," I gasped. "Please tell me more."

"My mouth would be on you, all over you. My tongue would thrust inside you."

My body tensed in anticipation of my release, and I moaned into the phone.

"You're close, Kathleen. Whatever you're doing to yourself, don't stop. Keep going. Say my name when you come."

As he finished with his request, my orgasm overtook my entire being. I lost my grip on the phone, and it slid off my shoulder as I grasped the sheets. The intensity of the moment consumed me, and if Jack said anything else, I didn't know it. But I damn well made sure he heard me and called out his name several times until my body began to relax.

I took several, slow deep breaths as the lingering pleasure radiated throughout my body. The last thing I expected to receive from Jack during this call was phone sex, but I was so very happy at this turn of events.

When I retrieved the phone, I was sated and smiling.

"Are you there?" I asked.

"How could I hang up on that?"

I flushed. He sounded relaxed and happy. I was tempted to ask if he'd changed his mind about joining in with me, but I was overcome with emotion and appreciation.

"Thank you, Jack … for this."

"Thank you for trusting me, Kathleen."

"Now what?" I asked him. His sweetness was intoxicating. I'd never met anyone quite like this man.

"I'd be happy to listen to you again if you need more."

The persistent smile on my face grew bigger.

"I could be talked into another one," I answered, "but I'd like to save it for you."

"You would, huh?" Jack's tone was quiet, but still playful.

"Yes."

"Now I really want that dinner date."

I laughed for a few seconds before I said, "Soon."

"I'm glad you're happy."

"Me, too."

"I'm going to let you rest now, Kathleen. I want you to take this feeling and go to sleep with it."

It was the most romantic thing any man had ever said to me. My eyes filled with tears and my heart began to pound. I was euphoric. "Is it odd that I'd rather fall asleep with you still on the phone?"

"I think it's nice. Thank you for saying that."

"You're welcome."

"Are you all right?" While this wasn't the first time Jack had asked this question, it was the first time he wasn't asking out of deep concern.

The thought of him checking on my current level of happiness was another new and welcome form of realism.

"I am," I said with confidence. "I'll let you go. I'll see you tomorrow."

"Good night, Kathleen," Jack said in a voice so soft that I envisioned him kissing my forehead as he spoke the words.

Tonight I would sleep well. "Good night, Jack."

chapter  Twelve

THREE WEEKS after the awkward conference room meeting, Robert had left me alone, much to my surprise. There were no demands made on me at the office, and there were no awkward phone calls in the evenings or during the weekends. For the most part, he ignored me and I was fine with that. I was even tempted to relax.

I entertained theories about his change in behavior and even considered his unexpected retreat was because he had taken my offense to heart. In the end, however, my instincts and experience with Robert convinced me that I was in the midst of a deadly calm. This was the eye of the storm, and it would be wise to prepare myself for the inevitable backlash.

I speculated that Robert was offended by me and laying low while calculating his next move. Our argument in the conference room differed from others because I had dared to challenge him. The last time I had done so, I had been a child. The whys were fuzzy now, but I'd learned an important lesson. My father reacted to such tests with searing anger. My challenge had not been perceived as the natural progression of growth and independence for a child. He saw it as an act of betrayal, a declaration of disrespect. Perhaps now that I was an adult and could no longer be punished like a child had emboldened me to push back, but there was no way of predicting how Robert would respond.

The unknown should have kept me awake at night, but the soothing presence of Jack Evans shielded me from stress. We were still finding our way, but the tension we'd experienced after spending the night together had receded.

Jack often brought Heide to the office after she finished her day at school, and I found myself fascinated by his interactions with her. His daughter was blossoming despite the divorce, and this was in large part because of him. Jack was supportive and nurturing and not at all like Robert.

He even extended his protection and kindness toward me by following through on his pledge to make sure I wasn't alone with Robert. With care and expertise, Jack kept close to me without raising eyebrows at the office. He arrived at work most mornings with two coffees, one for me from Dutch Bros. and one for him from Starbucks, and throughout the ensuing days, we'd focus our energies on the upcoming luncheon.

I was beginning to realize that there was a precious intimacy forming between us. Jack Evans was becoming a good friend. He was patient and bided his time before asking me on another date. A week before the Portland event, I received an invitation to spend time with Jack and Heide at their home for dinner. I accepted with enthusiasm.

We hadn't slept together or engaged in phone sex again, yet I was certain I would be spending the night with him. We made plans for Wednesday evening so we could take advantage of the Farmer's Market, which had just opened for the season. He encouraged me to find a way to leave the office in the afternoon so we could shop at the market without being rushed, and we began to refer to the upcoming Wednesday with a tone of unmistakable anticipation and excitement.

When the day arrived, I drove home during the noon hour and exchanged my work clothes for a loose gray blouse paired with dark skinny jeans. On a whim, I rolled up the cuffs and completed the outfit with a white pair of Converse low top sneakers. I also prepared a discreet overnight bag, opting not to include a pair of pajamas.

Jack and Heide arrived at my condo after he picked her up from school, and together we rode into the heart of the city during that warm and sunny late afternoon. After parking the car, we made our way to the Brooks Street Alleyway and meandered through the small crowd of shoppers and vendors. As we strolled through the market, Heide asked me about the mountains surrounding Bend.

"Have you been to the top of all four of them?" she asked, her eyes full of excitement.

"No, I haven't. I did climb one of the Sisters though."

"You did?" Jack and Heide spoke in unison, impressed.

"It was a long time ago. I did it for a fundraising drive. I don't think I could do it again. I was lucky I made it back."

"I'm going to climb all four of them," Heide declared with a great deal of enthusiasm. "All Three Sisters and Mount Bachelor."

"Well, you know there are more than four mountains around here," I teased. "You should add those to your list, too."

"Like what?"

"Mount Washington is nearby. Mount Jefferson and Mount Hood aren't all that far away from here either." I paused as the name of another local peak flashed in my mind. "There's even Three Fingered Jack." I couldn't help but waggle an eyebrow at Jack when I said it. He blushed, and the color of his cheeks contrasted beautifully with his dark shirt.

"What?" Heide stared in disbelief. "Is that mountain named after you, Dad?"

Jack shook his head, while trying to suppress a grin.

"It used to be called Mount Marion, but someone changed the name," I explained.

"Why?"

"Some say it was renamed after a beaver trapper." I smirked once again in Jack's direction. "But it's probably because of the three big peaks on top of it. It's one of the oldest volcanoes around here."

"Maybe I should climb that one first."

"I'd save it for last. I hear it's kind of hard."

Jack coughed, and this time I couldn't keep myself from laughing. Heide was clueless to my innuendos, and was distracted by a booth offering an exotic variety of jellies.

When we returned to the Evans house, Heide led me inside while Jack gathered our purchases from the trunk of his car.

As we opened the front door, the home's sentry, the family cat, greeted us. The fluffy gray feline with a flat Persian face and suspicious blue eyes wasn't animated, but since she didn't hiss and run away as soon as I walked inside, I considered this a success. The cat didn't block my way into the living room as much as she forced me to step around her.

"I just realized I don't know your cat's name," I whispered to Heide, while sidestepping the animal.

"Kitty Hawk," she said in a casual tone.

That didn't make much sense to me. "You mean like the place the Wright Brothers took off from?"

Heide looked as confused as I felt when she shook her head. "I don't know. She's just a good bird hunter."

"Yes, I see."

When Jack entered the house, I offered to help him unload the groceries, but he steered me away.

"Kathleen! Come here! I'll show you Minecraft," Heide said, seizing the opportunity to continue our conversation from several weeks ago.

I followed her to the living room and joined her on the sofa. She grabbed her tablet and gave me a brief tutorial of the game until Jack reminded her to get her homework done before dinner. Heide frowned at the interruption in her duties as hostess.

"What kind of assignments do you have to work on?" I asked, deciding to back up her father's suggestion.

She pushed her hair away from her face as she answered. "Just math."

"Maybe I could help. Then we can we come back to Minecraft later."

She looked at me with skeptical eyes. "Did you go to college?"

Somehow I managed to keep a straight face, even though I wanted to bust out laughing. "I did. I even graduated."

"Where'd you go?" It felt like she was taking my offer of help with a fair amount of skepticism.

"I went to the University of Oregon. In Eugene."

"So you're a Duck?" Jack asked from his station in the kitchen. The distinct sound of a wine cork popping followed his comment.

I raised my voice enough so hc could hear my reply. "I guess. I would have preferred to go to school in Portland. I'm more of a platypus."

"What does that mean?" he asked, appearing from the kitchen with an amused smile and carrying a glass of white wine.

As he offered me the glass, I responded, "It just means that I can cheer for either the Beavers or the Ducks. I don't have a strong loyalty one way or the other."

"Given what I know about the Civil War, that sounds dangerous," he commented.

"It can be, so you'd better never share that with anyone. I'll deny it." I was somewhat joking.

Jack looked back at his daughter. "Will you need our help with your homework, Heide?"

Jack's use of the word "our" caused an exhilarated shiver to surge through me.

"Nah. I know what to do."

"That's good. Why don't you go finish up and get it over with for the evening."

"What about Kathleen?" she asked.

"Kathleen can keep me company while I make dinner."

"Okay." Heide bounded off the sofa, grabbed her backpack from the floor and flew off in the direction of her bedroom.

I followed Jack as he returned to the kitchen, but declined a proffered seat. Instead I leaned against the breakfast bar, more than ready to watch him prepare another meal with a graceful expertise I could never replicate, even on my best cooking day.

As he prepared our meal, I sipped my wine and allowed the alcohol to relax my body and my mind. We established a playful banter, and I was grateful when Jack avoided office and family politics. With dinner well underway and a small lull in his culinary duties, Jack washed his hands before closing the distance between us.

I watched in silent anticipation as he took the wine glass from my hand and set it down on the counter.

"Don't you want a taste?" I asked him, my voice husky.

"Absolutely," he confirmed before covering my lips with his own.

As I opened to him, he caressed my neck. Having just washed his hands, their touch was cool and soothing on my heated skin. When he touched my tongue with his after far too long, I gripped his hips and pulled his body closer. This was our first kiss since I'd last left his home, and in that time so much had taken place. I wanted to possess him and tightened my grasp. I was now holding a man I wasn't worthy of.

Jack had been easygoing and tender with me when I wasn't capable of treating him with the same consideration. He alone had brought me through a challenging time as my relationship with Robert hit a new low. Somehow, despite my frustrations and flare-ups, he still found something appealing about me.

Kissing this man in his kitchen, I found it was impossible to deny our emotional bond had strengthened. My connection to Jack was closer than ever before, and I was so happy to express this to him physically. I hummed my abundant appreciation and Jack deepened our kiss in instantaneous response.

He pressed against me even more, and I rejoiced as my breasts made contact with his chest. I answered by tightening my hold on his lower body, pulling him flush against me and was pleased to discover he was as aroused as I was. This insight was all it took for me to forget all sense of self and propriety. Our first night together had been incredible with its spontaneity, and now I was determined to show him just how grateful I was to have him.

Over the previous few weeks, I'd had plenty of time to myself, at night, in my bed. Often, I'd imagined what it would be like to kiss Jack again. Even though I'd already known his touch and his taste, this moment exceeded all expectation. Having him back in my arms with our bodies responding to one another meant more to me than my most detailed fantasies.

I lost myself in his kiss and the worry I carried with me disappeared in an instant. I couldn't care less about dinner; he was all I needed. All I yearned for was the opportunity to undress one another and fall back into his bed. I moved my hand down and slid it over the front of his trousers, communicating my truest desires. When Jack pushed his erection into my palm, I felt triumphant. I would make him mine again tonight.

The shrill noise of the phone on the kitchen counter jarred us both from the kiss. Jack rested his forehead against mine, and I closed my eyes while I attempted to regain my senses. When I attempted to match my shallow breaths with his, I realized he was holding his own. His body was tense, but not with desire. I opened my eyes. His were also open, but he wasn't looking at me.

He was listening for something, and my first thought was Heide discovering us in the middle of a heated embrace. The theory was confirmed when I heard his daughter's voice travel from the hallway into the living room.

"He's cooking dinner, Mom. And Kathleen is keeping him company."

Jack retreated to the stove without a word or a single reassuring gesture.

As Heide entered the kitchen, chatting away on the phone to her mother, I was in the throes of a different kind of shock and recovery.

I was frozen in place, not just because Jack's daughter had returned, but also because the emotional shift in the room was seismic. I gripped the countertop until my fingernails weakened under the pressure.

86

Heide held out the phone to her father as he glanced at her over his shoulder. "Mom wants to talk to you."

Jack smiled at Heide and reached for the phone. As soon as his fingers made contact, he began strolling from the kitchen with Heide following.

"How are you doing?" he asked. I bristled. It was the same greeting he used with me on the phone. Jack made his way through the living room and proceeded down the hallway. Even though I realized he was heading for his bedroom, I flinched when I heard the door close behind him.

I was alone in the kitchen. Not even the cat was around to stare at me. I heard a bird chirping from the yard and, after several moments, I stepped toward the living room with a touch of caution. It was empty, and I surmised that Heide had followed her father into his room. It was a perfect reminder I was an outsider and I had forgotten my place.

Unsure of when they would rejoin me in the kitchen, I wandered back to the counter and resumed my spot. I helped myself to another glass of wine until my mutinous hand began to shake mid-pour.

The few minutes until Jack returned to check on the dinner's progress were torturous. He made his way to the stove with just a passing grin in my direction.

I waited a few agonizing seconds for him to say something, but found myself unable to keep the awful silence. "Where's Heide?"

Jack answered without turning around. "She's just finishing up her phone call. She'll be along in a minute." His voice was quiet and controlled.

I recognized the tone from his conference room interaction with Robert. Was he attempting to disguise his strain?

"Is everything all right with Allison?" I couldn't stop myself from asking even though I feared broaching the subject of his ex-wife.

"She's fine," he supplied.

I took a big sip of wine as I pondered how to move forward with the evening. An unnerving silence dragged on until Heide reappeared for dinner.

"Do you want me to set the table?" she asked.

Jack nodded and told her that would be great, so I offered to help. I needed something to distract me from the awkwardness. Leave it to the seven-year-old to provide the perfect solution.

During dinner, the easiest thing to do would have been to yield to my personal insecurities and be angry with Jack. It was a real temptation.

Rather than focus on my own disappointment with the unpredictable turn in the evening, I put all my effort into easing Jack into contentment. There was something new in his eyes as we sat down to the table, something I interpreted as a mixture of worry and sadness. Something had upset him to the point of distraction, and it was this more than anything else that compelled me to make the meal as enjoyable as possible.

I turned most of my attention to Heide and picked up our earlier conversation about mountain climbing, a subject she was more than eager to discuss and one that allowed Jack time to process whatever was on his mind.

Talking with Heide was effortless and I enjoyed listening to her. As dinner wound down and we began clearing the table, Jack's posture loosened. He even hazarded a smile or two in my direction, but I was also no fool. Whatever hopes there had been for this night were off the table along with the dishes.

When Heide made herself scarce just as the cleanup was about to begin, I followed her direction.

"I could use some fresh air," I admitted. "Do you mind if I step outside for a minute?"

Jack looked surprised, but nodded. "Sure."

I smiled with what I hoped was a welcoming expression. "Join me when you're ready?"

He nodded again before looking down to inspect the impending workload.

I opened the door off Jack's kitchen and stepped onto a courtyard. Pulling the door shut behind me, I observed that the space was an outdoor seating area, complete with padded seating and a fire pit. I chose a spot on a swinging bench seat, closed my eyes and took a deep breath, hoping my plan would fall into place without a great deal of manipulation.

When we had made plans for this evening, there had been no talk of my going home. Now, in the wake of Jack's emotional detachment, I had to extract myself from the situation. I didn't want to argue with Jack. I was prepared to call a taxi if need be, but I'd prefer Jack to drive me home. I tried to clear my mind by listening to the evening breeze blow through a nearby tree line, a pleasant sound that kept me company until Jack opened the door.

I opened my eyes and studied him as he took a seat next to me on the bench swing. He was still out of sorts but began talking just as soon as he settled.

"It's early to see the stars."

I considered Jack's words, remembering his knack for evading uncomfortable subject matter.

"True," I began slowly. "But you're also in town. It wouldn't be the best view anyhow." I hesitated before picking up the thread of conversation. "When I was little, we lived outside of town above the river. I swear I spent every summer night, sitting outside studying the sky. I could see it all—planets, comets, meteor showers, the Milky Way, Andromeda, even passing satellites."

"I've always been in a city, so I don't know that much about constellations."

"The sky was endless. I didn't comprehend that until I tried to keep track of each speck of light I saw. I've forgotten a lot of it, but I could teach you a few things if you're interested."

My nerves got the better of me, and I crossed my arms over my chest.

Jack frowned as he rubbed his chin. "I've made a mess of things this evening. I wasn't prepared for that phone call."

I shrugged. "Dating is complicated."

"Yeah."

"Was Allison upset because of me?"

"I suppose," he answered. "But that isn't the point. She left me. It shouldn't matter if she's upset." Jack sounded hurt.

I took a few moments to consider what that meant before I asked him another question.

"Has she been dating anyone since she returned to Baltimore?"

Jack blinked as though the thought had never occurred to him. "I don't know."

"Would you be upset if she started dating again?"

Jack didn't answer the question, so I tried to fill the void in conversation.

"You were married to one another. You have a child together. If she is upset, it does matter. She is Heide's mother, and she doesn't know anything about who I am or what I want from you. If Allison started dating another man, you'd have the same questions about him because your daughter would be in contact with him. I can't take that personally."

Jack reached for my hand and wrapped his fingers around mine. "Thank you, Kathleen."

I'd been concerned about how Heide would welcome me into her father's life. But it was Allison's reaction that was increasingly important to me. She was a complication I had considered with a great deal of thought, and this was the first opportunity I'd had to talk with Jack about it. "I need to tell you something. Do you mind?"

He looked anxious, but said, "Please."

"We weren't prepared to date one another, so there have been more than a few bumps along the way. But I've enjoyed getting to know you and Heide, and I care about you both. I don't want you to worry about me interfering with your family. I told you this the morning after we slept together and I meant it. I refuse to be a troublemaker."

Jack turned to face me. "Do you think that's why I was upset tonight?"

"No, but it's still important you understand this about me. I'm not interested in making things difficult. I hope that helps you."

"It does."

"Good." I took in a deep breath. "Keeping that in mind, I hope you'll understand if I ask you to take me home this evening." I offered a tentative smile.

After a few moments of contemplation, Jack replied, "I suppose that's for the best. But please know that I wish tonight had turned out differently."

"So do I, Jack. I did enjoy some good wine and one hell of a kiss before dinner though, so it wasn't a total loss."

Jack chuckled and I leaned over and pecked him on the cheek. I allowed my lips to linger on his skin for an extra beat or two before pulling away. He had done the same to me in his bedroom when I had been upset with him, and I remembered how the sensation had soothed my anxiety.

"You made such a good dinner. Let me help you with the rest of the dishes, and then I'll treat us to some ice cream on the way home. I think we've all earned it tonight."

"That does sound good," he said. Jack rose from the bench and held out a hand to me. As soon as I was on my feet, he encircled me in his arms.

I looked into his dark eyes. I was encouraged by how relaxed he was now that we'd cleared the air.

"What are your plans after the event next week?"

"Why?" I asked.

"Heide isn't coming with me to Portland, and I'm spending the night there."

"Oh?" I squeaked.

"Please think about it." Jack released me and walked back into the house.

chapter

Thirteen

I SPENT the following week thinking about Jack's offer.

We didn't speak of the upcoming business trip in anything other than professional terms, but away from work I planned my outfit for the luncheon with a great deal of consideration and excitement. As the day drew closer, I anticipated the best and planned for the worst. Things with Jack could, and did, turn on a dime, and the one thing I could count on with certainty was the uncertainty of Jack Evans.

After several long days and nights, I arrived in downtown Portland. My family had relocated from the city years earlier, but my grandfather's reputation had kept those business relationships alive so we were welcomed back each spring for this all-important luncheon. I took the assignment seriously and set my personal agenda aside to work my way through Robert's logistical checklist.

Once I was satisfied the details were under control, I occupied an empty office to dress for the event. I was eager to get the day moving, but forced myself to remain patient for the moment Jack and I would see one another again. As I donned each item of my ensemble, the idea of Jack undoing it all aroused me. With my transformation completed, I went to the rooftop garden off the main event room.

I wanted to enjoy a few peaceful moments outside in the sunshine. Although I'd been happy living in Bend, I also enjoyed my time in Portland. From my vantage point, I could hear the urban noise several stories below. As I meandered through the garden, I could see the nearby Willamette River. It was a clear, warm day with Mount Hood visible to the east. I also had a spectacular view of Mount Saint Helens to the north.

This rooftop oasis had been a favorite place of mine since the first time my grandfather had shown it to me. As a child, I'd been fascinated with the idea of a playground on a skyscraper. As an adolescent, I'd found the garden a perfect place to indulge my daydreams of a glamourous life as an adult. I smiled as I realized this day was the closest I'd ever come to achieving my romantic fantasies.

I paused to make a final, somewhat nervous, assessment of my outfit, one of the most lavish I'd ever purchased. I wore a black dress with a dramatic scarlet V-neck. It was damn near impossible for the bright accent not to draw the eye to my cleavage, and I'd brought it with this in mind. The dress cinched at the waist, and although the skirt flared, it highlighted my legs in a pleasing way. My favorite, but seldom worn pair of black high heels completed the look. I rarely had the opportunity to wear these sexy shoes at home.

The outfit was a daring choice for a business lunch, and it would draw attention in a crowd. But I didn't care about the crowd's attention. I was concerned with capturing the eye of just one man.

Jack opened the terrace door and approached me. He was dressed in an attractive suit accented with a dark necktie and shoes that were both well shined and expensive. He'd cut his hair since I'd seen him at the office, and he'd indulged in a close shave.

I caught my breath in exhilaration, because not only was he so handsome, but because his eyes roamed up and down my figure. My appearance was having the same effect on him. I stood still as he moved in my direction. Everything about his demeanor, his tailored appearance and especially the intense warmth of his eyes as they stared back at me was mesmerizing. I softened with complete happiness, and the closer he came to me, the more my eyes widened in desire. My lips parted in welcome, and Jack responded with a knowing, half-smile. Without a word, he walked confidently to me, grasped me by the waist and pulled me into his arms. My hands moved as if they were floating, and rested on his shoulders.

"You look beautiful," he said.

It had been my goal to dazzle Jack and I'd succeeded. Nevertheless, his words forced me to blink and look away even as I smiled. "Thank you."

Jack tightened his hold. "Is this all right?"

"I'm holding you back."

"True." Jack chuckled, sounding nervous. When I turned my gaze back to him, he continued, "I've missed you. We see each other at the office, but I like having you back in my arms. I've missed you," he repeated.

"This is good," I said.

"You surprise me."

"How so?"

"You have a streak of daring in you. You're just really good at keeping it quiet."

"Only with a select few," I whispered, as heat rushed to my cheeks.

"I want to kiss you," he confessed. "I think about it more than I should."

I glanced around at our surroundings. "We seem to be alone for now."

Jack slid his hands upward, over the curve of my waist and paused just below my breasts. His thumbs stroked the bottom of my bra, and he looked into my eyes, making sure he had my full attention.

We stared at one another, words unspoken, our passion strengthening between us. I moved a hand to caress his jawline. Jack's skin was smooth, and I could smell his scented soap in the light breeze. I slid my hand around the back of his neck and tugged him toward me in greeting.

Jack didn't resist. He leaned in and brought his lips to mine. I could sense his respect, but I was confident his desire to kiss me was strong. I opened my mouth, eager to receive him. After a passage of time, Jack decided either we were alone or that he didn't care whether someone noticed us. He pressed in closer to me and our tongues connected and explored, gentle yet ambitious.

He pulled back from the kiss far too soon for my liking, but we kept our arms locked around one another. I played with the shortened hair along his neckline in the hope of relaxing him with my touch.

We were content in our embrace. Having shared so few intimate moments together, we both reveled in the newness and excitement of our connection. Jack watched my mouth intently. His desires were obvious.

"Jack?"

"Hmm?"

"Kiss me again."

He obliged, and this time he was more aggressive, planting his feet on the ground and pulling my body flush with his.

We kissed for a prolonged period, and I was grateful for the uninterrupted time. When Jack pulled back, his long fingers traveled all the way down to my thighs. I was surprised, but delighted when his grip tightened on my legs. I held still, enjoying the sensation of his strong hands on this part of my body once more.

"Every time I see you in a dress," he murmured. "I remember how you wore a garter the night we were together. It makes me wonder what you're wearing under your skirt."

Jack stretched his hands to roam around my legs, exploring, searching for the answer. I waited, allowing him to enjoy his quest.

He made his determination. "No garter today?"

I shook my head and then attempted to hide my amusement as mild disappoint flickered across his face. He glanced down to make another observation.

"You're wearing stockings."

"Thigh highs."

"No garter though?" he asked again, as if hoping the item would magically appear on my frame.

"Not today."

I decided to share one of my secrets. "On days like this, I'm more confident with fewer undergarments in place."

"Oh?"

I shrugged. "Maybe if things go well this afternoon, I'll let you have a look."

This was going to be the longest luncheon of my career. Whenever I looked his way, Jack was engaged in conversation with a different woman. One was wearing a violet colored dress that accented her bust line. Still another was in a black wrap dress, which flattered her athletic figure. I grew upset when I saw more than one feminine hand make contact with Jack's arm, but I was pleased to see Jack keeping his hands to himself.

Nevertheless, he was engaging the women with his personality. They laughed at his jokes, they stared back with interest and all the while, they made sure their best assets were on full display.

Not that I acted like a wallflower. My outfit was a hit with the men in the room and I found myself speaking with quite a few gentlemen. I sensed Jack watching me just as I'd watched him.

After a while, I wandered to safe ground with Theresa Mayfair, a longtime friend and client. She was a petite brunette who possessed one of the biggest hearts I'd ever known. Theresa was a reliable presence in my life, and I was closer to her than just about anyone else in my own family. She had been there for me during some of my most frightening days, and I'd been grateful for her protection.

While I chatted with her, Jack had removed his jacket and sat on a bench near the terrace door. His white dress shirt clung to his torso, and even though I was halfway across the room, I could see his well-defined chest muscles.

Another woman sat down next to him, her skirt sporting a high slit that just happened to expose her toned thigh within direct view of his line of sight. Her bare leg rested mere inches from his, and the image made me seethe.

The two began to talk, but were soon interrupted by a middle-aged man who drew Jack's attention away, much to the chagrin of the woman. I made a mental note to say thank you to the man before he departed the luncheon. Satisfied with this turn of events, I smiled at no one in particular.

"I take it that's your firm's newest acquisition?" my astute friend asked, determining the source of my happiness.

"Jack Evans. Yes. Robert recruited him from back East."

"He's striking, and he watches you almost as much you watch him."

I wasn't sure how to respond, so I sipped some water.

"Is he married? I can't tell from here."

"No." It was the one answer I was comfortable providing.

Robert approached us, and for once it was a relief to welcome him into the conversation. He greeted Theresa before saying hello to me.

Theresa looked at Robert. "I was just getting ready to tell Kathleen that she's outdone herself planning this year's lunch. This is one of the biggest turnouts I've seen. I do hope you've shown her your appreciation."

Robert glanced around the room before looking at me. "She's always done a good job." As my father finished his statement, he looked me over from head to toe. A severe look of disapproval formed in the process.

"Laying it on a bit thick with that dress, don't you think?"

Theresa scoffed. "Don't be ridiculous, Robert. Kathleen is a gorgeous, accomplished woman. She's sophisticated and forward thinking. She's just what this party needs."

I remained silent and watched this exchange. Theresa had known Robert since before I was born, and she had played this game with him before. Robert had a healthy dose of respect when it came to Theresa. He may not have admired her per se, but my father seemed to know better than to push the woman. Theresa's inner strength and her refusal to be intimidated by Robert were the main reasons I sought refuge at the woman's side. I'd done so for as long as I could remember. Since growing into adulthood, I'd wondered more about their history, but I had yet to ask Theresa for any of the details.

My father glanced at his watch. "Kathleen, it's time to have the servers bring out the food."

I nodded and gave Theresa a quick hug before moving on to speak with the catering manager.

Robert had a long-standing policy at these events of assigning his staff to sit at separate tables. In the past, I hadn't minded the policy because it ensured I wouldn't be forced to sit with my father. But this year was different. This was the first time I'd suffer because Jack and I wouldn't be sitting together. And after our intimate encounter on the rooftop followed by the non-stop female attention he was receiving, sitting away from him would be utter agony.

I went to my assigned table and offered my greetings to those already gathered.

"Is this seat taken?" I looked up to see a man my own age standing behind the unclaimed chair to my right and smiling down at me.

"No. Please." I gestured at the chair.

He settled into place with a polite nod. He wore dark trousers and a light blue dress shirt. Despite his relaxed looking outfit, his clothes were affluent. He was also a good-looking man, with a thick head of blond hair, sparkling blue eyes and a contented successful air.

As it turned out, his manners were as flawless as his appearance. Once seated, he introduced himself, offering me his hand.

"Ryan Murray."

I accepted his handshake. He held my hand confidently and with respect.

"Nice to meet you, Ryan. My name is Kathleen Brighton."

When Ryan released my hand, he leaned in just a little. My curiosity allowed me to lean toward him.

"Please pardon me for saying so, Kathleen, but you look exquisite. Is it sad to say I find it nice when I see elegance and boldness applied to an advertising company's lunch?" Ryan's compliment wasn't sexual.

"Thank you. I'll admit it's dressier than I'm accustomed to," I replied with warmth.

"You have impeccable taste."

Ryan struck up a conversation with me during our meal, and I was delighted. His intentions felt like genuine interest and not pursuit. I relaxed further and we fell into an easy discussion.

"I've never seen you at this event before. Where do you work?" I inquired.

"I'm from Denver. I own a marketing firm there."

"Portland is one hell of a trek just for some lunch."

Ryan laughed before answering, "I'm in town on business. A client of mine invited me here as his guest. I'm not here to spy, but I may borrow an idea or two if you don't mind."

"I won't tell anyone. I won't even ask who your client is."

We continued to talk as the lunch progressed. In fact, I had to remind myself to address the other table occupants from time to time. I was also pleased when Ryan began to make sure my basic needs were met at the table. He passed me items that were outside my reach and helped me to clear space when needed, all without a single request from me.

When Robert finished eating, he rose and worked the room as he made his way to a centrally placed podium. My father monitored my interactions with Ryan and gave me a satisfied nod. This was as good as I'd get from him all day.

When Robert began his post-meal presentation, Ryan leaned in close to me and said, "I see some iced tea over there by the wall. Can I pour you a glass?"

The air had warmed up with the midday sunshine and numerous bodies in the room, not to mention my own internal heat.

"Yes. That would be perfect. Thank you."

Having attended this event for many years, I tuned out Robert. Instead, I let my new friend's movements distract me as he prepared two glasses of iced tea. I was having a good time with Ryan and hoped to chat with him again before the lunch wound down.

I opted not to stare at the man as he returned to our table, and as I attempted to resettle in my seat, I made eye contact with Jack. It was the first time I'd acknowledged him since meeting Ryan. Jack sat a few tables away, staring at me and wearing a slight frown.

I wanted to reassure him, but flirting with him from across the room wasn't the way to do it. Instead, I offered Jack a quick smile before Ryan returned to the table with my glass. Ryan raised his glass and I lifted mine, and we clinked them together before each taking a sip. When I returned my glass to the table, I snuck another look at Jack. His attention was on Robert's speech as he sat back in his chair with his arms crossed.

At the end of the lunch, Ryan offered me his business card and asked for mine in return. I took one from my small stack of cards on the table and handed it to him. We shook hands once again and he surprised me by kissing both my cheeks while holding my hand.

It was impulsive, but I walked him to the elevator to say a proper farewell.

"I'm so glad you accepted your client's invitation, Ryan."

He smiled. "It wasn't planned, but I'm so pleased to have met you, Kathleen. I enjoyed your company. Meeting you has been a highlight of my week." When the elevator door opened, he stepped inside.

"Have a safe trip home, Ryan."

We waved to one another as the doors closed.

I returned to the event room and helped Jack, Robert and the rest of the staff see our guests off with a thank you and an assurance of future meetings.

Together, Jack and I found ways to linger in the room while the rest of the staff sought escape. The sooner they left, the sooner they could enjoy an afternoon off in the city. Once the crowd departed and Robert left to entertain some of his most valued clients, Jack and I were alone.

Jack made no pretenses, much to my immediate relief.

"I'm going back to my hotel now." He stared down at my high heels. "Can you walk a few blocks in those shoes? Or should I call us a taxi?"

We were already out in the lobby, and I pressed the button for the elevator. "I don't want to wait for a cab. I can walk."

We stared at one another as we waited for the elevator to arrive, but maintained our physical distance. When we emerged onto the street, we walked without speaking. I didn't want to think about work and focused on making my way to our destination.

At the hotel, we took a second elevator ride in anticipatory silence and when we arrived on his floor, I followed Jack down the hallway to his suite. He opened the door and held it open for me to pass through. I began undressing as soon as I cleared the doorway.

chapter  Fourteen

"STOP."

I paused the moment Jack's gruff voice touched my ears. My fantasies of this particular moment had included loving caresses, whispered affections and the slow, erotic removal of one another's elegant outfits. The reality was much more abrupt.

Most of my clothes were already off, and although I was afraid to look up, I did anyway. My worries were for nothing.

Jack was still undressing, having only removed his suit jacket, shoes and socks. I watched without shame as he methodically took off his trousers and then unbuttoned his white dress shirt. He pulled his white undershirt up and over his head with deliberate slowness, and didn't hesitate to push down his boxer briefs almost as soon as his tee shirt hit the floor.

Once Jack was naked, he sat on the edge of the king-sized bed. He didn't even bother to pull back the duvet. I stared at him, having forgotten there wasn't one part of his body that didn't fascinate me. With his dark hair and eyes, olive complexion, broad shoulders and toned muscles, Jack was my ideal man.

"Come here," he commanded. "Now."

Jack's eyes were intense and his face displayed a rare ruggedness that had me obeying him. Under another set of circumstances, I might have found his tone too aggressive, but this energy had been building between us for weeks. I understood his impatience.

I still wore my sheer stockings and despite the barest layer of clothing covering me, I felt more exposed to him than I ever had. As soon as I was within arm's length, Jack grasped my hips. He glanced down at my legs, furrowing his brow, and I ran my fingers through his thick hair.

"What's wrong?" I whispered.

"Nothing." Jack traced the scarlet paisley and floral designs at the top of my thigh highs. My heart raced as his unhurried touch drifted along my legs. I tried to follow Jack's lead and took in a controlled breath. I wanted to savor each second with him, to enjoy his caresses, but I found it difficult to relax.

"Where did you get these?" He rested his warm palm on my bare backside.

"They came from Paris," I rasped. "I've been saving them for a special occasion."

Without another word, Jack pulled me down to the mattress and rolled me onto my back. He lowered his body on top of mine, and the contact of our bare skin was overpowering. Jack brought his lips to my neck. As his sensual mouth traveled across my skin, I tightened my embrace. I'd held him like this once before and had been waiting too long for another chance.

Jack's hands roamed over my body, and his thoroughness delighted me. After a time, he rose and knelt back between my legs. He massaged my breasts before trailing his long fingers down my stomach and over my thighs. When his fingertips reached my stockings, he bowed his head over my leg. The pleasurable sensation of his tongue gliding slowly along the scalloped border of my silk stocking followed his warm breath. He moved his mouth from the top of my leg down to my inner thigh before he dropped down to the most sensitive part of my being.

He had sworn to pleasure me with his mouth. The caress of Jack's tongue was measured and determined, and I welcomed the sensation. This intimate act required more trust than I was willing to offer any man, and yet with Jack I questioned nothing. I didn't close my legs to him or try to pull away from his touch.

I was his. And this realization startled me. The experience was foreign, and almost as soon as I comprehended this, I came. I came hard.

Once my orgasm subsided, Jack rose back up and lifted my leg from under the knee. He took hold of my stocking, slowly pushed it down my calf and off my foot before releasing my leg. He repeated the gesture with my other leg before lying next to me on the bed.

I should have been sated by that one incredible act, but it only fueled my desire to have this man once and for all. As soon as I caught my breath, I rolled onto his body and straddled him. We both inhaled sharply when our lower bodies made direct contact.

"Is this what you want?" I asked with a breathy voice. "Me on top?"

"Yes."

"Why?"

"I want to see you. I want you over me."

"You want me in control."

"Yes."

I rubbed against him.

A groan escaped his lips.

"Put your hands behind your head," I instructed, elated in the power I had over him.

When he did, I eased myself onto him, but just enough to keep my focus. He moaned again, thrilling me to no end. My newfound bravery flourished as I watched this beautiful man surrender to my impulses.

"Tell me something, Jack."

"What?"

"Before me. When was the last time you had sex?"

I held my body still as I waited for his answer.

His face altered, reflecting his apprehension. "What do you mean?"

"You know what I mean. The question is clear enough."

"Is it?"

"Don't be evasive, Jack," I warned him. "No matter what the answer is, this is still going to happen." I swiveled my hips a little to punctuate my statement. "I just need to know."

He scrutinized me. When he didn't respond, I pulled away from him a bit and asked a more direct question.

"Have you been with other women since your marriage ended?"

"No."

"Do you miss sex, Jack?"

"Kathleen ..." Jack's voice was a combination of reprove and surprise. He was shocked by my inquiry in this moment of intimacy, but remained beneath me. Even more important, he hardened.

"Is this happening because you miss sex?" I pushed my hips forward again, just a bit.

"No."

"You're an attractive man. You proved that today. Any of those women would've slept with you if you asked."

Jack blinked at my statement, but kept his silence.

"Is there more to what's happening between us?"

"I don't know what's happening," he said. "All I can think about is being with you again. I want you, Kathleen."

"You want sex from me?"

He pushed up inside me just a bit more as he answered. "Yes. So much."

I pulled backward from him once again. "I'm not good with casual, Jack. Is what's happening between us casual?"

"No."

"But this moment, this is simply about lust. Am I wrong?"

"No. You're not wrong."

"And you want this from me?"

Although Jack kept his hands above his head as requested, he stretched his body in anticipation.

"Only from you, Kathleen. I want you riding me. I want you to enjoy me. I want you to tighten around me, and then I want you to make me come."

"You could have chosen some other woman at that lunch."

"Maybe. But I choose you. You're the one I want to please. You're the one I want to please me."

I pushed forward again, emotionally satisfied, when Jack brought down his hands and pressed his fingers into my thighs.

"What about you, Kathleen?" he challenged. "You had that man wrapped around your finger at lunch. You even followed him out the door."

It was now my turn to maintain silence while Jack resisted pushing himself inside me.

"I've never seen that man before," he told me. "Do you even know who he is?"

"I do now," I admitted while tilting my hips toward him again.

Jack's hold on my legs tightened, halting my movements. "Are you sure I'm the man you want?"

"Yes," I told him. "Only you."

"Did you wake up this morning anticipating this?" He pushed inside me just a little bit more. "Did you look forward to seducing me this afternoon?"

"Yes," I confessed. "Yes, I did, and I'm not going to waste the opportunity." I wriggled my hips and this time Jack did not resist. I enjoyed his full and glorious penetration of my body. We both responded loudly, and I arched my back as I pushed my hips forward.

"We'll worry about the rest later," I gasped.

Jack didn't object, so I began to move with ambition. My body was still sensitive from my orgasm, and my pleasure overtook me after a few gyrations. As I began to pant, Jack cupped my breasts. His thumbs brushed over my nipples, and they constricted from his contact. He stirred beneath me, and I leaned forward and offered them to his waiting mouth.

Jack closed his lips around my right breast and halted my movements by firmly placing his hands on my backside. As I brought my hand to the back of his head to encourage his kisses, Jack began thrusting upward. With each ambitious stroke, Jack edged me ever closer to another powerful orgasm.

"You're gorgeous," he rasped. "Incredible. So tight."

"I missed this."

"Anything for you."

"Don't stop," I gasped. "Don't you dare stop."

He responded by increasing the speed and depth of his thrusts. The bed began to creak in protest, but we were both beyond caring.

From where our bodies were joined, warmth and pleasure began to radiate throughout my entire being. A distinctive tingling rippled over my breasts, and I yearned for Jack's release within me before this tremendous moment ebbed away.

"Please, Jack," I begged. "Come with me."

My body tightened as the tingling exploded into another orgasm. My mouth dropped open, and I threw my head back and arched my body so far my hair tickled my lower back as I cried out. Jack grunted and somehow managed to push himself deeper into my body with one final, forceful lunge. His release was strong as his body pulsed inside of mine, but even so my ecstasy wasn't complete until my name tumbled from his lips. As Jack called my name over and over again, a wave of gratitude washed over me.

Finally.

After our initial lust-fueled frenzy subsided and Jack withdrew from my body, I moved to his side and lightly dozed while he ran his fingers along my back.

Sometime later, I stirred awake and turned my head toward him. My eyes met his, and I was happy to see he'd been watching me.

I couldn't help myself. I smiled, and Jack returned with a grin of his own. There was little space between our bodies, but even so he moved closer and pulled me into his arms. I settled my cheek over his heart and idly played with the hairs on his chest with my fingers.

Jack began to drag his fingers through my long tresses.

My eyes drifted closed as I bathed in the serenity of the moment.

"Kathleen?" Jack's voice was quiet. Reflective. Sexy.

"Yes?"

"Last time you said birth control was taken care of, but I was wondering if you'd tell me how."

In my drowsiness, I was confused. Then I remembered that Jack wasn't there when it all went to hell.

"You don't have to worry," I mumbled. "Pregnancy is impossible."

"Why?"

I was tempted to sit up and examine his face, to see how interested he was in the details. But I was too sated to move. He'd been married and was the father of a daughter, so I decided he could handle the full explanation.

"I had trouble with my cycles, even from the beginning. They just got worse over time, and I could never get a doctor to listen to me. One day I was at the office, sick. I stood up from my desk to get a file and everything went dark."

"You collapsed?" Jack's voice was full of concern, but the soothing movements of his fingers in my hair continued.

I nodded. "The next thing I remember is waking up in a recovery room."

"What happened?"

"An ovary ruptured and I almost bled to death at work. I had to receive a blood transfusion. But that wasn't the end of my problems. While they were operating on me, my uterus began to bleed, too. They didn't know why. It's a mystery."

"How old were you?"

"Thirty." It was the first time I'd talked about the incident in years, and I was compelled to share more.

"When I was returned to my hospital room, my father was waiting for me. I think he sat with me all evening."

"Oh?" Jack was unable to hide his astonishment.

"I was in and out of it for hours, but Robert was there whenever I woke up. He was holding my hand. The next day I found out I'd had a hysterectomy."

"Was that difficult for you?"

"No. I think in many ways, my mind already knew my body wasn't capable. I never had the desire to be a mother. Not like my friends. I never was focused on it or excited about it like they all were. It's just as well. I don't have a maternal instinct. "

"That's not true."

I opened my eyes but couldn't look up at Jack. "What do you mean?"

"You're a natural with Heide. She likes you."

I grinned. "I like her. She's feisty."

"You'd be a wonderful mother, Kathleen."

I shrugged. I didn't believe what he was saying. "It's not in the cards for me," I reiterated.

"You don't know that. There's more than one way to become a parent."

I opted not to pursue the conversation.

I was terrified that Jack meant something other than a future with him.

We had sex a second time that afternoon and experimented with several positions for more than an hour. By the time we climaxed, our bodies were slick with perspiration and one another's kisses. Afterward, we fell asleep where we had collapsed in a tangle of limbs on the ravaged bed.

When I roused myself back into consciousness, I was sated, but sore and fatigued. I attempted to straighten my arms and legs, but my body was slow to respond. The room had grown darker during our nap.

"What time is it?" he asked while reaching for his phone on the bedside table.

"You tell me," I responded.

Jack glanced at it before setting it back down on the mattress. "Late enough. We should think about what to do for dinner."

"I don't care about food," I confessed. "I'd prefer a bubble bath."

Jack rose from the bed and stretched. I watched his backside as he raised his arms toward the ceiling. When he turned to face me, I watched his front.

"Your body is amazing," I said.

"Thank you." He grinned. "Why don't you take that bath? I should see how Heide's day went. Do you mind?"

"Not at all." I started to get up, but Jack held up his hand.

"Let me start the bath for you. I want you to relax."

"Are you sure?"

He was already making his way into the bathroom. "How warm should I make the water?"

"As hot as you can stand it. And then I'll kick it up a couple of degrees."

As the water poured into the tub, I grew eager to let the bath soothe me. I rolled onto my stomach and listened to the white noise, allowing it to lull me into another brief doze.

The soft touch of Jack's lips on my bare shoulder brought me back.

"Come, Kathleen," Jack whispered as he helped me up from the mattress. He guided me through the suite and into the bathroom and held my hand as I stepped into the hot water and lowered myself into the bubbles. Ever resourceful, Jack had given me the perfect temperature. I moaned in appreciation as I sank farther into the tub.

"This is wonderful. Thank you."

"I want you to stay here tonight. Will you?"

I nodded without hesitation. "I'll need to go back to the event room though. I left my bag behind."

"Is your car in the garage there?"

"Yes. My keys are in the bag."

"I'll go get your bag and move your car here."

"I'm sorry. I should have planned better."

"Don't apologize. It's not that far and a walk sounds good. You'll be fine while I'm gone?"

"Oh, yes."

Jack knelt down next to the tub and rubbed my neck with his strong hands.

"I want you to think about eating something this evening. We can order room service if you're tired. But if you're up to it, I have a particular restaurant in mind. If you want to get some fresh air and a good meal, I'd be happy to make us a reservation. It's nearby, so we can walk. Or I can call a cab to take us there. I'll leave it up to you."

I was somewhat reluctant to leave Jack's room, concerned that doing so would derail our momentum. But Jack sounded so eager to take me out for a proper meal I decided to indulge his wishes.

"If I can have another small nap after my bath, we can walk to the restaurant. That sounds nice."

"I'll make our reservation for eight o'clock. I don't want you to be rushed."

"Be careful, Jack. You're spoiling me. I won't want to go back home."

Jack smiled and kissed me on the forehead before rising and sauntering from the bathroom. I paid particular attention to his ass as he went. I wanted that image forever imprinted in my memory.

When I emerged from the bubble bath, Jack was gone but he'd surprised me by picking up my clothes and placing them in the closet. He'd also repaired the bed and arranged the pillows in an inviting way. He'd made it all too easy to lie down and rest until it was time to get ready for our evening out.

chapter
Fifteen

WHEN I roused from my nap, Jack was sitting nearby on a comfortable looking chaise lounge. He was dressed for dinner and reading the newspaper. As I raised my arms to stretch them over my head, I inhaled the pleasant combination of his soap and my bubble bath. I slipped from under the covers, stark naked, and approached him to place a light kiss on his forehead. Jack grinned, but kept his hands to himself.

"I was just thinking about waking you," he said.

A slow smile spread across my face as his eyes lingered on my nude form.

When his gaze returned to my face, he asked, "What is that look all about? I've never seen you look at me quite like that before."

I tapped his newspaper. "This."

Jack's expression was puzzled. "The paper?"

"You're such a grown-up."

Jack released the newspaper and it withered as he skimmed his fingers over and down my hip. He dropped his thumb just enough to exert a glorious bit of pressure against my sex.

"So are you," he replied, his voice low.

I closed my eyes and sighed over his skilled caresses.

"No, I'm not," I murmured while reopening my eyes, "but I could play one on TV."

Jack chuckled, but couldn't disguise the automatic furrowing of his brow. "Your bag is on the bathroom counter," he said, changing subjects as he was prone to do. "If you still want to walk, we should leave in thirty minutes."

"Perfect. Thanks." As I turned toward the bathroom, I trailed my fingers down the sleeve of his blazer and was rewarded with the barest touch of his hand across my backside before I walked out of reach.

It was a warm summer evening in downtown Portland with no breeze to stir up a chill from the Willamette River. I wore a cotton dress and light sweater to complement Jack's choice of denim jeans, blue shirt and navy blazer. As soon as we stepped outside the hotel lobby and onto the sidewalk, Jack wrapped his arm around my waist.

"Do you want me to tell you where we're going?" Jack inquired. "Or do you enjoy surprises?"

"You could march me over to the food trucks and I wouldn't care. I'm just happy to be with you tonight."

"Me, too. But no food trucks this evening."

"VooDoo Doughnuts, then?" I ventured.

He chuckled. "Maybe tomorrow."

"Lead the way, Mr. Evans."

Jack turned us east, and we began making our way toward the river. The streets of downtown Portland were quieting down for the evening. Most of the people who spent their workdays in the city center had vacated for the night, allowing us to stroll through the city in near privacy. We walked and chatted, enjoying the warmth of the summer evening and one another's company.

When the familiar golden VQ sign came into view, I pointed to it. "Is this where we're going?"

Jack nodded. He'd chosen none other than Veritable Quandary.

"Have you been here before?" I asked.

"No. Have you?" There was a slight tinge of worry on his normally relaxed features.

"I've been here for family dinners, but never on a date."

"Good." Jack tightened his grip on my waist.

"I have to commend you on your ability to secure a last minute reservation. Do you have any idea how popular this place is?"

Jack shrugged off the compliment. "I couldn't secure a spot on the outdoor patio. Truth be told, we may have to settle for something in the lounge."

"I don't care." I was relaxed and happy just to be with Jack. Nothing mattered but him. I'd never felt so close and connected to him, or to anyone, for that matter. I was beginning to believe we were becoming a couple.

Jack held the door open for me and after speaking with a young woman, we were led straight to the dining room. As we settled in our seats, I nodded toward the floor to ceiling windows across from our table.

"It's a view of the patio. Well done."

Jack grinned. "I have to give credit to our generous hostess."

As we perused our menus, he glanced my way. "You've been here before. What do you recommend?"

"You can't go wrong with anything on the menu," I deflected.

"Shall I surprise you once again?"

I set the menu down with a smile. "Please. I'd love to see what you'd choose for us."

Our waiter returned and Jack placed our order — grilled wild prawns, sweet black rice, and spicy Asian slaw. He also selected a bottle of sauvignon blanc, which we enjoyed while we waited for our meal to arrive.

As we waited for dinner, our conversation was light and fun, focusing on the city we were visiting and some of its quirkier yet endearing traits.

"Did you speak with Heide?" I asked after our food arrived.

"Yes." Jack's eyes sparkled at the mention of his daughter, and he smiled as he relayed his story. "She tolerated my questions about her day, but she had other things going on. Don't get me wrong. It's good to hear she's doing fine."

"She seems to like it in Bend," I commented as I lifted a delectable morsel to my lips.

Jack paused before he answered with a loving sincerity. "She's handled everything so well. She inspires me."

I shifted my posture, hoping it would import my seriousness. "You've been going through some big changes."

"Yeah," Jack replied with a rare display of casualness.

I was apprehensive to broach the subject of his personal life, but this one word answer demonstrated a sense of serenity in Jack.

I jumped into the deep end. "How long were you and Allison married?"

"Not quite seven years." I paused to connect the dots.

Jack smirked. "We got married after we found out Allison was pregnant."

My eyes grew wide in amused surprise.

Jack rubbed the back of his neck as he plodded on with his explanation. "We'd been together about six months. We weren't even living together yet, but given enough time, I would have proposed."

"How did you meet her?"

"We were introduced by a mutual friend at a barbecue, and I'll admit I fell in love with her almost immediately. But there were complications in our relationship. At first, I found the differences between us small and attractive." Jack's voice drifted off.

I wanted more of the story. Hoping he would provide more details, I asked, "Then what?"

"After Heide was born, we began arguing more and more. I tried to dismiss our troubles as part of the adjustment to parenthood, but spent too much time denying our fundamental problems instead of trying to find a way to fix them."

Jack paused and took a few contemplative sips of his wine. "The move out here was my idea. I'd been restless and looking at other opportunities for a while, but never jumped on a single one until I heard about the job here. We'd never even been to Oregon."

A small part of me was pleased to hear Jack say this. My reaction to this revelation was selfish. I knew it, but I couldn't help myself. Here he was, recounting the end of his marriage and somehow I was experiencing happiness over it. My emotions in this moment were an unwelcome reminder that half my DNA came from Robert. I squirmed in my seat, frantic to shake off the sentiment.

Jack continued with his story, and my anxiety escaped his attention. "I intended the move to be a new chance for the three of us. I thought the change of pace and scenery would bring the excitement back to our lives. But it ended up being the last straw for Allison. She went through the motions, but it was the last thing she wanted to do. I think she believed I wouldn't go through with it. Once we were here and she realized I liked the new job, she admitted this wasn't the life she wanted."

"I'm sorry, Jack. I've wondered about your divorce, but I never meant to pry." This was the truth, and I hoped that Jack understood that.

He leveled his determined gaze on me. "Allison isn't the villain, Kathleen."

I opened my mouth to respond, but Jack held up his hand. "It seems to me that you may understand this, but I still need to make that clear."

I nodded and proceeded with my original thought. "You're not the villain either, Jack. Life doesn't always go the way we expect it to."

"The marriage is over. We're each building new lives now, and I like it here." Jack's eyes bored into mine, and I held his look with equaled resolve.

He continued once again. "Allison went back to Baltimore, and she's working hard to make a good life for herself. She wants a comfortable future for our daughter, and at some point, I'll have to be prepared that Heide might return to her mom back East."

Jack's voice caught on his last sentence, and he swallowed hard before continuing, "I'm determined to do all I can to make this a happy time in Heide's life. She means more to me than anything. Raising her will be the lasting legacy of my time with Allison."

"You have the right idea, Jack. Never let anyone tell you otherwise."

Jack looked at me with something like astonishment. It was the only encouragement I needed.

"When parents divorce, they seem to forget the fact that having a child together makes them blood related. At least it seems that way to me." Tension had increased with each word so that by the time I finished this brief statement, my anger coursed through my veins. I glanced down at the white linen tablecloth for a few moments and willed myself to remain calm. When I looked back up, Jack was watching me.

"My parents split up when I was young, like Heide," I confessed. "I've been in her shoes."

Jack nodded, but otherwise remained quiet.

"Your love for Heide is evident. Believe me, no one was the least bit concerned with my well-being the way you are about hers. I'm telling you, she's thriving despite the challenges. I admire the hell out of her, and you deserve the credit for your commitment to your daughter.

Your attention and your love now will radiate from her for the rest of her life."

"May I ask what happened?" Jack asked.

I glanced around our table while I considered my answer. Jack had shared so much with me over dinner, and it hadn't been easy for him. When I brought my attention back to him, I saw the growing concern in his rich brown eyes.

"I don't mind you asking," I whispered as a single tear escaped from my right eye, "but this isn't the evening to share that story."

Jack noticed the tear glistening on my skin. He slid from his seat and knelt beside mine. Jack leaned over and brushed his lips next to my eye over the top of my tear. He then wiped the rest of it away with his thumb and took my face in the palm of his steady hand.

He looked into my eyes. "I thought I kissed that away on our first night together."

I leaned my cheek deeper into his grasp at the mention of the bittersweet memory. We remained silent and I was content with his comfort. Jack soothingly caressed my face with his thumb. He took hold of my hand in my lap with his other. We stayed like that for a while, ignoring the bustle of the dinner crowd. The restaurant was small and full of good-natured diners, but that all seemed to fall away. As my composure began to fall back into place, I registered the distinctive shift in the energy between Jack and me.

The lust of the afternoon had now given way to a more loving evening.

And all I cared about now was our total privacy.

"I'm ready to go back to the hotel, Jack. I want you to take me to bed. I want you to hold me, and I want us to be gentle with one another."

"Of course," he whispered. "Anything for you."

chapter Sixteen

STANDING NAKED in the bathroom of our hotel room with my side turned toward the reflection of the round wall mirror, I stared at my breast from a view I seldom glimpsed. It was shallow of me, but I wondered what Jack thought of my looks.

Clad in black boxer briefs, Jack wandered into the small room as if on cue.

I glanced at him over my shoulder and smiled, a touch embarrassed at being caught.

He smirked as he paused at the sink. "Don't let me interrupt. I enjoy looking at you, too."

"That's because you're insatiable."

"Be careful or I'll take you right now." Jack winked, before removing the contact lenses from his eyes. As soon as the task was done, he strolled back out into the main room.

I gnawed on the inside of my cheek and mulled over how I never realized he wore the lenses until this moment.

He turned off the lamps in the other room and then soft music filled the space.

Surprised and curious, I forgot my minor awkwardness and walked into the bedroom. The song was relaxing and melodic, just a man singing along with his piano.

Jack had discarded his boxer briefs and stood in the open space between our bed and the chaise lounge. The curtains in the window were parted just enough to allow the city's illumination into the room. The soft light complemented Jack's lean body. He was confident and serene — enthralling.

I went to him and encircled my arms around Jack's neck. He smiled and chuckled as he wrapped his arms around me.

"When a body meets a body, walking through the suite."

I grinned as he began to sway us in time with the romantic tune.

As his hold on my waist tightened, Jack swept his mouth against my ear. "I can't think of anything sexy to whisper. I just know that I want to."

We both laughed, enjoying the moment of spontaneity and lightness. Many of the day's events had been full of intensity. It was so good to relax with Jack especially after my weepiness during our dinner. As I reflected over our meal, I realized I had something important to say.

"It means a lot to me that you shared some things about Allison and your marriage," I said without concern and massaged the back of his neck. "I'll tell you more about my life soon. Just not now. I want to spend the rest of tonight like this."

Jack swept his eyes over my face with the searching expression I'd now come to recognize. He'd examined me in this way several times since we'd become lovers, and whenever he did, I felt cared for.

Jack ran his hand through my hair. "I'm ready to listen whenever you're ready to share your story. I don't ever want you to reveal things until you're willing."

And with those words, we returned our attention to our naked dancing. Jack's hands began to roam along my curves, exploring my hips and torso.

"Kathleen?" he murmured.

"Yes?"

"I didn't notice a scar earlier. I was just wondering where it is."

Overcome by shyness, I ducked my chin downward. "There isn't one," I explained. "Not externally, anyhow."

Jack lifted my chin with his finger and I offered no resistance. "I'm sorry. That was dumb of me. I didn't mean to make you uncomfortable."

"I don't mind. You just surprised me, that's all."

Jack's fingers migrated to my back, brushing along my spine. "Is what happened to you a bad memory?" he asked in a concerned tone.

I supposed he had good reason to be worried, but Jack was naïve. He couldn't begin to comprehend how bad some of my memories were. I snuggled into his chest and closed my eyes.

"It's a fuzzy memory. It seems so long ago, so detached. I couldn't say it's bad. Just old."

We both fell silent once again and caressed one another as we danced. Serenity and intimacy were effortless. It was as though dancing naked together was the most natural thing in the world. As the song began to wind down, Jack lifted his head.

"Can I kiss you?" His voice was gentle.

"When your mouth is involved, it's hard to say no," I said with blatant desire.

Jack brought his lips to mine. Our bare chests pressed together and our arms tightened around one another's bodies. After a few moments, I rose on my toes to pull him closer.

This was one of my favorite kisses with Jack. Even in the midst of the experience, I recognized this kiss would remain in each beat of my heart for the rest of my life. Our mouths opened and our tongues connected, but in a delicate way, it was different from any of our previous encounters. We explored one another, savoring each moment of the precious contact. When Jack withdrew from me, his regret at having done so was obvious. My immediate concern for his emotion made me forget my own pang of disappointment.

"Do you still want gentleness, Kathleen?" Jack whispered just above my lips, the sensation tingling through my entire body.

"Yes," I said as his hands traced my backside.

Jack brought his hands back up my body with deliberate slowness until they encircled my forearms. I unwound my hands from his neck without additional prompting, and he moved his fingers down my arms to entwine around mine. He lifted each hand one at a time and kissed them with reverence.

"I want you relaxed. Let's lie down." Jack helped me onto the bed and positioned me on my back. True to his word, he eased my mood with soothing caresses of my legs and arms. My eyes drifted closed, and I surrendered to his touch.

After a time, he asked, "Can I share a story with you?"

I hummed my approval, and Jack knelt between my legs. My eyes opened to enjoy his new proximity. "What's your story about?"

"You. I'm going to tell you about the first time I was attracted to you."

I was astounded and my heart stuttered in response.

"It happened at Robert's home. During the firm's holiday party."

"You noticed me then? All those months ago?" This was surprising.

"Yes."

"It's odd to hear you say that."

"Why?"

"It was such an uncomfortable evening. I haven't been back to his house since then."

Jack nodded, but didn't press for details. He moved forward with his recollections. "It was awkward for me, too. Allison had left a few weeks earlier, and I was still new to the job. I didn't know anyone well, and I wasn't in a good frame of mind, so I arrived without a date. I noticed you because you appeared to be the only other person there who arrived alone."

I nodded.

"You were in the living room, sitting on the hearth of the fireplace. You were wearing a beautiful, dark blue, cocktail dress. You looked elegant, but out of place. At first, I thought it was your choice of seat, but then it hit me."

I swallowed, and even though I knew what was coming next, I prompted him for it. "What did you see?"

"Sadness. You looked as miserable as I felt."

"I'm sorry you were unhappy, Jack."

He grinned before continuing. "I considered approaching you then and there. I'd even talked myself into it. I took several steps in your direction, but then I stopped."

"Why?"

"My logic began to argue with my emotions. My divorce wasn't final. I had a daughter waiting for me at home. My complications didn't need to become yours. I lost the nerve."

"For what it's worth, you made the right decision that night. I wouldn't have been good company and couldn't see past my own nose."

"I didn't speak with you, but I studied you. I saw so much that I'd never noticed before. I took in as much of you as I could and memorized everything I liked — your long neck, your breasts, the curve of your hip, your slender legs. You have no idea how sexy you were just sitting there by the fire. But more than anything else, I was captivated by your profile. I would have been content to spend the entire evening watching the firelight dance across your face. Watching you that night made me realize I could find enjoyment in this new life."

"I'd admired you by then," I said. "You've been such a welcome addition to my life. Bringing you onboard is one of the few things I'd thank Robert for over and over again."

"I've wondered why you were sad. Did you argue with Robert that night?"

"No. But the holidays can be hard to get through. Some years go better than others."

Jack changed the subject. "You were angry with me. That morning at my house."

"I was."

"Why?"

"That's a good question."

Jack waited as I considered my answer. Did I want to ruin this romantic moment by telling him I felt ignored that morning? I didn't, but not just because I was wary of hurting him. In the weeks since we'd first slept together, I'd thought about that morning many times. I'd also thought about how Jack was capable of evoking such strong reactions from me. Enough time had passed that I began to doubt my own perceptions of that encounter, and as a result, I'd wondered how I could have been so warped.

I shrugged. "I'm used to men treating me in a certain way. My mind just went there."

"You thought I treated you poorly?"

I recalled my chaotic emotions of that day and found I was too ashamed to answer his question. Jack's hand on my thigh drew my attention back to the present.

When he had my full attention, he said, "Whatever it was I did to make you upset, I'm sorry."

"It wasn't you, Jack. I wasn't being fair—"

"I upset you. That's enough to warrant an apology," he said in a remorseful whisper.

I sat up on the mattress and looked into his eyes. "I've upset you now. I'm sorry, too."

I wrapped my arms around Jack's neck and kissed him. He relaxed within my embrace, and I lowered us both back onto the mattress. We kissed for some time, and I held Jack against me. Lying underneath him, I was cocooned in ecstasy. In the past, we'd been vocal during sex, but this time was different. We communicated via touch and emotion.

After a time, Jack began to chart a new course along my body, skimming his lips down my neck. I ran my fingers through his hair and soon his attentions drifted to my breasts. His kisses were erotic and tender. As his smooth lips concentrated on my nipples, Jack's hand drifted down and grasped the curve of my waist. His grip was strong and with a subtle nudge of his knee, he coaxed my legs to open. I wrapped my legs around him, enjoying the touch of both masculine muscle and the short hairs on his skin.

With our lower bodies now entwined, Jack returned to my mouth once more and emitted a gruff sigh against my lips as he entered me slowly. His emotional desire matched his physical pleasure, and I was in awe of him. Jack didn't thrust hard into me, but moved deep within me, his elbows resting on either side of my head. As my own delight grew, I arched my back, prompting Jack to rise up on his arms. Jack opened his eyes and hummed his appreciation as my breasts pushed against his chest. As my body stretched taut, my head fell back into the pillows, and I surrendered to him. We both began to pant, and my heart rate increased with the tempo of our bodies.

Being with Jack was unlike any other sexual experience I'd had before. Despite the newness of our romance, he knew how to please me as though we'd always been together. When we made love, there was no awkwardness, just pure bliss. And our time together earlier in the day now had an unexpected, delightful result in this moment. We were unhurried. There was no impatient frenzy. We endured and as the minutes floated by, I found myself overcome by desire over and over again.

Jack was in good physical shape and with measured continual strokes, he maintained our mutual pleasure and enjoyment. On occasion, he stilled his movements and placed his head on my chest for a few moments of rest, but he never withdrew from my body.

During one of these restful moments, he hardened even more within me, and I urged him back into action with a lift of my hips. I was now consumed with pleasing Jack. I pressed my body flush against his and moved in perfect synch with him. As his self-control diminished, my own happiness increased, amplified by the intensity of our raw emotions. Together, we reached a mutual climax, my final orgasm fueled by his release.

Moments later, Jack spooned with me, but kept enough distance between our upper bodies so he could kiss my back and shoulders.

I smiled at the unexpected shower of affection and shivered when he ran the tip of his tongue along my bare skin.

He stilled his movements and tightened his grip. "Are you cold?"

I laughed. "Hardly."

He laughed in return and refocused his attentions on my shoulder and the back of my neck. In between kisses, he asked me a series of questions.

"Are you warm?"

"Yes."
"Are you cared for?"
"Yes."
"Are you protected?"
"Yes."
"Do you feel beautiful?"
"Yes."
"Tell me how you are now."
"I'm a little afraid."
Jack stilled his movements.
"Why?"
"I keep finding new ways to fall for you."
He smiled against my skin. "Good."

chapter Seventeen

I WOKE up in the middle of the night with sore muscles. I needed to stretch and eased from the bed, careful not to disturb Jack. His soft snores reassured me of my success, and I walked away from our bed to look out the window.

I pulled the curtains back to take in the view. I wasn't concerned about being seen by anyone. There were offices in the building across the street from our hotel room, and they were all dark. The streets below were deserted. After several minutes a satisfying form of fatigue began to set in.

Rather than returning to the bed, I opted to sit on the chaise lounge Jack had occupied earlier. I drew my knees up to my chin as I stared out the window at the city and thought about everything that had happened in just a few short hours.

Caring, generosity and intimacy were concepts I understood in theory, but had seldom experienced firsthand. Sex had always been enjoyable, but this was different.

I didn't understand how, but I did grasp that my connection with Jack Evans was life altering. I was forever changed by my relationship with him, and I didn't know if this was a good thing or not.

My feelings for him were undeniable and strong. I'd never experienced such intensity with any man. We had known each other for almost a year, working side by side.

I'd admired him, but hadn't lusted after him. An innocent and spontaneous dinner had triggered a staggering series of events over the course of the past several weeks, and in that short span of time, my life had changed.

In the quietest of ways, Jack had taken hold of me—heart, body and soul. In doing so, he'd triggered an emotional tsunami. Over time, I'd become so comfortable setting my emotions aside that the coping mechanism was automatic. Jack Evans had the innate ability to dredge all my anxieties back to the surface. Positive and negative emotions were swirled in a frenzied vortex within me.

I'd never been so happy and so frightened.

As if my thoughts were loud enough to wake him, there was a rustling of the sheets and a sharp inhalation as Jack awoke. I turned in his direction and waited, taking advantage of the time to corral my thoughts.

He rolled onto his side toward me and opened his eyes. When he saw me, he propped himself up on an elbow, smiled, but remained in the bed. I smiled back and held my position on the chaise lounge.

"What are you doing?" he asked.

I shrugged as I answered. "Thinking, I guess."

"What an incredible day this was."

Jack's comment encouraged me to offer him a glimpse of my true mood. "I don't want to let it go."

Jack picked up his phone and narrowed his eyes to glance at the time. "We don't have to yet. We have hours still."

"What are you doing tomorrow?" I needed to prepare myself for the inevitable. Accepting this night would soon retreat into the past was not an easy thing to do.

Jack's eyes drifted to the wall in front of our bed as he answered, "I was going to drop in on a few clients. Then head for home in the afternoon."

A new and important question occurred to me—one that needed answering. "Who is Heide staying with?"

Jack returned his gaze to me. "I'm friends with a single mom on Heide's soccer team. We've been helping each other out. I'm giving her next weekend off in exchange."

"Oh." My voice was timid and I regretted its tone.

"Oh, what?" he prodded.

"Nothing," I whispered. Every raw nerve in my body was irrational and stinging with resentment.

"Are you worried?"

Fearful tears burned my eyes, and I turned my face away from Jack toward the window.

I couldn't stand the possibility of another woman developing an attraction for him like I had. I suffered from more than simple jealousy. I was also certain of something else. Most other woman my age had their lives under much better control than I did. By comparison, I was lacking. Despite his reassurances to the contrary, I was apprehensive that Jack would discover this truth soon enough.

When I didn't answer him, Jack threw the covers away from his body. He drew my full attention back, and as he strolled over to where I was sitting, I ogled him without shame. Considering how much sex we'd engaged in during the day and evening, I was surprised by his semi-aroused state.

He bent at the waist and brought his face close to mine. Our eyes locked and he said succinctly, "Never worry."

He kissed me, but instead of focusing on his gentle touch, I was thinking about how I'd have to let him go in the morning. And how much I didn't want to.

I took hold of him by the legs and drew him down on top of me as I positioned myself on my back on the chair. Jack's hand moved to my backside to guide me, and I whimpered at his strong grip.

I slid my hands over his lower back and settled them on his hips, pulling him toward me. He pushed my legs apart and the moment he touched me, he was hard.

I was still wet after spending hours in bed with Jack. When he entered me, he glided inside without resistance. I slid my hands down and pressed on his firm ass with my fingers to encourage his movements.

Jack reared up and removed my hands from his body. He placed my arms above my head, draping them over the back edge of the chaise lounge. He began thrusting hard as he held my arms in place. I cried out in passionate excitement, my fingers pressing into the upholstery of the chair as his body claimed mine. Jack pushed down on my wrists as he continued his unrelenting pace, drawing my attention with the amplified pressure.

"Leave your arms like this," he instructed.

"Yes," I panted.

Jack removed his grasp, brought one of his hands to my chest and caressed me as our momentum picked up. We increased our rhythm every few moments. Our initial murmurs of pleasure escalated into unapologetic grunts and groans. We didn't worry if neighbors heard our lovemaking or if the chaise lounge survived.

All I cared about was how quickly Jack could push himself back into me.

When the perspiration of our slick bodies threatened to interfere with our incessant connection, I pressed my legs against his. With my hands still clutching the back of the chair I arched my back, bringing our chests into direct contact once again.

"I could do this with you all night," I confessed, telling him my deepest desires.

Without warning, Jack rose up on his knees, but did not withdraw from my body. He grabbed my legs and pulled them upward, along the length of his torso. Once my ankles rose above his shoulder, he took hold of both with one hand and braced his other hand on top of the chaise lounge, near my outstretched arms. Astoundingly, he increased his speed again. The combination of his feverish pace along with the deep penetration from the new angle evaporated all rational thought. I yelled out in surprise as the intensity of my impending orgasm took complete control of my senses.

"Should I keep doing this?" Jack asked with a voice thick with arousal.

"Please," I begged.

"Will you come like this?"

I gasped at his words, at his tone of voice, at the stunning control he held — not only over his body but also over mine — and at my complete surrender to his whims.

"Kathleen?" he said, punctuating my name with an aggressive thrust.

"Yes! Jack!"

"Tell me when you come," he commanded. "I want to know when it happens."

"Soon," I breathed.

"Do you understand how much I want you, Kathleen?"

Jack was fucking me into incoherence. I couldn't answer him intelligently and cried out my acknowledgement. He lifted my legs in response, my bottom hovering in the air just above the seat of the chaise lounge. This final shift in position was enough to throw me over the edge. I had a second or two to comply with Jack's request and managed to do so by sheer miracle.

I cried out his name with heat, and his own control swayed as my orgasm claimed every ounce of me. My body tightened even more around his and he moaned, the sound emanating from deep within his chest. I knew him well enough to know his own climax was underway.

"Don't let me go!" I cried out.

Jack tightened his grip on my ankles. After several vigorous thrusts that ensured my final orgasm, he pushed himself deep inside me. His glorious body stilled and the strength of his release overpowered us both. He surrendered to the desire of the moment and it was beautiful. My own esteem blossomed. His usual careful demeanor all but evaporated whenever we had sex. This is what I did to him, and the euphoria was profoundly addictive.

His grip on me relaxed, and he lowered my body onto the cushion of the chair. I drew my legs down, aware of a sudden onset of weakness.

Jack remained on his knees between my legs with his eyes closed and his body glistening with sweat. He was breathless, so I pulled on his arm, coaxing his body back onto mine. He collapsed into my embrace.

I held him, unconcerned with the weight of him upon my chest or to the heat that radiated off his body. I wrapped my legs back around Jack's with my feet resting on the backs of his knees. Tracing my fingertips along his back, I whispered my gratitude to him over and over again in hopes of relaxing him. It worked and soon his arms reciprocated the embrace. We were both quiet, and as I held onto him my thoughts began to wander.

I wanted to tell Jack Evans I had fallen in love with him, but I couldn't find a way to do so. I doubted my ability to make him happy, so I kept the words to myself.

chapter Eighteen

WHEN THE sunlight appeared, I did my best to put on a brave face. The prospect of sleeping alone at day's end was an unwelcome one. Just thinking about that empty bed in my condominium brought tears to my eyes.

Jack was still in this bed with me, so I placed an arm over my eyes in an effort to disguise my emotions. Almost immediately, the soothing touch of his fingers slid along my arm.

"Good morning." His voice was happy.

I raised my arm just enough to uncover one eye and turned my head in his direction.

"Hey." Compared to his, my voice was croaked and thick.

His eyes took in my guarded expression. "Is something wrong?"

I shook my head and cleared my throat. "It's just … um … it's just so bright in here."

We watched one another for a few seconds.

"Are you hungry?"

I shook my head as my arm dropped back down over my eye. "I'm too ravaged to be hungry."

Jack laughed and I smiled, my sadness now forgotten. Emerging from my shell, I rolled on top of him and hovered just above him with the tips of my breasts skimming his chest.

"What about you?" I asked as he caressed my backside.

"Starving," he whispered.

"Well. I can't blame you for that," I said, playing it safe. "You've earned your breakfast. What do you want to do?"

Jack raised his hips to meet mine and smiled. There was nothing subtle about that.

I pursed my lips in mock seriousness and playfully waggled a finger. "Don't distract yourself now."

He pushed against my body again but with more insistence and coaxed a low moan from me.

"Do you want anything?" he asked.

"I'll always want you. But let's worry about feeding you first. Where do you want to go?"

I went to move to the edge of the bed, but Jack's arms held me in place. I looked at him with amused curiosity.

"I don't want to waste our morning getting dressed and going out. Let's order room service."

I arched an eyebrow and grinned. "Naked breakfast?"

Jack sat up and kissed the tip of my nose before flipping me on my back.

"We didn't get breakfast in bed last time, remember? I'll grab the menu." Jack rose from the mattress, and I was delighted to reacquaint my eyes with his lean body in the light of day. As soon as he found the room service menu, he returned to my side and I snuggled up against him.

"I chose our breakfast before." He opened the menu above us. "So why don't you choose this time?"

"I don't bother with much more than coffee when I travel," I confessed. "If anything, I just have some fruit and toast."

Jack mumbled disapprovingly.

I took the hint. "We both need a protein boost though, so add some scrambled eggs and bacon."

"I'm adding some potatoes, too. Do you want some juice?"

"Orange juice sounds good."

Jack set the menu aside and ran his fingers through my hair. "I'll call it in. Do you want to take another bubble bath while we wait? I'll run it for you."

"That's sweet, but you don't have to."

"Sure I do. I don't want you to get dressed yet, and I can't have anyone else seeing you naked when they bring our food up."

Jack enjoyed taking care of me, and despite my fair level of independence, I found that I enjoyed it. He didn't make me feel childish or helpless. In fact, I felt beautiful. Celebrated.

I agreed and within a few minutes, I was settled in the tub, determined to cherish each remaining second of our morning together. I let go of the lingering tension and even giggled as Jack closed the bathroom door when our meal arrived. As Jack directed the placement of our breakfast dishes, I stepped from the tub.

I dried myself with one towel before wrapping my body with another. As I returned to the main room, our breakfast waited on the work desk. Jack was sitting up in the bed, shirtless, the sheets drawn up to his waist.

I strolled over to him and lifted the edge of the sheets. "Still naked, I see. Did you answer the door like that?"

He hooked one finger into the seam of my towel.

"Speaking of which," he murmured. "You're a little overdressed." He yanked the bath towel from my body and tossed it to the floor.

I casually glanced down at my body. "I don't know, Jack. I'm not sure naked breakfast is considered good naked."

Jack tilted his head to better observe my breasts. "Jerry Seinfeld didn't have you to look at. Believe me, there is no such thing as bad naked."

"I'll remember you said that."

"Please do," he answered with sincerity before patting my side of the mattress. "Come back to bed, and I'll bring our food over."

"No crumbs in the sheets. I may not be done with you just yet." I settled myself on the bed, and soon we were enjoying our breakfast. I was hungrier than I'd realized. For a few minutes, all conversation halted as we satisfied our appetites.

Once our eating slowed, Jack said, "I want to talk with you about something. I was going to wait, but maybe it's better to talk now while we still have some privacy."

I paused mid-bite on a strawberry and tried not to jump to any immediate conclusions. "Okay."

Jack stroked my knee. "Please don't worry."

I nodded, swallowing my fruit and waiting for him to continue.

"We haven't said this to each other yet, but I think you feel the same way I do. I want to see you exclusively."

My heart filled with happiness at his words. "That's what I want, too."

Jack smiled and leaned over to kiss my lips before resuming his place. "Good. There's more." He hesitated and then added, "I want us to be open about our relationship. I need to be upfront with Allison about you, and I need to explain to Heide that we're a couple now." Jack paused again and searched my face.

I glanced down at my lap. Allison was far away, and Heide did appear to like me. I looked back up at Jack. "If you think that's for the best, but please remember, I'm not interested in complicating things between the three of you."

"There's nothing to worry about between Heide and me. Allison already knows about you, and I don't think she'll be surprised to learn that I'm making this commitment."

A tinge of nervousness gripped me and I shrugged. "Are you sure?"

"Yes. There's just one other thing."

"What?"

"I don't think it's a good idea to hide our relationship at the office."

I immediately opened my mouth to object.

Jack held up his hand. "Think about this for a minute before you answer. We don't need to flaunt ourselves at work. But I've mulled this over a lot, and it's important Robert finds out about us under our own control. I don't want to sneak around at the office because these things never stay hidden for long, and I won't have him think we've been deceiving him. That won't help anything between the two of you."

"You've mulled this over?" I repeated his words, somewhat stunned. "For how long?"

Jack smirked. "At least since you dropped teriyaki sauce down your shirt."

I reached out and playfully smacked his arm. "Be serious," I chided, but I was flattered.

"Have you thought about how Robert should find out?" I asked.

"A little bit. I thought we could arrange a dinner with your family. That way we'd say it once and be done with it."

I frowned and bit the inside of my cheek as I tried to imagine the proposed evening. "I don't like that idea."

"Why not?" he asked, but it wasn't accusatory.

"I'm not concerned about my grandparents. I already know they'll approve of you. Robert's wife and I can't be in a room together for ten minutes before one of us storms away. I couldn't care less what she thinks about anything. And aside from them, there's no other family."

"What about your mother?"

Jack's question shocked me into silence. No one had asked about my mother in eons. I just shook my head. She was a nonfactor.

I sighed. "We'll go see Robert together, but you have to accept that things with him will not go well. They never do."

"Do you think my job will be in danger once he knows?" His calm tone indicated he'd been mulling that scenario over as well.

I owed it to Jack to think about my answer, and so I did. "No, your job will be safe as long as we're the ones to tell him of our situation."

With reluctance, I accepted that Jack was right. Robert's criticism would be directed at me, but I decided against saying this to Jack. I didn't want to deter him from his idea because it would never matter to Robert what choices in life I made. He would find a way to dredge up my worst fears. Robert would leave Jack alone. But I would not be so fortunate.

"What are you thinking about?" Jack asked, drawing my attention back to our conversation.

"I'll do this on one condition."

"What is that?"

"Whatever we set up with Robert, Heide cannot be a part of it. Robert is too unpredictable where I'm concerned. I don't want her exposed to his harshness."

Jack stared at me for several long agonizing moments.

Perhaps he was reconsidering his decision. Maybe I'd just lost him for good, and the prospect of this was frightening, although I wouldn't blame him one bit for wanting to keep his daughter far away from my crazy family.

"Agreed," Jack answered. "Thank you for thinking of her."

I nodded, too overcome with relief to be able to say anything else.

Jack's lips pressed into a hard line. "You know Robert best. Is there something we could arrange that would be relaxing for him? Something that would make the news easier to accept?"

"Yeah," I mumbled in resignation. "I know what we could do."

Jack's brown eyes brightened with anticipation. "What?"

"What do you think about a round of golf at Widgi Creek?"

chapter Nineteen

ONCE WE agreed on announcing our news to Robert during a golf outing, I was content to let Jack work out the specifics. We left the hotel just before the lunch hour, and it was with great difficulty that I parted company with him. With one last lingering kiss, Jack went to his client appointments.

I decided to take in a little shopping before driving back to Bend, but I was antsy, not to mention sleep deprived, and couldn't focus on buying anything for myself. However, I did purchase a gift for Heide after spotting the whimsical item through a shop's window. I considered stopping by the Evans house that night to deliver it to her, but decided the gift could wait. Better to let Jack and Heide spend their evening together.

The following morning, I was back in the office and catching up on my e-mail when Jack arrived with my coffee. He closed my office door behind him and set a Dutch Bros. windmill cup on my desk. Before I could even offer my thanks, he lowered his head to mine for a surprisingly passionate kiss. I had arrived at work lonely after just one night away from him, but his eager mouth restored my happiness. He held my face with his hands, and I relaxed within his embrace. After a time, he withdrew.

"How did you sleep?" he asked.

"Better than I thought I would," I told him. "But I missed you."

"I missed you, too. Will you come over tonight?"

I blinked in surprise. "I'd love that. Are you sure?"

His expression turned playful. "Yes. I want something to look forward to. It's going to be hell keeping a respectful distance from you."

I grinned. "That would make things tolerable today."

Jack kissed my forehead before stepping to the door. "Robert asked me to stop by his office this afternoon. I'm going to invite him to play golf."

I nodded, trying to keep my nervousness at bay.

"Are you having second thoughts?"

"No, are you?"

"Nope," he said as he opened the door and returned to reality.

In the wake of the Portland luncheon, there was plenty of work to keep me busy and the hours flew by. Before I knew it, Jack was back at my office door, offering a quick wave on his way to his meeting with Robert. I mouthed good luck and blew him a kiss.

My office was only a few doors away, and since my door was open, I heard my father welcome Jack into his office along with the distinctive click of his door as it closed. I needed something to do to keep me distracted from the meeting inside my father's office. I glanced around. When my eyes landed on my purse, I remembered the various business cards I'd collected during the Portland trip.

I closed the day by e-mailing the new contacts. It was a perfect task in its important simplicity. I took the cards out and set them down on my desk and grabbed one at random. The name brought a smile to my face.

Ryan Murray
Owner / CEO
Innovative West Media & Marketing
44 Cook Street, Suite 1300
Denver, CO 80206
303.555.0141
Ryan.Murray@Iwmm.Com

Turning my attention to my monitor, I began a new e-mail.

Hello Ryan,

Thank you once again for stopping by our event in Oregon this week. It was nice speaking with you. If I can ever be of any service, please don't hesitate to contact me.

I don't know if you've returned to Denver, but I hope your trip back home proves to be uneventful.

If you should ever find your way back to Portland (or even better, Bend) please let me know. I would enjoy the opportunity to share another meal and talk shop.

You can even choose the restaurant next time!

With Warm Regards,

Kathleen Brighton

Senior Target Marketing Strategist

Aurora Advertising

Just as soon as Ryan's e-mail was on its way to him, my office phone rang. The caller ID said Robert.

Hell.

I picked up the receiver and stared at the ceiling. "This is Kathleen." It was my standard office greeting, and Robert was no exception.

"Come over to my office for a minute." No standard greeting, no pause for my answer, just his command and a click when he hung up. That was Robert.

As I walked to Robert's closed door, I listened for raised voices or other noises associated with conflict. Nothing. The tranquility made me anxious as I knocked and opened the door.

"You rang?" I asked as I attempted to gauge the mood in my father's office.

Robert sat behind his desk, leaning back in his executive chair. His expression was masked by indifference. Jack sat, facing Robert with his back to me. He looked over his shoulder as I made my way to stand behind the empty chair to his right. Robert gestured for me to sit down, and as I did I kept my eyes trained on my father and away from Jack Evans. It nearly killed me.

Once I was settled in my chair, Robert resumed the meeting. "We were just talking about Portland. I think this year's lunch was one of our best yet, and Jack here thinks you deserve most of the credit."

I nodded in Jack's direction before turning back to Robert. "I'm glad to hear you think it went well, too. We had some new faces in the room this year. I'm happy about that."

"So am I," Robert said. "You talked a lot with a man at your table. I didn't recognize him. Who was he?"

From the corner of my eye, I noticed Jack shift in his chair.

"Honestly, he was a party crasher."

Robert angled his chair in my direction and leveled me with a serious look. "Competition?"

Jack cleared his throat and I glanced in his direction.

"I don't think so," I murmured, turning my attention back to Robert. "The gentleman owns a marketing firm based in Colorado and was in Portland visiting a client. But he was dragged along to the lunch."

Robert narrowed is eyes. "Who brought him?"

Shit.

"I didn't ask."

Robert expression morphed into an aggravated stare. "I don't understand. You didn't ask him who he was with?"

I shook my head. In fact, I had chosen not to ask, but Robert would never understand.

"He didn't seem interested in getting the inside scoop on us," I offered.

"Nevertheless. Did you volunteer any information to this guy?"

"Of course not," I replied defensively. "We chatted and exchanged cards. That's all."

"If he contacts you, let me know. Best to be wary of someone like that. The whole thing sounds suspicious."

I nodded once. However, I couldn't bring myself to agree with his assessment. It was obvious both men in the room viewed Ryan as a threat for different reasons. I found this commonality perplexing and attempted to shift the conversation in another direction.

"I've already been mulling over a few ideas for next year's luncheon. Maybe we should schedule a wrap-up meeting next week and brainstorm."

Robert bristled. "Fine, but let's make it the last meeting about the event for a while. I don't want this one day to eat up too much of my time."

"Sure," I replied.

"I have a thought," Jack interjected.

Now, I was the one squirming in my seat.

"Yeah?" Robert looked over at Jack.

"I was thinking about taking you up on your offer to play a round of golf. That is, if your invitation still stands."

"Sure it does." Robert grinned.

I couldn't figure out how Jack was going to set up this golf date with Robert and include a good reason for inviting me along, too. Perhaps he thought Robert would be willing to golf and brainstorm at the same time. I knew otherwise.

"Maybe I'll go with you two," I said before Jack could speak.

Robert turned to look at me, his forehead wrinkling. "Why do you want to go?" His tone was cool.

"I don't have to go." I shrugged one shoulder in chagrin. I was going to have to navigate the rest of our conversation with care.

"Well … you don't golf." Robert was a tad reticent and confused.

"Maybe I could caddy for you like I used to. That's all I was thinking."

Robert studied me for a long moment. "Yeah? You serious?"

"Sure." I glanced at Jack, eager to draw him back into the conversation. "I could caddy for both of you."

"That sounds good to me," Jack supplied as we looked back at Robert.

"Okay," he agreed with a light tap on his desk. "Tell you what? I'll set up the tee time for us. It's going to be eighteen holes. Are you up for that?"

"That's fine," Jack said.

"It's settled then," Robert declared. "We'll go later this week."

chapter

Twenty

AS I approached the front door of the Evans house with an overnight bag on one shoulder and a gift bag in the opposite hand, I smiled. Since returning to Bend, I'd felt out of place in my own home. Before seeing Jack at the office that morning, it had become imperative to fill my waking time with one small task after another. It kept me from fixating on when I could see him again. For reasons I couldn't pinpoint, I hadn't expected an invitation back to his house so soon after our trip. His offer gave me great joy, and it was flattering to think he was just as anxious to spend time together as I was.

Spring was in full bull bloom and summer was almost underway. I found something perfect about beginning a romance during my favorite time of year. The flowers were colorful and the days were long and full of sunshine. My senses were attuned to the vibrancy all around me, and I was experiencing true happiness.

Before I could ring the doorbell, the front door opened.

"Hello, Heide."

"Hi, Kathleen!" The smug tone of Heide's voice hinted she was someone with valuable information. She stepped aside to allow me entrance, and she honed in on the gift bag.

"How was your day?" I asked, pretending not to notice her interest.

"Good," she said, swaying back and forth.

"How was school?"

"Good."

"Are you getting excited for summer break?"

"Yep!" She offered a broad smile. "I'm going to go stay with my mom."

Although this was the first I'd heard of Heide's summer plans, I wasn't surprised by them. My school holidays often involved me shuttling from one relative's house to another. I recalled several fond memories of camping trips, treks to the cities of the Pacific Northwest and many days at one swimming hole or another.

"I bet you're looking forward to that."

"Yep. And I bet you're looking forward to hanging out with my dad." Heide's perceptive remark took me by complete surprise.

"Uh …"

"Heide," Jack called with perfect timing as he emerged from his bedroom. "Please close the door before Kitty Hawk runs back outside."

"Oh, yeah!" Heide bounded over to the door.

"Hey," Jack greeted me warmly. "Let me take your bag." He gestured to my shoulder before kissing me on the forehead. His lips on my skin, even for that brief moment, sent my already good mood soaring.

I slid the tote off my arm without another word into his capable hands. As Jack retreated to his bedroom, I held out the gift bag in Heide's direction.

"I got you something when I was in Portland the other day. I hope you like it."

"Yeah!" she exclaimed. "My dad got me something, too."

"Oh? What was it?"

"Some new books," she said while relieving me of my package. "Since you're staying over tonight, maybe we can read one at bedtime."

"Wow, I'd like that."

I hoped my response wasn't too lame, but since she'd turned her full attention to her new gift, I doubted she heard a word.

"Awesome!" Heide yelled just as Jack returned to the living room. She pulled out the distinguishable green pair of Minecraft Creeper socks and inspected them with glee.

I'd taken a big risk purchasing a child clothing and was relieved that Heide was excited. Even so, I'd padded the package with another few items just in case the socks went over like a lead balloon.

"There are a couple of other things in there, too." I nodded to the tipped over and forgotten gift bag.

"Really?" Heide dove back into the bag, throwing tissue sheets in several directions.

From her secured post on the arm of the sofa, Kitty Hawk pounced on one particular sheet as it floated in the cat's general direction. The cat and tissue paper tumbled to the floor together with a loud thud.

"Awesome again!" Heide yelled, discovering several Minecraft action figures inside the gift bag. "Steve! Iron Gollum! Creeper! And ... look, Dad! An ocelot!"

"I didn't know if you had those already, but they seemed like your kind of toy."

"I don't have them! I mean, I do now!"

"What do you say, Heide?" her father prompted.

"Thank you, Kathleen!"

"You're welcome."

"Can I go play with them?" She glanced at her father.

He grinned. "Pick everything up first."

"Okay!" She made a frenzied dash through the living room, picking up the pieces of tissue paper and sending the cat tearing down the hall ahead of her in the process.

Jack laughed as soon as Heide disappeared into her bedroom. "You scored."

"I should have asked you ahead of time if Minecraft was appropriate."

"They're perfect. I appreciate you thinking of her like that. It's sweet." Jack leaned in for a brief kiss on the lips.

I blushed from the compliment and the contact.

"Maybe she'll only ask to play on the computer once every twenty minutes instead of every five," he murmured as he pulled back. "Wine?"

"Please."

Jack took my hand, and I followed him to the kitchen. "How are you feeling about today?"

"Okay. It scared me when Robert called my office though."

"Yeah. Sorry about that." Jack grimaced with a touch of awkwardness. "I thought you needed to hear what he was saying. I get the impression that no one reminds him enough to speak positively."

He studied me as he opened a cupboard and reached for our wineglasses.

"Because people are too scared to nudge him."

Jack didn't answer. Instead, he poured our wine and handed me my glass.

I took my first sip and asked, "Aren't you nervous around him?"

He shook his head. "Not yet. Maybe that will change in a few days."

I frowned and Jack cupped my cheek.

"I'm not worried about Robert. And now that we're together, you can count on me to keep you safe."

"Let's read a story together," Heide announced a few hours later. We'd been in the living room since dinner, talking and watching television. It was enjoyable and dreamlike and the kind of family time I was unaccustomed to.

Jack shifted from his spot next to me on the sofa as if to follow Heide, but she put a halt to that. "I just meant Kathleen, Dad."

Jack flashed a brilliant grin as he sat back against the cushions. "By all means," he said while reaching for the remote control. "Enjoy your girl time."

"It's not girly girl time," Heide emphasized this with total seriousness, looking at both of us.

"Got it," I agreed. I followed Heide to her room and entered her space for the first time.

Her bed was chaotically made in a way that said she was in charge of keeping her room together. There were a few Minecraft posters on the walls, and her room also included a collection of soccer team photos and medals. All but two of the photographs had been taken in Maryland. When I spotted a poster of the Three Sisters and Mount Bachelor, I felt some hometown pride.

Caught up in the gravity of its familiarity, I wandered over for a closer look, dodging a few toys and shoes along the way. "Has your dad taken you up to Mount Bachelor yet?"

"Nope." Heide had paused in the center of her room, locking her hands behind her back.

"Maybe we can plan an afternoon up there before you go to your mom's."

"Really?" Heide's voice was full of excitement.

"Sure," I answered. "There's all kinds of stuff we can do there."

She tilted her head. "Even though it's summer?"

"You bet. We could take a chairlift ride and hike some trails. We can even have dinner up there at sunset if you want to."

"Cool!"

"I'll talk to your dad about it. I think he'll like it there, too."

I spotted a silver portrait frame sitting on Heide's bedside table. Inside was a photo of a smiling woman, hugging a slightly younger Heide.

Allison.

I crossed the room and took a seat on the twin-sized mattress. "What book are we reading?" I asked, distracted by Allison's picture.

Heide turned her attention to the bookshelf, and I took advantage to study the photograph. My memory of Allison had faded due both to the passage of time and the lack of opportunity to be around her before she left Oregon. I wanted to see if there were any physical similarities between Allison and me.

Allison had medium-length blond hair that was shorter than mine and an identical color to her daughter's. Her complexion was neither pale nor olive, just sun kissed. Her eyes were blue and sparkled, and her overall appearance was meticulous. Allison's makeup was well maintained and her nails were manicured. There was no denying her natural beauty, but it also was clear she was the kind of woman who wouldn't be caught looking anything but her absolute best. I admired the woman's polished look, having never committed to the effort to achieve that particular image myself. Allison looked to be a woman who had it all together, and it left me wondering why Jack wasn't good enough for her.

How could Allison give up such a prize as him?

"Heide?" I said before I had a chance to think about the conversation I was initiating.

Her teasing earlier plus her father's relaxed demeanor indicated that Jack had explained that I was his girlfriend. I wanted to know what she thought about this development. I knew how terrible it was not to like my father's numerous girlfriends over the years. Heide's acceptance of me was crucial if I was going to commit to a relationship with her father. There was no question that I held Heide's opinion in high esteem.

"Yeah?" She glanced over her shoulder before turning back to her bookshelf.

I turned away from Allison's photo and asked, "What has your dad said to you about me?" I watched for any signs of uncertainty.

She turned around to face me full as she answered, "That you are his girlfriend and that he cares about you."

I smiled. "I care about him, too. And I care about you. I want us to be friends."

She tilted her head slightly and her expression changed. Her eyes were soft but serious. "Will you be friends with my mom?"

Her insightful question took me by surprise, and I had to think for a few moments before responding. "Well. I'm not sure. We don't know each other, and she lives in Baltimore and I live here. That might make it tough for us to be friends."

"My mom's a nice person."

I had no reason to believe otherwise and pointed toward the picture of her mom. "I can see that in her picture. And you're a nice person. I'm guessing you learned that from both your mom and your dad."

"And my teachers," Heide added with finality.

I laughed, glad for the positive release of nervousness. "I'll bet. Of course they helped out, too." I took a deep breath and decided to move forward. "Being your dad's girlfriend means I'll be spending more time with both of you."

"Like tonight?" I was relieved to hear the levity in her voice. I expected her to have some curiosity about this news, but not much. She was too young to understand what a relationship between her father and another woman fully meant, but I was relieved that she accepted the situation.

"Yeah," I answered. "Is that okay?"

"Sure."

"Good. And if you ever think I'm hanging out here too much, just tell one of us you need a break."

"Okay."

"Promise?"

"Yep."

"Shake hands on it?"

"Nah. Let's fist bump."

"Okay."

Heide bounded over and we sealed our deal with a brief touch of our knuckles.

"Did you find a book you wanted to read?" I reminded her.

"Yes!" Heide plucked an orange paperback off her shelf and jumped onto the bed with Diary of a Wimpy Kid in her hands. She extended the book to me.

As I took the novel and opened the cover, she snuggled in close to my side. Without even thinking, I wrapped my arm around her.

In my joy of being accepted by Jack's daughter, I soon forgot about Allison.

chapter Twenty-One

LESS THAN an hour after Heide had been tucked into bed by her father, I stretched my arms upward as I sat on Jack's sofa. "I'm going to go lay down," I announced.

Jack turned his head in my direction and furrowed his brow.

I leaned in close enough to kiss him, but miraculously restrained myself. "I'm done wearing clothes for the day," I elaborated.

Jack grinned. "Now, there's a sentence every man wants to hear."

Together, we rose from the couch. Jack secured the house while I made sure to turn off the television and the lights. He took my hand as we walked down the hall toward his bedroom, but as soon as we entered, he let go and snapped his fingers.

"I forgot one thing. Give me a minute." He turned and left me alone in his bedroom.

My eyes were drawn to the mirrored closet doors. Allison's closet.

I made my way to one reflective door and slowly slid it open. It was empty, and I let go of the breath I'd been holding. I ended my examination of the space and closed the door. Then I took a seat on the corner of Jack's bed. I wasn't exactly sure how to proceed with my bedtime routine, so I folded my hands in my lap and waited for his return.

After a couple of minutes, Jack reappeared. He carried napkins, two bottles of water, and a small bowl filled with orange slices. He set them down on his dresser across from the bed and then turned around.

"I have something to return to you," he said.

"You do?" My brow quirked up.

Jack nodded, opened a drawer and motioned me over to look inside. I approached his side and spotted the stockings and garter belt I'd worn to his house the first time I'd spent the night with him. One hand covered my mouth to stifle my laughter while the other reached up and squeezed his arm.

"I forgot about them. Heide knocked on the door and asked to come in after I finished my shower. I didn't have time to put them back on, so I just shoved them underneath the pillow." My giggles were interrupted by a scary thought. "She wasn't the one who found them, was she?"

Jack shook his head, and his eyes lit up with amusement. "I found them when I went to bed that night. Way better than anything the tooth fairy ever left me."

"That was such a weird morning," I confessed. "I'm surprised you wanted to see me again after that."

Jack shut the dresser drawer and closed the small distance between us, sliding his arm around my waist and pulling me up against him. "It wasn't weird. It was an emotional night for both of us. I'm glad you're willing to give me another chance. This time, I expect you to wake up feeling very happy."

He kissed my neck just below my ear. I closed my eyes in relaxation and massaged his scalp with my fingers as he wove an intricate pattern of kisses over my skin.

"I've never undressed you," Jack whispered as his mouth passed near my ear. "May I?"

I hummed my approval and he pulled away. "Wait here, I won't be long."

164

I waited patiently as Jack circled the mattress and pulled back the covers on both sides before returning to stand between the bed and me. With measured movements, Jack removed his shirt before sitting down on the bed and reaching down to slip off his socks. He then stood back up, unbuttoning his trousers and sliding them down his muscular legs. Wearing only his black boxer briefs, he gathered his clothes and stepped toward me. I allowed him to back me up against his dresser, and he reached past my body to set the garments down on its surface.

"Your turn." His voice was low and sensual.

I glanced down at my casual outfit and bristled.

"What is it?" he asked with a touch of worry.

"I was in a hurry to get over here after work. I didn't stop to think about wearing anything sexy for you."

"Doesn't matter," he said with a smile. "I'm all too eager to get you out of whatever you have on. Knowing you, I'm sure I'll discover a sweet surprise." Jack took my hands and encouraged me to step away from the dresser. He then moved and stood behind me, pressing his bare chest to my back. His erection rubbed against my backside, and my body tingled in response.

"Raise your arms and close your eyes." Jack's hushed words were warm as they brushed the slope of my shoulder.

I complied without a single word, savoring the happiness that radiated from somewhere deep within.

He slid his fingers underneath the hem of my black cotton shirt. He lifted it up while tracing his fingers deliciously along my skin. I shivered in response and Jack paused.

"Please don't stop," I begged.

Jack chuckled, vibrating his body against mine in the process, but I kept my eyes closed and my arms raised. In one swift movement, Jack removed the obstructing shirt from my body.

I reached back with my arms and encircled them around Jack's neck, pulling his chest flush with my mostly naked back. Jack brought his hands around my stomach to cup my breasts, his fingers gently exploring the satin of my pale pink bra.

"I like this color," he whispered. "Even your simplest choices are sexy." He squeezed both sides of my chest with a tantalizing amount of pressure. "Your breasts are beautiful."

"Thank you," I replied.

He caressed me for a few precious moments, and I enjoyed the pleasure of his skilled touch. Gradually, his hands moved down to the waistband of my jeans.

"Are you ready for me to see what's under here?"

I opened my eyes. "I am."

Jack circled around to my front, and I brought my hands down and undid my button and zipper. He repositioned his hands on the curve of my hips and pulled us toward the bed. He took a seat on the edge of the mattress and guided me to stand between his thighs before sliding my pants down my legs. I placed a hand on his shoulder for balance as I stepped from the denim.

He ran his hands over and up my legs. His thumbs soon came to rest on my matching pink satin panties. "You never disappoint me," he said affectionately. "In fact, I think you're spoiling me."

He leaned forward and kissed my stomach. It was a foreign sensation, and I couldn't recall anyone doing this to me before. His kisses were cool against my warm skin, and I enjoyed his slow movements and loving attention.

I wanted so much to do something new for him and was suddenly inspired. I slid my hand from his shoulder to skim my fingers along his strong jaw.

"Jack?"

"Yes," he murmured just before allowing his tongue to explore my navel.

"I'm ready."

"Ready for what?" He punctuated his question with a pleasant nip of my skin.

"To tell you my story."

Jack slowed his kisses, lingering in place for a second or two. He gave me one final kiss on my abdomen before pulling down my underwear. He rose from the bed, reached behind me and unclasped my bra. It fell to the floor.

"Are you ready to tell me now?"

I nodded, my gaze locked onto his dark eyes. I cupped his cheek in my hand. My heart was pounding, but whether it was from arousal or nervousness I couldn't tell.

"It will change how you think about my family. About me."

Jack kept his eyes locked on mine, but he pulled my hand away from his face and kissed my palm. "Something tells me I'll only admire you more."

We stood still for a few moments, and in that time I felt our emotional bond grow more secure.

"You should know these things before we talk to Robert," I explained. "I want you to know what happened."

"Come lie down, let me hold you, and you can tell me everything you want me to know."

I nodded and Jack held my hand as I situated myself on the bed. He stepped over to the dimmer switch and dialed the lighting down to its lowest level. He walked around to his side of the bed and stripped off his underwear before joining me under the cool sheets. I turned on my side to face him, the covers resting comfortably on my hips.

Jack reached over to pull the blankets up my body, but I set my hand on his arm. "I'm fine."

He nodded and settled himself on his side. Our legs sought contact, and I began to massage Jack's forearm in appreciation and contemplation. I wanted to gather my thoughts and figure out how to begin. The silence between us dragged on, although not uncomfortably.

Jack ended my deliberations and offered me a launching pad for our conversation when he asked, "How long were your parents married?"

That was a simple question to answer, and I was grateful to Jack for easing me into things. "Almost thirteen years."

"And you're their only child?"

I nodded.

"That was a good choice on their part," Jack observed. "There was no way any sibling could hold a candle to their big sister."

I rolled my eyes, but thanked him for the compliment.

"My mom convinced Robert to have a vasectomy when I was three. Rumor has it she sensed the divorce would happen. I guess she wanted to make sure I was the only heir."

Jack laughed at this. "That was really clever of her."

I smiled, too. No other woman had ever held so much power over Robert Brighton.

"Where is your mother now? Did she remarry later on?"

"No," I replied. "She's dead."

Any remaining traces of humor vanished from Jack's expression, and he maneuvered his arm away from my caresses to entwine his fingers with mine.

"I'm sorry, Kathleen."

I shrugged. It was a matter of time before the emotional dam broke. The crying was all but inevitable, but I did my best to keep my breathing slow and measured. It was easier to keep the tears at bay when I did so.

"I'm afraid that's part of my story," I said.

"It's all right. Take your time." Jack squeezed my hand.

"I don't speak of it," I whispered. "Not even a therapist could get it from me. I'm not sure I can put it all into words."

"It's up to you, Kathleen."

I continued on before I could think about it too much. "I was used to their fighting. And as awful as that was, it rarely involved me. I had a huge closet in my room. Over time, I figured the space out pretty well. As long as I had a place for a lamp, blankets, books and a small stash of snacks, I could disappear for hours. Between closing my bedroom door and the closet door, I could muffle ninety percent of the noise."

"Didn't they know how upsetting it was for you?"

"I doubt it. They were both drunk, a lot, and they enabled one another's bad habits. I don't think they were coherent enough to think about what I was up to."

I took another break, and Jack leaned over and kissed my forehead. When he pulled back, I dove back in.

"When I turned ten the fighting got really bad. Considering how numb I was to it by then, that's saying something." I tried to make the story as light as I could, but Jack's face was unyielding in its seriousness. I looked over at his pillow to focus on getting the words out without succumbing to the sadness.

"Robert went away for a few days. I remembered it because it was such a relief. I didn't have to worry about when the next fight was going to break out. As long as he was away, it would be fine. But when he returned, the house was too quiet. I didn't know what the hell was going on." I glanced at Jack with hesitation.

"It sounds like the calm before the storm," Jack said.

I nodded. "One morning, my mom left home. Before she went out the door, she told me Robert was sleeping, and I needed to be as quiet as I could. That wasn't a problem because by this point in my life, the last thing I ever wanted to do was draw attention to myself. A few hours later, the phone started ringing. I was terrified because there was a phone in the room on Robert's bedside table. I ran like hell to answer it before it woke him." I halted my recollections to wipe a stray tear from my eye.

"Do you want a sip of water?" Jack asked with concern.

"No, thank you," I answered. "But I think I'm going to sit up for this next part."

At this, Jack rose up and positioned himself so that his back was against the headboard. He beckoned me to rest between his legs and drew me in to recline on his chest. He draped himself loosely around me, securing me in his arms without closing in. I allowed myself the luxury of enjoying the tranquility of his comfort.

"Who was on the line?"

"I don't know exactly. A woman. She asked to speak to Robert, and I told her he wasn't able to come to the phone. She wouldn't take no for an answer, insisted on speaking to him, and when I resisted, she told me she was calling from a hospital and it was an emergency."

Jack's embrace strengthened around me.

"The last thing I wanted to do was wake him up. But somehow I managed to do it."

"How did he react?"

"Surprisingly well. When his eyes opened, I handed him the receiver and ran away. I returned to the living room and hoped that was the end of it."

Jack leaned forward and placed several tender kisses on my shoulder. His gentle efforts soothed me.

"A little while later, Robert walked into the living room. He was dressed and he told me we had to go over to the Willamette Valley. That my mom was in the hospital there."

"What was your mom doing so far from home?"

"At the time, Robert wouldn't tell me. I found out later that she had been discovered unconscious in her car, sitting on the side of the highway. She'd taken an entire bottle of sleeping pills. A passerby decided to pull over and check on the car. If they hadn't, she probably would have died that morning."

Jack wove his fingers into my hair and delicately stroked my scalp.

"We were at the hospital all afternoon, but Robert wouldn't allow me to see my mom or go in her room. So he stayed with her while I wandered around. I walked through the whole building several times. I'd never been there before, but I knew the whole place by the time we finally left. On the way home, he stopped at one of our favorite restaurants, but we didn't stay to eat. Robert ordered something to go and then he brought me home. We ate dinner and afterward he told me that he was divorcing my mother. I should have seen it coming, but I didn't. I was completely surprised. He sent me off to bed, and I cried myself to sleep."

Jack froze his movements, and I wondered if he'd had a similar conversation with Heide. While I was certain that conversation was a painful one for both Jack and Heide, I was not convinced that same conversation with me had been difficult for my father.

"It was summer and Robert stayed home with me for the next few days, but he was busy. Preparing to leave." I spat the words and took a moment to settle my anger.

"He left the house one afternoon, and a short time later my mother came home. By herself. She went straight to their bedroom and shut herself inside."

"No one was looking after her?" Jack sounded perplexed.

I shook my head in response.

"I knocked on her door more than once that evening, but she didn't answer me. It never occurred to me to try turning the doorknob." I shuddered at this admission before moving forward.

"I waited for a long time, but it was getting late. I knew how to cook a few basic things for myself so I finally made some dinner. I tried to bring some to her, but she wouldn't open the door. I put her plate back on the kitchen table and took my food to the living room. I remembered turning on the TV so there was some noise to drown out the silence. I sat on the sofa and was in the middle of taking a bite when this god-awful loud noise went off in the house. It startled me so much that I bit my tongue and dropped my dinner on the floor. The pain was intense, and I was bleeding so I ran to get my mom. I didn't bother to knock on the door. I just burst into the room."

I stopped speaking, having become aware I had pulled away from Jack. I was still sitting between his legs, but was ramrod straight and disengaged from his protection. I glanced over my shoulder to look at him and saw the dawning realization of horror in his eyes. There was no going back now.

"She shot herself. In the heart."

"Jesus Christ," he uttered.

"She died almost immediately." My eyes strayed toward the carpet. "I recognized the gun. Robert kept it in his bedside table. Mom had told me to stay away from it, and I always did."

Jack was silent, and eerily motionless. I felt compelled to fill the dreadful silence.

"I didn't know where Robert had gone. I had no idea how to get a hold of him. I pulled the phone from his bedside table as far as the cord would let me. I knew my mother was dead, but I had this crazy thought that if I turned my back, she would sit up and follow me. So I sat across the room from her body and called Theresa Mayfair. I don't know what I said to her, but she showed up to our house, wearing a red bathrobe and rollers in her hair. I remember feeling bad for making her come over in her pajamas."

I took a deep breath as Jack continued to sit in silence. "You've met Theresa, right?" Somehow, it was vital for me to confirm this with Jack. Or perhaps it was just vital to hear his voice.

"Yes," he whispered.

"She took me to the living room and held me on her lap while her husband called the police. There was a lot of activity, but I tuned it all out. Theresa held me and tended to my injured mouth. I was calm, but when Robert burst into the house, I lost it. He was drunk and crazy looking. I started screaming my head off and clung to Theresa for dear life."

"Why?" Jack's voice was full of strained emotion, and as I formulated an answer, I worried about the toll my memories were taking on him.

"I was terrified he was going to blame me. It was my responsibility to look after my mother and I failed. Robert tried to pull me from Theresa's arms and I panicked. I fought him because I got it in my head that he was going to hurt me. I kicked and punched and yelled even louder. Theresa pushed Robert away and took me to her house. She wouldn't let him see me until he sobered up."

Having recalled the incident for the first time in decades, I was overcome by weariness. "There's not much more I can share about that night. Suffice it to say, things between Robert and me have been supremely fucked up ever since."

Jack's expression was flooded by a variety of emotions.

I had never seen him so affected, and I felt guilty for being the source of his distress. "I'm sorry, Jack. Maybe I should have thought this through before telling you. It was impulsive."

He shook his head. "Please don't apologize. I know that wasn't easy for you to share."

"I've told you something deeply personal about me, but also about my father. Our boss. I've entrusted all of this to you. Perhaps that isn't fair."

"Are you having regrets?"

"Not on my account. All I ask is that you keep this between us. Forever."

"I can do that."

"Thank you. Did I ruin our evening?"

"No."

"Will you hold me now?"

"I will hold you anytime you ask."

We continued to stare at one another, but neither of us made a move. Finally, I shifted on the mattress. "I'll get the light."

Jack gently grabbed my wrist. "There's so much I want to say to you, Kathleen. I just don't have the words right now."

"I get it," I said, trying to reassure him. "I lived it and look how long it's taken me to find the words." A new realization dawned on me then, and it must have registered on my face.

"What is it?" Jack asked me with urgency.

"I can't believe I'm not crying right now," I confessed. "I must be more fucked up than I thought."

"You are not fucked up. You're the strongest person I've ever known."

chapter

Twenty-Two

IN THE wake of reliving my mother's death, it was a struggle for us to ease back into one another's company.

I believed Jack when he told me he lacked the words to express his feelings. I was concerned for him, but thankful he was the one I'd chosen to say these things to. Even so, we needed to move away from the subject of my childhood.

"Is it all right if we have something to eat?"

Jack nodded, and dashed from the bed to the dresser where he had placed our snack. A few weeks before, I would have thought he was trying to escape from me, but now I knew otherwise. He was eager to see to my needs, and I was more than happy to encourage him. Allowing Jack to be a man of action was important.

It had been a while since I enjoyed a good orange, and I savored the treat. The citrus scent and juiciness of the fruit filled my senses with the comfortable familiarity of warmth and happiness. To my relief, Jack relaxed as we shared the slices. I didn't understand what had motivated him to prepare the snack in the first place, but was grateful for the distraction and simple joy it provided us.

Afterward, we settled into bed and began to kiss. Within a matter of minutes, we were making love. We explored one another's bodies with tenderness as we tasted the sweet juice on one another's lips. I'd never look at oranges again without thinking of him.

We didn't have the luxury of sleeping in the following morning. It was a workday and a school day, and Jack woke up just before dawn to begin his regular routine. When his movements roused my attention, he kissed my forehead.

"It's early," he confirmed. "Stay in bed a while longer. Get some more rest."

Unaccustomed to looking after anyone but myself, I complied without protest.

In time, the fresh sunlight combined with the irresistible aroma of Jack's cooking, lured me to full consciousness. I dressed in the conservative pajamas I had brought for Heide's sake and made my way to the kitchen. When I turned the corner to the room, I stopped in my tracks and smiled.

Heide had woken up before me and stood just behind her father as he prepared breakfast. Like me, they were both wearing pajamas—he in a white tee shirt and blue plaid bottoms and she in a bright Angry Birds ensemble. Being the wonderful father he was, Jack sensed her presence and glanced over his shoulder at his daughter. As he did so, remnants of the lingering emotion from the night before overtook his handsome features as if he was looking at Heide and recalling what I had been through as a child. Jack watched Heide, and the intensity of his love for his daughter filled me with wonder.

"Come here," he requested softly.

Heide shuffled over to her father's side, and he held out his arms to her. "Jump," he instructed.

She did and Jack swept her up into his strong embrace. She snuggled her head into the crook of his neck as he settled her weight on his left side. Her arms and legs were long and dangled across her father's body. He likely wouldn't be able to hold her like this for much longer. Perhaps another year or two at most.

"Morning, Dad," she mumbled.

"Good morning." Jack smiled into her mussed, blond hair. "Did you sleep well?"

Heide nodded without lifting her head from its resting place.

"How hungry are you this morning?"

"Only a little bit."

"Yeah?"

She nodded again.

"Okay. Just a light breakfast before school then."

"Okay."

Jack kept a tight hold on his daughter with one arm while he returned to cooking breakfast with the other. It would have been far easier to set her down, but he wasn't letting go of her just yet, and she was content to remain with him.

"I love you," he said.

It was the first time I'd heard him say the words, and my heart fluttered even though the declaration wasn't meant for me.

"I love you, too."

The affirmations between Jack and Heide were brief but sincere, and I knew by this one exchange they were made often. It wasn't something I could relate to from my own personal experiences, but it was something I could appreciate.

As quietly as possible, I backed out of the kitchen and left Jack and Heide alone to spend some precious time together. Looking for something to occupy my time, I wandered into the living room and retrieved my cell phone from the coffee table. A text message was waiting for me. When I swiped the screen, Robert's name appeared. His message informed me that our golf date had been set for the next day at twelve o'clock.

High Noon.

"Naturally," I grumbled, tossing my phone on to the sofa. Eighteen holes of golf, plus a round or two of drinks afterward meant spending at least four hours underneath Robert's scrutiny. I would need every second of today and tomorrow morning to prepare for the inevitable.

I looked back in the direction of the kitchen and frowned with anxiety. I anticipated my mother's story would give Jack pause about telling my father about our new relationship. It would be far easier and preferable to avoid any new conflict with Robert, but there was also something else brewing within me — hope.

I'd spent years wondering when or if things would ever change between Robert and me. It couldn't happen without an outside influence to reshape the dynamics of our dysfunctional relationship. Perhaps with the support of Jack Evans, I could find my way from the quagmire my life had become.

The weeks I'd spent allowing Jack into my heart were among the most romantic and significant I'd ever experienced. There was no denying it. Things between us hadn't been hassle free. I'd thrown any number of roadblocks his way, and yet here we were. He'd endured my uncertainties and worries, and now my involvement with Jack was among one of the most enjoyable times of my life. Our relationship strengthened me in a way that nothing else had been able to. He'd welcomed me not only into his life, but also his daughter's. Heide was the most important person in his world, and he trusted me with her.

Despite the ugliness that saturated my family and my reluctance to expose Jack to more of my painful recollections, I owed him nothing less than the same amount of trust he had extended to me.

If not now, when?

If not him, who?

Spending the night at Jack's house had been eventful once again, and I was experiencing a certain amount of lightness after having shared so much. Although I wasn't joyful, I was content. Heide left on the school bus that morning, and we enjoyed our own breakfast. Later, I retrieved my phone from the sofa and answered Robert's text. "Noon on Friday it is. I'm looking forward to an afternoon out of the office."

Almost immediately, he answered back, "I'll drive you out there."

I set my phone back on the kitchen island and reached for my cup of coffee.

Jack nodded toward it. "Was that Robert?"

"Yeah." I took a very small sip of the Starbucks brew. "He wants me to ride to the golf course with him."

"That's good."

I smirked. Robert had informed me, not asked me, about the driving arrangements.

"Try to think about the positive side of it."

Finding the silver lining was not a habit I'd developed over the years, so it took me a few moments to find it. Accepting Robert's terms meant I was spared the complication of how to get to the golf course. I was certain I would need a ride home from Jack once we'd made our disclosure to my father. I needn't worry about Robert leaving me stranded once he stormed away. It was the best I could come up with under the circumstances.

I nodded. "You're right. I'll try to work on that."

I attempted once more to channel my concerns through a different canyon of thought when a new question occurred to me.

"Do you ever find it hard?" I murmured my words as I was still contemplating them.

"What?"

"Raising a daughter by yourself."

Jack shook his head without deliberation. "Hard isn't the right word. I never think about it in terms of easy or hard."

"What is the right word?"

"Meaningful."

The morning of the game was sunny and warm. I chose to wear a navy skort with small white polka dots along with a matching, sleeveless, navy shirt. The outfit was suggestive for the office, but I covered up the figure-hugging top with a light sweater and made sure anyone I came into contact with understood I'd be spending the afternoon at Widgi Creek with Robert. Most smiled and told me to have a good time golfing, while a select few paused as if unsure of how to respond. I couldn't really blame them.

Although I had worked through the morning, Robert only appeared in time to pick me up. He was wearing one of an endless number of golf outfits he kept ready in his closet. Today's choice was a green shirt paired with khaki knee-length shorts.

"You ready?" he asked, and simultaneously clapped his hands. The gesture reminded me of a master summoning his dog, and I bit the inside of my cheek to keep from snapping at him.

"Sure," I replied, forcing a smile.

Robert turned and walked toward the exit with me following behind. The air in the office was stifling, and I welcomed the fresh breeze as soon as we entered the parking lot.

When I opened the door to his luxury SUV and stepped up into the vehicle, I noticed his clubs peeking up from behind the back seat. My father's passion for golfing was well known and he had it down to a science. For several months of the year, Widgi Creek was Robert's preferred office space, and he always brought along the newest equipment. Not for the first time, I wondered how Jack's game would compare to my father's.

Robert was in a good mood as he drove to the golf course, and I coached myself to lower my guard, trying to appear as casual as he was.

"When was the last time we did this together?"

I couldn't be insulted by his lack of memory. I wasn't sure myself. "At the end of middle school? Maybe the beginning of high school? Something like that."

"More than twenty years then." It was a statement devoid of emotion. Nothing more than a simple fact.

Our conversation fizzled for a minute or two, and I began to assume the rest of our journey would be a silent one. Surprisingly, Robert attempted small talk once again.

"I moved here because I wanted to spend more time outdoors."

"I remember lots of time outside," I said.

"I thought it would be good for you. I wanted to raise you in a place most people only enjoy on their vacations."

This revelation was new to me. As I processed my father's words, I related it to what Jack had said about moving his family to Oregon. In some ways, the two men shared similar experiences. The fundamental difference was the outcomes. Allison had left the state to escape her husband, while my mother had made a more bewildering and irreversible decision.

Robert looked over at me. "What do you do when you're not at work? Do you do anything outdoors?"

I blinked as he drew me back into the discussion. "I've always enjoyed being out on the water."

"I don't remember you doing anything like that recently."

"I haven't," I confirmed. "It was always something to do with friends, but my friends are busy with their families these days."

"Ah." Robert connected the dots. My friends had married and gone on to have children. Even though I wasn't opposed to marriage, there would never be children for me.

The second pause in our conversation was longer and heavier with all that my final statement implied. I should have been all right with letting the talk slide away, but I racked my brain for a way to salvage the uncharacteristic lightness between my father and me. Jack was determined to start things out on the right foot with Robert. It was for his sake, not mine, that I plodded forward.

"I'm thinking of going up to Mount Bachelor for a hike."

"When? You shouldn't go alone, you know."

"You don't need to worry," I said, watching the road in front of us. It was the only information I was willing to supply.

From the corner of my eye, I saw Robert shake his head. "You never want to talk."

I shrugged. "I've always been quiet."

"Not always," he countered in a reflective voice.

My emotions were still raw from sharing my family's story with Jack, and I reminded myself that Robert couldn't know any of that. I didn't answer my father and turned my gaze once more to look out the passenger side window.

"You weren't always this way," he reiterated.

A bitter impulse overcame me. "Being a father is hard?"

He answered as he slowed down to make the final turn toward the golf course, "Immensely. But hey, if today goes well, maybe we can think about doing this again."

"Maybe," I said. It was the only response that seemed adequate, and I was grateful when he didn't read into my answer.

chapter

Twenty-Three

WHEN WE pulled into the parking lot at Widgi Creek, a quick scan for Jack's car confirmed we had arrived before him.

He spent the morning meeting with clients and was away from the office. I hadn't seen him since work the evening before. I was restless and yearned to bask in the comfort of his close proximity.

Robert and I exited his car, and I stood at the back of the vehicle while he retrieved his clubs. As he organized his golf bag, Jack arrived and parked nearby. As much as I yearned to drift away from my father to greet him, my apprehension of drawing too much attention kept my feet locked in place.

Jack waved as he got out of his car and opened the trunk. He pulled his golf bag out and slung it over his shoulder. After securing his blue BMW sedan, he walked over and joined us. He carried a vintage set of clubs with the gold initials A.E. engraved on the worn leather of the coffee and cream-colored bag. After he set down his bag, he shook hands with Robert.

"I'm glad we could do this," Jack said. "I've been looking for an opportunity to get back into the game."

"Just watch out for elk," I chimed in, smiling.

Robert chuckled and Jack turned to me with interest. "Are you serious?"

"I remember seeing elk pass by us more than once out here."

Robert nodded. "She's not lying."

Jack's eyes sparkled with amusement. He was dressed smartly in a gray pencil-striped polo and navy slacks. I had no choice but to resist the urge to kiss him.

"Do they ever get hit by balls?" he asked.

"Not by me," Robert answered. "I sure as hell don't want to piss off an elk."

I laughed at this and, judging by the quick glance I received from both men, the sound was unexpected.

Robert smiled. "I'll get us all squared away with a cart. This is all on me today."

Jack nodded, knowing my father well enough not to argue. "Thank you, Robert."

"No problem."

Jack turned in my direction. "Shall I keep you company?"

"Sure." In an effort to avoid appearing too interested in Jack, I occupied myself with removing my sweater.

My father headed into the clubhouse, and when I turned my attention to Jack he was watching me.

"Why did you wear a sweater today?" he asked as we began the walk to the first tee.

"I didn't want to," I answered while folding the garment over my arm, "but I needed to look somewhat modest at work."

Jack's expression turned prim. "You wore this to the office?"

"It's Friday. It's casual." I arched an eyebrow, warning Jack not to push the subject any further.

He leaned in close to me as we continued to walk, but he refrained from touching me.

"You look stunning in the sunshine," he said. "You'll be tempting me all afternoon."

"Don't flirt." I nodded to the infinitesimal space between us. "I'm having a tough time keeping my distance as it is."

"I'm not going to hold out until Sunday." His voice was gruff with arousal, and the confidence in his tone sent my desire into overdrive.

"Are you suggesting we sneak off into the woods?" I said as a dare. "I'm not sure the elk will like that."

"Who's flirting now?" Having reached our destination, Jack's gaze drifted down.

I followed his gaze to my polka-dotted mini-skort. "I know what you're thinking," I teased.

"Tell me," he challenged.

"You're wondering what underwear I have on."

"And?"

"And I'd tell you, but you need to get your game face under control before you tee off."

"You're right about that." He sighed. "But you should know that I'll be thinking about how much I want you for the rest of the afternoon."

"I want you, too," I said, nodding toward a nearby bench. "Now don't forget to put on your cleats."

Jack grinned and, as he was changing his shoes, my eyes drifted back to his bag of golf clubs.

"Whose initials are those?" I asked.

Jack glanced up at me as he answered. "My father's."

"What's his name?"

"Andrew."

He returned to his shoes without another word, and I recognized the subtle shift in his mood. Jack's answers grew shorter when he was nervous.

I looked back to the clubs, and it occurred to me that Jack would not have brought them all the way to Oregon if his father still used them.

I shifted my glance back to him. "Did your father pass away?"

Jack stood up. He strolled closer to me, nodded and placed his hands in his pockets. I wondered if he'd done so to avoid taking hold of mine.

Melancholy rippled through me at his revelation. We'd each lost a parent, and it became clear why Jack had trouble articulating his feelings earlier in the week. He understood my loss all too well.

I longed to touch Jack, to take him in my arms and press our bodies together in affection and security, but under the circumstances it was impossible. Robert was only steps away. Instead, I reached out to trace my finger gently over the letter E imprinted on Jack's bag.

"I'm sorry," I said.

Jack's eyes rested on the letter I outlined.

"He taught me to golf when I was twelve," he recalled with fondness. "We played together, and I learned a lot from him. I enjoyed the game so much I went on to play in high school and college. He was proud of that. He always took the credit."

I smiled, happy that Jack was sharing his memories with me.

"He died during my second year of college right before winter finals. I've only played on and off since then. Almost thirty years ago." Jack frowned. "Wow."

"Your father must have been young," I surmised.

"He was."

"What happened?" I nudged.

"He had a brain aneurism. It was unpredictable."

Although our situations were vastly different, Jack's story resonated with me. He'd lost a parent in his youth and under shocking circumstances. Just like I had.

"You didn't deserve that," I said.

"Neither did you, Kathleen.

"Andrew sounds like a good man. I wish I could have met him."

"He was a great man."

"So are you."

Jack self-consciously dropped his head. "I don't know about that."

"You are," I affirmed. "I watch you with Heide, and you're such a good father. You're so devoted to her. I think your father had a lot to do with that."

Jack lifted his head and he looked toward the clubhouse. "Thank you. He would've adored her. And he would've adored you, too."

"I want to kiss you. Right now," I blurted.

Jack's warm eyes connected with mine and, for a second or two, I thought he was going to allow me to do just that.

"I missed you last night," he responded. "Once today is done and this weekend is behind us, I want to talk about more frequent sleepovers."

My melancholy was replaced by excitement. "How frequent?"

"We'll ease into it," he said. "Five. Six. Seven nights a week."

"I'd never be home," I quipped.

"Of course you would. You'd be home all the time."

Before I could respond, Robert's boisterous laughter reached our ears. He was driving a golf cart right alongside another occupied by two men — Widgi Creek regulars. Jack took the opportunity to retrieve a single glove and a Ginty driver from his bag. He pulled on the glove as wandered over to the tee. He stretched his muscles and began practicing his swing. My eyes were glued to his movements, and I was content to soak up the sun and watch him.

I could hear Robert nearby, talking to his friends, but kept my eyes locked on Jack as he prepared to play. Jack possessed the athlete's grace and focus, the muscles of his lean form on fine display. Given everything that had passed between us, I was certain a stop at my condo would be necessary before I allowed him to go home for the weekend. As I watched his appealing movements, I visualized another scenario.

I wanted to take him to my room, undress him and position our bodies so I could watch the reflection of his powerful back in my bureau mirror. I wanted him to lose control like he had on the chaise lounge, and I wanted to watch his body perform in all its magnificence while I came all around him.

My nostrils filled with pungent smoke, disrupting my fantasy. I turned in time to see Robert accept a cigar from a friend who was smoking his own. After lighting it up, Robert turned toward Jack and called him over to make a quick introduction. I waited in place, wondering if I would be asked to join the rest of the Boys' Club. Jack shook a couple of hands, and his new acquaintance also offered him a cigar. He declined to smoke it, but pocketed the gift with an appreciative nod.

"Kathleen!" Robert waved his hand, gesturing for me to join the rest of the group and I wandered over. As soon as I reached his side, Robert surprised me by placing a loose yet friendly arm around my shoulders. We were taking some downtime before the game began and as the men continued to talk, I fell into an odd sense of contentment.

Not unlike Jack and his father, golf games with Robert were one of the few fond memories I had of time spent with my father. Having returned to Widgi Creek once more, I was ashamed to admit I hadn't thought about those memories in many years. I risked making eye contact with Jack only to discover he was watching me with interest. I smiled to indicate that I was all right.

My acceptance of Robert at this moment was the last thing I could have predicted for the day. Was Jack's presence in my life contributing to my improved good mood toward my father? Or was Robert just so perfectly in his element that even I could let down my guard?

"Load up your clubs, Jack," Robert instructed. "Let's get moving."

The well-designed golf course meandered through a thin forest of evergreen trees. Between the manicured grounds and the surrounding wooded area, it was easy to forget we were spending a summer afternoon in the high desert country of central Oregon. My favorite spot had always been the tee box on the fifteenth hole where I could peer down a canyon to watch the constant, shifting rapids of the Deschutes River. Between the natural setting and the wildlife, the trek through Widgi Creek was always a beautiful one.

My interest in the technicalities of golf had recessed halfway through the game. Robert and Jack had bonded over their shared interest in golf and I was glad of it. They were enjoying themselves, discussing strategy and reacting to one another's shots. Although Jack wasn't at the top of his game, he was able to hold his own against Robert.

And he looked incredibly sexy while doing so.

"Line up on your left nut," Robert advised Jack on the fairway of the fourteenth hole. "As opposed to dead center."

Robert had no qualms that I was standing just a few feet away when he offered this choice piece of wisdom. I pretended I didn't hear anything in order to spare Jack any discomfort.

It was, however, the kind of comment that kept my attentions riveted on my lover's body.

Jack repositioned his body according to Robert's direction and took his shot, which was impressive. I lost track of the ball briefly before watching it land near the intended target.

My father beamed at having coached him right on to the green. "There you go! Works for me every time."

"Is that a trade secret I missed hearing somewhere?" Jack kidded. "Where did you pick that up?"

"Don't remember," Robert answered. "But it works like a charm."

Robert wandered toward his own ball, which was farther ahead, while Jack walked back to the golf cart and me. The afternoon sun was almost too warm for comfort, and Jack wiped his brow as he approached.

I reached into the cart and pulled out a bottle of water. As I traded Jack his club for the water, he swooped in for a light playful kiss, his tongue stealthily skimming my lips. I'd thought of little else but Jack's touch for the past two hours, and I was more than ready to hold him close against me.

He suddenly pulled back. "Fuck," he whispered, upset with himself.

We both glanced in Robert's last known location. We'd avoided detection, but it was a perfect reminder of why it was better to clear the air with my father.

"You were saying?" I encouraged.

Jack watched me keenly while he drank his water. I held his gaze with what I hoped was a lustful expression.

"What time is it?" he asked after lowering his water bottle.

"Just after three. When do you have to be home?"

"I'm on my own until six."

"Will you have time to stop at my place?"

"I'll make the time," he said. "Incidentally, I'm blaming your outfit for my loss today. I plan to take out my aggression on it."

"Whatever," I responded. "It's smarter to let the boss win the first game anyway."

Jack offered me the water bottle and took back his club. "I don't let anyone win. Ever."

Robert did win with Jack performing well enough to garner my father's admiration.

"We should play together more, if you're interested," Robert offered as we walked away from the eighteenth and final hole.

"I am," Jack responded, and judging by this tone, he meant it.

I took in a deep breath to settle the increasing flurry of nerves in my stomach. I hoped Robert would still feel that way once he knew Jack and I were seeing each other.

After the cart was returned and the two men had reloaded their golf clubs into their respective automobiles, Jack moved toward Robert.

"Do you have time for a beer or two," he asked, tilting his head toward the clubhouse. "I lost the game, so drinks are on me today."

Robert looked at me. "Is that all right with you?"

My father's consideration for my schedule took me by surprise.

"Sure," I stammered.

The matter settled, Jack and Robert turned toward the lounge. I followed behind them and my eyes drifted to Jack's hand. I longed to take hold of it as we made our way inside. With each step closer to the clubhouse, my nervousness evolved into dread. It was agonizing that I couldn't comfort myself with Jack's physical reassurance.

As we entered the bar, I did my best to calm myself down with a single thought.

When I leave this room, I'll be able to hold Jack's hand any time I want.

chapter

Twenty-Four

CONFIDENT AS ever, Jack led the way to the window side of the lounge. The table he selected was low to the floor and designed more for resting drinks on than enjoying a meal. He gestured for me to sit next to the window before taking his place on my right. Robert sat across from us.

When the server approached to take our order, the young man looked to me first.

"I'd like an unsweetened iced tea, please."

Jack looked surprised by my order, while Robert appeared impassive.

"You don't want a beer?" Jack asked me before offering an impish grin. "I'm buying, remember?"

"I don't drink beer. But thanks."

Jack quirked his eyebrows in surprise and persisted. "Wine?"

I shook my head and turned my attention to the window, pretending to take in the view. I was hopeful Jack would take the hint and drop the matter. I hated beer and couldn't even stand the smell of it. I could have ordered the wine, but I'd never swallowed an ounce of alcohol in my father's presence, and I wasn't about to begin now. Robert rarely offered me the same courtesy.

I was relieved when the waiter switched his focus from me to Jack.

"An Inversion IPA, please."

I cringed when Jack ordered his beer. It could make kissing him later unpleasant.

The server nodded and turned to Robert. "The usual?"

"Yep." Robert pointed at Jack. "And he's the one paying today so make sure he gets the bill."

"Good deal." The waiter grinned before turning toward the bar.

"What's the usual?" Jack inquired.

"Deschutes River Ale," I replied in monotone, my eyes still fixated on the nearby tree line. I answered the question before Robert could.

Talons of tension dug into my shoulder, and I was helpless to control my growing anxiety.

"She knows me so well," Robert jokingly replied to Jack.

I crossed one leg over the other. I did my best to hold still in my seat, but my leg began to bounce as the inevitable conversation was now underway. The day had gone well, so I did my best to hold on to the more enjoyable moments.

"Thanks for letting me tag along today," I said to my father, doing my best to remind him of a good afternoon spent together.

"Maybe one of these days I'll talk you into playing, too."

I didn't see that happening. However, I wasn't rude enough to say so. "One of these days. I'll have to retire sooner or later. Maybe then you'll have the time you'll need to teach me properly."

Robert chortled as our server reappeared with our drinks. "I'll be ordering you around when I'm ninety and in a wheelchair."

"Hmm." The thought was not an exciting prospect.

Jack reached for his beer and raised it up in the air to offer a toast. Robert and I followed suit.

"Thanks for a good game today." Jack nodded toward my father. "And here's to many future afternoons of you paying the bar bill."

"Keep lining up on that left nut and maybe I will," Robert returned.

The three of us tapped our drinks together and indulged in a few sips before Jack set his beer down on the table. He sat back in his chair and turned to look at me, a signal that the time had come to make our announcement. Jack smiled and turned back toward my father.

"I enjoyed our game today, Robert. I would like to keep playing with you."

"Absolutely," Robert responded. "Let's figure out a schedule for the rest of the summer."

"Sounds good. My daughter will be in Baltimore with her mother, so I'll have plenty of open afternoons."

Robert nodded as he took a significant swig of his ale.

Jack leaned forward and rested his arms on his knees as he tented his fingers. "There is something else I'd like to talk to you about. I hope you don't mind. I wanted to have this conversation away from the office."

Robert glanced in my direction as though to remind Jack that I would be overhearing their conversation. "Sure."

I looked back and forth between the two men as Jack set the scene for the conversation. Jack paused and rubbed his chin as a nervous laughter escaped him. He turned his head and his brown eyes met my green ones. Several anxious moments passed by as we watched one another.

"I thought this would be easier," he confessed.

I hadn't seen Jack so nervous since he'd discovered me half-naked and angry in his bedroom many weeks before. This sudden shift was surprising. He'd been so adamant about leading this conversation with Robert and assured me of his ability to do so. I had offered up no resistance with his decision, and I'd been relying on Jack's fortitude to hold my own resolve intact. Without it, I wasn't sure how best to proceed. But we were in this together and now the time had come for me to prove it to him. And to me.

Before another consideration stopped me, I reached for Jack's hand. He entwined his fingers around mine. I turned back to my father. His eyes were locked on our joined hands. Jack and I were a united front, and as Robert began to comprehend this, the smile slid off his face.

I waited to speak until my father raised his eyes to meet mine. "Jack and I are seeing each other."

"Since when?" Robert's voice was low. His tone soft, but also infuriated. I wondered who he was most let down by. Me? Or Jack?

Jack's grip tightened around my fingers. "Not long," he said, "but long enough to know we're serious about one another."

Robert didn't respond to Jack. He was far too concentrated on me, his eyes sharpening into ferocity. It was a look I'd come to know well over the years. I braced myself.

"Well," he scoffed. "You're back to acting like a fifteen-year-old, I see."

Jack remained motionless while I held my father's gaze. I sensed no fear from him, and the slight tightening of his grip hinted that Jack was awaiting the opportune moment to interject.

"How many other men from the office have you slept with?" Robert spat, grabbed his beer and took another long pull from the bottle.

Jack sat forward, prepared with his response. I strengthened my hold on him as a deterrent, knowing my knuckles were turning white with the effort. I wanted to stand up, end the discussion with Robert and walk away, but I didn't. I didn't give a fuck what my father believed, but I did care about what Jack believed.

"You tell me, Robert," I retorted with suppressed rage. "When was the last time I went out with you to share any kind of good news?"

Robert slammed his bottle down onto the table, momentarily drawing the attention of several other members of the golf club. When I chanced a quick peek in their direction, they averted their eyes immediately.

"I asked how many," he hissed. "And I want a number. Now."

"None," I seethed.

"Just him?" Robert jabbed a thumb toward Jack, while his livid gaze remained on me. "Are you sure about that?"

"I'm not like one of your girlfriends," I snapped in a voice laced with acid anger. "Don't talk about me like I'm easy."

"You're certainly no saint, are you?"

Robert blinked and acknowledged Jack. "You know, she hasn't been a virgin in a very long time."

Jack let go of my hand and the sudden disconnection frightened me. I whipped my head in his direction and observed that his face was flush with anger. His nostrils flared as he fought to control his temper.

"Stop," Jack said in a tone ice cold and vicious in its delivery.

Taking in the sight of an enraged Jack Evans was one of the most frightening moments of my life. Jack's countenance terrified me more than any of Robert's confrontational remarks. I'd been raised by Robert, and I expected my father to be a prick. I never counted on Jack Evans to strike back with equal force.

And neither did Robert, whose focus returned to me. "Jack has a complicated situation with his family. Did you stop to think about the damage you could do?"

Despite all the coaching during the week I'd given myself not to take his bait, my temper broke. I possessed more loyalty to Jack and Heide than I'd ever had for my father. Robert had just made a terrible mistake.

"Don't you dare ever lecture me on family," I warned him. "Don't you ever talk to me about his family again."

"Control yourself, Kathleen," Robert fumed.

I leaned forward, closing the distance between us at the exact moment I most wanted to separate from this miserable excuse of a father. "Look at me, Robert. I am in complete control. After everything you did to my mother? To me? You're lucky I'm even giving you the chance to throw this ridiculous fit."

Robert stood up and swept his beer bottle off the table in the process. Suspicious of what he might do next, I didn't take my eyes off him even when I felt Jack's hand take hold of mine again.

Robert looked at our reunited hands as he gulped the rest of his beer. He rocked on his feet for a few silent moments before setting the empty bottle on the table.

He offered a final look at Jack and said in a frigid empty tone, "Good luck with her." Robert walked away without a backward glance.

I turned my attention back to the window, but I knew Jack kept his eyes on Robert until he left the clubhouse.

"Are you all right?" I asked. I was concerned for Jack but too afraid of his answer to look at him.

"I want to get you out of here," he replied. "I just wanted to give Robert time to leave first."

"Fine." I kept my face to the window and tried to cool my anger.

"What about you?" he asked. "How are you doing?" Jack's voice was calm once again, and I found the courage to face him.

"I've been through worse."

"I'm glad we did this on a Friday."

"His anger is always situational," I tried to reassure Jack. "He'll calm down over the weekend."

"You think so?"

I nodded.

"Should I call a cab?" I asked him. "Let you get on your way?" My question was impulsive.

Jack's eyes flashed with offense. "Of course not."

"After all that? Are you sure you still want to take me home?"

His dark eyes softened. "I do. Is that what you want?"

I nodded.

"Do you still want me to come in for a while?" he asked. "Or do you want to be alone?"

"I don't want to be alone."

"Good."

chapter

Twenty-Five

I SPENT the afternoon planning to take Jack to my bed and watch us in the mirror, but as it turned out, we never made it that far.

As soon as the front door of my condo closed, I lunged at him, releasing every ounce of the afternoon's tension into our kiss. I was frantic as I guided him to my sofa, where I pushed him down before settling myself on his lap. We were breathless as we devoured each other with our kisses. I unbuttoned my shirt, and Jack pulled the front of my bra down to expose my breasts. As soon as my nipples were freed, he took me in his mouth.

As he skimmed his teeth over my skin, I arched my back and reached down between us to stroke his already hard and immense erection. I had to have him now. Withdrawing from his mouth, I stepped back just enough to drop to my knees in front of him. My intentions took him by surprise, and his reaction was visceral. He helped me to unfasten his pants, and I released him from his clothing. He breathed heavy with anticipation, but allowed me to control the moment.

Once I held him in my hands, I delighted in the warmth of his skin. He was beautiful to behold—healthy, pink, smooth and vigorous. I couldn't wait and took him into my mouth. I'd never done this to him, and I lost myself in the passion of pleasing him with my tongue.

His hips lurched enthusiastically forward, and he grasped me by the shoulders. His breath caught, followed by a throaty moan. Encouraged by his lust, I closed my lips tightly around him and worked him more aggressively. Jack panted as he throbbed in my mouth, and I figured, within a matter of several strokes, he would erupt inside me. I craved him and triumphed in Jack's impending orgasm.

"Kathleen," he breathed.

I'd never heard anything so erotic.

"God. Hold on. Wait."

I pulled back, but kept my lips pressed to his tip. I didn't have the willpower to break our contact.

"I need you," I confessed against his skin. "I need you so much. Let me do this."

"You're amazing, but not right now. Not yet. I need to slow this down. Please."

Heavy tears rolled down my face as I pulled away. My desire and emotion were one and the same in this intense moment. Over the course of the day I had missed Jack, yearned for his touch, and watched his ire and bravery unfurl in the face of my father, his boss. All I could think about was the sense of fulfillment I had whenever we had sex.

"Kathleen. No. Don't cry." He pulled me up into his arms before I could retreat. "Come here. Let me hold you."

I wrapped my arms around his neck and allowed my emotions free rein. I cried hard in his embrace, indulging in the relief brought on by the release. "Don't leave me."

His arms wrapped around my back and pulled me even tighter against him. "I'm here. I have you."

"I need you."

"I need you, too, but there's been too much intensity today. We need to relax. Let me hold you."

I was highly aroused and shifted in an effort to ease my physical discomfort. The movement proved to be more agonizing and I inhaled in surprise.

"What's wrong?" Jack asked with nervous concern.

"I'm throbbing."

"I'm sorry. What can I do?"

"I need you to fuck me, Jack."

"I want you, Kathleen. I do, but let's calm things down first."

He shifted our bodies and lowered me to the sofa. He pulled off my shoes, followed by my skort and the midnight blue thong. He placed his palm between my open legs as he lowered his lips to mine. I squeezed my eyes shut, whimpered and pushed my wild body against his hand.

He kissed me softly once, twice, and then once more. His third kiss lingered on my mouth and his patient tongue sought to subdue my fervent one. Soon, he coaxed me into a tender mood and my body reacted accordingly. After our kiss wound down, I opened my eyes. He was watching me, his eyes sparkling and kind.

"I'll be right back," he said, tracing my lower lip with a finger. "Don't move. I'm coming right back."

"Okay."

Jack removed his hand from between my legs, stood up and adjusted himself back into his clothes before exiting the living room.

He stepped into the bathroom down the hall just across from my guest room. He opened and closed several cupboards before the faucet turned on. The water ran for a short time before it turned off again, and Jack reemerged, carrying a wet washcloth.

He lifted my calves and elegantly sat down on the couch, guiding my feet to rest on his lap. He then reached between my thighs with the washcloth and rested it against me. The wet heat of the towel made contact with my delicate aching skin, delivering relief for the pain. I closed my eyes and enjoyed the warmth of the treatment and the pressure of Jack's hand holding the cloth in place.

"Did I get the temperature right?" Jack's voice was quiet and tranquil.

"Yes. You always do. You have a talent for it."

He smiled and began to caress my knee with his other hand. "Good. Let me know when I need to warm it again."

We sat for a few minutes and when the washcloth began to cool, Jack didn't wait for my instruction. He returned to the bathroom and ran it under the hot water one more time before returning for a second round of treatment as he pressed the warm cotton against my sex.

"Why did Robert make that remark about your virginity?"

Jack's care of me had been affectionate and soothing, so I didn't hesitate with my answer.

"I was in high school when it happened. He wasn't happy."

He tilted his head toward me. "You're hardly the first person to lose their virginity in high school."

"How old were you?" I asked.

He blushed and said, "My answer won't prove my point. Sorry."

"No?"

Jack shook his head and looked at my ankles. "I was shy. I didn't date much."

I smiled at the thought, inconceivable as it was. "You're kidding? I assumed the girls would have been all over you."

Jack laughed solidly, but self-consciously. "No. Not at all."

"Did you wait until you were in love?"

"No. Just until my loneliness got the better of me. It was in college after my father died."

"You were nineteen?"

Jack nodded, still unwilling to meet my eyes.

"I was fifteen."

Jack looked at me with consideration, and I knew he was replaying more of the heated exchange from Widgi Creek.

"That's what Robert meant back in the lounge? About you acting like a fifteen-year-old?"

"I suppose so. Although I wouldn't say he influenced that particular decision." It was my turn to break eye contact. I was suddenly fascinated by my own fingers. "I didn't do it to get back at my father over anything."

"Were you in love with the boy?"

"No. And I even kind of knew it. But I liked being his girlfriend, and I thought he liked being my boyfriend. The chemistry was there, but I wasn't interested in teenage pregnancy, so I tried to slow things down after the fact. That's when I realized he was more interested in the sex than me. We broke up."

"He's a moron."

I laughed. "I figured that out after about ten years. For the longest time, I was fixated on figuring out what I'd done wrong."

"You did nothing wrong."

"Tell that to Robert."

"Kathleen?" Jack waited to speak until he had my full attention.

"Yes?"

"Robert won't scare me away. I don't want you to ever worry about that."

"What about me? Will I scare you away?"

"I don't think so." Jack's fingers drifted away from my knee, proceeding to my inner thigh. "Do you feel better?"

"Yes."

"I'm sorry I can't stay tonight. I don't like the idea of leaving you here alone."

"You promised to watch Heide's friend this weekend. It's all right."

"I want to bring you home with me, but I haven't had a chance to explain things to Lydia yet. It wouldn't be fair to her or her daughter."

"Lydia is the soccer mom?"

"Yeah. I'll tell her about you tonight. We'll get through this weekend, and then we'll start making our plans together."

"Before Heide goes to visit Allison, I want to take you both hiking on Mount Bachelor. I might have already mentioned it to her."

Jack flashed a brilliant smile. "Perfect. She'd love that."

"Thank you, Jack"

"For what?"

"For taking such a gigantic risk on me."

"I've never considered you risky, but I understand what you mean. I could easily say the same thing to you." He removed his hand from the center of my body, and the washcloth crumpled without his support.

Jack lifted my legs from his lap and rose to stand next to his end of the sofa. I watched him with unwavering interest as he removed his clothes. Once he was naked and fully roused, he reached for my hand and pulled me up from the couch. With only my unbuttoned blouse and bra left on my body, undressing me was a matter of formality.

As the last of my clothing hit the floor, he pulled me into his arms, pressing our chests together and capturing my mouth in a sensual, searing kiss. When he pulled back, he looked into my eyes.

"Do you want me here? Or in your bed?"

"Here."

"Turn around."

I did as Jack requested. He rested his damp palm on my back and directed me to bend over the arm of the couch with just his touch. He then moved to stand between my legs and carefully tested my flesh with his fingers before entering me from behind.

He held still for a long, delicious moment before pulling back. He moved with great control, pausing only just before he fell away from me. He swept his hands up my back, into my hair, and drifted back down along my sides to glide along my breasts in the process. His fingers settled on my hips, which he grasped with intention.

"I will always be gentle with my touch," he whispered. "I will always be sincere with my words."

Jack pushed himself back into me. I moaned from the deliberate pleasure and contentment he offered me, and I trembled when Jack bent over my back to place several warm kisses between my shoulder blades.

"I'll give you everything you ask of me," he vowed. "And today you asked me to fuck you. So hold on."

I seized the cushion nearest to me just as Jack began thrusting into my body. He was strong and focused with his movements, and with each penetration, I was consumed by desire. He moved quickly and deeply with each stroke, hurtling me toward a considerable orgasm. I was losing control while he maintained it. The more I responded to him, the more he performed.

Our position. Our speed. Our slick bodies. Our sounds. All combined, these things should have been interpreted as nothing more than pure carnality, and yet there was much more happening between us. Jack's every move was devoted to satisfying me — body and soul. I surrendered to him. He lavished me with every bit of pleasure he could offer, and I was as overcome by my gratitude for this man as I was with the ecstasy he was giving me.

Jack was relentless, and over the course of several minutes, I had straightened my legs until I was standing on my tiptoes. My back stretched taut as my orgasm exploded throughout my body, and still Jack found the ability to move even faster. He pushed into me even deeper, and I cried out his name from underneath him each time he did so.

When the thunder in my blood finally receded, I heard Jack's breathing change. His guarded control was waning, and I reached back to cover his hand with my own to encourage him to enjoy his own release.

He withdrew from my body and the shock of the action jolted me. Before I could react, however, he pulled me up from the sofa and turned me around to face him. Without a word, he swept me into his arms and carried me into the guest room, the master bedroom evidently too far away. He set me down on my feet at the side of the bed, and together we lowered ourselves onto the mattress, facing one another as Jack entered me once again. I held him as close to me as possible, alternating between kissing his neck and voicing my praise in his ear.

We soon achieved a fierce and wild rhythm, committed to reaching Jack's climax, and as he began to come, he stilled my efforts by collapsing on top of me. He shuddered within me numerous times as I tightened my legs around his hips. He was breathless with his exertion when he withdrew from me one last time and kissed my forehead before rolling to my side.

I turned to Jack and waited until he'd caught his breath before I said, "I'm going to start a shower for you, but you'll need to use the master bathroom."

"Why?"

I kissed his lips and ran my fingers through his damp hair. "Because it's my turn to look after you, and it's the only shower big enough for the both of us."

chapter

Twenty-Six

DESPITE JACK'S declarations to the contrary, finding time to spend with one another over the next two weeks proved elusive. However, I didn't mind the reason why.

School had let out for the summer, which meant Heide would soon be leaving to spend two months in Baltimore. The upcoming weekend would be her last in Oregon before traveling back East. Although Jack would miss her terribly, he knew it was much-needed quality time for mother and daughter.

Jack and Heide would only spend a few days of her summer vacation together, so Jack took time off from work to make the most of it. He kept in touch with me during the day by texting photos of their adventures together. In one of our late night phone conversations, Jack and I solidified plans for the upcoming weekend and were both excited to surprise his daughter with a day trip to the mountains.

With Jack away from work and me spending the evenings back at my condo, I experienced bouts of loneliness, but I was careful not to wallow in it. My temporary displeasure was nothing compared with the impeding separation Jack was about to endure.

I was content with the progress of our romance and embraced the opportunity to look after Jack as he adjusted to having his daughter on the other side of the country. I was also determined to do something positive with my downtime, and Jack's absence from the office provided me with an unexpected opportunity.

After Robert had stormed away from us at Widgi Creek, I began contemplating ways to mend the fences. I was tired of our arguments and concerned about subjecting the Evans family to our tumultuous relationship. I wasn't certain if Robert would ever commit to improving things between us. One way to know for sure was to extend the olive branch and gauge his receptiveness.

I tested my initial attempts with caution. Starting the Monday after the eruption in the clubhouse, I stopped by Robert's office for a hello or two during the day. I never lingered. I paused long enough to say hello and ask how things were going. He received my greetings with equal reserve, but never sent me away.

After a week, I took a calculated risk and asked my father about tagging along to another golf game, perhaps even with just the two of us.

"Perhaps," he said.

I acknowledged this with a nod before returning to my work.

I progressed through another few days, securing the building blocks for a longer conversation with Robert. Before I knew it, Jack's vacation time had wound down. With him set to return to work the following morning, the time to achieve my short-term goal was running out. Near the end of the day, I approached Robert's office and paused in the doorway.

"Hi," I began, holding onto the doorframe for support.

"Hey," he answered.

"How did your afternoon go?"

Robert sat back and pointed to the laptop sitting on his desk. "Working my way through e-mails." He frowned. "I'd rather be out there golfing."

"Are you busy? Should I leave you alone?"

He shook his head. "I could use a break."

"I was thinking of going next door for a smoothie. Do you want to join me?"

Robert's jaw began to drop open, but then he caught himself. My invitation was something he wasn't expecting.

"Yeah. Okay. Sure." He rose up from this seat with awkward immediacy in case I reconsidered.

As we exited the building, my mind whirled. It was important to me to maintain a certain level of composure. I didn't want Robert to think I was desperate for his approval. I wanted to quell the storm between us, but not at the cost of my own self-worth. After we ordered our drinks and took our seats at an outdoor bistro table, I struggled for a way to begin an important conversation. To my surprise, it was Robert who initiated our talk.

"Jack returns from his vacation tomorrow?" Robert stretched his long legs in front of him, crossing them at the ankles.

"Yes." I smiled.

"I'm surprised you didn't take time off together. You've accrued plenty of vacation days."

I shrugged. "His daughter is going to Maryland next week. She'll be gone for most of the summer. They need to spend time together, but we're all going up to Mount Bachelor this weekend."

A flicker of recognition passed over Robert's face. "Now I understand why you didn't want to say anything about your plans there."

"I'm sorry about that," I said with sincerity. "That's a prime example why Jack and I decided to be honest about our relationship. We didn't want to deceive anyone." I paused before making my next admission. "Telling you about us at Widgi Creek was my idea. I thought it would be easier on you to hear the news there."

My father was quiet for a moment before responding. "I felt set up."

"That wasn't my intention." My resolve to maintain my composure began to flounder. "The three of us had a good afternoon. It was just the end of the day that got fucked up."

My father winced, but I wasn't sure if it was over my use of an expletive or something else. "You wanted to tell me," he replied, "but you were also trying to make sure I wouldn't blow up. You expected me to lose my temper. As moronic as it sounds, that's what pissed me off the most."

"I'm sorry that you were upset."

We fell into a tense silence, and I distracted myself with my beverage.

After several moments had passed, Robert said, "It was a good afternoon."

"I'd like it if you and Jack golfed together more. It's an important game to him, and he should play more often."

Robert nodded before asking, "Have you dated a father before?"

"Never."

"How's that going? Between you and the girl?"

"Her name is Heide."

"Between you and Heide," he restated.

"It's going well. I like her. A lot."

"That's good."

"It's important that she approves of me."

This statement produced an inadvertent lull in the conversation. I had never approved of Robert's current wife, Courtney, and doubted I ever would.

"I should go. I have a few e-mails to deal with myself." I began to rise from my chair.

"Hold on a second."

Robert's tone was soft so I sat back down. "Yes?"

"I'm supposed to meet with Don Taylor tomorrow morning about the Hydro Flask account. You're pretty familiar with the project by now."

"I am."

"Why don't you take the meeting instead? We need to get people used to dealing with you in a leadership capacity. This is a good opportunity for that."

I stared at my father, stunned.

"That is, if you have the time."

"I have the time."

"Good. I'll call him when we go back and let him know."

"Thank you."

"You're good at your job. I don't know if advertising is your true passion, but you've always done right by the firm," he said.

"I'm glad you think so."

"I'd never hand the agency off to anyone just because they're family. You've earned your success here."

Robert began to stretch his hand in my direction, but then drew it back. Instead, he patted the table before standing up and drawing our monumental discussion to a close.

"Stop by my office tomorrow after the meeting. I'll want to know how it all goes."

"I will."

We returned to work, and Robert secured my breakfast meeting for the following morning. I left the office less than an hour later and went straight home. I was in a good mood and wanted to share the developments with my father with Jack. I reached into the pocket of my purse that held my phone and found it empty. I then searched the pocket to confirm my phone wasn't hiding deep within.

"Shit," I mumbled. I emptied the contents of my entire purse. I'd left my phone at the office. I glanced down at my pajamas and commenced an internal debate. Did I want my phone enough to change back into regular clothes and drive back to work?

I didn't have a landline at my condo, so I kind of did. I missed speaking with Jack and wanted to have his baritone voice to tickle my ear. On the other hand, he was enjoying the last hours of his vacation time with Heide, and what I had to say wasn't urgent. It could all wait until the morning. With extreme reluctance I got used to being cut off from Jack for the night.

I retrieved my phone charger from my bedside table and repacked my purse. There was no doubt my phone battery would be drained by the time I returned to the office.

chapter

Twenty-Seven

TO MY delight, Don Taylor suggested that we meet at Chow. The restaurant was well known for its farm to table approach and was one of Bend's most popular places for locals and tourists alike. The restaurant featured large windows, colored walls coupled with white wainscoting, hardwood floors and fresh flowers on each table. Although I took the time to enjoy breakfast, Chow made the experience divine.

I savored each bite of my blueberry pancakes while Don opted for the buttermilk biscuits 'n' gravy. The pleasing aromas of various dishes lingered in the air and our conversation was productive yet light. Before I knew it we were back outside, preparing to part ways. Our good-byes were interrupted by the ominous sound of multiple emergency vehicles. Curious, we watched in silence as an ambulance raced by, followed by a fire truck and two police cars.

"Someone's having a bad morning," Don said as he chewed on a toothpick.

I glanced around at our surroundings and even the horizon. "I don't see any smoke, do you?"

Wildfires were a constant threat during the summer months. Now that I took the time to think about the possibility, it was surprising that one or two hadn't already broken out nearby.

"Nope," Don confirmed. "It's probably a car crash. People are in a big damn rush these days. Looks like you're headed in their direction. Better watch the road on your way back to work."

"I will. Drive safe."

We waved to one another and went our separate ways.

My meeting with Don had taken place midmorning and had run into the lunch hour. It was half past eleven when I pulled into the parking lot at the firm. I was relieved when I hadn't encountered an accident on the drive over, but a sweeping glance at the surrounding cars left me disappointed. Jack's car was nowhere to be seen. I shouldn't have been surprised. He took his midday break like clockwork, and I had missed another opportunity to be with him.

I took my time making my way inside the building. With Jack gone, there was no reason to hurry. I entered my office and pulled my charger from my purse. I was going to get myself back on the grid and send a text to Jack just as soon as my phone powered up. Before I could even complete that one simple task, Robert appeared in my doorway.

I observed his impatient demeanor with a rapid glance and experienced another churning swell of disappointment and anger. Not even one day had passed since our talk and we were already back at square one.

"Have you checked your phone?" he asked without preamble.

Annoyed by too many things in that moment, I swiped the device from my desk and held out the blank screen in my father's direction. "I need to charge it."

"I've been trying to get a hold of you—" he began but I cut him off.

"I wasn't ignoring you," I huffed. "I left my phone here last night, and then I was meeting with Don about the Hydro Flask account this morning. Remember? I know you want a debriefing, but can I please get organized and see you after lunch?"

"This isn't about that." Robert's voice remained stern. Serious. "Jack is at the hospital. In the emergency room."

"What?"

Without another word from either of us, I dropped my phone into my purse along with the charger. I slung my bag over my shoulder with shaking hands and pushed past my father. Without looking back, I made for the nearest exit.

"Kathleen!" Robert yelled.

I could hear Robert's footfalls on the carpet behind me, but Jack was in the ER.

I didn't need to know anything else.

I didn't want to stop.

I didn't want to waste a second.

So I didn't.

I broke into a run before my father could catch up to me and delay my departure. I burst through the exit into the parking lot. As I unlocked my car and tossed my purse on the passenger seat, Don's words echoed in my ears. "Someone's having a bad morning... It's probably a car crash."

I took a deep breath as I put my car into reverse and stepped on the gas pedal. Whatever had happened to Jack, I needed to remain calm. I wouldn't do either of us any good by wrecking my own car on the way to the hospital.

By now, the lunch hour in Bend was underway, and I navigated the increased traffic clenching the steering wheel. Stopping for red lights was infuriating. Getting stuck behind drivers who had all the fucking time in the world was maddening. Whenever I was forced to bring my car to a halt, I squirmed in my seat. My nerves got the better of me in the end, and I passed someone illegally at the final intersection before the hospital. I couldn't stand to wait any longer.

Even my arrival at the hospital was stressful. Finding a parking space was a hassle, and I had to settle for a spot on the street on the opposite side of the building from the emergency room. I left my car and jogged in the general direction of the ER. I was crossing a second street when a low noise reached my ears. When I was halfway across the road, the true meaning of the increasing volume of the noise registered.

I stopped in the middle of the street, mindless of any approaching traffic. I'd heard that exact noise so many times during my years in Bend that I'd become all but immune to it. That afternoon, however, the disturbing scream of the familiar engine rattled me to the core.

I didn't need to look up to determine the source, but I did anyway, just in time to see the medical helicopter fly overhead. The helicopter was far too close and the powerful roar of the machine grew so loud I no longer recognized the tone. The chopper was descending onto the hospital's landing pad.

The fear that had been percolating within me now exploded into full-blown terror.

When I made my way into the ER, my eyes froze on the secure entrance to the examination rooms. The wooden windowless door was the final barrier between Jack and me.

"Can I help you?" A woman's voice called from behind a glass-partitioned reception desk.

I whipped my head in her direction. "I hope so. I was told Jack Evans was brought here this morning." I glanced down at my ringless finger and dropped my hands from the clerk's view as I approached her desk. "I'm his fiancée."

Fuck it. He'll understand.

"Your name?"

"Kathleen Brighton. Please. I need to see him."

The woman nodded and held up her hand. "If you could have a seat in the waiting area, I'll check with a nurse."

It wasn't the answer I wanted to hear, but it wasn't a denial either. I nodded and forced a grim smile, willing every ounce of strength and patience within me to remain polite with my lone ally in the room.

"Thank you."

The clerk picked up her phone and dialed an extension while I took the nearest available seat to the exam room door. I forced myself to sit still and take in slow controlled breaths. I would never receive permission to enter the exam room if I couldn't maintain my own self-control. I glanced nervously around. There were just a few people on the surrounding chairs and they all appeared bored rather than distressed. I hoped beyond hope that the dull serenity of the reception area would bode well in my favor.

The woman's muffled voice drifted through the small opening in her partition, drawing my full attention. I strained to hear her words.

"Mr. Evans' fiancée is here. Can I send her back?"

Please God. Please God. Please God.

"Yes … I understand … I'll let her know."

Please God. Please God. Please God.

I watched the clerk with anticipation as she hung up her phone. I was certain anxiety had blossomed all over my face, but I was also certain I couldn't do anything to disguise it.

The woman looked up with an unreadable expression. "Kathleen? Can you come over here, please?"

I rose on rubbery legs and walked with deliberate restraint to the reception desk. My panic was escalating by the second, and I was too frightened to speak. I knew my voice would betray me and reveal my suppressed horror.

The woman met my eyes with a serious face. "The nurse manager will allow you in to see your fiancé, but please stay with him and do not wander away. Things are hectic in there right now."

I nearly burst out laughing with relief. Not only was I going to see Jack, but I was sure my worst fears had just been put to rest.

"Yes. Thank you. Thank you so much."

The clerk gestured to the door. "I'll buzz you in. He's in Exam Room 5. Stay with him."

"Room 5. Yes. Thank you. I appreciate this so much." I made my way to the door. It clicked as I reached for the push bar and opened without resistance. I was determined to get to Jack.

I was unfamiliar with this part of the hospital. When my ovary had ruptured several years before, I'd been brought to this ER as a patient, but I had no memory of the incident. Mercifully, locating Jack was not a difficult task. I just knew where to find him as though pulled by gravity.

He sat upright on the side of an exam bed, still dressed in his work attire, his shined shoes touching the linoleum floor. I dropped my purse on a single folding chair and approached him. He'd been left unattended, much to my annoyance, and he appeared dazed. Jack showed no obvious signs of physical injury, so I began my own timid examination.

I inspected his body with my hands, starting with his heart. I set my palm flat against his mint green dress shirt and closed my eyes for a brief moment, seeking solace in the warmth of his body. His heart was beating fast, but strong.

"I'm sorry, Jack," I began as tears threatened to overtake me. "I was stupid. I left my phone at the office last night. I should have gone back for it when I realized what I'd done. But I was too fucking lazy. I'm so sorry."

My fingers roamed over his torso and traveled down his arms. He did not flinch in pain or voice any distress at my touch. In fact, I couldn't find a damn thing wrong with him. My confusion melded into resentment when I reached his wrists. I blinked, and stared at one and then the other and back again. There was no hospital band. Something was wrong with him, and yet here he was sitting in an exam room, neglected. I needed to get him help. Now.

"Jack," I said firmly, hoping to capture his attention. "My friend, Sarah, works here. Remember? She's the one I've been helping with a fundraiser. I'm going to call her and ask her to get a doctor for you right away."

I began to reach for my bag when Jack grasped onto my arms, his fingers digging into my flesh in an unfamiliar and terrifying way. He wanted my undivided attention and now he had it.

I studied his face once again, this time with intensity. He wasn't injured. He was watching something. Something behind me. I shifted my focus to listen to the sounds over my shoulder. There were several voices and a great deal of activity in the exam room across the corridor. I peered over my shoulder and followed Jack's gaze. When I took in the rush of chaos just a few feet away, I reciprocated his hard grasp.

Across the way was a frenzy of doctors and nurses attending to a body on another gurney. Their efforts were obvious. They were fighting to save the life of a small child whose tiny feet were still clad in a pair of Minecraft Creeper socks.

chapter

Twenty-Eight

"HEIDE!" I turned in a vain attempt to wrench myself from Jack's hold. My logic in that moment was asinine. There was nothing I could do to help her or those trying to save her, but I was desperate to run to her side. I almost broke free, but then Jack's strong arms encircled me and pinned my back to his chest.

"We have to stay here," he whispered, pained as though the wind had been knocked from him.

As Jack finished his words, three men in dark blue flight suits appeared from another hallway, pushing a large orange gurney. The tallest of the three spoke with one of the ER nurses. The other two men inserted themselves into the group working on Jack's daughter, inciting my immediate jealousy. The nurse rattled off Heide's vitals and other pertinent news regarding her condition, but I was already too deep in shock to absorb anything she said. She may as well have been speaking a different language.

"Where are they taking her?" I asked, not knowing whether Jack would hear me or not.

"To Portland. I took her to Lydia's this morning before work. The girls were playing at the park and she was hurt." Jack's voice broke on the final word.

I stopped asking questions for the time being.

A couple of agonizing minutes later, the man who'd been speaking to the ER nurse approached us.

"You're Heide's father?" he asked Jack.

Jack simply nodded.

"My name is Keith. I'm one of the flight nurses that will be taking your daughter to Portland."

"Which hospital?" I interrupted. "Legacy Emmanuel or OHSU?"

Keith looked at me for a brief moment as he answered. "OHSU."

Keith returned his attention to Jack. "Do you understand what's happened to Heide and why she's being transferred to another hospital?"

"Not completely," Jack said. "I know she fell and has internal injuries. But they've been so busy helping her I didn't want to interfere."

Keith nodded. "Sure. Let me explain. Your daughter has multiple severe injuries, and the doctors here are concerned about her lungs. They've both collapsed and she can't breathe on her own. Her condition is critical. Although St. Charles has a Level II trauma unit, the ICU here is full. We can fly her to Portland in less than an hour."

"What happened to her?" I asked.

"The first responders reported that she was climbing on a backstop when it tipped over and crushed her. When her friend couldn't pull her out, she ran for help."

My comprehension was frazzled, and I shook my head as I tried to process what Keith had just said. "A backstop? You mean like on a baseball field? Behind home plate?"

"Exactly. When help arrived, she was unconscious and not breathing. The EMT's at the scene were unable to insert a breathing tube down her windpipe, so they performed a tracheostomy. She's been stabilized as best she can in the ER, but we need to take her to Portland now."

"Can I fly with her?" Jack asked.

Keith hesitated and glanced over his shoulder at Heide before answering.

"I can't authorize that," he explained after turning to face us. "I'll ask the pilot, but it's his call. I wouldn't get your hopes up. They sent four of us over. I'm not sure the pilot will want the extra weight."

If Jack's request was denied that meant the only way to reach Heide in Portland was to drive there. The journey would take several hours by car, and there was no question that I would be going with Jack. He was in no shape to drive home, let alone to Portland.

"Let me make the final preparations for the flight," Keith said. "I'll let you know what the pilot's decision is."

"Thanks," Jack replied with a chilling lack of hope.

We waited, helpless to do anything but observe the medical team prepare Heide for her flight. The clock in the exam room indicated it was not yet one in the afternoon.

How had such a normal morning given way to this level of hell?

As promised, Keith returned within a few minutes. "I'm sorry," he said to Jack without pretense. "The pilot says we can't bring you onboard."

Jack nodded, having already prepared himself for this decision. Keith carried a clipboard and grimaced as he removed a pen from his chest pocket.

"I know there's a lot to take in right now, but I'll need you to sign a couple of forms to authorize your daughter's transfer."

Freed from Jack's tense embrace, I reclaimed my purse in preparation to leave one hospital for another. Keith walked Jack through the specifics, and Jack numbly added his signature whenever he was asked. I turned in Heide's direction just as one of the ER nurses approached us, carrying a bag in her hand.

Jack was still preoccupied with Keith's paperwork, so she offered the clear plastic bag containing Heide's socks and soccer cleats to me. The bottoms of her cleats were caked in thick mud and grass. I glanced over the nurse's shoulder to peer at Heide, worried that her naked feet would grow cold. I was relieved to see they'd been covered by a blanket.

"Where are the rest of her clothes?" I asked the nurse.

"They were ruined. We had to cut them off her. We'll dispose of them."

"I see." The nurse patted my arm in sympathy before returning to Heide's bedside.

Keith and Jack were finished with their paperwork, and the flight nurse pulled a business card from the same pocket he kept his pen in. He offered the card to Jack.

"This is the ICU where your daughter will be admitted. I know it's a bit of a drive from here. You can call that number and check on her status while you're making your way to Portland."

"What will happen when she arrives at the hospital?" Jack asked Keith.

"With an injury like hers, emergency surgery could be necessary. She'll undergo more tests when she arrives at OHSU, and then we'll know more about the extent of her injuries. Do you have any other questions before I leave?"

"No," Jack mumbled.

Keith made eye contact with Jack as he offered his farewell. "I'll take good care of your daughter. We'll land in Portland in about forty-five minutes. You call that number and the staff there will let you know that we have arrived. They'll keep you well informed of Heide's condition. All right?"

"Yes," Jack said. "Thank you for your help."

"Stay strong," Keith advised. "Drive safe."

"Can we follow you out? To see her off?" I inquired this without considering if the request made any kind of sense. I just knew that it was important enough to ask. Jack reached for my hand and squeezed it. It was important to him, too.

Once again, Keith made no assurances. When he returned to Heide's exam room however, we saw him speak with the same nurse who'd brought me her belongings. Within moments, we heard Keith ask if his colleagues were ready to go, and both answered in the affirmative. They secured all the machines, tubes and wires that were connected to Heide and began to push her bright orange gurney out into the corridor.

As the flight crew made their way back down the same hallway they had come from, the ER nurse stepped out from Heide's exam room and beckoned us to join her.

"I can't let you go the full distance, but follow me. I'll lead you as far as I can."

Jack and I followed without a single word. Ahead of us, the three men from Portland were focused on their patient. It was difficult to be grateful for anything as I watched her being navigated through an unfamiliar set of hallways, but there was some relief that this crew had been the one sent to care for her. Keith had been direct, yet comforting, and I was confident in his abilities to help save Heide's life.

The walk to the landing pad turned out to be a short one, and the ER nurse stopped us just outside the exit door. "This is it. You'll need to wait here."

"Thank you," Jack replied. His eyes locked on his daughter as she was taken farther and farther away from him. The nurse stepped just inside the doorway, offering us the smallest bit of privacy. I stepped closer to Jack and slid my arm through his. I squeezed, hoping the effort would deliver what little strength I had to him.

We watched in silence as Heide was loaded into the chopper. The door to the craft was closed and secured just as soon as the final flight nurse was inside, blocking her from our sight. Seconds later, the helicopter lifted off the ground away from the landing pad with precision. We both craned our necks as Jack's daughter drifted away from the ground. It wasn't more than a minute before it left our sight completely.

I drew in a rickety breath. Standing in the afternoon sun holding onto Jack, I was as helpless as I had been when my mother died. I didn't know if I was capable of doing everything that would see Heide and Jack safely through this crisis. Despite my own personal demons, I understood that I'd never been involved in an emergency like this. I was afraid for Heide's life. I was afraid for Jack's well-being. And I was afraid of failing them both. I didn't know what to expect going forward, but at least I knew where to begin.

"If you're ready, we should go. I'll drive you home to pack a few things, and then I'll drive you to Portland. I know exactly where Heide's going. I'll take you right to her."

Jack didn't answer me, but turned his back on the landing pad. Five minutes later, we were in my car, pulling away from St. Charles for the beginning of a very long journey.

chapter

Twenty-Nine

WHEN WE arrived at Jack's house, I opted to leave the hospital bag with Heide's items in the trunk of my car. In his daze, he hadn't paid attention to what I was carrying from the ER, and I'd been able to stow it away from him. I walked with Jack to the front door and when he opened it, Kitty Hawk meowed her usual greeting.

"Damn it," he muttered. "What am I going to do about the cat?"

That was a good question, but I didn't want Jack to linger on it. "I'll handle it. You go pack."

As we stepped into the living room, I pulled my useless phone from my bag and stared at the blank screen.

"Do you have your phone with you?" I asked, worried he might have forgotten it somewhere. Jack opened his blazer and checked the inside pocket. "Yes."

He began to pull it from his jacket, but I waved him off. "We need to keep your line free. Can I use the phone in your kitchen?"

"Go ahead." Jack was already making his way down the hallway.

"Don't forget your charger!" I yelled after him. After the debacle from yesterday, it was unlikely I would forget these things ever again.

"Got it!" he called from the bedroom.

Satisfied, I went straight to the landline and called the office. I was comforted when a familiar voice answered the call.

"Aurora Advertising. This is Tracie. How may I direct your call?"

"Tracie, it's Kathleen."

"Oh my God! Robert told me Jack's daughter was in an accident. Is everything all right?"

"No, it isn't." I paused to swallow the lump of emotion lodged in my throat. "She was just airlifted to Portland. I have to drive Jack up there."

"Oh no!"

"Listen, you need to know we'll both be out of the office for a while. Jack and I are seeing each other, and I'm not about to let him go through this alone."

Tracie dropped her voice to a whisper. "Your secret is safe with me. Don't worry about anything there."

"I'm not worried. We were getting ready to go public, but I don't think now is the time. I'd appreciate your discretion until things calm down."

"Is there anything I can do?"

"Yes. I really need your help with a couple of things."

"You got it."

"Do you still have the key to my condo?"

"Yes. It's on my keyring."

I closed my eyes, savoring this one small fluke in an otherwise terrible day. "Great. I'm going to have Jack leave his keys at my place. I'll put them on my coffee table. You'll need to take someone with you to the hospital and pick up Jack's car from the parking lot and drive it back to his house."

"Sure thing. No problem."

"Also, he's going to need someone to look after his cat until one of us comes back. I'll be honest, Tracie. I don't know when that will be."

"Don't worry about it."

"Thank you. I'm here at his house now. He's packing, and I'll make sure the cat has enough food and water until you can make it over."

"Is there anything else?"

"Not right now, but I may think of other things later. I don't want to be a pest but I might need to be."

"Whatever. Just call me or text me. I'm here and I'm not going anywhere."

"Thanks so much, Tracie."

"Is Jack's daughter going to be all right?"

"I really don't know," I whispered.

"Not to stress you out or anything, but Robert instructed me to put you through to him immediately if you called."

"That's fine. I was going to call him at some point. Put me through now. Otherwise, I won't be able to speak to him until this evening."

"Okay. Be careful on the way to Portland. I'll talk to you later and tell Jack not to worry about anything. I've got it all covered."

"You're awesome. Thanks."

"Sending you over now."

The line went silent and I waited for my father to answer the phone. I was going to have to rush our conversation, but there were things I needed to say. Important things.

"Kathleen?" Robert picked up the line and interrupted my thoughts. "What's happening?"

"It's bad. Heide had to be flown to OHSU. I'm going to drive Jack to Portland. I can't let him go on his own."

"Shit. How awful."

"We're just packing some things and then getting on the road. I'm hoping to be out of town in less than an hour. I don't know when either of us will be back."

"Don't worry about it," he said. "Do what you have to do. I'll call you later this evening, but don't worry about answering if it isn't a good time. Just text something so I know you both made it up there."

"Dad?" I hadn't used the word in years and it was foreign to my own ears.

Robert's breath hitched on the other end of the line. "What is it?"

"It was terrible of me to run away from you. I realize now you were trying to tell me about Heide. I need to apologize for—"

"We can talk about these things later," Robert interjected. "When you're back to work."

I wanted to express regret for not giving my father a chance. Not today, when he tried to tell me that Heide was hurt. And not decades ago, when my mother died. Robert was right, however, that needed to be a much longer conversation and probably one held in person.

"Okay," I conceded. "Jack should be almost ready. I better get going. My phone is still"—Don't say dead. Not right now.—"not working. I'll charge it in the car."

"Have you figured out where you're staying?"

"Um … no. I hadn't gotten that far yet. All we care about is getting to the hospital."

"I'll tell you what. I'll have Tracie arrange it for you."

I shook my head even though Robert wasn't there to see me do so. "I've already given her a list of things. I don't want to add to it."

"Then I'll do it," Robert said with determination. "I'll find you a room downtown and e-mail the reservation to you. It's probably the closest you're going to get to the hospital."

"Thanks. That would be helpful. If you could try the Sentinel first, I'd prefer to stay there. I'll give them my credit card number when we arrive. I don't mean to bolt, but I have a couple of things to help Jack with here before we stop by my place."

"Go. I'll get a hold of you later."

"Bye, Dad."

"Bye."

After ending my call, I proceeded to the mudroom to check on Kitty Hawk's food supply. Her water was low, so I plucked the bowl from the floor. The cat followed my every move as I walked over to the utility sink and refilled it. She grumbled over each effort I made. When I set the water bowl back down, she stared at me as though I had done it all wrong. Very, very wrong.

"I'm trying," I explained. "I promise to learn the rules when we come back."

The cat watched me until I left the room.

"Jack?" I called. "How are you doing back there? Do you need help?"

"Almost done," he answered. "I just need another minute."

"Okay."

It was now or never. I dashed back to my car, opened my trunk using the key fob and grabbed the hospital bag. I jogged back into the house and went straight to Heide's room. I made a mental note to have Tracie take the bag to my condo. I wanted to clean the cleats and socks myself and spare Jack the task. It would have been simpler to leave them in my car, but I was compelled to keep it from Jack's sight.

I set the bag down on the bedroom floor, near her closet. As I did so, my eyes took in Heide's empty shoes. She should have been outside playing in the summer sun. Instead, her abandoned shoes were here and she was somewhere over the skies of Oregon, fighting for her life.

I tore my eyes away from the cleats and looked around Heide's bedroom while I tried to settle my feelings. My eyes came to rest on the poster of Bend's surrounding mountains, and I was overcome by a horrible thought. Ever since I had known Heide, she had been so eager to climb the peaks near her new home. Was that why this was happening? Had she been pretending to climb mountains when she was hurt?

I rubbed my temple as a bout of fatigue struck me. Then I walked from Heide's room and made my way to Jack's. His suitcase had been pitched on the bed with items randomly tossed inside it. I heard him moving around his bathroom, but didn't want to interfere with his movements. Cautiously I opted to wait in his doorway until he was done. Sure enough, he appeared within a heartbeat or two.

Jack walked right to his suitcase without acknowledging my presence, but this time I refused to take the action personally. He set his toiletry bag on top of his clothes before pulling the lid over and zipping the suitcase closed.

"Let's go," he said, taking hold of the handle. "If I've forgotten something, I'll figure it out later."

"What about your phone charger?" I prompted.

"It's the first thing I put in the suitcase."

"Good," I answered. "I'll only need five minutes at my place. I keep some things packed all the time for business trips. I'll just need to grab a few clothes."

I turned and walked to the front door with Jack close on my heels.

Fifteen minutes later, we were walking into my condo. Jack moved toward my sofa, the same one we'd had sex on. At the last second, he veered course and sat in my reading chair instead.

"I have to call Allison," he said. "I should do it now before we get on the road. I don't want to risk dropping the call in the middle of the conversation."

"Sure," I said, while wondering if she was the reason why he'd changed his mind about where to sit. "Go ahead."

But Jack was already dialing, so I went to my bedroom to get my own things organized. I closed my bedroom door to offer Heide's parents the privacy they deserved. I didn't want to move too slowly, but I moved slow enough to allow Jack the time he needed to explain to Allison what had happened.

I was sad for Heide's mother. She'd been preparing for her daughter's arrival, and now her world was turned upside down. Jack was making the type of call to his ex-wife every parent feared.

Once I was set to leave, I made my way to the kitchen. It would be a good idea to bring some food and drinks along with us. I was still full from my breakfast at Chow, but I wasn't sure when Jack had last eaten or when we might have the opportunity to do so again.

I began packing what few things I had to take on a road trip. As I did this, I was no longer able to avoid overhearing Jack's discussion with Allison. From where I stood in the kitchen, I could see him. I was an intruder on an intimate family moment, and I was reticent to draw attention to myself.

"Do you have the confirmation number for Heide's plane ticket?" he asked, his voice thick with emotion.

Jack paused while Allison answered his question. He sniffled between statements.

"Good. While I'm driving to the hospital, I want you to call the airline and explain what's happened. You need to ask them to put that ticket in your name and change flights. Then you get them to book you on the first available plane to Portland."

Jack attempted to hold back a sob and failed. The initial shock of Heide's accident was ebbing away. Having to explain to Allison what had taken place that morning had broken Jack's emotional dam. I wanted to stop everything and go to him. Kneel in front of him on the floor and hug him, but then I wondered if doing so while he was speaking to Allison would make him feel awkward. Besides, I told myself, the action would delay me from completing my task. As soon as Jack was done with his call, we could leave town.

"I need you to get to Oregon as soon as you can," he said to her in an ambitious effort to regain his composure. "If the airline wants to charge more or whatever, don't argue with them. Just give them our American Express card and make it happen."

There was another pause as Allison responded. "It's fine. I haven't used that account in months. I know I was supposed to cancel it, but I just didn't get around to it. It will work fine. Call me when you get the flight booked, and tell me when you'll be here."

There was another short pause while Allison made a request of her own. Jack closed his eyes and dropped his head as he answered her. "I promise. As soon as I know something, I'll call you. I'll call you with every update until you're here. Just please … get here soon. I need to go. The sooner I do, the sooner I can call you with some news."

There was one last pause before Jack ended the call. "I will. You, too. Bye."

Cleared for reentry into the living room, I moved toward the front door with several bags in hand. "I'm going to take these to the car. Why don't you call the hospital before we get on the road? They've probably landed by now."

Jack looked back at his phone and then to me. His face was conflicted. "I should help you load those in the car."

"It's fine. I can handle this."

"I'm sorry, Kathleen." Jack's voice was emotional, and I suspected that he didn't even know what he was apologizing for.

"Don't be sorry. Make your call and then we can talk in the car if you want."

He nodded and pulled the ICU's business card from his jacket pocket. He dialed the number and then looked my way as he waited for someone to answer him.

"Remember to leave your keys on the coffee table," I added before walking out the door.

Two hours after I arrived at the emergency room, Jack and I were on the road to Portland. Jack was frustrated and I couldn't blame him. His call to the ICU had been short. He'd been able to confirm that Heide had landed at OHSU, but she was still undergoing testing, and there were no new developments regarding her condition. She was in critical condition, still unable to breathe on her own. And that was all we knew.

Finding something to talk about was difficult. Nothing seemed appropriate or interesting, and we were both too tired to energize one another. I opted for listening to satellite radio and tuned in to a news channel, just to fill the conversational void. I had done the same thing the night my mother shot herself. It was now a habit.

Shortly before reaching the I-5, Jack's phone rang. "That must be Allison calling about her flight." He swiped the screen before bothering to check the display.

"Hello?"

I risked a glance at Jack, just in time to see his forehead furrow in confusion. "I'm sorry. Who is this?"

Jack reached out and grasped the dashboard. The odd movement unsettled me.

"I see. I appreciate the call. Thank you. I'm on the road so maybe we can talk when I get there? Thanks again. Bye." Jack ended the call and set his phone down inside a cup holder with too much force.

"What's happened?" I asked him with increasing fear.

"That was a chaplain, calling from the hospital. He wanted to introduce himself and offer his services." As soon as Jack told me this, he broke down. He pitched forward, trying to bring his head to his knees, but the seat belt restrained him.

"Do you need me to pull over, Jack?"

"No!" he yelled. Then he violently lurched back against his seat and spoke again. "Yes. Do it."

Jack's voice was so poisoned by anger that I stopped the car at the first opportunity. As he unbuckled his seat belt, he spoke to me again. "Promise me we'll only stop for one minute. One minute, and then we need to get back on the road."

"Okay," I whispered.

Jack bolted from the car and made his way over to the nearest tree. He commenced taking out his rage on the trunk of the evergreen, kicking, yelling and crying all at the same time. His emotional pain was overwhelming us both, and as much as I wanted to join him—to scream right along with him—I kept my eyes locked on the digital display inside the car. He'd asked for this minute, and I was allowing him to have it.

When his time was up, I went to Jack. Pine needles crunched under my shoes as I approached, and he ended his tirade before I reached him. I hugged him briefly from behind before leading him back to the car. I held the door open as he retook his seat and noticed he was perspiring. Once again, I was tempted to kneel down so I could kiss him, wipe his forehead and speak comforting words. But I knew better than to waste any time indulging my own desires. As soon as his feet were back inside the car, I closed his door and walked around to the driver's side. I opened the back door, reached into a bag resting behind my seat and retrieved a bottle of water. When I resumed my place behind the wheel, I uncapped the water and handed it to Jack.

"Take a few sips of this. I'm worried you'll get a headache."

He did as he was told while I pulled back out onto the highway.

After a few minutes, he voiced his fears. "They must not expect her to live. We're trying to get to her, and they're preparing to tell us the worst. What if she dies before we get there?"

I removed one hand from the steering wheel and took Jack's. "She's strong," I said while squeezing his hand. "She's full of fight and nowhere near done making her mark on this world. She's at one of the best hospitals in the state. She's going to survive this, Jack."

She has to.

chapter

Thirty

IT WAS late in the afternoon when we arrived in Portland. Rush hour was well underway and, even with my knowledge of the suburban side streets, we were forced to accept the inevitable stop-and-go traffic that clogged the southwest section of the Rose City.

The hospital was located atop the West Hills with an agonizing trek up the steep and curvy road that led to the campus. We parked the car in a garage and began navigating the massive complex on our way to the pediatric ICU. After close to two hundred miles, we reached Heide's room only to discover that she and her bed were both gone.

The space where we hoped to find her was stark and empty. Frightened, Jack smacked the doorframe with his palm before making his way to the nurse's station located just out of sight from her room. A brunette nurse was alone at the station, concentrating on the computer monitor in front of her. Our approach didn't go unnoticed for long, however.

"May I help you?" she asked with a friendly countenance.

"I'm Jack Evans. I'm looking for my daughter, Heide. She was flown here from Bend this afternoon."

"Hello, Mr. Evans. Heide is in surgery. The surgeon had her taken to the OR as soon as her test results were complete. He knew you were driving up here, but her condition is critical, and he didn't want to risk waiting for your arrival. I'm sorry. I know you've been through so much already."

"What exactly did she need surgery for?" Jack asked, doing his best to remain calm. "How long has she been in there?"

"There is severe damage to her chest." The nurse reached forward and opened a file on her computer. "She has many broken ribs, some of which punctured her lungs and caused them to collapse. She also has a lacerated liver, bruised kidneys and a ruptured spleen."

"How's her heart?" I heard myself asking in a weak voice. Jack glanced in my direction and pulled me close to his side. I held on.

"That's where she was lucky," the nurse replied. "Her heart appears to be fine with no signs of trauma. She's been in surgery for a couple of hours now. Let me see if I can get an update for you both."

"Thank you ..." Jack's voice drifted off, unsure how to address the nurse.

"Terry," she supplied. "I'll be here until midnight so if you need anything, just let me know."

Terry picked up the phone and dialed an extension. As we waited, I drifted deeper into Jack's embrace, knowing it wasn't fair to do so. I should be holding him up, not the other way around. After hours of nonstop stress, I was fighting a losing battle. There had been no peace since my breakfast with Don Taylor, and my mind's exhaustion was now spreading throughout my body. While Terry completed her call, my eyes fluttered closed and my breathing slowed. I was at risk of falling asleep on my feet and only the sound of Terry hanging up the phone jarred me back to full consciousness.

"Heide's surgery should be over soon. She'll need to spend some time in recovery before she'll be brought back to the ICU. It's probably going to be a couple of hours before she's back here." Terry angled her head to study my face, and I pulled myself back into an attentive stance. "When was the last time either of you had something to eat?"

"Too long," Jack answered, his arm still locked around my waist.

"You are more than welcome to remain here. I understand if you'll want to sit with your daughter tonight, but if you do have a hotel room I'm sure there's time for you to both freshen up and have something for dinner. You have to take care of yourselves in order to help your daughter heal. It's important that you stick to your routines as much as possible."

"We haven't had time to think about those things," Jack mumbled.

I pulled out my phone, now fully charged, and opened my e-mail. Sure enough, Robert had come through.

"My father booked us a room downtown. There's a restaurant in the building. It's up to you, Jack. We can stay here and wait, or we can check in and come back later."

Jack pulled away from me and used his familiar sweeping glance of my features to assess the situation. "When did you eat last?" he whispered, reiterating Terry's concern. He also knew I usually skipped a morning meal on weekdays.

"Believe it or not, I had a huge breakfast this morning. It's held me most of the day."

Jack nodded, a sure sign he'd made up his mind. He turned back to Terry. "If Heide comes back here before we do, will you call me immediately?"

"Yes. I'd be happy to do that." Terry pulled out a post it note and took down both our phone numbers.

"She'll be coming back to this room?" Jack pointed to the empty space.

"Yes. That's her room."

"We'll go get some dinner, and then we'll come back here."

Jack took my hand in his and together we meandered our way back to my car. As I unlocked the doors, he looked my way once again.

"You really do look exhausted," he said. "Do you want me to drive to the hotel?"

I shook my head. "I'll get us there. You can drive us back."

"Where are we staying?" he asked as we took seats once again.

"The Sentinel. It's between Tenth and Eleventh. It'll only take a few minutes to go back and forth."

"What made Robert choose that place?"

"I asked him to. It has good beds, good restaurants and Target is just across the street in case we forgot anything. It even has a Starbucks."

"No Dutch Bros.?" Jack's voice was tired, but I recognized his attempt at humor.

I rolled my eyes in return as I shifted the car into reverse. "Sadly. No."

As soon as we emerged from the parking garage, Jack retrieved his phone. "I'm going to call Allison and tell her what's happening."

"Ask if she's booked her flight. We should probably find her a hotel room, too."

Jack twisted in his seat in response to my statement with his ear to the phone, but I kept my eyes on the treacherous downhill curves of the road.

"Yes. We need to help her with that, too. Thank you."

I began to reply, but Allison answered Jack's call before I could say another word.

"How are you doing?" he asked her. "I made it to the hospital, but Heide is in surgery now."

As Jack told Allison about the known extent of Heide's condition, I drove the car into downtown Portland. By the time they had updated one another on their news, we were approaching the Sentinel.

"The hospital is called OHSU," Jack said. "Oregon Health Sciences University. It's huge. I'm certain any cab driver will know how to find it."

I nodded in agreement to Jack's statement.

"I'll meet you there. We'll get your hotel squared away after you've seen Heide. Please travel safe."

Jack paused to listen to Allison. "I will. I promise. I'll tell her whether she's awake or not."

Allison said something else as I pulled up to the hotel's front door. I risked a glance at Jack. His sadness over whatever she was telling him was apparent.

"For what?" he asked her, perplexed.

"You know I don't believe that. Don't do that to yourself. You're a wonderful mother. I'd never think that about you. I'm sorry I didn't just take the rest of the week off. I should have insisted on staying home with her for two more days. I should have been with her this morning. I never would have let her near that fucking thing if I'd been there. If there's anyone who should be pleading forgiveness here, it's me."

The valet clerk approached our car, and I intercepted him by stepping out on the sidewalk.

"If you could just give us both a moment, please." I nodded toward the passenger seat. "He's finishing up an important phone call."

The valet glanced behind my car and smiled. "Not much traffic at the moment. Just let me know when you're ready."

"Thank you." I reminded myself to return the blond man's smile before sitting back down in the driver's seat. Jack didn't look at me, but did hold up his finger, indicating he was nearly done on the phone.

"I don't want to hang up unless I know you're going to be fine. Are you alone?"

He closed his eyes in relief. "Good. I'm glad she's there with you. I know it's hard to relax, but you need to get some sleep before your flight. I won't be back to the hospital for a little while yet. Do you want me to call you tonight once I have more news?"

His pause was a brief one. "I'll find out everything I can for the evening and then give you one last call for tonight. It will probably be several hours before I call again. Try to rest in the meantime."

He opened his door and stepped from the car as she spoke her parting words. "I promise you, it will be the first thing I tell her when I see her. I'll call you back tonight."

He hung up as we entered the hotel lobby.

"She couldn't get a flight out tonight, but she'll be on her way here first thing in the morning. The sooner, the better. She's having a rough time."

I reached out and placed my hand between Jack's shoulder blades. Even through his blazer, I could sense his tension. "She'll calm down once she's here. You'll both feel better once you see Heide again."

Jack nodded, but didn't answer.

"Can I help you?" asked the young man in hipster glasses behind the front desk that was disguised as a library shelf.

I dropped my arm from Jack and moved to the counter. "Reservation for Kathleen Brighton, please."

The gentleman turned to read his computer monitor while I reached into my purse for my wallet.

"Ms. Brighton. I have you booked into the City Terrace Studio Suite for ten nights."

I jerked up my head at this news. "You do?" My exhaustion was to blame for my lack of decorum.

Unfazed, the young man nodded. "Fully booked and paid for. I just need to see some ID please."

Now I was in genuine shock. My mind was a blank, and I stood at the front desk, staring at the poor college kid. He glanced from me to Jack and back again.

"Will two keys be enough?"

"Yeah." I was still dumbfounded, but snapped from my trance in order to hand over my driver's license.

"Wonderful. If you could just sign this form for me please, we'll get you on your way up to your suite."

The desk clerk gestured and a second young man appeared to collect our luggage. Jack and I were both too tired to argue humility. I accepted the room keys and followed the bellman to our top floor suite. Safely delivered to our room, Jack fumbled for some cash to tip our bellman while I stepped onto the terrace for some fresh air.

I was hopeful the light breeze would spark some energy back into my useless muscles. My body was shutting down more and more by the minute, and yet I knew we still had a very long night ahead. I raised my arms and stretched them as far as I could before going back inside.

Jack was standing in the middle of the room, staring at the dark green walls of our suite. I took a few steps back in, but stopped across the room from him.

"I can't believe this is where I am tonight," he said. "This is where I'll be for who knows how long."

I nodded. "I don't even know where to begin. Or what to say."

"How hungry are you?" he asked after taking his eyes away from the walls.

I set my hand down on the work desk, leaned into it for support and shrugged. "I'm not hungry, but my energy is running low. Maybe I should eat."

"Me, too."

The thought of going back downstairs was overwhelming, not because I was tired but because I couldn't see myself sitting in a restaurant, surrounded by people who cared about nothing more than celebrating the beginning of their weekend. "Let's not fuss with going downstairs. We can order room service. It will give us a chance to decompress until our food arrives. Then we can go back to the hospital and see if Heide's out of recovery."

"That's a good idea. Plus we can change out of our work clothes." Jack nodded toward my dress and wedge heels.

"A shower sounds good," I said. "But I can't decide between that or laying down for a few minutes."

"Let's do both. We can shower in shifts. That way one of us can keep an ear out for the phone."

"Good plan. Let's order our food and then you shower first."

Jack peered at the digital clock on the bedside table. "Unless the hospital calls, let's give ourselves two hours. We'll leave in two hours if Terry hasn't called us back."

"Got it."

"Kathleen?"

"Yes?"

"Thank you for everything you've done today. I'm not sure how I would have made it here without you."

"Anything for you, and for her."

Jack closed the distance between us and pressed his lips to my forehead. He kept them there, potentially due to sheer exhaustion. I closed my eyes and held still until he drew back.

"Let's order dinner," he declared with renewed energy.

chapter
Thirty-One

WE RETURNED to the ICU after eight that evening, feeling stronger than we had that day. Terry hadn't called Jack during our two-hour break, so we'd allowed ourselves the time to recuperate by resting and eating a protein rich meal of Alaskan halibut. We each showered and redressed in more comfortable apparel, and when we retrieved my car from the valet, I offered Jack the driver's seat. I directed him through the streets of downtown and up to the hospital. I wanted him to be able to take my car at any time and get to OHSU on his own if need be.

Heide's room was full of activity as we approached. I took Jack's hand in mine as we stopped just outside the door. Inside, Terry and another nurse moved around the room, which now also contained a bed along with its young patient.

Terry looked up. "You can come in."

Jack entered the room first and I followed, still holding his hand until Terry directed Jack to stand on the right side of Heide's bed. There was more space to maneuver there, and he took his assigned spot while I opted to stand at the corner of the bed. I took a gentle hold of her foot as I tried to absorb the sight of the small and broken body before me. It was the first good look I'd had of Heide following the accident, and what I saw was jolting.

She was unconscious and still on a ventilator connected to the tracheostomy in her neck. Machines were breathing for her and their loud and precise efforts were haunting. The monitors stationed on the left side of her bed tracked both her heart rate and blood pressure while a bag of IV fluids constantly dripped fluids into a tube connected to Heide's arm.

These things were somewhat expected, but what upset me most was seeing her naked chest. An angry red scar ran down the middle with staples holding it shut. Her incision was significant, and there was no doubt that it, along with the hole in her neck, would form impressive scars. Whatever Heide remembered later on, these marks would forever be reminders of this horrible day.

I watched Jack as he took careful hold of Heide's hand while stroking her limp blond hair. Having become accustomed to Heide's near-constant animation and boundless energy, I had a difficult time watching her inert form.

"Sweetheart," Jack spoke with an elevated voice over noise of the machines. "Mom doesn't want you to worry about missing your plane. She's on her way here, and she's decided to spend the whole summer with us."

I blinked several times at this revelation, but did nothing more.

"By this time tomorrow night, Mom will be here with us. I'm hoping you'll open your gorgeous blue eyes and let her know you can see her. Mom loves you so much. And I love you, too. We're both going to help you get well."

Jack looked over his daughter's still figure, lifted up her arm and kissed her hand.

"Kathleen is here, too. She's spent all afternoon telling me how strong you are and how you're going to come back from this. She's absolutely right. We can see how much you've been fighting today and you're doing great."

I squeezed Heide's foot as he spoke. Even if she was unable to respond, perhaps she could hear us or feel our touch.

"Today is going to be the most difficult day of them all. Every day will be a little easier than the one before, and soon you'll be back home and ready to play soccer again."

Jack paused and cleared his throat before continuing.

"You're strong and sweet, and I'm never going to let another day go by without telling you how much you mean to me. You're the best part of my life. I love being your dad. I'm so proud of you, and I know you're going to impress everyone here at this hospital with your recovery."

Jack gazed at his daughter, displaying every bit of strength and sweetness he had just credited her with possessing. She was every bit her father's daughter.

In that one precious moment I realized I loved her just as much as I adored Jack.

Terry finished her various tasks and stopped across from Jack. "I'm sorry you missed the doctor, but he'll back in the morning to check on her progress."

"Is she likely to wake up tonight?" Jack asked.

"There are no guarantees, but my guess is probably not. It may be tomorrow, but it may be longer. Every patient is different."

Jack glanced to me and then back to his daughter, and I understood he was trying to decide between remaining at the hospital or taking me back to the hotel for the evening.

"You don't need to choose," I said. "If you want to stay, then you should. I can look after myself."

Terry pointed behind Jack to a cushioned window seat. "Parents often choose to sleep here, and that's fine if you want to do that. Personally, it's a fine spot for a nap, but I prefer a real bed for a good night's rest. Your daughter is going to be in the ICU for a while yet. Keep that in mind as much as possible."

"Try to stick to the routine," Jack remarked, quoting Terry's words from earlier. He watched his daughter for several more minutes before rubbing his eyes.

"What if she wakes up and I'm not here? She's not going to know where she is or what's happened to her."

"She's injured and also on heavy medication. When she wakes up, she'll do it slowly. We'll keep her calm and call you immediately. In the few minutes it will take for you to get here, she'll still be trying to figure out if she's even awake."

Jack nodded. He leaned over and lightly stroked Heide's cheek. "You seem to be getting a good rest right now, so I'm going to go lie down, too. But the nurse will call me if you wake up, and I can come back here in just a couple of minutes. Tomorrow you'll see Mom. All right?"

I glanced at Heide, looking for any sign that she could hear her father's voice. Other than the rising and falling of her bruised chest, there was no movement at all. Tears flooded my eyes, and I looked away from everyone else in the room to wipe them away.

"I love you, sweetheart." Jack's voice quaked with strong emotion. "You keep sleeping well tonight, and I'll do the same. Kathleen and I will come back first thing in the morning, and we're going to spend the whole day with you. You'll get tired of hearing me talk."

Jack set Heide's hand back down on the bed and kissed her forehead. When he straightened back up, he turned to me. "Let's go."

I nodded and gave Heide's foot one last squeeze before walking to the door.

"You both rest well," Terry said. Heide is in good hands here."

"Thank you," Jack replied. "I'll sleep better knowing she's receiving superb care."

As we stepped back into the corridor and made our way to the exit, Jack's hand drifted down to the small of my back. Nevertheless, he looked over his shoulder at Heide's room.

"Are you sure you want to leave?" I asked after pressing the button for the elevator.

He turned to me. "The night Heide was born, our nurse came to the birthing suite and offered to take her to the nursery so we could both get some sleep. At first we refused, but the nurse just gave us both this look. And then she reminded us we wouldn't be getting much sleep at all once we took her home. The nurses looked after her and after us. She convinced us not to feel guilty about letting them perform their job, and so we let her go to the nursery. Other than a couple of feedings, we slept pretty well that night."

I smiled as the elevator doors opened.

"Do I want to leave her?" he continued as we stepped inside the elevator car. "No, but Terry is right. She's not going to wake up tonight, and she's not going home tomorrow or by the end of the weekend. Exhausting ourselves won't be helpful to anyone. I told Allison to rest, and now Terry has told me to do the same. I know someone will call if there's a change in her condition."

When we returned to the parking garage, Jack asked to drive back to the hotel so he could also find his way back to our base camp. When we returned to our suite, he stepped out onto the terrace to call Allison one last time before she left Baltimore. It was after midnight on her end of the line, but she answered almost as soon as Jack pressed the call button.

The next time they would speak to one another, they would be in the same room. It was at this point I wondered how wise it would be for me to remain in

Portland. I knew I should speak to Jack about it, but far too much had happened during the long day. The conversation could wait until the morning. Instead, I turned on the television to offer Jack and Allison another few moments of privacy.

I undressed for bed without ceremony, tossing my clothes onto a nearby chair before crawling into the sheets, naked. I stretched out on the king-sized mattress and was overcome by how good it was to lie down. My muscles ached and I considered taking a hot bath, but I managed to doze off while Jack was still outside on the patio.

A short time later, I awakened flat on my back with Jack bent over my chest. My nipple was in his mouth and his hand was caressing me gently between my legs. I stirred beneath him in surprise and when I did, he brought his lips to mine. He was naked and hard against my leg.

"I should let you sleep," he murmured. "I know you're as exhausted as I am. I didn't mean to start anything, but I just reached over and found you were already wet. I shouldn't want this, but I can't resist you when I know you're ready for me."

"I'm always ready for you," I said, opening my legs wider. Encouraged, he glided into me, and yet we both froze once he was fully inside me. We were both hesitant to proceed, but we were also both hesitant to break the connection. We explored one another's bodies with our hands as we contemplated our next moves.

"Sex should be the last thing I'm thinking about tonight," he mumbled as he ducked his head against the side of my neck.

I tightened my hold on his back. "Don't feel guilty about what you want," I said. "Today has been a terrible day and sex is a comfort, not to mention a distraction. I'll leave it up to you. I'm here for you, Jack. In any way you need me to be."

He raised himself up on his elbows and stared into my eyes with gentle desire. I kept my hands still on his back as I awaited his decision. After a moment, he lowered his head to mine and we kissed. As we did so, he moved his hips back and forward. Back and forward again. Back and forward once more. I scratched his back and ran my hands from his back to his chest and rested them over his heart. Unlike previous encounters where I had reveled in Jack's ability to push my physical limits, we made love this time with delicacy.

This moment wasn't about making Jack come, it was about offering all my love to him. Our bodies melded into one another, and we rocked together within our new home away from home. I held him as closely as I could, and he continued to thrust into me with tender insistence for several minutes. We were both hushed except for the occasional soft sigh, and I held my hands to his heart the entire time. Eventually, his movements wound down, slower and slower. He pressed back into me one final time before wrapping his arms around my shoulders and drawing me up to his chest.

We held on to one another for several long moments before he withdrew from me and rolled back to his side of the bed. Before he could roam too far, I drew him back to me, inviting him to rest his head on my breast. Our legs entwined and my fingers drifted into his wavy hair as he stretched a lazy but large hand to cover my other breast. I massaged his scalp even as I began to drift off to sleep.

"You know what this moment needs?" I asked him, dreamily.

"What?"

"Orange slices. I want some."

He chuckled.

"I mean it. I'm going to pick up a few oranges from Safeway tomorrow."

"That does sound good."

"Oranges are our thing," I declared. "We need to keep some in our room."

"That can be our thing, but I need you more than the oranges. I'm so glad you're here."

"I wouldn't be anywhere else," I whispered as his body relaxed against mine.

chapter

Thirty-Two

THE REST of our night was dominated by power naps. Jack would doze for a short while before stirring back awake. His constant movements disturbed my own light sleep. Each time he turned to the bedside table, grabbed his phone and looked for messages only to discover there were none. After several such checks, he gave in and called the ICU for an update.

The night shift nurse informed him that Heide was still unconscious and her vitals were holding stable. This proved to be among the first good bits of news we'd heard since the accident. After ending his call, Jack sent Allison a text message. She replied within seconds and Jack acknowledged her answer before setting his phone back down.

"Allison's at the airport," he said. "She's sitting at the gate waiting to board her flight."

"I hope her trip goes well." I yawned. "It's going to be another long day for her."

Jack attempted to settle in the bed and spooned up behind me. I reached back and caressed his hip, and he kissed my shoulder.

"I don't mean to keep you awake. I just can't seem to relax."

"Do you want to go back to the hospital?"

He tightened his hold on me and nestled his chin on my shoulder. "Let's try to get some more sleep. We'll be there all day, and I want to be ready for Allison's arrival. You're right. She's going to need support."

I opened my eyes and rolled over to face Jack. "Maybe I shouldn't go to the hospital."

His response was immediate and harsh. "What do you mean by that?"

My hand searched for his. "I don't want things to be stressful for you. Or her."

Jack shook his head. "You should be there."

I sighed. "It's asking a lot of Allison. Does she even know I'm here with you?"

Jack's eyes closed for several moments. "It didn't exactly come up," he admitted.

I pulled my hand back in surprise. "She's about to get on a plane thinking about her injured daughter," I scolded him. "I don't think blindsiding her with us is the way to go."

"You're right, but let me handle her."

I rolled back to my original position, and Jack tightened his grip around my waist.

"Are you upset with me?" he asked. His voice was quiet and cautious.

I was upset, but given everything he was going through, I opted to spare Jack the reality of my disappointment.

"You know her and I don't," I responded. "I'm sure you'll figure out what to say." I patted his hip once again. "We both need to rest."

Satisfied with this answer, Jack drifted into another doze. Long after Jack had fallen back asleep, I lay in his embrace with my eyes wide open and my mind racing. Knowing Allison was unprepared for my presence at the hospital, I prepared for the endless potential outcomes the moment I came face to face with Jack's ex-wife.

Jack and I spent the morning at Heide's bedside, sitting in chairs provided by the nursing staff. At times, we occupied ourselves with light talk about the office or by discussing a show playing on the television. Other times, we silently watched Heide, hoping to spot one indication she was regaining consciousness. The ventilator continued to breathe for her and provided the only sign of movement from her.

An hour after our arrival, a middle-aged man with salt-and-pepper hair and smooth features walked into the room. He was dressed in a white doctor's coat and dark brown trousers.

"Hello, Mr. Evans," he greeted Jack. "I'm Dr. Avery. I treated Heide yesterday."

Jack rose from his seat and shook the doctor's hand. "Hello. Please call me Jack, and thank you for everything you've done for her."

"Your daughter is strong, but she has a long recovery ahead of her."

"How long do you think she'll be here?" Jack asked, getting to the point.

"I would plan on her remaining in the hospital for a while. Probably three or four weeks, and then we'll have to make a decision about whether she'll return home or transition into a rehabilitation center."

"Can you tell me more about her surgery?"

"We don't know when she stopped breathing, but it was before the EMTs arrived at the scene. From the time of the accident until Heide arrived here, her lungs were compromised. Her tests revealed that a portion of her right lung tissue was permanently damaged. That's why she was rushed to surgery."

Jack gave Dr. Avery a worried look. "What does that mean—permanent damage?"

"The lung tissue was dead, and we had no other choice but to remove it."

"She lost part of her lung?" Jack looked horrified by this discovery.

"I'm afraid so. To be specific, she lost a quarter of her right lung."

Upon hearing this news, I reached out and massaged Heide's foot.

"What does that mean for her long term?" The fear in Jack's voice elevated.

"She can recover from the injury and go on to live a mostly normal life."

"Mostly normal?"

"There will be some limitations. For example, is she athletic?"

"She likes to play soccer."

"That will be difficult for her in the short run. It will take several months for her lungs to recover and for her ribs to mend. Even when she does feel better, she'll become winded more easily. Her endurance for physical activities may be somewhat limited."

"What about her other injuries?"

"Everything looks good there. I don't predict any long-term damage to her other organs. They will all heal well before her ribs do."

"Should I be concerned that she hasn't woken up yet?"

"Not at this point. She's been through a lot, and we're managing her pain with morphine. Based on my experience, she'll most likely wake up within the next day or two. Let's see where things are Monday morning."

"What can I expect from this point on?"

"Once she comes off the ventilator, breathing will be uncomfortable. She'll be weak for a while, but her energy and strength will grow by the day." Dr. Avery pointed toward Heide's chest, while maintaining eye contact with Jack. "This incision also needs time to heal. We need to make sure she doesn't contract an infection, and her activity cannot put any stress on the incision for about eight weeks."

Jack turned his full attention back to Heide, and I watched as his face expressed apprehension and vulnerability. A new level of reality had been layered into the situation, and the impending complications would not be resolved any time soon. It would take months, possibly even years, for her to recover from this one mistake.

Dr. Avery stepped closer to Heide's bed, recapturing Jack's attention. "I'm sure it doesn't seem like it now, but all things considered, your daughter is fortunate. Frankly speaking, everything I've heard from the flight crew was incredible. Being crushed beneath that backstop should have killed her."

The doctor allowed Jack to process these words for a few moments before moving forward. "Do you mind if I look her over for a minute or two?"

"Not at all. Please." Jack stood back and resumed his seat.

Dr. Avery listened to Heide's heart and lungs. Afterward, he checked each of her pupils along with several of her reflexes. Once the brief exam was complete, Dr. Avery turned to Jack.

"Her heart sounds good and her blood pressure is about where I would expect it to be. I'm not seeing any signs of brain damage, either. We just need to keep watching her and give her body some more time to recover. I know it's tough to keep calm in a situation like this, but that's exactly what we need to do."

Jack smiled with effort and nodded.

"I'll be back tomorrow morning to check on her again, but if something significant changes in her condition, I've left instructions for the nurse to contact me. I'll be available to pop in if need be. Do you have any other questions before I go?"

"I can't think of any right now."

"I'm sorry this happened to your daughter, but she's tough."

"Thank you."

"Take care."

Dr. Avery left the room as quietly as he'd entered a few minutes before.

Jack returned to Heide's bedside. He gathered one of her small hands in both of his. I studied him and noted his posture was slouched in an unfamiliar manner. His face was drawn and somber.

"You look tired, Jack."

"A little bit," he confessed.

I peered at my phone to check the time. "Why don't you go to the cafeteria and get something to eat? I'll sit here with Heide. When you return, I'll take a break."

He used one of his hands to rub his face. "Yeah, all right. That sounds like a good plan."

I stood from my chair, stepped over to Jack and wrapped my arms around his shoulders. He closed one arm around me but kept holding his daughter's hand with the other, unwilling to let her go.

I detached and took a step back. "I'll text you if anything happens."

"Thanks."

"No worries."

He kissed Heide's hand and then kissed me briefly on the lips before wandering from the room.

Once Jack left, I found sitting on my own difficult so I occupied myself by tidying up Heide's room. I disposed of the Starbucks coffee cups we'd brought with us from the hotel and organized a few of the miscellaneous items on the small bedside table. It was while I was attending to this particular task that I heard someone enter the room and gasp. I turned.

Allison stood just inside the doorway. She was dressed in dark jeans, a purple shirt and a slate gray jacket. Her hair was pulled into a simple yet chic ponytail but her face was devoid of cosmetics. With her hair pulled away from her face, it was easy to see she was exhausted. Her cheeks and lips were both pale, and the dark circles underneath her eyes were the only spots of color in her face.

Heide's mother didn't take notice of me at all. Every bit of her attention was on her daughter, lying unconscious and severely injured in a hospital bed. Allison left the single suitcase in the doorway without a second thought as she approached her daughter. As soon as she was within arm's reach of Heide, Allison raised a shaking hand to caress her daughter's cheek. Tears fell from her eyes as she took in the bright red incision that ran almost the full length of Heide's chest.

"Has she woken up at all?" she asked without looking at me. Her voice was sad, but still soft and almost melodic. I knew without hearing another syllable it was a well-trained voice for public speaking.

"Not yet," I answered. "But she's expected to."

"How soon?"

"Perhaps another day or two. The surgeon was just here a few minutes ago and he is optimistic about her outcome."

Allison nodded as I spoke, and then she unexpectedly pulled her hand back from Heide and grasped the bedrail with both hands. I watched as each of her knuckles turned white. She was holding on to the bed as though it were some sort of lifeline.

"Are you okay?" I asked.

"It's so warm in here," she muttered.

I looked at Allison's face. If she had been pale upon walking into the room, she was now shockingly barren of color.

"Do you need to take your jacket off?"

The tempo of her breathing increased. "My ears are ringing."

Without delay I hurried around the bed and grasped her by the elbow. "Allison." My tone was raised and serious, but not too stern, I hoped. "I'm worried you're going to faint. I want you to lie down for a moment. Can you walk with me?"

Allison didn't respond, but she let go of the bedrail and allowed me to guide her away from Heide. Her knees buckled several times as I helped her to the cushioned window seat. I encouraged her to sit down before instructing her to lie back. Once she was secure, I let go of her arm and rushed over to Heide's bed. I pushed the call button for the nurse and grabbed Jack's blazer from his chair before making my way back to Allison's side.

I rolled the coat into a makeshift pillow and lifted Allison's head to place it underneath her.

"I'm sorry," she said between hurried breaths. "I'm a wreck. I'm sorry."

I placed my palm on Allison's forehead. Her skin was clammy. As I withdrew my hand, Terry came dashing into the room, nearly colliding with Allison's abandoned suitcase. She looked at me, perplexed.

I gestured to the woman lying on her back on the window seat. "Heide's mother just arrived from the airport. I think she nearly passed out."

Terry wandered over and performed a quick check of Allison's vitals before turning to a cupboard across the room and pulling out a washcloth. She turned on a nearby sink and ran the cloth underneath the faucet. After she turned off the water, she extended the small towel in my direction.

"Put this on her forehead. I'll grab some juice."

I did as instructed while Terry moved the suitcase out of the way as she left the room.

As soon as the washcloth covered Allison's eyes, she reached up and held it in place.

"How are you doing?" I asked her. "Feeling any better?"

"A little bit," she whispered.

"We're going to get you some juice, so just lay here for now and try to relax. I know seeing Heide like this is a shock, and you've had a rough couple of days to get here."

Allison bit her lip and nodded. New tears appeared from underneath the white cotton of the washcloth and rolled down her cheek. Although I was hard put to explain how, I recognized something in Allison's forehead. It was the determined set of her expression, one that I had seen on Heide's face but hadn't noticed until it was mimicked by her mother. Already missing Heide's personality so much, I couldn't help myself. I stroked Allison's hair with delicate yet cautious movements.

Terry returned to the room carrying a small juice box with a straw. "I have some orange juice. Do you think you can hold it and take a few sips?"

"Yes." Allison began to sit up and I pulled my hand back.

Terry brushed the bottom of the juice box against Allison's hands, stopping her from pulling herself upright. "I want you to stay down for a couple of minutes. Let's take things nice and slow for the time being."

Allison took hold of her juice and rested back against Jack's blazer. She obediently sipped from the straw and went quiet for several minutes while she concentrated on making herself better.

I remained at her side, unsure of what to do next.

"I can smell Jack. Are you in here?"

Her statement caught me off guard. "No, you're using his coat as a pillow," I whispered.

Allison went still for several heartbeats before pulling the washcloth away from her eyes and looking up at my face. "Who are you?" Her voice was now cool.

"Kathleen Brighton," I responded, not wishing to elaborate beyond that. We both understood any additional designations were unnecessary.

"Where is Jack?" she demanded. "Why isn't he with our daughter?"

"He's here in the cafeteria. We decided to eat lunch in shifts so one of us could stay with Heide. I sent him to eat first," I explained.

Allison didn't respond. She was trying not to glare at me. If I had been less experienced in holding back my own vicious looks, I wouldn't have recognized the effort she was making to hide her true emotions. Her energy renewed, Allison moved into a sitting position and began to stand up.

I retreated to my chair and gathered my phone and my purse. "You seem to be doing better," I said while avoiding eye contact. "I'll go and tell Jack that you're here."

I made my way toward the door while Allison took her rightful place at Heide's bedside. As I left the room, she said, "I hate it here."

chapter

Thirty-Three

I MADE my way to the cafeteria in a daze, walking without paying attention to anything or anyone else around me. When I entered the space, I easily spotted Jack's form fitting tee shirt in a room filled with hospital professionals. He was sitting alone at a table, motionless and unobservant of the activity around him.

Instead of approaching to tell him Allison was here, I veered into the food line. As I selected my items, I attempted to get my frazzled nerves under control. Finding nothing much that appealed to me, I picked up an apple, a bag of pretzels and a diet soda, mostly because I could take them all with me when I left. I paid the cashier and then made my way over to Jack. When I took my seat next to him, he looked at me in surprise.

I held the granny smith apple in both hands and kept my gaze locked on the stem. "Allison is here."

Jack was surprised. "Already? Her plane must have landed early."

I nodded. "She was pretty upset when she saw Heide. She almost fainted."

Jack sat back in his seat and wrapped his arm around my shoulders. "That's not good. I've never known her to do that. Not even during pregnancy."

I turned to look at Jack's face. His calm casualness at Allison's condition irritated me, although I couldn't pinpoint why. "When was the last time she saw Heide?"

He hesitated, as though considering whether to divulge an answer. "They spent spring break together."

"Well," I snipped, "it's a drastic change from the last memory she has of her daughter."

Jack's forehead wrinkled as he tried to make sense of my mood. "What's the matter?"

"I've decided to make myself scarce this afternoon," I announced.

"Why?" Jack was agitated. "What did she say to you?"

"She didn't say anything, but it's only common sense that she doesn't want me hovering nearby."

Jack was stubborn and refused to accept this development. "You have a right to be here."

My mind was made up, so I offered another piece of logic before our discussion disintegrated into an argument. "Allison is tired, even more so than we are today. My presence will only wear on her nerves more."

"She'll calm down once she gets some rest."

I set my apple down and placed my palm against Jack's cheek. I waited until he met my eyes before expressing my most important point. "Remember when I told you I wouldn't interfere with your family? That I refused to be a troublemaker?"

"Yeah," he mumbled.

"This is precisely the moment I need to honor that promise."

"I wish you would stay here," he whispered. "You bring me peace."

I leaned forward and pressed my lips against his for several seconds, unconcerned with showing my affection for him in public. When I pulled back, Jack appeared to be more relaxed.

"I want there to be peace today, and I'm convinced that if you insist on your ex-wife sharing the afternoon with your girlfriend, there will be none. She's so upset about Heide, and she needs to sit at her daughter's side. Believe me, I don't want to walk away from you and Heide, but I'm the low one on the totem pole here."

"You're not low," he responded. "Never think that."

I changed the subject as I pulled back from him. "I do have some errands I can run."

"Like what?" Jack tested me, looking dubious. "We've only been here one day."

"I told you last night I wanted to go to the grocery store. We should have a few things handy in the room so we don't have to go out if we're too tired. And I can send some of our clothes down for laundry service. If we're here for a week or more, I just want to make sure we're both as comfortable as possible. Besides, I should also give Robert a call and let him know what's going on. I forgot to check in with him last night."

"Will you thank him for our hotel room?" Jack wasn't smiling, and his question suggested he'd accepted I was leaving for the afternoon.

"Sure."

Jack slid his hand into the front pocket of his jeans to get my car keys, and I rested my hand on his forearm to stop him. His skin was warm and his muscles were firm. I couldn't resist drifting my fingers over the exposed portion of his arm.

"I can take a cab back to the hotel. I'll leave my car with you. That way you can decide what you need to do without worrying about how to do it."

"Are you sure? What about your trip to the grocery store?"

"It's fine. The store is just a few blocks away from the Sentinel. I can walk."

"I'll bring Allison down to the hotel this afternoon so she can check in and get some rest," Jack said. "You and I will go out to dinner tonight, and then we'll figure things out from there."

"That sounds good. Will you call me if Heide wakes up?"

"Of course I will."

Jack leaned over and we kissed once again. As our kiss lingered, I was torn between finding a way to be available to Jack, and respecting Allison's need to re-bond with her family. I was wary of upsetting him with my departure, but it was easier to coax Jack to understand my decision than to force myself upon Allison.

Leaving the hospital was the safe and respectful thing to do.

When I returned to the Sentinel a short time later, I wasn't quite ready to return to our hotel room or walk to the grocery store. It was early afternoon, but I wasn't interested in either of the hotel's lounges, so I opted for the in-house Starbucks. I approached the counter and ordered Earl Grey tea before occupying a comfortable seat near the window. I stared out at the activity on Eleventh Avenue for a few moments, but soon checked out, lost in my own thoughts of how to handle the situation between Jack and Allison. I had managed to avoid conflict today, but I was increasingly concerned about my ability to navigate the terrain in the days and weeks to come.

Allison would be spending the summer in Oregon.

In yesterday's frantic urge to reunite Jack with Heide, I never paused to consider how the dynamic between Jack and I would have to shift once Allison arrived. Dr. Avery mentioned that Heide would remain hospitalized for several weeks, and from the sound of things, she would need continued care even after leaving OHSU. Despite the emerging differences between the three of us, nothing would matter more than seeing Heide healed. It meant that Jack and I would be forced to make major adjustments in our relationship just when everything had begun to fall into place.

"Kathleen?"

I snapped from my thoughts at the surprised sound of my name. I recognized the voice, though I had trouble placing it. I craned my neck and found myself face-to-face with the party crasher from Denver.

"Hi," I uttered with equal surprise. Ryan Murray stood a few feet away from me, newly acquired Starbucks coffee in hand and looking as immaculate and polished as he did the afternoon we met. Today, he was wearing black trousers with a gray V-neck sweater.

"What are you doing here?" he asked.

Overdue for a good laugh, I allowed myself to indulge in one. "Shouldn't I be asking you that question?"

He joined in with my laughter, although he was more reserved. "I suppose so. It's just ..." Ryan paused and stepped in closer to clear the walkway for another patron. "I'm glad to run into you. I sent you an e-mail Thursday night to tell you I was coming back to Oregon, but I didn't hear anything back. I was worried I'd overstepped my boundaries."

"Not at all," I reassured him. "I've been on emergency leave and haven't been checking my e-mails."

Ryan's frown reflected his sincere concern. "Emergency? Is everything all right?"

I shook my head. "I don't know yet. I hope so."

Ryan took the seat next to mine. "Do you want to talk about it?"

I smiled and considered my choices. "Yes and no. I don't want to keep you from anything."

"You're not. I flew in this morning and just settled in. I don't have any appointments until this evening."

"Are you staying here?"

"Yeah. You?"

I nodded.

"Well," Ryan smiled back. "That sounds like fate to me."

I couldn't disagree with him, and so I found myself mentioning that I was in Portland because a coworker's daughter had been involved in a serious accident. Although I trusted Ryan enough to share more with him about my relationship with Jack and Heide, I held the information back. I held it back because I remembered how both Jack and Robert had been wary of Ryan Murray without ever speaking with him. Instead, I focused on sharing the details of Heide's accident and all the events that had followed in its wake over the past day.

"My God," Ryan said after I finished my story. "That's terrible."

"Do you have any children?" I asked him.

"Not yet. Hopefully one day. I can't imagine what a horror that is, watching your daughter fight for her life."

Tears were beginning to well up in my eyes and I took a long sip of my tea, hoping to halt their progress. Ryan watched me, and once I had regained my composure, he grinned with a smile that reached his eyes.

"It's good of you to drive to Portland to check on her. Your commitment to your coworker speaks well of you and your family's business."

I accepted Ryan's compliment with my thanks and nothing more. I felt guilty for not telling Ryan the whole truth about Jack, even though doing so meant maintaining my loyalty to my company and my lover.

"How long are you in town?" I asked, changing the subject.

"All week. I fly back next Friday."

"You must be really interested in the Portland market," I prodded, knowing Robert would be seeking the same information if he were sitting here.

"Yes and no." Ryan copied my answer from a few moments before. "My biggest client relocated to Portland, but his company remains headquartered in Denver. The big ad firms here are chomping at the bit to get his business, so I work a little bit harder to keep it. I'm out here almost every other month."

Ryan took a sip of his coffee, and his blue eyes locked onto mine. "What about you? Are you just here for the weekend?"

"Longer, actually."

Ryan paused for a moment, before he said, "Maybe we could meet up for dinner before you go back to Bend. I'm dying to check out Departure."

"You should," I said without making a commitment. "That's a great place."

Ryan leveled a determined gaze at me. "A great place is made even greater with pleasant company."

I blushed at Ryan's compliment. I couldn't help it.

"I'm not really in a work frame of mind right now. It'd be a waste of your time. I wouldn't be able to contribute much."

Ryan set his coffee cup down on our table. "The last thing I talk about at dinner is work."

This comment intrigued me, and before I could stop to think, I retorted, "What do you talk about?"

"Anything else."

I smiled, hoping to regain my self-control. "I like speaking with you, and I am always interested in dinner at Departure, but I don't know how things are going to play out. I've made promises, and I can't really make any new plans."

Ryan accepted my answer. "I'm staying in room two oh five," he revealed, not giving up entirely. "If an opportunity comes up, call me there. I'll move forward with my week, but I'll save Departure for you. Just in case."

I agreed, certain there was no conceivable scenario in which this dinner plan would be solidified. I stood up, deciding to make my exit before Ryan and I could find anything else to discuss. "I'm glad we ran into each other."

"Me, too."

"I'd stay longer, but I have some errands to run this afternoon and then I'm going back to the hospital."

"I'll keep the little girl and her family in my thoughts."

"Thank you. I know they would appreciate that."

Ryan rose, leaned in and kissed me on the cheek. "Bye, Kathleen."

I stepped back and waved before making my way back to the hotel lobby.

I strolled to the elevators and pressed the up button, intending to freshen up before leaving for the store. While I waited, I checked my phone for messages.

A text from Robert had arrived. "I'm in Portland. At the Sentinel. Call me when you have a moment."

"Holy shit," I said just as the elevator door opened. Embarrassed, I turned away from the other hotel guests as they disembarked. I stepped away from the open door and walked toward the main lobby as I called my father. Robert picked up on the second ring.

"Kathleen, how is everyone?" Robert's voice contained a mixture of concern and relief.

I fumbled my way through my response. "Hi. Yes. We're fine. I'm sorry I didn't call last night. We didn't get back to the hotel until late in the evening."

"That's okay."

I furrowed my eyebrows. "You're here?"

"Yes. I'm sitting in Jake's right now."

I glanced to my left. Robert was only a few steps away, sitting on the Tenth Avenue side of the building.

"I'm in the lobby. I'll walk over."

"You're not at the hospital?" This time Robert's concern was tinged with admonishment.

Patience, Kathleen. Strength, Kathleen.

"I'll see you in a minute. I'll explain everything."

"Okay."

"Bye." I disconnected the call before he could respond.

The walk to Jake's was meandering, but I promptly found Robert, sitting on a stool at the wooden bar, sipping a beer and staring at the various specimens of taxidermy placed near the ceiling. I walked over, undetected, and took the seat next to his.

"Hey," I began.

"Hey yourself." Robert leaned slightly forward as though to offer me a hug, but then retreated back into his own personal space. I considered leaning toward him, but couldn't quite bring myself to do so.

All in due time.

We sat for a couple of moments, each struggling to find a place to begin.

"Do you want a drink?" Robert began to raise his arm for the bartender.

"No, thanks." I smiled, hoping to show him I appreciated the offer. "I just left Starbucks."

Robert lowered his arm and twisted his body in my direction. "I thought about going to the hospital first. But I didn't want to intrude."

I attempted to mirror Robert's casual stance and stretched my arm out on the bar as my fingers drifted along its shiny surface. "I'm surprised you're here, but I'm glad I can thank you in person for getting us the suite. That was really nice of you."

"You're welcome. I've always liked that floor."

"I didn't know that," I said. "Are you staying in one of those tonight?"

"Not this time." Robert took a swift sip of his beer before plodding onward. "How's Heide?" The concern had returned to Robert's voice.

"She's in critical condition, but she's a strong girl. I think she'll live, but she's got a long recovery ahead of her. I don't know if she'll be able to return to school on time."

Robert sat and listened as I updated him on everything Heide had been through. I also explained that Allison had arrived from Baltimore and I had left the hospital to let her spend time with Heide and Jack.

Robert nodded in understanding, but didn't elaborate.

"I'd like to speak to Jack while I'm here. Can you help me find a good time to do that?"

Although I was working on improving my relationship with Robert, I couldn't stop my initial suspicion of his request. I stilled and processed his mood. He was quiet and unusually patient. He had also asked for my help rather than expect it. In return, I decided to help him, not punish him.

"We have plans to meet up for dinner tonight. Why don't you join us?"

"If you're both up for it, I'd like that."

"Sure. We haven't figured it all out yet, but I'll keep you in the loop."

"Good."

I nodded and rose from the barstool. "I need to go pick up a few groceries, and then I was going to take a small nap. What room are you in?"

"Three ten. Do you want me to take you to the store?"

I shook my head and offered another smile. "I could use the walk and the fresh air."

"Sure." Robert turned his body back toward the bar. I placed my hand between his shoulder blades. It wasn't a hug, but it was the first time we'd made such contact since our afternoon at Widgi Creek. My father turned his head and looked me in the eyes.

"Thank you, anyway," I said. "I'll call you just as soon I know what's going on for dinner."

Robert grinned, and we left one another's company on a good note.

chapter

Thirty-Four

AFTER MY trek to the store, I returned to our suite, unpacked the groceries and turned my attention to emptying our suitcases. Once all our clothes and other items were put away, I stretched out on the bed for a brief nap. Consumed by the physical and emotional fatigue of the past day, I soon fell into a deep sleep, bereft of dreams.

I only awoke when a sudden tilt of the mattress alerted me to someone's presence. Jack had returned from the hospital and was sitting on the side of the bed with his back to me and removing his shoes. I waited in silence until he reclined beside me and then I drew close to him for a kiss hello. His arms wrapped around my back but he held me loosely and kissed me much too passively. I pulled back from his mouth and ran my fingers through his hair. His brown eyes drifted shut in response.

"Do you want to talk?" I asked, watching his face with interest. "Or do you just want to sleep?"

"Both," he mumbled.

"How's Heide doing?"

Jack's eyes remained shut while he answered, "She's still unconscious. I'm trying to stay calm, but it's getting harder."

I sympathized. "I know."

"I'm scared," he whispered.

"What can I do for you?"

"Just lie here with me for now."

"Okay."

We rested for a time, listening to one another breathe. Jack began to return some of my affectionate caresses, and I moved forward with more conversation.

"How did things go with Allison?"

"Fine, I guess. We didn't talk much. I think we're both too tired. We mostly just sat there with Heide and waited for anything to happen."

I kissed Jack's forehead. "I have to tell you something."

Jack opened his eyes. "What's that?"

"Robert's here. He drove up this morning."

"Are you serious?"

"Yep."

"Did you see him?"

I nodded. "He's staying here. I met him in Jake's for a few minutes."

"How did that go?"

"A little awkward, but fine."

Jack brought his hand from my back to my face and cupped my cheek.

I couldn't help but relax under his touch. "He wants to see you, but he didn't want to approach you at the wrong time. I invited him to dinner with us tonight. I hope you don't mind."

"I don't, except I was going to ask to stay in."

"Room service is turning into our thing," I kidded.

"Yeah," he responded without indulging my joke.

I rubbed a thumb underneath Jack's eye. "You're so tired. I can explain that to Robert. I'll make him understand and ask for a rain check."

"No. That's fine. We need to eat either way."

"I haven't had the chance to talk with you about him since you've been away from work but something is changing between him and me. We've both been trying to do the right thing. Now more than ever, I need to give him that chance."

"I agree." Jack opened his mouth to say more but hesitated and took my hand in his while he thought about what to say next. "I want to help you with him however I can. I just don't know what I can promise right now."

"Heide is the priority no matter what. Even my father would agree with that."

"Thank you, Kathleen."

"You need to rest. I'll tell Robert we'll eat at Jake's tonight. We'll keep it short and casual."

Jack nodded. "Afterward, I want to go back to the hospital and say good night to Heide. I told Allison that she could come along when I go back, but that I intended to bring you with me."

"I don't know Jack—" I began.

"Please, don't argue with me about this," he interrupted. "I've already worked it out with Allison."

Jack sounded agitated once again, so I backed down. "Okay."

We both fell silent, the atmosphere tingling with increasing tension.

"I would like to see Heide again," I told him as I dropped my hand to pull on a wrinkle of Jack's tee shirt. "I got a present for her this afternoon. I'm saving it for when she wakes up."

Jack pulled me to him while I was still talking and kissed me just as I finished my sentence, this time with more intensity. Although surprised, I grabbed on to him and was happy when he did the same in return. Our clothed bodies pressed together, and Jack rolled me onto my back to deepen our kiss. During our brief romance, I'd come to realize how much he expressed his emotions in this way and so I found myself paying particular attention to whatever he was saying now. His movements were not frenzied or aggressive. He was not offering himself to me or trying to end our conversation. I only perceived close intimacy and profound connection.

Unity.

I'd been close to telling Jack I was in love with him several times, and as I lay underneath him, receiving his devotion I wanted to say it more than ever before. I wanted to tell him I loved him so much that when he ended the kiss, I swore I felt his honest love in our embrace and was convinced I could see this same love in his eyes as we looked at one another.

I'd never been in love with a man before. I never understood anything about love until Jack and Heide had come into my life. What made me worthy of them? I didn't know, and I also comprehended that I might never know the answer to that question. Jack held himself above me, and gazed at me as if waiting for something. I grasped him by the waist, at a total loss for words.

"It's all right," he whispered. "Take all the time you need."

"I've never said it," I confessed. "I've never felt it until you."

"Never?"

I shook my head.

"When did you first feel it?" he asked me. "What was the moment?"

"It was our first night together. At your house. In your bedroom, actually."

"Tell me," he encouraged.

"On your bedside table was a photo of you holding Heide when she was a baby."

"That was taken on her first birthday."

"Your foreheads are pressed together and your eyes are locked on hers for eternity." Tears fell from both of my eyes, but I did nothing to wipe them away or break my contact with Jack. "I looked at that one photo, and I thought about how there are no pictures like that of me and Robert."

"Is that why you cried that night? Because you were sad about your family?"

"No, I was crying because I saw how much you love your daughter and how much she loves you back. I saw your unconditional love for your daughter, and I fell in love with you that night because of it."

Jack swallowed as his eyes grew watery. I waited, not knowing what to do or say next. We both held our breath, our eyes locked on one another, as Jack lowered his head.

When his forehead rested against mine, he said, "I love you, Kathleen. I love you because you went through hell as a child, and instead of allowing tragedy to destroy you, you turned into an extraordinary woman. You are intelligent. Strong. Passionate. Brave. I wish you could see yourself through my eyes for even just one minute so that you would never doubt yourself again. There is no one I want with me right now more than you. With you at my side, at Heide's side, I know we'll get through this. I know my daughter will be whole again."

"I love you, Jack. I love Heide, too. And I'll do whatever it takes to see you both happy."

chapter

Thirty-Five

THAT EVENING, Jack and I left our suite to meet my father for dinner. We held hands as we made our way down the corridor. Sadness and worry for Heide still dominated our moods, but we'd declared our love to one another and there was a powerful comfort in that.

When the elevator doors opened, we stepped inside the empty car, and I pressed against Jack's side as he pushed the button for the lobby.

"Should we see if Allison wants to join us?" I asked. "Do we need to make sure she eats?"

Jack looked down at me and smiled. "She told me she was going to Clyde Common after she had some rest. I'll give her a call when our meal is winding down and see when she'll be ready to go back to the hospital."

"Okay."

Jack leaned down and kissed me with modesty. "I love you," he whispered.

"I love you, too."

He held my gaze and caressed my cheek as he spoke once again. "I know things didn't go well the last time we tried this with Robert. Tonight will be better."

"I think you're right."

The elevator door opened and we continued to Jake's with our hands intertwined.

When we entered the lounge, Robert was sitting at a table next to the window but close to the bar.

He stood up and shook hands with Jack. "Thanks for coming," he said. "I won't keep you here any longer than need be." As if to prove his point, Robert waved to our server and pointed to our table.

"Thank you, Robert. I'm trying to follow sage advice and keep to a schedule as much as possible. I'm looking forward to a good dinner."

We occupied ourselves with updates on Heide's condition until our drinks were served and our meal was ordered.

As soon as our waitress left the table, Robert turned to Jack. "I've been thinking about a lot of things since Kathleen told me about your daughter. For instance, you'd just used all your vacation time before this accident."

Jack nodded with a somber face. "I need to take family leave, possibly the full twelve weeks. I apologize for leaving you in a lurch like that."

Robert shook his head. "The last thing I want you to worry about is how to juggle everything else while you're up here looking after your daughter. I want you to take as much family leave as you need. If you need more than the twelve weeks, we'll work that out. And the firm will continue to pay your salary in full during your leave of absence."

If Jack was stunned by this news, I was flabbergasted. Although our company had a good reputation of taking care of its own, I'd never heard of Robert being quite so generous.

"That's incredible, Robert." Jack sat back in astonishment, his eyes growing wide. "Saying thank you seems wholly inadequate."

Robert looked at me when he said, "Years ago, we lost Kathleen's mother. And once I almost lost Kathleen." Robert turned back to Jack. "Heide's care is what's most important. I can't do much to heal your daughter, but I want to give you the opportunity to focus on her recovery."

As I listened to my father, I realized he was seizing an opportunity of his own. We had done wrong by each other over the course of my life, and now my father had the chance to begin making up for some of his less than stellar behavior. By offering Jack reassurance and removing multiple obstacles from our path, he was also easing my mind and reducing my stress.

"Thank you, Dad," I said.

"You're welcome." Then he added, "There's more."

"What's that?" I asked.

"Our health insurance program is good, but something like this always results in bills. Whatever they are, I want you to consider them paid. Just bring them to me, and it will be taken care of."

"That's a substantial offer," Jack replied, "but I couldn't—"

Robert held up his hand once again. "I don't normally brag, Jack, but the money isn't a problem. The family has amassed a tad of wealth over the years. You're with Kathleen now, and if you two are as serious as you claim to be, then I consider you and your daughter a part of this family. The bills will be taken care of."

Jack looked to me with an anxious expression, unsure how to proceed. I nodded and smiled.

"It's true," I confirmed. I leaned forward and whispered, hoping to lighten Jack's mood. "I don't brag, either."

"One last thing, and then we can enjoy our meal," Robert announced.

Jack shook his head. "I'm not sure I can handle one more thing," he semi-joked.

"From what you've both mentioned, you'll need to stay in Portland longer than your reservation here. I arranged to have my apartment in the Pearl readied for you to move into. You can remain there as long as you need to. It has three bedrooms, so there should be plenty of room if you and Heide need to stay there after she leaves the hospital."

My father turned to me once again. "You can stay up here and work remotely from the apartment. I'll let you determine your own schedule, and we'll work through any kinks that might come up. Do you have your laptop?"

"No," I answered. "I wasn't thinking that far ahead when we left town."

"I'll get it to you."

"Are you sure?" I asked.

"I'm sure I don't want you roaming back and forth between here and Bend for the next couple of months."

I smiled and was overcome with relief. Despite the reason for our coming together that night, the mood between the three of us was lighter. Robert accomplished what he'd set out to do in Portland, and Jack and I were now in the clear to be there for his daughter, and each other. After dinner, Jack excused himself to step outside and call Allison, allowing Robert and I our own bit of privacy.

As I considered my own words, my father surprised me and said, "We seem to be making some headway. You and I."

"I agree."

"I like it."

"Me, too."

"I don't want to screw things up between us. I just want you to know that I intend to keep building on this good will we've established."

"I want that, too."

"I'm glad."

I glanced down at the table. "I'll mess things up once in a while," I warned him. "You need to let me know when I start down that slope."

"The same goes for me."

I nodded as Jack rejoined us.

"Allison ate earlier and napped after. She's on her way to meet us in the lobby."

I looked to my father, and he rose from his seat to shake Jack's hand. "I hope things go well for Heide tonight. If you don't mind I'd like to stop by and see her tomorrow before I head back home."

"You're welcome to stop by anytime," Jack said. "No need to ask."

Robert turned to me as I stood up and gathered my purse.

"Thanks for coming all the way up here," I said. "I know you could have dealt with all this over the phone."

"You're both capable individuals, but I wanted to see for myself that you were both taken care of."

I stepped forward and gave my father a brief but heartfelt hug. We were both unaccustomed to overt affection, so I pulled back before the mood became awkward for either of us.

I grinned. "We'll see you in the morning."

"Good night."

I turned to exit the lounge and Jack followed my lead, taking my hand in his.

"That went well." I smiled at Jack.

"Very well. I'm still in shock," he admitted. "I don't know how I'll every pay any of this back. Or forward."

"You're clever. You'll think of something."

As we made our way to the main lobby, I attempted to detach my hand from Jack's. I was startled when he grasped my hand with more strength.

"You don't want to hold my hand?" Jack's expression crinkled with curiosity.

"Of course I do." I hesitated. "I just thought maybe we shouldn't in front of Allison. At least, not right now."

Jack halted and we faced one another. "I appreciate your consideration of her, but I've been upfront with her about what's developed between us."

He pulled my hand up to his lips and kissed the skin there, all the while holding my gaze.

"You don't need to be afraid of upsetting her. She told me how you helped her this morning, and I wasn't the least bit surprised to hear about it. You're so cautious about exposing your own vulnerabilities, but you'd move heaven and earth to help others."

I wanted so much to trust Jack about Allison, but right then I found doing so difficult. We lowered our hands and resumed our walk, fingers still laced. I did my best to keep my hand from shaking within his grasp, so my anxiety coiled around my heart in exchange.

Allison was waiting near the entrance to Starbucks, close to the Eleventh Avenue doors. When Jack said hello to her, she swiveled in our direction.

"Hi." She looked over each of us, greeting us both with one word. Her tone was as unreadable as her expression. If she noticed our public display of affection, her face gave nothing away.

"Feeling refreshed?" he asked as we paused to stand beside her.

"You were right. I needed the break," she said. "Thanks for putting your foot down on that one."

"Is your room nice?" I ventured, nervously.

Allison nodded and swallowed before answering. "Yes. Thanks for asking."

I turned to Jack. "Do you have the valet ticket? I'll go ask for the car so you two can talk."

Jack nodded and handed it to me, although he leveled me with a somber stare. I clutched the ticket and retreated outside before he could think of a reason to stop me. My respite was brief, but long enough for me to figure out how to survive the next few minutes. The two of them joined me right when the car pulled up to the curb. As the valet emerged from the vehicle, I announced my intention.

"I'll drive us there."

I ducked into the driver's seat, sheepish. I'd chosen to sit behind the wheel because I didn't want Jack to. If he'd opted to do so, it would have forced Allison and me to decide who would sit next to him and who would take the back seat.

Allison chose to sit behind me. Jack walked around the back of the car and settled into the front passenger seat. From her place in the back, Allison could see Jack perfectly. I pulled out into traffic and began navigating through the streets of downtown, making our way toward the West Hills along Broadway.

"Kathleen? I want to thank you for your help this morning when I arrived. My condition took us both by surprise, but I appreciate you not letting me fall on the floor in front of Heide."

I believed Allison was sincere, but I couldn't help but wonder if she'd chosen to say this in the car so she didn't have to make eye contact with me.

"You're welcome. I'm glad you're feeling better now."

Jack turned in his seat, and even with my periphery vision, I saw him offer Allison a grin. There wasn't much conversation between the three of us during our short drive. As we made our way up the steep hill to OHSU, we all prepared ourselves for the evening ahead. My day in particular had been long with several unanticipated twists and turns. I had left Heide's side that morning and was eager to sit with her again.

As we approached her room, Terry intercepted us in the corridor with a smile on her face. "I was just heading back to the desk to call you both."

"What is it?" Jack asked, attempting to restrain his growing excitement, but Terry's optimism was palpable.

"Heide is showing signs of waking up. I'm glad you're all here now. It will be good for her family to be with her when she does."

Allison dashed into Heide's room without another word, and Jack reached behind him to take my hand as we followed her. Terry was right behind us.

"It may take a little bit," she added, preparing us, "but if you can stay in the room until Heide comes around, it should help her remain calm."

Jack took his usual place on the right side of the bed, while Allison stood across from him on the left. I watched with quiet anticipation as Heide stretched her legs. The movement was small and slow, but compared to her complete inactivity since the accident it was significant to us. Jack and Allison reached out to their daughter, offering soft words of encouragement while I retreated to take a seat on the window bench. I wanted to respect the Evans family unit during this critical point in time.

As predicted, Heide woke up within the hour. She was unable to speak because of the ventilator, and Terry and her parents explained this to her several times, offering her guidance and advice on how to relax in spite of the confusing situation.

After a few minutes, Jack looked at me. "She's groggy and mouthing words. It took me a few tries before I realized she's asking for you."

At this, I stood up and made my way over to Jack's side. Heide's blue eyes were partially open and languidly looking between her parents.

"Hello, Heide," I greeted her as I placed a hand on her knee. "It's Kathleen."

She tried to open her eyes wider but was having difficulty. Between the pain medication and the fluorescent lighting above her head, I sympathized with her inability to focus. After several more attempts, she made eye contact with me before groggily pointing toward her mother. Jack and Allison didn't understand what Heide was communicating, but I did. I peered over at Allison, who was smiling but also perplexed.

"Heide and I were talking in her room a few weeks ago," I explained. "She asked me if you and I would be friends."

Allison looked down at her daughter and bit her lip in an effort to hold back tears.

I turned back to Heide in order to offer Allison time to process this. "Yes, your mom and I met this morning, and now the four of us are all together."

Jack's hand slid back into mine, and this time I offered no resistance.

chapter
Thirty-Six

"GOOD EVENING, everyone," Dr. Avery announced with a smile as he walked into the room. Terry followed close behind. "I decided not to wait until the morning to examine your daughter."

"By all means," Jack replied.

We all stepped away from Heide's bed to give the medical team an opportunity to assess her current condition. It was close to eleven o'clock, and the doctor's impromptu late hour visit gave the three of us an opportunity to discuss our plans for the rest of the night.

"I'm going to stay here with Heide," Allison announced. "I don't want her awake and alone."

Jack nodded and added, "I'm staying, too."

I was compelled to give the family their space and pointed in the direction of the cushioned window seat and the reclining rocker that had been added to the room after my previous departure. "You'll both have comfortable places to rest, so I'll call a cab in a few minutes and go back to the hotel."

"It's almost midnight," Allison remarked. "I don't like the idea of you taking a cab alone so late at night."

I was surprised by her insistence and addressed her with a gentle voice, "I'll be fine. I know this city well. I'm not concerned."

Allison directed her attention to Jack. "You should drive Kathleen back to the hotel, and then you can come back."

He looked at me. "I'd prefer to drive you," he coaxed. "It will give me a chance to grab a few things for the night."

Jack glanced back at Allison. "If you give me your room key, I can bring you some things, too."

"That'd be perfect." Allison rattled off a small list of items that Jack had no trouble committing to memory.

Dr. Avery finished his examination of Heide and regarded us all with a smile. "She's making good progress. Setbacks can and do occur in trauma cases like hers, but I'm hopeful she's through the worst of it now."

"That's wonderful to hear. Thank you so much," Allison answered. She walked back over to her daughter and grasped her small hand. I watched their fingers with rapt attention and was pleased when I saw Heide squeeze her mother's hand back. Every little movement Heide made was a true delight to behold.

"Are you ready now?" Jack asked.

"Yes. Let's go."

As the elevator doors closed shut on the Sentinel's main lobby, Jack pressed the buttons for two different floors.

"I'm going to stop by Allison's room first. I'll meet you back at the suite."

"Sure." The plan made sense, but I couldn't stop the nagging thought that Jack didn't want me in Allison's hotel room. I attempted to shake the negativity away as though it were a nagging insect.

We waved to each other when he exited a few moments later, and I continued the journey to our room in tortured silence. My back and shoulders ached, a combination of both stress and fatigue. My usual refuge for pain management was a steaming hot shower, but instead I found myself drawn out onto the terrace and its rectangular, stone tiled fire pit.

I turned on the flames and went back inside to change into the one nightgown I'd brought with me. It was a satin, mint-green ankle-length garment. Something I'd picked up on a previous business trip. I seldom wore it, opting to keep it packed in a suitcase at all times. The gown's lace was minimal and what little there was clung to my bustline. It was also the perfect choice for the summer with its thin spaghetti straps. Once changed, I brushed out my hair and returned to the balcony.

The city air was warm and buzzed with late night weekend activity. I stretched out along the wicker sofa on the terrace and rolled onto my side, exposing my full back to the welcome heat of the fire. I relaxed, considered the possibility of sleeping in this spot for the next little while, and I drifted into a meditative state.

Jack returned to our room several minutes later. I listened as he gathered things for his night at OHSU, but I made no effort to rouse from my spot outside. The terrace door was open and wasn't surprised when he stepped out to join me. He didn't speak at first, probably wondering if I was asleep.

"I'm awake," I murmured without budging.

Jack's gentle footsteps approached me and a few seconds later the delicate touch of his fingers rested on my shoulder. He proceeded to trace the outline of the satin covering my body. His touch glided down the side that was available to his examination, next to my breast, down and back up the curve of my waistline before coming to rest at the top of my hip.

"I'll miss you tonight," he whispered, "but I'm glad you understand why I have to go."

I opened my eyes and rolled over to face him. I smiled when our gazes met and pulled myself up to a sitting position.

"Sit with me for a minute."

As soon as he was settled on the sofa, I faced him and reclined once again with my head on his lap. "I won't keep you. I know you're anxious to get back to Heide."

Jack ran his hand through my hair with soft deliberation. "I love your hair like this. It was the first thing I noticed about you. You should always keep it long."

"For you, I will."

He smiled broadly at this. Between this simple moment of happiness and his impending departure, I was overtaken by impulse

"I want to touch you," I confessed. "May I?"

His hand continued to sweep through my hair, massaging my scalp undeterred.

"What did you have in mind?" His voice was husky. Excited.

"We can stay right here. Like this." I skimmed the waistband of the athletic pants he'd changed into with my finger.

Easy access.

Jack broke eye contact with me and turned his head to examine the cityscape beyond our balcony.

I watched his handsome profile with interest as I tried to read his thoughts. "No one is watching us," I offered, hoping to convince him.

I rose up and waited until his eyes met mine. "Only if you're sure."

I placed my hands on his waist and tucked my fingers underneath the hem of his pants. I pulled them down as he briefly raised his hips and backside away from the cushions of the sofa. By the time we repositioned ourselves, he was fully aroused.

I ran my hand along the length of him, delighting in my close proximity. His breaths grew shallow as the anticipation blossomed between us.

"I've only had one taste of you," I said. "And I want so much more."

I leaned forward and ran my tongue around the tip of him. Jack's fingers dug into the wicker as his head fell back. I smiled with pride before closing my lips around the area I had just licked. I sucked gently and enjoyed the slow introduction to a new experience for us. I pulled back, withdrawing all but the tip before pushing back down on him. I did this several times, taking a little more of his skin into my mouth with each descent.

Jack's hands found my hair once more and swept it all away from my face. I opened my eyes and was delighted to see he was watching me with unblinking intensity. Assured of his undivided attention, I went back to pleasing him. I savored the opportunity to explore Jack intimately and took my time. Whenever he moaned with desire, I did the same. Listening to Jack as he grew closer and closer to his climax was ecstasy.

After a short while, Jack dropped his hands on my shoulders. "Let me take you to our bed. You need something, too."

I pulled back just enough to say, "If I let you, it will take me longer to let you go."

"No. It … it really won't," he breathed. His disclosure provided me with infinite joy, and I closed my mouth back over him before he could dislodge us from our current position.

"Kathleen," he panted.

I raised an arm and determinedly placed my palm against his chest, pushing him back against the cushions of the sofa. I pulled back again to add, "I want this more than anything else. Relax. Enjoy."

Jack offered no objection. Underneath me, he began to cooperate with my movements and within several heated moments, he was lost in desire. His hips moved in perfect synch with my own body. As his orgasm drew near, my pace became more frenzied. All the while, Jack's hands in my hair remained loving and delicate.

His increasing sighs, his tightened muscles and his tender hands were magical elements of an erotic chorus. All combined, I was thoroughly satisfied and when his release overtook him, I received it with utter joy. I only withdrew from him when my continued touch became too sensitive for him to endure.

He was still attempting to catch his breath when I rose from his lap, drew him close and whispered my appreciation and assurances in his ear. Once he came back to his senses, I sat back and watched as he clothed his body. Together, we stood up from the sofa and he pulled me into his strong arms.

My eyes closed within his embrace and I clung to him. Nights away from Jack Evans were becoming increasingly painful, but I was anxious for him to return to Heide's bedside.

"I love you," he said, pulling me to him even closer.

"I love you so much." I bit my lip to keep my tears hidden.

He continued to hold me, and I realized he wasn't going to let me go until I was ready. I was far from ready, but I patted his back to signal the end of our evening together. He withdrew, but took me by the hand and led me inside the suite and back to our bed. Jack pulled back the duvet and looked over his shoulder to meet my gaze.

"Come, lie down."

I did as requested, and he pulled the covers back over me before turning down the lights and the fire outside.

Before he left for the night, Jack sat down on the edge of the bed next to me.

He stroked my face as he said good night. He leaned down and ran his nose along my cheek before moving his lips next to my ear. "Get a hold of me in the morning as soon as you're awake. I want to shower with you."

"I will."

Jack kissed me on the forehead. Then he rose from the mattress and returned to the hospital.

chapter

Thirty-Seven

"**GOOD MORNING.**" My text to Jack was a simple greeting often used with so many it was automatic. For once, however, I understood a deeper meaning behind those two words. After everything I'd watched Jack and Allison go through, it was a relief to wake up knowing that Heide was conscious.

I sent him my message that Sunday morning, and then I prepared an impromptu breakfast as I waited for his response. He did not keep me waiting for long. I was standing at the foot of the bed, still dressed in my nightgown when Jack entered our suite. He made his way right into my arms, almost as though we hadn't held one another in days.

"Good morning," he whispered, our foreheads touching.

"How's Heide? How did things go last night?"

"She's doing well. She dozes on and off, but she always knows we're there."

I caressed Jack's cheek, noting his tired eyes. "Did you sleep at all?"

"Not much, but Allison and I decided to split the day. I'll rest here for a couple of hours and then she'll come back to the hotel for the afternoon. We don't want Heide left alone for the time being."

"That makes sense. Is there something I can do to help?"

Jack's eyes lit up with determination. "You can help me now."

"How so?"

"First, we'll help each other from these clothes so I can return your favor from last night. Then we'll help each other in the shower."

Jack eagerly tugged at the material of my satin gown while I raised my arms in compliance. Within a heartbeat I was standing naked before Jack and assisting him with his clothes. As I undressed him, I wondered about his uncharacteristic impatience.

It had been a long weekend filled with little sleep, much fear and an onslaught of obstacles to manage. The only moments of peace for Jack had revolved around the few private ones we'd shared since arriving in Portland. Although I was perplexed over his insistence, I wasn't about to deny the man I loved his much-needed dose of serenity.

We tumbled onto the bed as soon as we were both naked, and Jack brought me to orgasm with his mouth twice before sauntering into the bathroom to turn on the water.

Show off.

During our shower we shared passionate kisses, all the while massaging one another's tired muscles. Although we'd shared some loving encounters since arriving in Portland, we hadn't succumbed to our truest urges since the afternoon in my living room more than two weeks before. We couldn't stand the separation any longer, so we devoured each other.

Jack pressed my back against the shower wall. The cool tile on my skin kept me from overheating as steam drifted all around us. He curled his fingers around mine and pinned my arms above my head. Our wet bodies pressed tightly together, my heavy breasts flattening against his chest and his thighs straining against mine.

Jack crashed his mouth into mine, his tongue caressing my own in rapturous frenzy. We remained in this pose, kissing and rubbing against each other until my arms began to tremble underneath Jack's restraining hold.

He released my arms and I wrapped them around his waist. I wasn't ready to let him pull away. Our kisses continued, but slowed to a luxurious pace. Jack brought a firm hand up to my neck, and I dropped my fingers to Jack's strong backside and squeezed. He pulled back with a smile, and I was relieved to see that the more intense edges of his thirst were quenched.

"I'd let you do this to me all day, but you need to rest," I reminded him.

Jack maintained his hold on me and gave me a final kiss while I shut off the water. I stepped from the shower and grabbed a towel. When he followed, I began to dry him off.

"Are you hungry?" I asked. "I have some oranges."

"Perfect."

"I could run downstairs and get you something from Starbucks."

Jack shook his head. "Later. I need you. I want to make the most of our time."

I began to wrap Jack's towel around his waist, but he stopped my efforts with a touch of his hand. Instead, he pulled the linen away from his body and dropped it to the floor. He then reached for another clean towel and wiped away the beads of water from my own skin.

"No clothes for now," he requested as he completed the task at hand.

"So I guess breakfast on the terrace is out of the question," I teased.

"For today."

After he dropped the second towel to the floor, I left the bathroom to retrieve a small bowl of orange slices from the mini fridge. When I turned back to the bed, Jack had stretched out across the mattress, and I paused to admire his form.

Jack was an attractive man but there was something particularly sexy about him in that moment. Perhaps it was the contrast of his olive complexion against the bright white of the comforter. With the morning sun streaming into the room, Jack's unclothed body was striking to me in a whole new way.

He was the man of my fantasies come to life. He was long, lean and firm with just the perfect amount of hair over his chest. Even though he'd been blessed with natural good looks, he took care of himself, and by the subtle definition of his muscles, it appeared as if he always had.

He caught me watching him, and although he smiled, he was the one to drop his gaze first. He was suddenly preoccupied with the bedding, and this unpretentious reaction elevated his sex appeal.

"You really are gorgeous," I said.

"Are you sure?" he asked with surprising timidity, his eyes still riveted to the sheets.

"What do you mean?"

He shrugged and I knelt on the bed next to him. I took an orange slice from the bowl and brought it to his mouth. He allowed me to feed him, establishing eye contact with me in the process.

"I've never been more sure of anything, Jack."

I kissed him and savored the sweetness that lingered on my lips after.

"I'm not exactly young anymore," he murmured while looking at my shoulder.

Normally Jack was the one offering me assurance. I was unaccustomed to his vulnerabilities and wondered once again what was going on in his mind this morning. It seemed the most logical explanation was the fatigue wearing on his emotions.

"You're incredible," I replied. "In every way. The stars have aligned for us. I believe this was meant to be our time and, aside from Heide's accident, I've never been happier."

"Thank you," he whispered.

"When do you think we should go back to the hospital?" I asked, opting to spare him from more ogling.

A muscle twitched in Jack's jawline. It was yet another uncharacteristic reaction, but his face remained otherwise impassive. "We should be there around noon. Allison hasn't had much rest since this whole thing began. She's stubborn and digging in her heels. I know better than to talk her out of things when she's this tired, but I have to convince her to sleep at the hotel tonight. It won't be easy."

"Maybe you should remind her of the night Heide was born. It's a marathon, not a sprint."

"I'll try." Jack's short answer made me wonder if I was treading into unwelcome territory. I glanced at the clock as I fed him another orange slice.

"We have a good hour of downtime. I'll help you figure out a plan for Allison when we leave the room. Until then, let's just enjoy ourselves."

Jack grabbed the bowl of fruit and rolled over to place it on his bedside table. I remained on my knees and when he rolled back to me, he closed the distance and kissed my breast.

"We don't have much time," he mumbled as he navigated from one side of my chest to the other. "We better get started."

We arrived at the hospital on time, and I brought my gift for Heide. When we entered her room, Allison was standing at her daughter's bedside, holding her hand. She looked up and a visibly hostile frown overtook her features.

Jack ignored his ex-wife and spoke to Heide. "Hello, beautiful. Were you able to sleep for a little while?"

"She woke up an hour ago," Allison retorted without looking in his direction.

"Why don't you gather up your things?" he suggested in a cool tone without looking away from his daughter. "Get ready to go back to the hotel."

"Don't be so anxious to get rid of me," she huffed.

I remained frozen to the spot where Allison's glare had landed on me. I was stunned by her change in demeanor from the evening before and confused by Jack's sudden aloofness upon seeing her. I had expected both of their moods to be lighter now that Heide was awake, but there was no indication of that. Heide's parents were both exhausted. Their strain rose rapidly to the surface, and they both needed sufficient time to rest.

"What is that?" Allison nodded to the gift bag I held. She sounded testy.

"A present for Heide. I wanted her to have it now that she's awake."

Allison rolled her eyes without attempting to disguise her annoyance. "It's nice you had time to do a little shopping."

I was speechless and struggled to find an appropriate response, but it was Jack's reaction that stupefied me.

"Stop." It was the same word, spoken in the same tone that Jack had used when Robert had become so upset at Widgi Creek. Jack was furious with Allison, but it was the ease in which he expressed this in front of Heide that brought my hackles up.

Allison glared at Jack in silent, seething anger, and he matched her scowl. It bothered me that they were doing so within their daughter's line of sight.

"Don't start again," he warned her in a low voice. His entire body was tense. "We've already dealt with this."

Jack's statement confirmed everything I suspected. Jack and Allison had argued sometime during the night and things had not yet been resolved between them. I understood enough from my own family dynamics to theorize that their conflict had something to do with me. Until Jack was willing to share the details, anything I did or said would fuel the anger and resentment between them.

The three of us turned at the sound of a light knock on the door behind me and discovered Robert standing in the open doorway.

Allison set Heide's hand back down on the bed and turned away to collect her personal items.

"Hi, Dad," I said, mostly to inform Allison who he was. Whether she would remember my father was also Jack's boss was another matter.

"Allison," Jack called across the small room. He was struggling to find a calm demeanor. "You remember Robert Brighton? He owns the firm."

I swallowed as Allison took in a breath before flashing my father a polite smile.

"Yes, of course," she said. "It's good to see you again. Jack explained to me all the wonderful things you are doing to support Heide's recovery. It's amazing of you. Thank you so much."

Robert strolled into the room to shake Allison's hand while Jack joined the duo to form a conversational circle. I stepped aside and approached Heide.

Her eyes were open and her attention was more focused than when I had last seen her. She looked at me and lifted her hand, reaching in my direction. I took her small fingers in mine and grinned down at her.

"Good morning, Heide. It's good to see you awake."

She squeezed my fingers in return.

I lifted my gift bag up so she could see it. "I brought you a present. Do you want to see it?"

Although her face was pale, she nodded. I set the bag down on the bed and reached inside. When I pulled out the Minecraft Zombie Plush, I watched as happiness filled her eyes. Heide reached for the stuffed creature, and I placed it in the crook of her arm.

"Did I pick out a good one for you?"

Heide nodded, the smallest hint of a smile trying to break through her physical discomfort.

I reached into the gift bag once more, this time retrieving a replacement pair of Minecraft Creeper socks. I was nervous about this offering, uncertain if they might trigger a bad memory for her. My fears, however, were put to rest. Heide raised a foot from the covers, inviting me to put the new apparel to immediate use.

I moved down the length of the bed and dressed Heide's feet with the new socks. As I did so, I risked a glance at the small group assembled nearby. Allison was watching me attend to her daughter.

"I'm going to head back downtown and get some rest," Allison announced. "It's been a long few days, and I think it's catching up to me."

"I'd be happy to give you a lift," Robert offered. "I'm on my way out of town, so it's no trouble."

"That's kind of you, Mr. Brighton, but I've already called a cab. I should probably get downstairs to see if it's arrived."

Confusion flashed over Jack's already strained features, and I wondered if Allison's declaration about the taxi was true. She detached herself from the small talk with Jack and Robert and finished collecting her things.

She then approached Heide's bedside and commented about her new gifts before kissing her daughter on the cheek.

"Dad and Kathleen are going to sit with you for a while, and I'm going to get something to eat and rest up. But if you need me for anything just have Dad call me, okay?"

Heide nodded.

"You're doing so well. Pretty soon we're going to get that tube removed, and you'll be talking up a storm again."

Heide offered a thumbs-up to her mother, and all the adults gathered in the room chuckled in relief.

"At least allow me to walk you downstairs," Robert offered.

"Sure," Allison agreed. "That would be nice."

Robert angled his body in my direction. "Is there anything you need me to check on when I get back home?"

"Maybe just call Don Taylor and thank him for the meeting. I didn't get a chance to brief you on it yet, but I'll put something down in an e-mail."

"Don't worry about it. I'll explain to Don what's happened and he can catch me up." My father turned to Jack. "You always do a good job of keeping me up to speed on your work, so I'll take it over from here. You just focus on your daughter."

Jack nodded. "Will do."

Allison made her way to the doorway and waved to us, but nothing more. I opted to keep quiet while Jack waved back. I wanted to pull him aside and ask about what had happened during the night, but before I could, Jack had returned to Heide, offering his full attention.

Instead, I took a seat nearby. I attempted to corral my mounting concerns and failed miserably.

chapter Thirty-Eight

THE SUMMER drifted by and over the weeks Heide's condition improved. Each achievement in her recovery was celebrated, but her progress was slow. Two weeks passed before the ventilator was removed, and it took several more for the gaping hole in her neck to seal itself. Her ability to endure simple physical tasks proved to be a consistent challenge. With a significant portion of one lung removed, Heide was easily fatigued and often frustrated.

As a result, tensions between her parents and me continued to rise. It was difficult for Allison to accept me into her intimate circle, and she was dealing with the stress far away from her comfort zone in Maryland. She was often tired, and continued to treat her ex-husband with contempt. One afternoon, after I voiced my concerns to Jack, he was forced to admit what had Allison so upset.

"She was mad because my breaks away from Heide were taking longer than expected."

"I don't understand?"

"She confronted me when I returned to the hospital. After our encounter on the terrace."

"How so?"

"It occurred to her that we were having sex away from the hospital. It pissed her off."

"Why? Is she jealous? Does she want you back?"

"Not even close, but that's probably because I'm just a selfish prick of a father."

Adrift on these undulating waves of pressure, the three of us relocated to my father's apartment in the Pearl District. Out of respect for Allison's feelings, Jack and I had settled into separate bedrooms, and we stopped having sex. It was an awkward situation for all of us, and we navigated the unfamiliar terrain with caution.

Interactions between Allison and I were limited and strained. Jack filtered the majority of her communications with me. Based on what little he'd shared with me, Allison respected everything my family was doing on Heide's behalf, but he suspected she felt guilty for not being there when Heide's accident occurred.

As the day for Heide's discharge from the hospital grew closer, I began to make plans for the next phase of our journey. She was going to need a bedroom, and I needed to make other living arrangements. My inclination was to return to Bend, but Jack pleaded with me to stay in Portland. Logically, I believed this to be a bad idea, but I was too softhearted to turn him down. When Dr. Avery announced that Heide would be leaving the hospital in mid-August, I reserved a suite at the Sentinel.

On the morning of her discharge, I remained behind at the apartment while Jack and Allison went to the hospital to bring their daughter home. I packed up most of my things, cleaned up the space and ordered some groceries for delivery, hoping it would ease the day for all. I had just finished putting away all the items from the store when the family arrived.

Jack was carrying his daughter in his arms. Her head rested in its usual place in the crook of his neck, and she cradled her Minecraft Zombie against her chest. Allison went straight to Heide's bedroom and began organizing the space.

I couldn't resist. I walked up to Jack and Heide and hugged them both in gratitude and love.

"I'm so happy to see you here," I said as I ran my fingers through her golden blond hair.

"I'm so happy to be out of that place," she said without lifting her head from her father.

Jack held the three of us together for several heartbeats longer than necessary, and I basked in the extraordinary moment. Two months earlier, Jack and I had arrived in Portland unsure if he would ever hold his daughter again. He wasn't bringing her home to Bend yet, but it was easy to see he was enjoying his happiest moment since the night Heide regained consciousness.

"Are you hungry?" he asked her.

"I want pizza."

"I'll make you one," he said before setting her down on the floor. "Why don't you sit on the couch and watch some TV?"

"Okay," she answered as she reached out for my hand. "Come on, Kathleen. Let's see if SpongeBob is on."

We walked to the sofa, and I handed her the remote control. I instructed her on how to find her favorite channels, and together we located her show.

"This is a cool place," Heide said, glancing around the living room. "Mom says this belongs to you? How come we've never been here before?"

"This is my father's apartment. He stays here when he works in Portland."

"Oh." Her voice was quiet.

I studied Heide's face and ascertained that she was tired. "Why don't you stretch out on the couch and rest for a few minutes? Do you want some lemonade?"

"Okay."

"I'll be right back."

When I rounded the corner to the kitchen, Jack surprised me with a firm but quick kiss on the lips. His tongue encircled mine briefly before he pulled away. Deprived of his touch for so long, my body's primal reaction was instantaneous. Nevertheless, I wagged a finger at him in mock anger and shook my head, trying to suppress a laugh while opening the refrigerator. He returned to his culinary duties.

"When are you heading over to the hotel?" he asked after I retrieved the lemonade and opened the cupboard to reach for a small glass.

"After lunch. Heide seems tired already, so I want to make sure she can relax this afternoon."

Jack put the finishing touches on Heide's homemade pepperoni pizza and placed it in the oven.

"I'm going to go talk to Allison while that's cooking. Can you help me keep an eye on it?"

"Sure."

Jack disappeared into Heide's new bedroom while I placed a bendy straw in her glass and delivered her drink. Heide took a couple of sips as she watched Patrick Star annoy Squidward Tentacles.

"Patrick isn't very bright," I commented.

"Nope. Sometimes I'm not very bright either." Heide's hand drifted up to the healing wound in the center of her throat, a gesture that concerned me.

"Do you remember the accident?" I'd been curious about the answer for weeks.

"No. I just woke up in the hospital. It's weird. I don't know why I did that."

"We all do things we wonder about later."

"Even when you're already a grown-up?"

"Definitely."

"Sometimes I feel smarter than adults."

I grinned. "That's because you are."

Behind a closed bedroom door, the sound of Allison's angry voice reached the living room. I grasped the remote control, and I turned up the volume of Heide's cartoon before standing up.

"I'm going to check on your pizza," I said louder than usual. It was my subtle way of reminding Heide's parents that their voices could be overheard. It failed.

I walked into the kitchen and peeked in the stove, knowing that the pizza would not yet be finished. As I returned to the living room, Allison's voice rose up once again.

"Why weren't you watching Heide more closely, Jack? Do you want to know my theory? I think your new girlfriend is the reason why!"

I flinched at Allison's harsh comment. It wasn't rational, but she was cracking under the stress of the entire situation. Allison needed to vent somehow and my relationship with Jack was an easy target.

"Is it so terrible that I want to spend an evening with her?" Jack responded. His words rattled me more than Allison's had.

"Yes, Jack. Yes, it's terrible! Your daughter hasn't been out of the hospital for an hour before you've decided to run off for a celebratory lay!"

Perturbed and embarrassed, I crossed my arms and stepped into the living room just far enough to check on Heide. She was no longer paying attention to her cartoon. Instead, she was sitting up on the couch, staring toward the sound of her mother and father's argument.

"You have a lot of fucking nerve, Allison! You know that?"

"What do you mean by that?" she demanded.

"You left us! You ran back to Baltimore without any worry for her! You've been gone for close to a year, and you'll go back the first chance you get! I'm talking about a few hours off for a breather! God dammit, you owe me this! You've been on a breather for months!"

I marched over to the living room sofa with the intention of distracting us both from eavesdropping. I took my seat next to Heide and reached for the remote control once again.

"Why are they so upset with each other?"

"They're both tired. Adults get cranky when they worry too much about things."

"They're yelling because they're worried about me?"

"They're tired because they've been worried about you, but they're yelling because of other reasons."

Heide's hand returned to the scar tissue on her throat and squeezed her wound.

I took her hand in mine. "You have to remember that your neck is still healing. You shouldn't touch it with your bare hands for the time being."

"Sorry."

I patted her hand. "Don't be sorry, Heide."

Much to our mutual dismay, Jack and Allison's loud exchange continued for several minutes. It was the first time I'd experienced this volatile side of Jack's personality, and I didn't like what I was hearing. My own anger rose.

Jack hadn't spoken to me about an evening out prior to bringing it up with Allison. I would have discouraged him from following through on the idea and considered he hadn't mentioned it to me because he already knew I would resist.

The argument disintegrated into a screaming match. I struggled with choosing the best option to ease the situation for Heide.

"You know what, Jack? Just take your girlfriend and all her things and leave right now! Leave and go downtown and let her suck your cock for as long you need her to!" Allison's rage was palpable.

Heide may not have understood what her mother's words meant, but regardless she dropped her chin to her chest and sobbed. I carefully took her small face in my hands before kissing her on the head.

"I'm going to go stop this now," I explained. "But I'm going to have to raise my voice, too. Just hold still for a minute."

She nodded.

Then I stormed my way into their fight. I shoved the bedroom door hard enough so that it swung wide and bounced back off the wall.

"Stop it! Both of you! Now!"

Jack and Allison were at the foot of the bed in the center of the room. He glared at her, his face red and his eyes blazing. She was glaring right back, their faces so close that one might have guessed they were on the verge of kissing. At my entrance, they both looked at me, startled, but it didn't last long.

Allison narrowed her eyes and opened her mouth, but I cut her off. "If you two want to fight, fine! But do it somewhere where your daughter isn't forced to listen!" Then I whispered fiercely. "You're scaring her!"

Realization flickered across Allison's face. She glanced over my shoulder to the hallway beyond with a growing look of worry.

"You need to apologize to Kathleen." Jack's voice was low, but still raging with fury.

Naturally, this comment pissed off Allison, but it also embarrassed me. I quickly closed the door to the bedroom as Allison turned back for her rebuttal but I beat her to it.

"For fuck's sake, Jack!" I yelled. "Don't even try to make this about me. Both of you need to calm down. Go back into the living room and put Heide at ease. She's the important one here. Not me. And not either of you!"

Jack glared at me as he jabbed a finger toward Allison, his nostrils flaring. "I won't have anyone speak about you like that! It's despicable!"

"I really don't give a shit, Jack!" I walked to the door and grabbed the knob before looking over my shoulder. "No one is the villain here. Remember that."

I opened the door and marched out, satisfied that I had derailed their fight. The entire incident had dredged up long-suppressed emotions in me. I returned to Heide's side. It took every ounce of my self-control to sit with Heide and present a tranquil face. I held her hand while we waited to see what happened next.

The bedroom door clicked closed once more. After a minute or two of agonized silence, Allison and Jack walked into the living room together. Their ire had deflated and a tense truce hung in the air.

Allison sheepishly focused her attention on Heide, who let her guard down upon seeing her parents and began another round of fatigue-induced crying. I abandoned my seat on the sofa and allowed her mother to comfort her.

I retreated to the kitchen and pulled Heide's pizza from the oven. The edges of the crust had begun to darken but her lunch was salvageable. I concentrated on slicing the pizza with forceful yet shaky hands.

When I stepped back into the living room, carrying Heide's lunch on a plate, Jack was standing behind the sofa. He watched Heide intently but glanced at me. This only angered me more. I looked away from Jack and leaned against the wall for support, disappointed with his lack of common sense.

I wanted nothing more than to extricate myself from this place but refused to commit to the idea until Heide calmed down. I also needed the assurance that Jack and Allison were composed. I caught Jack watching me a second time. Annoyed, I pointed Jack in the direction of his daughter with an angry gesture of my hand.

He obeyed my command, but there was a certain amount of uneasiness in his posture. I knew him well enough by now to understand what he was thinking. I'd told Jack more than once I would not be the cause of trouble with his ex-wife and his daughter. Now, that was precisely what had happened.

I was mortified. I was anxious. But most of all, I was pissed off Jack was splitting his attention between his daughter and me. I couldn't take that.

I straightened up from the wall. "Heide? I'm going to go now. I'll see you later," I said, selecting words to emphasize my point to the girl's parents.

"Will you come back tomorrow?" she asked, still scared and uncertain.

Seeing this brave girl so upset tore my heart. "I'm planning to."

Heide lifted her arms for a hug, and Allison respected this, withdrawing from the couch with no fuss. I walked over to the sofa and set Heide's lunch on the coffee table before leaning in to hug her. When the tight squeeze of her arms pulled on my neck, I almost lost my nerve to walk away.

I whispered in her ear. "They're done being angry now. You'll be fine."

She nodded.

I knew Jack was watching the two of us, but I refused to meet his stare. When I pulled back, I gave her a kiss on the cheek along with a smile. Then I grabbed my suitcase from the entryway and left without speaking another word or sparing another glance at Jack or Allison.

chapter

Thirty-Nine

I CHECKED into the Sentinel and left word at the front desk that I was not to be disturbed. I abandoned my suitcase by the closet door and dropped into a wingback chair to indulge in a crying session of my own. Several minutes later, I wandered into the bathroom and splashed cool water on my face.

My phone pinged from inside my purse and I braced myself. It was a single text message from Jack. Too upset to open it, I scrolled through my contacts until I located Theresa Mayfair. I placed my free hand on my hip and pressed the green button to call her. She was as dependable as ever, answering within a couple of rings.

"Kathleen? What's happened?"

I made a miserable attempt at acting casual. "Why do you assume something has happened?"

"Dear," she chided, "do you ever call me otherwise?"

I covered my eyes with my hand and let another round of tears loose. "I'm sorry."

"Don't apologize. Where are you?"

I sniffled before answering her. "I'm at the Sentinel."

"Do you want me to come over there?"

"No. I just need to talk."

"I'm sorry you're so upset. I'd heard rumors that things between you and your father were improving."

"This isn't about him. For once."

"Well, then. We really do need to talk."

I told Theresa everything about my relationship with Jack. I told her because, outside of Robert, I hadn't spoken to anyone about falling in love. I spoke about Heide's accident and explained how I'd struggled to manage our relationship over the complicated summer. I also revealed everything about the blowup earlier in the day. Theresa listened without interruption, and as I processed my thoughts and described them, I realized something significant.

I'd become a defender of Heide just as Theresa had been a defender of me. All my life, Theresa had stood between my father's rages and me. It was difficult to accept that I'd had to intervene on Heide's behalf with her own father, a man I thought was the total opposite of Robert. The realization that even a devoted father like Jack could lose control in front of his daughter was more than I could bear.

"I need your advice," I said. "I need to figure out what to do next."

"Do you want to remain in Portland? Or do you want to go back to Bend?"

"Neither," I grumbled.

"Either way you need to speak with Jack."

I was paralyzed by the prospect—a terrified child all over again.

"Kathleen? Are you there?"

"Yes."

"You've come too far with this man and his daughter. You have to face this problem with him. You cannot run away from it."

I shook my head. I thought I knew who Jack was, but what I'd witnessed that afternoon was foreign and familiar all at once. "Heide still has a long road ahead of her. What happened today, it could just keep on happening and none of it will be beneficial to her. Everything is becoming thorny."

"I've known you all your life, Kathleen. I don't need to point out what you've endured from a young age. I understand better than most your strong desire to manage your own life and keep things simple. You've been surprised and disappointed today so the situation may feel complex to you, but in truth, it's simple. You either love this man and you want to figure this out with him. Or you don't."

"I do love him, but I can't stand the thought of subjecting Heide to another ugly incident like this afternoon. I won't stand for it, especially when I'm the source of struggle. I don't know if I'm strong enough to handle that. I just don't know what to do."

"Today? You don't do anything. Rest as much as possible this evening, and let everyone's emotions cool down. You'll make your decision tomorrow, and then you'll know what to do."

"I guess so," I mumbled.

"I wish I could give you the perfect answer, Kathleen. But in this case, I'm afraid you're going to have to figure it out with Jack."

"I suppose you're right."

"Of course I am. That's why you called me. I know you don't rest easily, but please try. Things will be better tomorrow."

Consumed by worry and despair, sleep was elusive that night. The following morning, after next to no rest, I made my decision.

The Evans family would attend physical therapy in the afternoon. I left my room at the Sentinel and drove back to my father's apartment to gather the remainder of my things while they were away.

I unlocked the apartment door and closed it behind me. I stood in the entryway for a minute and detected no signs of activity. Convinced that I was alone, I proceeded into the living room.

Jack was sitting on the sofa, facing the main hallway in silent expectation. He'd been waiting for my appearance.

I stopped dead in my tracks when we made eye contact. "What are you doing here?" I asked, caught and embarrassed.

His voice dripped with disappointment. "You never answered my text. I anticipated this would be your next move."

His presence had startled me and the realization he chose to remain behind pissed me off. Exhausted and defensive, I fired the first shot. "You should be with Heide."

I stormed down the hall to Heide's bedroom, and Jack hopped up from the sofa to follow me.

"You're better than that, Kathleen," he roared. "Stop playing the long-suffering martyr!"

Jack's words stung and I moved even faster, desperate to put any level of distance between us.

"Don't ignore me," he demanded. "We need to talk about what happened."

I glanced over my shoulder, but didn't halt my progress. "No, we don't! You need to be with Heide!"

I entered the bedroom and made my way to the closet, intent on following through with my plans. Jack paused in the doorway and spread his arms to brace either side of the frame, ensuring I couldn't leave the room without going through him.

"So let me get this straight," he began infuriated, "You have this unrealistic idea of how I should behave, and when I don't meet your expectations, or God forbid act human, you get mad?"

I kept my back to him as I responded. "Just stop it. I didn't come here to fight with you."

"What do you need?" he barked with impatience. "Tell me."

"I need to get my things and go back to Bend."

"Don't do this, Kathleen."

I whipped around to face him, as my tears threatened to spill. "Why did you do this? You're making things worse with Allison!"

"Fuck that!" he yelled, smacking his hand against the doorframe. "She's infuriated with me either way! After everything you and your father have done to accommodate her! I hate the way she treats you. I don't give a shit about her right now!"

I held a shoe in my hand and threw it to the other side of the bedroom in outrage. "You should give a shit, Jack! If not for her, then for your daughter!"

Jack looked over at the discarded ballet flat slumped against the wall. "What in the hell is wrong with you?"

"You just don't get it!" I screamed.

"I really don't," he said in a tremendous effort to maintain his composure. "Please tell me what's wrong."

I paced the bedroom like the trapped woman I was. "Sitting on the sofa with Heide? Listening to the two of you scream at each other? Watching your daughter worry and cry? It was like I was listening to my parents all over again!"

Jack had no response to this, and I paused in the middle of the room. I lowered my head to take a few calming breaths and placed my hands on my hips. "I'm not going to stay here and fuel your fighting. I care too much about Heide to allow my presence to set the two of you off like that again."

Jack's temporary sense of calm evaporated. "You think leaving Portland, leaving me behind is going to end all that?" he yelled. "You go back to your quiet condo in Bend, and poof Jack and Allison will get along just fine when you're gone? That's pretty fucking convenient, Kathleen!"

I lifted my head with deliberate slowness and glared at Jack. "How is any of this convenient?"

Jack was too angry to remain in the doorway and marched right up to me. He was as close to me now as he'd been to Allison when I interrupted them the day before. I held my ground and raised my head up to meet his red-hot stare.

"What is this all about, huh?" he demanded. "It's getting too hard for you so you're just going to run away? Well, why the hell not? You have no obligation here!"

"What about your obligation?" I countered. "I'm nothing but a distraction, Jack!"

"Bullshit!" he bellowed. He stepped back from me and turned away, raising his hands to pull his hair in frustration.

"You think I'm so full of shit?" I pushed. "Then why were you trying to take off with me last night? Why are you standing here screaming at me rather than helping your daughter with her therapy?"

Jack whirled around to face me once again, more enraged than I'd ever seen him. "Don't you dare!" he shouted at me while extending an angry finger toward me. "I am a good father! I am not Robert!"

Jack was rooted to his spot, fuming.

I held out a hand as I tried to clarify my point. "You're right. Your problems with Allison won't dissolve when I leave Portland, but if I go home you'll have more time with her to figure out how you two are going to help your daughter heal. Allison's not going back to Baltimore anytime soon. She's coming back to Bend with you.

330

Whatever kind of family you're going to be now is the time to lay down the foundation."

"Don't lecture me on parenthood, Kathleen! What the fuck do you know about family harmony?"

Jack's furious words struck me like a sucker punch. "Nothing," I whispered.

He paced the bedroom once again. "A negligent father! A suicidal mother! For fuck's sake, you'll never even have children!"

He smacked the bedroom wall for emphasis. When he did, my trust in Jack Evans shattered. The tears began to fall from my eyes before I could register the full impact of his offensive words. If his goal was to hurt me in the worst way imaginable, he'd just succeeded with flying colors.

Jack froze in place. Overcome by heartbreak, I cried in grief and agony as Jack stood nearby. He began mumbling words of sorrow and regret, but I was too lost in my pain to understand anything he was saying. After several minutes, he tentatively approached and reached out to embrace me.

I reached out with both hands, placed them on his chest and I violently pushed him away. "Leave me alone!" I shrieked.

"Listen to me," he begged. "Let me apologize."

"Go to hell!" I yelled.

Jack didn't back away, but he didn't attempt to touch me. I lost track of time and didn't know how many minutes dragged on, but eventually I gained slight control over my emotions.

I stepped around Jack and walked out of the bedroom. I moved toward the entryway, no longer concerned about the items I came to collect. I wobbled several times before reaching the front door because of the poisoned numbness radiating from my heart into my limbs.

"Wait. Please." Jack had followed me once again and this time there was sadness in his voice.

The damage done, I turned to look at him, knowing that my injury was plain to see.

Jack's brown eyes were full of regret and fear. "Just wait," he pleaded in a pained whisper.

I did with stone cold silence.

"Where are you going?"

"I'm going back to Bend. Back to the office. Back to my home."

"Are you leaving me for good?"

"I thought you were different."

"That's not an answer."

"I'll get your keys back from Tracie. I'll look after your house until you get back."

Jack nearly lost his temper again, and began shaking with the effort needed to maintain it. "Don't play mind games with me. I don't have the patience right now."

"I can't decide anything," I blurted with honesty. "Except that I'm leaving Portland. We'll worry about the rest later."

I left my father's apartment, and this time Jack didn't follow me.

chapter Forty

MY ORIGINAL plan had been to get the rest of my things, check out of the Sentinel and drive back to Bend that same day. I yearned to sleep in my own bed. I hadn't been back to my condo in months, and there were no lasting memories of Jack upon my own mattress. I wanted to leave the city, but the emotional toll our fight had taken on me was too severe.

The drive from Robert's apartment back to the hotel only took minutes, but by the time I returned to my suite, I was too overwhelmed to do anything but crawl into the king-sized bed and burrow underneath the covers. I fell into a deep sleep, and when I woke up, evening had set in.

Out of habit, I reached for my phone. There were now two unanswered text messages from Jack, but no missed calls. A new e-mail had arrived in my work account. Without thinking, I opened it. If nothing else, the message might provide a much-needed distraction.

After reading the e-mail, I crawled from the bed and went into the bathroom to freshen up. I opened my neglected suitcase and opted to change my clothes, desperately hoping that a new outfit would shed most of the past two days away from my suffering soul.

I combed my hair and tossed it up into a ponytail before brushing my teeth and deciding it was the best I could do under the circumstances. I wasn't one to indulge in heavy cosmetics and was confident enough in my appearance not to rely on them. I didn't see any point in going through the process for my planned evening indoors.

There was nothing to do and too much time to occupy. I convinced myself to make a trip down the hall to retrieve some ice. Better to go while I had a small amount of energy to do so. Knowing that the hotel pre-bagged their ice, I left the bucket behind, taking only my room key.

I took my time wandering the corridor. Instead of stopping at the ice freezer, I proceeded to the stairway and walked down to the second floor. I strolled around the corridor until I arrived at a corner room. I stood in front of it for several undecided moments, and then I curled my hand into a fist and knocked.

As soon as I drew my hand back, I second guessed my action and turned back to the elevator. I didn't even make it to the next suite down the hallway before the room's occupant opened the door. I forced myself not to look back and kept walking.

"Kathleen?"

I stopped and pivoted. Ryan Murray's head and shoulders were leaned into the hallway.

"Hey," I greeted him weakly.

His forehead wrinkled with confusion. "Were you walking away?"

"Yeah," I confessed, not yet willing to move in one direction or the other. "I didn't think before I came down here. I got your e-mail, but if now's not a good time …"

He smiled and waved a dismissive hand. "I wasn't doing anything but trying to figure out where to go for dinner. Come on back here."

Not knowing what else to do, I obeyed Ryan's request. He leaned against the doorframe, with his hands in his pockets. My legs felt heavy and uncertain but they carried me back to him.

"How fortunate for me that you're in town," he spoke with comforting warmth.

I glanced over my shoulder before turning to look into his friendly blue eyes.

"Would you like to come in?" he asked.

"Sure."

Ryan stepped aside and I entered his room. He closed the door behind me, and I paused in the middle of the room.

I didn't want to sit on Ryan's bed and there was just a lone chair sitting at the work desk. I chose to sit in the chair, figuring he could sit on the mattress. Instead, Ryan opted to lean against the closet door. He didn't want to sit on the bed either.

I tried to locate a coherent thought.

"You look upset," Ryan commented. "Would you like me to crack open the mini bar?"

"No, thank you. I couldn't subject you to that horrendous expense."

"It's not an offer I'd extend to just anyone, but desperate times call for desperate measures." He looked at me with expectation.

I shook my head a final time. "I'm too upset to consider alcohol tonight."

"Oh." Ryan straightened his posture and stepped a little closer.

Remaining quiet, he studied me and then made another suggestion. "You look exhausted. Why don't you lie down for a few minutes?"

I swallowed. "I've been lying down all afternoon. I need to move around."

Ryan approached me and my edginess ticked up. When he reached the desk, he was close enough for me to detect the lingering scent of his aftershave. He reached over my shoulder and collected his room key from the desk. I let out a small sigh of relief as he turned and walked back to his spot near the closet door.

When we made eye contact, he said, "Just give it a few minutes more." He pointed to his perfectly made bed. "You rest and I'll go down to Starbucks and get you some tea. Earl Grey, wasn't it?"

"How do you remember that?"

He grinned. "It's a gift. I'll be back in a few minutes." Ryan left his room without another word.

I could stand or pace around the room while I waited for him to return. I could do anything else but lie down on Ryan's bed. As soon as I was alone, I rose from the chair with rebellious intention—and too much ambition. Overcome with unexpected dizziness, it took an onslaught of lightheadedness to bring me back to my senses. Remembering how I had guided Allison through a similar spell, I stretched out on the bed. The coolness of the sheets against my clammy skin was welcome and refreshing. I closed my eyes and focused on my breathing, willing myself into a state of necessary calm.

Ryan returned with a single cup of tea. He approached my side of the bed and waited in patient silence as I rose to a sitting position. I accepted the proffered tea and attempted to move away from the bed, but he stopped my progress by taking a seat in the chair.

Instead, I resituated myself on the mattress, sitting on the corner just across from him. I sipped my tea and felt myself check out of reality as the warmth of the beverage soothed my jagged nerves. All the while, Ryan sat in the chair, waiting. It was several minutes before he initiated another conversation between us.

"When was the last time you ate something?" he prodded. "You look pale."

I looked down at the lid of my Starbucks cup. "Not recently."

Unsatisfied with my answer, he persisted with gentleness. "What have you had to eat today?"

"Today?" I held my tea aloft in a poor attempt at humor. "Just this."

Ryan frowned.

I glanced nervously toward the door. "I shouldn't be here."

"But you are," he responded. "So let me take you to dinner, and we'll figure out why that is."

I nodded. Ryan had been kind to me, as usual, and I wanted to honor that. I didn't want to linger in his hotel room. "Any place in particular?" I asked.

"I've been saving Departure for you. Remember?" He grinned. "I'll call and see if they're still taking reservations."

It was a Jack free zone, so I agreed to Ryan's suggestion. I rose to my feet and Ryan stood up with me. He reached out a tentative hand and took hold of my elbow. We both stilled as we anticipated the worst. As the seconds ticked by and I did not collapse to the floor, the tension lightened between us.

"What room are you staying in?"

"Six eighteen," I said. "I'll go get ready for dinner."

"I'll call you when I get our reservation set."

"Thank you for the tea, Ryan. It helped."

"I'm glad. You'll feel even better after you eat something."

I opened the door to Ryan's room and stepped into the hallway. I nodded, but didn't believe him. I was unconvinced that I would ever be whole again.

Several hours later, I returned to my room to spend one final night at the Sentinel.

I was sober, but well fed. Ryan and I had spoken about several things during our meal, but he was careful to avoid the subject of my greatest distress. He allowed me to direct the flow of conversation and never pushed for information I was unwilling to share.

I was stronger both physically and mentally. I prepared for bed, opting to take a sleeping aid. I sat down on my bed and spotted my neglected phone on the bedside table. It had been hours since I'd left Jack in my father's apartment. I didn't know if I was prepared to read the text messages he'd sent me but, good or bad, the time had come to see what he had to say.

I picked up my phone and found that Jack's unread messages had increased from two to four. I read them in order and noted how each one sounded more fearful than the last. It was the final message he'd sent, less than twenty minutes earlier that threatened to undo the slight progress I'd made during my evening out.

"Please let me know you're safe. I need to know nothing bad has happened to you. I'm scared."

I'd made a few decisions over the course of the evening. I feared calling Jack would unravel my fragile resolve, but it was also clear he'd become progressively frightened during the hours following our argument. I texted him, hoping it would ease his mind. "I didn't mean to worry you. I'm all right."

Jack's response was immediate, as though he'd been waiting for my reply. "Are you home? Can I call you?"

I was slow in offering my response. I needed to rest and couldn't change my plan. "I'll be home tomorrow. I'll call you then and let you know I'm safe. I'd like to say hello to Heide, too."

Jack replied, "You don't know how much I want to see you. To tell you how sorry I am. To kiss you and beg you to stay. But more than anything else, I want you to know that I listened to you today. I will fix everything. I promise."

I began to type out a response and found I wanted to ask Jack to come to the hotel for a little while, but I stopped short of hitting the send button. He wouldn't hesitate if I extended the invitation. Once I had Jack back in my arms, a little while would turn into the entire night. We'd succumb to our explosive desires and, no doubt, achieve a state of incredible bliss, but doing so would exacerbate our dilemma. Bringing Jack into my bed so soon would resolve nothing.

I deleted my unsent text and sent an alternate message. "Kiss your daughter's forehead for me. Good night."

I turned my phone off and set it back down on the bedside table. Within minutes, I fell into a deep and dreamless slumber.

chapter Forty-One

TWO DAYS later, I returned to the office, arriving early enough in the morning to avoid the awkwardness of my unexpected appearance. My desk was clear and there were no surprise projects waiting for me. Robert had promised to take care of things while I was in Portland.

Knowing I had e-mails to sort and respond to, I sat down at my computer and began the task of informing everyone I had returned to full-time work. Over the course of the next hour, people filtered into the firm and those who wandered by my open office door paused in amazement. Many stopped to say hello and some lingered to spend a few minutes catching me up with their summer activities.

I waited for my father to arrive, knowing he'd be more shocked than anyone would. When he appeared just before ten o'clock, he entered my office without pretense and closed the door behind him. I pushed away from my computer and waited for him to speak, already prepared to defend my decision.

"I wasn't expecting to see you back here today," he began. "When did you get home?"

"Yesterday."

"I wish you would've called me."

I shrugged, but not from irritation. "I had to put my place back together."

"How's Heide?"

"She's doing well. She left the hospital a few days ago."

"That's great news." Robert was genuine but also puzzled. Something about my sudden return wasn't making sense to him. "I take it everyone came back to Bend?"

"No. Just me. Heide is undergoing some physical therapy in Portland until she can get set up with someone here in town."

"Jack and Heide will be back soon? That's wonderful."

I nodded.

Robert hesitated before asking his next question. "And Jack's ex-wife?"

I bristled, unable to hide a flash of irritation. "What about her?"

"Is she going back to Maryland?"

"Not yet. Heide won't be strong enough to return to school right away. Allison is going to stay with Jack and help Heide with home schooling and doctor appointments for a while."

"Are things good between you and Jack?"

My father was beginning to connect the dots, but I did my best to protect the privacy of my complications with Jack. "Why would you ask that?"

"It just seems odd that after you commit yourself to this man and his daughter, spend the entire summer in Portland, helping them through a crisis, you'd come home alone now."

"I had to give up my bedroom at the apartment when Heide left the hospital. It made sense for me to come back."

Robert narrowed his eyes, and the realization that he knew I wasn't telling him everything annoyed me. Old emotions and bad habits began churning toward the surface and I sought my escape.

"I just remembered. I need to speak with Tracie."

"Sure." Robert's tone acknowledged a flicker of our former ways. He didn't want to drop the subject, but I was relieved when he did. He rose from his chair and opened my door. "Let me know if I can do anything to help you settle back in."

"Thanks," I said, my mind already moving to the next task on my list. I waited several seconds after Robert's exit before making my way to the reception area.

"Hey there!" Tracie jumped up and offered me a cheerful hug. "I was wondering when you'd make your way up to my desk. I was starting to think you'd forgotten me."

"I'm pretty sure that's impossible."

"I'm so glad you're back." She opened a desk drawer, pulled out Jack's keys and handed them to me.

"Jack's cat hates me," she said after sitting back down. "I think she's plotting."

"I don't know if I'll have any better luck with that cat than you," I said, "but you've earned some time off."

"I was over at the house this morning. Jack and his daughter must still be in Portland?"

"Yes." I bit the inside of my cheek. "For the time being."

"Is anything wrong?"

Tracie's question surprised me. I'd prepared for Robert to sense something was amiss, but not anyone else. I offered her a smile, hoping it would telegraph sincerity. "Jack's daughter will be home soon. That's the best news. Thanks again for all your help. I owe you a couple of nice dinners by now."

I waved and stepped away from Tracie's desk before she could sense anything else.

"Don't mention it," she said as she turned back to her computer monitor. "Although I really won't miss that cat."

I spent the remainder of the day in my office, reacquainting myself with my job and catching up with clients and colleagues. It was a day spent fielding phone calls and answering e-mails, but it kept me focused on something other than my personal problems and it was a welcome relief.

Shortly before the end of the workday, an e-mail from Jack's work account arrived in my inbox. When I opened the message, I saw that Robert was the primary recipient and Jack had blind carbon copied me. He wanted me to read the e-mail without Robert's knowledge. The subject read, "My Return Date."

Robert,

I'm happy to say that I will be returning to work full-time on Monday, September 20.

Heide's recovery has progressed to the point where she can return home. Her medical team in Portland is in the process of transferring her appointments to her pediatrician and a physical therapist in Bend.

I'm expecting to arrive back in town on Friday the 17th. I'll be sure to leave your apartment in excellent condition.

If you need anything else, please let me know.

Thank you for everything,

Jack

Jack's brief message was a tremendous milestone in a tumultuous summer. He was likely brimming with happiness over his daughter's good news, and although I was glad for the family, hearing the news in this fashion was bittersweet. I considered replying and offering my congratulations, but found myself shutting down my computer for the day instead.

Before I drove home, I stopped by Jack's house. I wanted to check on Kitty Hawk and see if there was anything I could do for the Evans family before they returned from Portland. I unlocked the front door and steeled myself for a charging cat, but she remained hidden.

I closed the door and made my way toward the mudroom to check on Kitty Hawk's food and water. Sure enough, a curious and grumpy furry face emerged from underneath a blanket resting on the living room sofa.

"Hey, Kitty Hawk." I smiled.

She hissed at me.

"I know. I'm sorry. You're probably wondering what the hell happened." I took a few careful steps toward the sofa.

Kitty Hawk hissed a second time and added a growl for good measure.

I reconsidered my approach. "Fair enough," I said. "I'm going to peek at your dish."

The cat didn't object so I went to the mudroom to replenish her food. Even if the cat's appetite was satisfied, I decided the effort couldn't hurt our tenuous relationship. Kitty Hawk didn't follow me to her food area, but she stopped hissing when I returned to the living room.

I decided to go from room to room and assess conditions, beginning with the kitchen. Tracie had taken good care of Jack's home over the summer, and I was thankful she had accepted the housesitting job. She had cleaned out Jack's refrigerator, washed and put away his dishes and taken out the garbage. Satisfied with the condition of the kitchen, I located a shopping bag and moved on.

Upon further inspection of the house, I realized that in addition to looking after Kitty Hawk's needs Tracie had completed Jack and Heide's forgotten laundry, including Heide's original pair of Minecraft socks. She'd also cleaned Heide's muddy soccer cleats.

The home was spotless, leaving only one task that needed my attention. I entered Jack's bedroom, overcome by the blatant loneliness of a space I had come to love. I indulged my sadness for the first time since returning to Bend and lied down on what I considered my side of his bed.

I didn't cry, but the substantial weight of my worries descended upon me almost as soon as I settled onto the mattress. I missed Jack terribly and wondered if I had made a colossal mistake leaving Portland the way I had. We hadn't communicated much since I walked away from our fight. I regretted not answering his e-mail, and I fought the urge to call him. I didn't have any idea of what I would say, and I was worried about what important thing I might interrupt. I glanced over to his bedside table and took in the photo of Jack and Heide that meant so much to me. I considered the photo and the love it conveyed while waiting for my selfish impulses to recede.

There was a sudden depression near the foot of the bed, followed by a curious chirp. Kitty Hawk had followed me down the hall. I held still while she cautiously made her way over to me. She took her time, sniffing me in various places, before deciding it was safe enough to step onto my stomach.

I scratched her head. Within moments, the cat was purring and kneading her sharp claws on my blouse. I indulged her, knowing she had missed social affection during the summer. I petted her until she stepped down from her perch and made her way to Jack's side of the bed. She curled into a contented ball and went to sleep.

Restless, I got up and decided it was time to finish my work. I went into Jack's bathroom and searched for the few toiletries and personal items I'd left behind after my last sleepover. I removed everything and packed the items into the shopping bag I'd brought from the kitchen before retrieving a single pair of pajamas from his dresser. I returned to the bed and added them to my stash.

Just as I finished the task, I glanced back to the dresser and remembered one last thing. I straightened and walked over to the drawer Jack had opened for me several months ago. I pulled it open and located the stockings and garter belt that I had worn the first time we'd slept together. It was strange, taking them back after so much time, but I'd committed to removing my things from Jack's house before Allison set foot inside it.

With nothing else left to do, I took my possessions and locked up Jack's house for the night. When I returned to my condo, I dropped the bag by the front door and went straight to bed.

chapter  Forty-Two

I LIMITED my interactions with Jack to phone updates on Heide, speaking with her more than I did with her father. She sounded stronger each time I called, and her improvement kept things light between Jack and me during our short conversations.

On the morning of Jack's return to work, there was a project team meeting. I made a brief stop at my office before making my way to the conference room. As I approached it, I thought about the room's recent significance in my life. It was the place where I had first met Jack Evans, the room where he'd become aware of my troubled family life, and now it was likely to be the room where I discovered if our relationship could be salvaged. My stomach was in knots as I stepped inside and those knots tightened when I discovered Jack already seated there.

He locked eyes with me while I locked eyes on his cup of Starbucks. I gripped my own windmill cup tighter before taking the first available seat.

We weren't alone in the conference room. There were already two coworkers seated and chatting away about their weekend. Once settled, I greeted everyone in the room, saving Jack for last.

"Welcome back to work."

"Thank you, Kathleen." His brown eyes leveled on my face. "I'm happy to be back."

"How did the trip home go? Was Heide all right?"

"Yes. She slept for most of it."

"That's good."

We both refrained from more small talk and soon Robert joined the group to run the meeting. He began by offering Jack a proper welcome back speech before everyone shifted gears to focus on our professional duties. It was impossible to avoid Jack during the hour, but somehow I managed to keep my concentration on the project at hand. When the meeting concluded, I offered a polite good-bye to everyone and returned to my office.

We gave one another space during the rest of the day. Jack had plenty to catch up on and he even worked through the lunch hour. Halfway through the afternoon, he sent me an e-mail.

Hello, Kathleen,
I wondered if you had a few minutes to speak with me.
Thanks,
Jack

I immediately hit the reply button.

Hi Jack,
Come over to my office when you're ready.
Kathleen

There was a knock at my door within five minutes. I grinned, remembering the time Heide had sat in my office and recognized her father's knocking. I now understood what she meant as I saw Jack standing at the threshold.

"Come in," I said encouragingly.

Jack stepped inside. "Do you mind if I close the door?" he asked with slight trepidation. He was as unsure of what to expect from me as I was from him.

"Please."

He did so and took a seat across from me. "I won't take much of your time. I have to leave early."

"Is everything okay?"

"Yes." He shifted in his seat. "We're meeting with Heide's new physical therapist at four."

"That's good."

"Yes. Things almost feel normal again."

I wasn't sure how to interpret this. My thoughts wandered toward Jack's ex-wife. "How's Allison?"

"We've settled back in at home. Allison likes it here better than Portland. It's progress."

Since their divorce, I'd always detected hurt in Jack's tone whenever he spoke of Allison, but in this moment there was none. He spoke of her without any sense of frustration, and the difference in both his demeanor and his posture was profound.

"I wanted to see how you were doing," he said, oblivious to my thoughts.

I couldn't hide my sadness from Jack. We knew each other too well. However, I put on a brave face. He carefully moved forward with our conversation, testing the waters with me just as I had tested them with Robert after our blowup at the golf course. I evaded answering any questions about my own well-being by changing subjects. I'd learned the tactic firsthand from Jack.

"I don't know if Robert mentioned this to you, but the firm is sponsoring an art festival at Heide's school tomorrow night. If she's up for it, it might be a good way for her to reconnect with her friends and teachers."

Jack nodded. "That's a perfect idea. Thank you for telling me."

"You're welcome."

Jack stood up, preparing to leave. I remained seated, and he paused in front of my desk. He tapped a contemplative finger on the corner of my work surface several times before walking around. Suddenly, he was on my side of the desk, approaching me.

I stood up from my chair and even took a step back, my chair rolling away as I bumped it. He halted his progress as soon as I retreated, dismayed. We stood still for several moments, staring at one another.

"I don't want to upset you," Jack said, breaking the silence.

"I'm not upset." My answer presented itself perhaps a bit too quickly. He studied my face as I fidgeted under his scrutiny.

"Are you sure?"

"You surprised me. That's all."

I gazed toward the closed office door.

"I had a nightmare last night," he revealed.

I brought my eyes back to his, concerned. "About what?"

"I dreamed I came back to work, and you'd cut off your hair." His brown eyes softened, but his apprehension was still obvious.

I didn't know how to respond to this, so I said nothing. Jack was undeterred by my silence. "Will you push me away if I touch you?"

I hadn't expected him to be this bold with me. I thought about his question for a moment, and then I shook my head.

"No. I won't ever push you again," I promised him. "But I'm not ready for you to touch me."

Jack took a tentative step forward.

I held out a trembling hand. "Please. Don't."

Jack's dismay turned to frustration. "What's the matter? Do you think I'm going to hurt you?"

"It's too late for that." I was nervous and semi-joking, but Jack didn't see the humor.

"You know, you're quite capable of hurt yourself."

I flinched.

"You have an appointment," I whispered. I didn't want to end our reunion this way, but an argument was brewing. I didn't want to fight with Jack at all and especially not at the office. Despite the tension of the moment, I hated the thought of breaking this delicate link between us. I didn't want him to leave.

Jack sighed before stepping back from me. We continued to stare at each other, although somewhat sadly.

"I didn't know if you'd welcome me back or slap me in the face," he said.

Once again, I was at a loss for words, rendered mute by his disclosure.

"I'm not ignoring the fact that we have problems," he continued as he closed his hand around the doorknob. "I just need you to understand that I'm going to earn your trust back."

He opened the door and left my office without another word. I was too frightened to hope and spent several minutes wondering why.

The following evening, I arrived at Deschutes River Elementary School and greeted the school principal with a warm handshake. He was dressed in khaki pants and a polo shirt featuring the school's porcupine mascot. Having come straight from the office, I wore a knee-length, taupe, business skirt, jacket and high heels.

"Ms. Brighton, I'm so glad you could make it this evening. Please allow me to provide you with a brief tour of our exhibits."

I nodded. "That would be wonderful. Lead the way."

The event had begun shortly before my arrival and was well underway.

"As you can see, Ms. Brighton, we have several education stations, each intended to offer hands-on interaction and engagement between the students and their families."

"Please, call me Kathleen." I nodded with appreciation. "The partnership is a natural one. Many of our staff members are creative professionals eager to encourage others to indulge their own artistic pursuits."

"Fundraising for the art program becomes more challenging by the year. Aurora's contribution means so much."

As our tour wound down, we entered the multipurpose room with a stage. The space was noisy with the excitement of the children and their families, but the din of the festivities evaporated when I spotted Heide on the opposite side of the room.

Surrounded protectively by her parents, she moved from one station to another with careful thought. She was attempting to protect both her energy and her delicate ribs, which were still healing. She wasn't bouncing with the level of energy I had become so accustomed to, but she was upright, and she was walking on her own. If I didn't know any better, I would have found it difficult to believe she had spent the summer fighting for her life in a hospital. She looked wonderful.

Thoughts of her father invaded my concentration as I conversed with the principal. Jack had spent another day at the office bogged down with work, and once again we kept our distance. Jack's words the afternoon before still consumed my thoughts and emotions. Disturbed that we'd both sidestepped the opportunity to talk through our troubles, I was somewhat glad for the reprieve. I couldn't make sense of our mutual hesitation.

I turned my attention back to my host before my romantic frustrations overwhelmed me. "Thank you for showing me around." I gestured in Heide's general direction. "Some of our staff has children attending your school, so we're more than happy to support events like this. If we can ever be of assistance, please, let us know."

"Thank you, Kathleen. I'm so glad you could stop by. I hope to see you again soon."

"You will," I promised. "Enjoy the rest of your night."

"You, too. Be sure to take a few minutes and work on some crafts."

I smiled. "I think I'll do that."

Another attendee intercepted the principal, and I turned my attention back to Heide and her family, intent on hugging her. As I made my way across the large room, my pace began to slow as my observations of the family began to take hold.

There was a certain air around the three, an intimacy, a familiarity that had all of them looking relaxed and at peace. As I studied them, Allison retrieved her phone from her purse and handed it over to the volunteer operating the station of their latest project. Jack, Allison and Heide all posed for a photo featuring Heide's completed craft, and what I saw took my breath away.

I saw the family that once existed. Even during the best moments of my parents' marriage, I had never glimpsed this level of harmony. Knowing what little I did about their life together, I could only assume the past year had been the most strenuous of Jack and Allison's relationship, and yet here they were, a unified family.

It was then the dense fog surrounding my doubts and hesitations began to clear, and I realized with shocking clarity what had been nagging. I froze just feet away from Jack and his family, unnoticed and reeling from the acknowledgement that Jack Evans might not be totally free from his marriage.

"Fuck," I whispered, before turning away from the trio and escaping from the school.

chapter  Forty-Three

AFTER THE art festival, my strained relationship with Jack continued to disintegrate.

We saw each other at work, but Jack was committed to both his career and his daughter's recovery. He had no downtime and I silently accepted this. He was being the responsible father I expected him to be. I wasn't about to question his course of action.

Nevertheless, I struggled with the severe disconnect between us. I missed being with him and my loneliness compounded my misery at work. My unhappiness followed the path of least resistance and threatened to undermine my fragile relationship with Robert. I attempted to keep my troubles with Jack away from my father, and the effort proved grueling and often tested my father's limited patience. I had no sanctuary away from either man, and my depression grew as a result.

Ever observant, Tracie noted my increased moodiness. "We're going out tomorrow night," she said to me on a Friday afternoon, a month after Jack's return. "You need a lot of drinks."

"I'll go out, but I don't promise to drink."

"We'll see about that. You know I'm an enabler."

The next evening we visited several popular nightspots. Tracie was adamant I should drink my worries away, but as she gradually become more intoxicated, I settled into driving her around town, and laughing at her antics. Over the course of the evening, she grew frustrated by the failure of her mission.

"I just want you to have fun," she whined as we arrived at the Astro Lounge. "You really need this."

"I promise I'm having fun. You're cracking me the hell up."

"Oh! I know!" she exclaimed, suddenly inspired. "Let's go to Seven for our seventh stop!"

"You think you're going to make it to seven stops?" I teased her. "You do that and I promise to take seven shots with you."

"You're totally on! I am motivated now! We're so gonna do this, Kathleen!"

"Uh-huh," I said as we made our way inside. At this rate, Tracie was going to be lucky to make it back to the car.

The place was crowded with Saturday night revelers and pulsing with live music. I held Tracie's hand and guided her to a table. She ordered a blended margarita while I stuck with a diet soda and a slice of lime.

I excused myself to visit the restroom and she began chatting with the occupants at the next table. I was making my way back to her when a man's hand reached out from the bar and took hold of me.

"Whoa!" I exclaimed, pulling my arm away from him. I was stunned beyond belief to discover the offending grabber was none other than Jack.

"What are you doing out on a Saturday night?" I asked him. "Entertaining clients?"

"Nnnooo," he slurred. "Is it impossible to believe I just needed some time to myself?"

My surprise now turned into mild concern as I glanced at the bar. He was working his way through a bottle of his favorite beer, although it clearly wasn't his first of the night. There were three cardboard coasters sitting in front of him along with a discarded pen. Jack's handwriting covered all of them.

I pointed to them. "Brainstorming? Are you working on the firm's next great ad campaign?"

Jack's eyebrows furrowed with drunken confusion. He wasn't following my words. He carefully turned his head as though it were heavy on his shoulders and stared at the bar for several moments.

Jack clumsily flipped the coasters over before turning to me. "Nah. That's nothing. Just me being silly." He grinned like a true inebriated goofball.

I tapped his beer bottle, sitting on top of another coaster. "Can I assume this is number four?"

"I wouldn't bet on it. You'd lose." Jack winked with poor coordination that was simultaneously adorable and alarming.

"More than four then?" I ventured.

"Yeah."

"Did you drive here?"

He shook his head. "I walked."

"From your house?" I asked with disbelief. "That's a bit of a hike."

"No. From dinner." Jack pointed randomly behind him. "Just down the street. Allison and I had a fight. Again. She drove off."

"I'm sorry."

Jack waved an annoyed hand at no one in particular.

"I'm out with Tracie," I shared. "We're winding things down for the night. I could take you home."

His response was painful with its yearning. "To your place?"

"No," I clarified. "To yours."

He nodded with an expression akin to surprised admiration. "You know, if we're quiet, we can sneak right past Allison's room."

I shook my head. "That's not what I meant, Jack."

He turned back to his beer and sulked. "I know."

He spoke next, his eyes still trained on his bottle of Inversion. "Why are you avoiding me, Kathleen?"

I shuffled my feet. "I'm not avoiding you. You're just busy."

"I don't believe you."

"Maybe we should talk about this later," I suggested. "When you're feeling back to normal."

Jack turned his entire body toward me, teasing me in more ways than one. "Avoider."

"I'm going back to my table. You can stay here and drink alone or you can join us and I'll drive you home in a few minutes. It's up to you."

Jack slid off his bar stool and wobbled as his feet hit the floor. I waited until he found his balance and looked my way once more. "You probably should drive me home," he agreed.

"Good man." I smiled while motioning to his forgotten items on the bar. "Is that your pen?"

"Nope. Bartender's."

"What about your notes there?"

"Just throw them in your purse. I'll get them later."

I scooped the coasters up in one hand before taking Jack's hand with the other. "C'mon. I'll escort you."

Jack's palm was sweaty as it rubbed against mine and his grip was sluggish, but still I enjoyed the sizzling touch of his skin against mine. When we arrived at the table, holding hands, Tracie pointedly stared at our entwined fingers before shaking her head vigorously.

"I'm so confused," she uttered.

"It turns out we could have been hanging out with Jack all night instead of running all over town," I said while depositing the coasters into my bag.

"Oh no! We suck!" Tracie yelled at him.

I pulled out the chair next to mine for Jack. He continued holding my hand even after we both sat down and Tracie took notice.

"That is so damn sweet!" she announced to anyone within earshot. "You need to do that at work! All the time! You'd both be happier!"

Jack took a swig of his beer while I pointed to Tracie's margarita. "You need to finish your drink."

She looked at me, dumbfounded at the turn of events. Then she looked over to Jack and back down to our hands before looking back at me with a smug smile. "Hell, yeah, I do!"

Tracie picked up her glass and drank with determination while Jack leaned over and said in my ear, "She thinks you're going to take advantage of me."

"I know."

"You don't have to lie to her, you know. I'll make the sacrifice and defend your honor."

"Maybe another time."

Jack appeared offended by my lackluster response. "I have sense enough to know what I'm committing to."

I leveled a serious expression at Jack. "I have something important to say to you, but I don't want to piss you off when I do."

He tightened his hold on my hand in what I assumed was a conscious effort to sharpen his focus. "Okay. I won't get pissed. What is it?"

I lowered my voice just enough to remove Tracie from earshot. "We're not sleeping together tonight because I can't stand the smell of beer on you."

Jack was baffled, but not angry. "You can't?"

"Beer is what my father drinks. What he used to drink a lot of."

Jack blinked twice over this revelation, before turning to include Tracie in his response. "Aw shit! Well, there goes that then!"

"Where goes what now?" Tracie yelled.

He waved her off. She shrugged. Discussion over.

"Are we ready to go?" I asked them both.

Jack and I stood up together, his hand still glued to mine. Tracie raised her arm into the air. "I'm drunk, too! I need your other hand!"

Begrudgingly, I took a hold of Tracie. Together, the three of us walked from the Astro Lounge and into the late summer evening.

I pulled into Jack's driveway and glanced at my passenger in exasperation. Somewhere between Tracie's apartment and his house, Jack had passed out and was snoring, loudly.

The porch light was on, as were the living room lights. It was just after midnight, and I was going to need help getting Jack into the house. I exited the car and as I stepped around the front of the vehicle, Allison opened the front door. She came out onto the front step, wrapping a gray sweater around her shoulders and crossing her arms against the chilled nighttime air of the high desert.

"Hello," she said in a reserved clip.

"Hi, Allison." I nodded toward the passenger side window. "I was out with a friend tonight and ran into Jack over on Bond Street. He needed a ride home."

"I take it he's drunk?" Allison was not amused.

"Uh. Yeah. I guess so. Anyway, he fell asleep on the way over here. Can you help me see him in?"

Allison pulled the front door shut before descending the stairs and making her way over to the car. She leaned down and observed Jack's head leaning against the window. She knocked on the glass experimentally. There was no movement.

"He's out cold." She straightened before taking a step closer to me.

"I realize I'm not in a position to ask favors of you, but I would appreciate one."

My stomach knotted in anxiety. "What's that?"

"Can you take him home with you tonight? Let him sleep it off there?"

"Why?"

"Jack doesn't often indulge in this level of intoxication. I don't want Heide to see him like this."

I looked back to the house and sighed. The thought of bringing Jack home with me was an awkward one, but I sympathized all too well with Allison's plight. It would have been nice if my own mother had made such requests on my behalf.

"Okay."

"Thank you."

"Sure." I walked back to the driver's seat before I could find an excuse to back out of the responsibility. Allison remained at the curb and when I opened the car door, I made eye contact with her.

"I've never seen him like this," I said. "Is there anything I should know? I don't like surprises when it comes to this kind of thing."

"He'll feel like hell in the morning. He'll probably be down most of the day. But he's never difficult or mean."

Months earlier, a few days after we first slept together, I'd asked Jack an impulsive question during our lunch at the Chinese restaurant. Standing in the street in the middle of the night, several feet from Allison, I impulsively asked it again.

"Why did you leave?"

Allison hesitated and I waited with anticipation. She opened her mouth to speak twice before changing her mind. Eventually, she shook her head.

"I don't know what he's told you about us, but as far as that goes? He should be the one to tell you. Not me."

"I asked him once," I revealed, "when we first began seeing each other."

"Did he answer you?"

"He gave me a reason."

"Do you believe him?"

"He hasn't given me reason not to."

"So why ask me?"

"I don't know."

We continued to stare at one another for a few moments before Allison turned away. "I'm going in. Thanks again, Kathleen."

My brief exchange with Allison brought up my guard even more. I woke up on and off during the night, partially to keep an ear out for Jack's well-being as he slept in my guest room and partially to mull over Allison's insinuation. Sound sleep evaded me until near dawn and only the sound of Jack rummaging through my kitchen lured me from my bed.

He stood next to my pantry, wearing a pair of forest green boxer briefs. Whatever he was looking for, he wasn't finding it, and impatiently moved from one cupboard to another.

"Can I help you with something?" I teased.

Jack wasn't in the mood for teasing. "Why don't you keep any coffee here?" he huffed, clearly wrestling with a major caffeine withdrawal. "Do you even own a coffeepot?"

"I don't need either because God invented Dutch Bros."

Jack abandoned his search and sought solace on my couch instead, lying down and bringing his arm up over his eyes.

I opened a tall narrow cupboard next to my sink and pulled out a bottle of ibuprofen. I shook three pills into my palm and grabbed a bottle of water from the fridge. I offered him the medication. He swallowed the pills eagerly.

"Drink the whole bottle of water," I said. "You passed out last night before I could give you any."

"Okay."

"Would you like a cool cloth for your eyes?"

"No, thanks."

"I'll throw on some clothes and go get your coffee."

"You're a lifesaver."

"Do you want anything else while I'm out? Something to help with your hangover?"

Jack opened his mouth to speak, but then hesitated to answer. The suggestion held some appeal to him, so I nudged further. "Whatever it is, believe me, I'll understand. I've been there."

"7UP. The cans, not the bottles."

"And?" I hedged.

"Cheetos Puffs."

"Original or White Cheddar?"

Jack removed his arm from his eyes and squinted at me. "They make White Cheddar Puffs?"

"Oh, yeah. They're really good, too."

He covered his eyes once more. "Get the White Cheddar ones. Those sound more sophisticated."

"You got it." My eyes swept the living room and came to rest on the shopping bag I'd dropped next to the front door several weeks before. I hadn't bothered to move it since bringing it back from Jack's house. I strolled over to the bag and swept it up off the floor.

"You should call Allison while I'm out. She knows you're here, but you should probably let her know when you'll be home."

Jack didn't respond to this, so I returned to my bedroom.

Jack's energy slowly began to return by the afternoon, and he asked me to drive him back to his house just before four o'clock. When we pulled into the driveway, his car was gone.

"The girls must have gone somewhere. Do you want to come in for a few minutes?"

"What for?" I challenged.

He shrugged. "I don't know. I guess I just need a few minutes to get used to the idea of you going back to your place. You don't have to."

"I'll come in."

"Great."

Out of habit, I followed Jack down the hallway to his bedroom but hesitated in the doorway. Jack made his way to his closet and chose a fresh outfit. He ceased his movements when he saw I didn't enter his room.

"It's all right, Kathleen."

I took two steps into the space, just barely clearing the doorway. Jack shook his head as he removed his clothes from the night before and carried them into the bathroom to place in the laundry hamper. Moments later, I heard the distinctive noise of an electric razor click on. I was surprised. I'd never seen Jack use one. I didn't even know he owned one. I took a few tentative steps toward him.

I had planned to observe Jack as he shaved and perhaps attempt to break through our ongoing awkwardness. Instead, I caught my reflection in the mirrored closet doors. Drawn to them, I slid the door on its track slowly, hoping to minimize any noise. As it turned out, I didn't have to move the doors much at all to confirm my theory.

The once empty closet now contained Allison's clothes.

With a heavy heart, I slid the door shut as slowly as I had opened it. I turned to look at Jack's bed and noticed for the first time that my side was unmade, the sheets and pillows rumpled from recent use.

I wondered what other portions of the household Allison had reclaimed.

Jack's razor clicked off but did not interrupt my jealous musings. When he reemerged from the bathroom, I was staring at his bed. He followed my gaze and his ensuing silence was as still as my own.

"Are you all right?" he asked after several difficult moments.

"I don't know," I said. "I should probably go."

I left Jack's bedroom before he could respond, but he was right behind me as I reached the living room.

"Kathleen—"

"It's none of my business, Jack."

He jumped in front of me before I could reach the front door and grasped me by the arms.

"Of course it's your business," he implored, his eyes pleading. "Don't run away from me. Especially now."

I glared my accusation without uttering a word.

"I am not sharing my bed with Allison. I am not having sex with her."

I held his gaze, waiting to spot any hint of his deception. As I did so, his expression changed.

"Please. Tell me you believe me."

I struggled against his hold, the instinct to flee crushing me. "Let go of me, Jack."

"Not until you answer me."

I didn't know what to say and continued to wriggle away from his hold.

"Kathleen?" he persisted, raising his voice just enough to startle me. His severe tone broke my resistance. We stared into one another's eyes while I regained my self-control and my common sense.

"I believe you about that," I finally answered. "But you're holding something back. Something important. I know it. I'm beginning to think I've always known it."

Jack didn't respond and my eyes filled with tears of frustration.

"Please don't deny it," I begged.

He looked down at the floor. I couldn't read Jack's thoughts, but my fear rose as his grip on my arms tightened. The wait felt interminable as he gathered his courage. "You're right. I'm not going to insult your intelligence by pretending otherwise."

I waited expectantly for him to share his secrets with me.

Jack released me, raised his head and cradled my face with his hands. He was on the verge of crying himself and shakily brought his forehead to touch mine.

"Can you give me some time?"

My temper snapped under weeks of agonized separation. "I've already given you months! Exactly how much more time do you need?"

Jack remained silent and it was one instance of stonewalling too many.

I angrily pulled back from his embrace, stepped around him and made my way to the front door.

"I need to go. Whenever you're ready to tell me the truth, come find me."

chapter  Forty-Four

THE REMAINDER of the day went by without any word from Jack. We both returned to the office on Monday morning, the dynamic between us irreparably altered. His silence endured for two days and reinforced my own personal commitments. It was Wednesday morning before he made an effort by calling my office.

"This is Kathleen," I answered with an impassive tone.

"Thank you for answering," he began.

"What do you need?" Under the current circumstances, it was a struggle to maintain my professional voice.

He cleared his throat before pushing forward. "I want to invite you to lunch. I'm thinking Chinese."

I closed my eyes and counted to three. There were things I needed to say, and the neighboring restaurant was the perfect choice.

"Do you want to go at the usual time?" I asked.

"Only if that works for you. I can be flexible."

"The usual time is fine. I'll meet you there."

Jack hesitated, unprepared for this stipulation. "Sure," he whispered.

"See you then," I said before hanging up.

I spent the next five minutes with my elbows pressed into the desk and my face buried in my shaking hands.

When I arrived at the restaurant, Jack was there and had already secured a corner table. He'd done his best to provide us with some privacy in the small open-concept restaurant.

He stood up as I approached him and reached for the chair next to his. I pulled out the chair across the table from him instead. His ensuing frown was evidence of his disappointment, but so was his acceptance of my choice. Once I settled in my seat, he returned to his.

"Hi," he said.

"Hi," I reciprocated.

Before our talk could begin we were interrupted by our server. She set hot tea down in front us and proceeded to take our order. Once she turned away, Jack set his hands on the table. He clasped them together and then he spoke.

"Whether you want to be with me or not, we have to start speaking again."

"Verbal communication has never been one of our strong suits," I muttered.

"You don't think so?"

"You do?"

"Why isn't it?" he asked, his curiosity genuine.

If there was ever a time to be direct, it was now. "I've spent a lot of time thinking you're holding back from me."

I took a sip of my tea as Jack set his elbow on the table and rested his cheek in the palm of his hand. He looked out the window until I set my teacup back down.

"We haven't known each other all that long," he said. "Not when you stop to think about it, but I think given enough time, you'll come to accept that you know me better than you think you do. You're a mystery to me, too. But there are some things I know about you."

"Such as?"

"The quieter your reactions, the deeper the hurt. And your silence right now since you left the house on Sunday, it terrifies me."

"Finally. Something you and Robert have in common other than golf."

"What does that mean?"

"He knows something is up between you and me. I've just been refusing to confirm it. It's getting to both of us."

"I'm sorry about that, Kathleen, although I do appreciate your discretion. Once we're on the other side of this mess, I'll speak to him and apologize for my part in all of it."

"There's something else you need to know," I revealed.

"What's that?"

"I'm leaving town for a few days."

Surprised, Jack straightened up in his seat. "When?"

"I fly out Friday afternoon."

"Flying out? Where are you going?"

"Denver."

"What for?"

"To meet with Ryan Murray."

The man's name never failed to initiate Jack's ire. "The marketing guy who crashed the Portland lunch?"

"Yes."

Jack's eyes narrowed as his suspicion widened. "Why do you need to meet with him?"

"To interview for a job."

"A job in Colorado?"

"Yes."

Jack's face registered his shock. "Why?"

There were so many reasons I could have given him in that moment. I could have explained staying at Aurora Advertising would destroy my hopes rather than fulfill them. I could have said that I needed the change. I could have told Jack I needed to clear my head somewhere else. Instead, I skewed the conversation in another direction by reaching into my purse and retrieving the three coasters from the Astro Lounge—the coasters that were covered in Jack's handwriting.

"These are yours. Do you remember them?"

"Yes," he admitted with a subdued tone.

"I'd almost forgotten about them, but when I went home on Sunday I saw them in my bag." I glanced down at the cardboard circles and tapped one for emphasis. "What you've written down here is quite erotic. You and a woman, swimming naked in a lake late at night. Making love to one another in the shallows."

Jack was painfully silent, and this time I couldn't fault him for it.

"This is far too detailed, Jack. I have a theory. Do you want to hear it?"

He rubbed his hands over his eyes, but didn't tell me no.

"This is a memory," I declared. "This is not a fantasy, and what's written here isn't about me."

Jack looked down, avoiding all eye contact. I slid the coasters toward his side of the table.

"These are about Allison," I concluded.

Jack was still looking down. "It's complicated," he whispered.

Now, he raised his eyes to meet mine. This was a make it or break it conversation for us, and although consumed by the frightful reality of our predicament, I pushed forward.

"Why do you think love stories always have such devastating moments?"

"All the best ones do."

"Did it ever occur to you that your involvement with me is the dark chapter in the love story with your wife?"

He stared at me in disbelief and hurt. "Never."

"You asked why I'm going to Denver. Do you really have no idea?"

"You think I want to be with Allison. And you won't interfere if you think that's the best thing for Heide."

I nodded and Jack began shaking his head. "Kathleen. Please be patient with me. I just need more time—"

"I know you need time, Jack. That's why I'm doing this. You tell me that I'm brave and strong, but now you can see how weak I really am. I don't know how much more of this I can take. I love you, but I can't be with you, and I can't just work with you, day in and day out. At least right now I can't. It's torture."

Jack's fist banged on the table in a physical display of his confusion and frustration. "Your tendencies lean toward flight rather than fight. Don't go to Colorado. Stay here and we'll work on this together."

"You just asked me for more time," I reminded him. "I can't hang on indefinitely waiting for you to make a commitment. You call it fleeing, but I'm going to Denver because I already feel isolated here."

This was our tipping point, and it reflected in his beautiful brown eyes. I saw the painful realization set in as he forced himself to accept my decision. It wasn't necessary for me to explain any more, but I was compelled to clarify my definitive point.

"I refuse to be a tragedy, Jack."

chapter  Forty-Five

I SAT inside Stanford's at the Portland International Airport, staring into my glass of untouched wine. It was the first drink I had ever agreed to share with my father. He was buying me lunch. I should take at least a sip or two.

I could feel Robert's eyes upon me, but I didn't have the willfulness to confront him.

"What is it?" I asked with exasperation. I didn't mean to be cross with him, but the toxicity had already begun to seep back into our fragile relationship.

The sooner I get out of this place, the better.

Robert was motionless in his seat. "Nothing." He was lying, and he made no real effort to hide it, but I detected none of his typical impatience either.

"Then why are you looking at me?" I was curious about his attention, but his interest was also unnerving.

"I see something in your face. I see it in your eyes and in your posture. Something I haven't seen often, but I recognize it."

I finally dragged my eyes to his. "What's that?"

"Your mother. You have the same countenance she did … near the end. It worries me."

I picked up my glass from the table and ended my self-imposed prohibition. "Don't worry. I'm not my mother."

"You're not me, either."

I grinned, despite myself. "No, I'm not," I answered, setting down my wine glass. "I have to find my own way."

"Are you absolutely sure you want to do this? If you're having even one doubt—"

I shook my head. "There are no doubts. This has nothing to do with what I want."

"Can I ask just one thing from you?" Robert's face was pensive, but I wasn't going to make any guarantees.

"Possibly."

"When he offers you the job—"

"If," I interrupted.

"When, Kathleen. When he offers you the job, just give it a day or two to mull it over. Don't make this decision too hastily."

"Will you forgive me if I say yes?"

My father crossed his arms. "I'm not going to pretend you leaving the family business wouldn't be a huge pain in my ass. But I get the need to make a change. I didn't leave the firm, but I was arrogant enough to pack it up and take it with me when I moved to Bend. I'm not going to fault you if finding your own way means finding it elsewhere."

"Thank you."

Robert sighed. "I've been trying to mind my own business, but where do things stand with Jack? What does he know? Do I need to be careful about what I say around him?"

"We went to lunch a couple of days ago. I told him what I was doing."

"How did that go?"

I shrugged and turned my attention back to my wine, hoping another sip or two would numb my heartache.

"He's not happy about it, but I think he understands I haven't been happy for a while."

"I'm the last person to offer up useful relationship advice, so I'll keep my nose out of it. Whatever is happening between the two of you, you'll both figure out how to deal with it."

"I think there's still a chance he can reunite his family," I revealed. "I refuse to stand in the way of that, and it's easier for me to walk away from Bend than it is for him. Heide needs to stay put while she heals. Allison isn't going to back Maryland any time soon."

"Is he going back to his wife?"

"I don't know what he's going to do. But I know she feels Jack was distracted by me enough to put Heide in danger."

"That's some major bullshit. Don't buy into it."

"She's not entirely wrong."

Robert leveled me with a serious look. "Many people influenced events here. Jack displaced his family and brought them out West. Allison left her husband and daughter in Oregon when she decided she didn't like it here. Jack left Heide in the care of another parent while he went to work. The woman took her eyes off those little girls for five minutes too long. And Heide decided to climb the wrong piece of playground equipment."

"I encouraged her interest in climbing." I angrily swiped a stray tear from my cheek. "If I had found other things to talk about with her, maybe she wouldn't have tried to scale that backstop."

"And I did more things to you than I can ever account or atone for. And all those things influenced how you conduct yourself in these relationships. No one person can take the blame for what happens in life. We all play a part, Kathleen. We all form a constellation."

We sat quiet for a few minutes, each lost in our own thoughts.

"Jack does love you," he continued with conviction. "I saw it that afternoon at Widgi Creek when he wanted to reach across the table and kick my ass. And I've seen it every day since."

"It took me a long time to believe it, but I know you're right."

"Then why go through all this?"

"Because something is off. Something is holding us both back, and I can't see any other way to work through it." I pulled my phone from my purse to check the time. "I should probably get going."

Robert nodded with a somber acceptance. He paid the lunch bill, and we made our way toward the airport security line. We stopped a few feet away from the entrance to bid our farewells.

Robert placed his hands on his hips and stared down at the floor, and that's when it hit me. Although we'd spent years emotionally distanced from one another, we'd never been physically far apart. With the exception of my years at the University of Oregon, Robert had always been by my side. I'd spent years angry with him for not being there for me when the simple truth was that he had tried to be.

He shook his head and lifted his eyes to look at me. I could see my realization had also dawned on him, and I waited to hear his parting words.

"I really hate the new carpet here," he mumbled.

I nodded. "Change sucks."

My father rubbed his face with his hand. "I hope things go the way you need them to. Try not to worry about things here. I'll make sure everything is taken care of."

"I know you will. Thank you."

I stepped forward and hugged my father. I didn't swoop in and back out again, Instead, I held on to him tightly and received a tight hug in return.

"I love you, Kathleen."

"Love you, too, Dad. Thank you for your support these past few months. I know I don't make it easy for you. I'm going to be better about it from now on."

"I'm sorry for all kinds of things," he added. "I'll try to do right by you going forward." My father patted me on the back and I disengaged from his arms.

"Time to go," he said.

"All right."

"Let me know that you landed safely. I'll leave you alone otherwise, and we can talk about what needs to be done when you get back."

I nodded. "I'll see you after the weekend."

chapter

Forty-Six

THIRTY MINUTES later, I was sitting in a black vinyl chair and staring absently out the terminal window as my plane pulled into the gate. My phone chimed with a text message, startling me from my daze.

I swiped the screen and read Jack's message. "There's something I need to say to you. Something I need you to hear before your interview. Please call me before then."

He was offering me the opportunity to call him much later, knowing my interview wouldn't be taking place until the following day. I decided to call him before I even left the state. I waited for him to answer and when he did, he dove right in to the conversation.

"Let me say these things before you speak," he began. "Listen to my words. You think I'm in the midst of making a choice between my former life and this one. Yes, I was in love with Allison once, and we'll always have a bond because we made the world's most beautiful daughter. But even so, what we had together wasn't what it should be. It was good enough at the time, but Allison and I aren't soul mates. We never were.

"You're right in that I don't have a lot of choice right now. Heide's future is on the line. She still has so much to overcome, and it scares the hell out of me that you believe you aren't an important part of her recovery. I'm afraid that I'm to blame for that.

"I was stupid, Kathleen. I was shortsighted and unfocused. I took your love and your generous heart for granted. Now I have to face the consequences of that mistake. I know I have a lot of work to do for us. I've given you plenty of reason to question my loyalty.

"I failed as a husband because I always thought I knew what was best and I was wrong. So now I'm putting my faith in you to know what's best for you. I hope beyond hope that you'll choose me. But if I'm not the best man for you, then I want you to find the best. You deserve nothing less."

He took a deep breath that rattled with nervousness. "I don't want you to go to Denver, but I also know I never want you to regret not going. I don't want you to regret passing up a good opportunity for yourself. Whatever choice you make after this weekend, I will support you. But I cannot have you walk into that interview thinking that I'm even close to considering a future without you. I love you, and I know you love me. I know you are my soul mate, Kathleen.

"After the first time we made love, you trembled in my arms and you asked me a question. Do you remember?"

"Yes," I whispered. "I'll never forget it."

"Then you remember my answer."

"Yes."

"Nothing has changed since the first time I held your beautiful body to mine. I will always feel that way about you."

My heart was beating heavy, eager to absorb the love it craved.

Jack's worried voice drew me back into reality. "Are you still there?"

"Yes. Thank you, Jack. You don't how much I needed to hear that."

"Just as much as I needed to say it. I love you, Kathleen."

"I love you. I do. I'm not doing this to hurt you."

"I understand that now. I'm not trying to talk you out of going to Denver."

"I know that." The gate clerk made an announcement through the loudspeaker, signaling the inevitable. "They're getting ready to board the plane, Jack. I better go."

"Have a safe trip."

"Jack?"

"Yes?"

"Robert asked me to think about things for a few days before I make any big decisions. I want you to know that's exactly what I'll do."

"I believe in you, Kathleen."

"Thank you. I'll see you next week."

"Bye."

I disconnected the phone call and rose from my seat, gathering my purse and my carry-on luggage. I watched as arriving passengers made their way toward the main terminal and considered blending in with them and calling Robert before he got any farther down the road. Jack had been sincere with his sentiments, and I believed everything he had told me. Emotionally, I wanted to return to Bend, go to his house and kiss him madly. There was just one thing stopping me.

Sadness can overshadow the brightest day.

Sorrow can smash you and tear you inside out.

Despondency can make everything else in your life inconsequential.

Consumed by despair, my mother arrived at the point where her friends, her family, her accomplishments, her love, and ultimately her life were no longer worthwhile endeavors. Swallowed whole by her unhappiness, her misery took her away from everything and everyone that once mattered.

When my mother died, she was thirty-six years old. My father took me to the funeral home. I sat alone next to her coffin while he wandered away. I was a child, yearning for words of comfort and because my father wasn't there to offer them, I had to come up with some of my own. That night, my child self struck a deal with my future adult self.

It was difficult to make sense from what my mother had done, but I knew it was important to remember what it was like to sit there with her lifeless body. If I had any hope of surviving beyond her age, I would forever need to remember how sadness could destroy someone.

I told myself to remember this because I was just as human as my mother was. I had to remain strong from that day forward because a time might come when I might be tempted to do the same.

Now, I was thirty-six and that frightful temptation had presented itself.

Now surrounded by dejection, and because of the promises I had made to my ten-year-old self, I rummaged for courage and introspection. By doing so, I made a surprising discovery. At the center of my emotional vortex, I stumbled upon stillness in the gloom. In the frenzy of melancholy, dismissing it could have been easy. Instead, I remembered the sight of my mother's coffin and embraced that pocket of stillness because it offered a bewildering version of tranquility. A type of peace.

I understood what was happening in my life now, and although I wasn't happy about it, I knew things were eventually going to get better. With my decision made, I simply had to accept the challenges standing in the way. In so many ways, Jack Evans was responsible for bringing me to this point. He was the one who opened my eyes and made me understand how much I was capable of accomplishing.

I loved Jack, but he confounded me. He had hurt me more than once. He'd essentially ignored me and infuriated me that first morning I had woken up in his bed. I'd been frustrated time and again by his varying degrees of elusiveness, but had ignored the reasons why he was holding a part of himself back.

For all that Jack had said during our call, there was still so much unsaid. He was still holding back from me, and still unwilling to address the issues from our initial argument many weeks earlier. The summer had finally ended, but there had been next to no progress in our relationship.

With everything said and done, I concluded we might never have belonged to one another. We were both in the midst of a transformational time, and now the time had come to move on. I had to move forward, because if I stubbornly hung on to him under the current circumstances I would lose everything. If I forced us to endure one another's presence, day in and day out without being able to love him freely, my love would turn toxic. My love would end up destroying me.

I'd promised myself to remember my mother's coffin, so I turned away from those who were taking their first steps into Oregon and boarded a flight for Colorado ready to see what opportunities awaited me there.

To Be Continued …

Acknowledgements

My long list of thanks begins with Kris, Morgan and Sue, who read this book in all its various stages. They selflessly contributed their time, advice and encouragement, and their wholehearted support of Jack and Kathleen's story convinced me I *could* write a trilogy.

Thank you to my online colleagues at "Argyle Empire" and "Bookish Temptations." As I devoted my attention to writing *Constellation* rather than blogging for AE, Coco, Iris and Mango were amazing. Special thanks also go to Tamie for reading the rawest version of the manuscript and offering a cover quote. You've all been amazing friends since the time we met, and this instance is no exception.

I am grateful to Colleen, who provided editorial direction despite her own hectic schedule. I asked for her help, assuming it was a longshot, and she eagerly took on the project. Her fingerprint is definitively on this book and the story is better as a result.

I also enjoyed my collaboration with Janine and Lauren at Write Divas. Their professionalism as editors is unequivocal and I look forward to working on this series with them. I'd also like to express my gratitude to Marla for her amazing copy edit skills. Carol (aka the Blurb Bitch) did a tremendous favor by drafting the synopsis for this book. Without her help, I'd still be trying to summarize this novel into a few eye-catching paragraphs. JM Walker took on the task of formatting the novel, and it's been a delight to work with someone who wants the inside of my book to be as appealing as the cover.

Jada D'Lee, Gel and Victoria all did something for this story that I never could. Jada's cover design, Gel's tempting illustrations and Victoria's illo have transformed my black and white words into vibrant pictures. The three of you were my top choices as visual artists for *Constellation,* and I'm honored you found this story worthy of your incredible talents.

Christine and Kelley from The Hype PR have been wonderful to work with and have provided me with amazing connections beyond my own personal circles. I love how we've worked together as a team and I can't wait to release other books with your help.

Melissa is not only my sister-in-law, she's also my personal assistant. We've known one another for most of our lives, but we're just beginning this particular journey together. She's a woman who can always get the job done and someone I trust completely. I'm thrilled to no end to have her help moving forward.

Since 2010, I've developed wonderful relationships with many readers, reviewers, bloggers, artists and authors. The people I've met both online and in person provide me with daily inspiration. I can't name you all here, but if we've ever spoken to one another, please know I'm speaking of you now. Because of your friendship, I am happier than I've ever been. My life has been a fantastic whirlwind since you welcomed me into the community. Thank you.

Having said all that, I'm including a special shout out to Ronnie. Beyoncé has nothing on her.

In that place we refer to as real life, I have a full-time career. While many authors fear losing their day jobs and conceal their published works from their employers, my personal experience differs. Not only do my work colleagues encourage my writing, they also allow me to do so under my own name. I wish to express particular thanks to Carrie, Caryl and Valencia. The three of you may not realize it, but the support you have so effortlessly given me is indeed an aberration in my publishing circles.

I need to express my love and appreciation to my children and my mother, who all patiently allow me to pursue random story ideas and all that comes with my writing endeavors. It isn't just about spending hours lost in a Word doc or spending time on social media. It's also about me leaving home on occasion to attend author events and other assorted shenanigans. You are all very good to me, and I hope I'm as good to you in return.

Finally, I wish to thank my husband. Morgan has been by my side ever since our introduction on a dance floor in 1988. Several years ago, he saw a spark of creativity in me and encouraged me to rekindle my connection to storytelling. Thinking about writing a novel is one thing. Sitting down to do so is quite another. Without Morgan's enthusiasm, love and effort to draw me into the spotlight, I guarantee you never would have heard a peep out of me.

~ Jennifer

Author Bio

Jennifer Locklear lives in the Pacific Northwest region of the United States. She married her high school sweetheart, Morgan, in 1995. She is the mother of two children, a son and daughter.

Jennifer enjoyed creative writing as an adolescent, but set aside her favorite hobby to concentrate on college studies, career and family. In 2010, she rediscovered her passion for writing when her husband recruited her to edit his own stories. They co-authored and published their debut novel, *Exposure*, in 2014.

Since 2000, Jennifer has been employed in fundraising and development for a non-profit organization. She has been a contributing reviewer for the "Bookish Temptations" book blog and is a founding moderator of "Argyle Empire," an approved fan site for author Sylvain Reynard. She also enjoys participating in charitable activities, both locally and online.

Constellation is Jennifer's first solo novel.

Team Constellation:
Jennifer Locklear
Website- **http://locklearbooks.com/**
Twitter- @RandomCran **https://twitter.com/RandomCran**
Twitter- @MJLocklear **https://twitter.com/MJLocklear**

Morgan & Jennifer Locklear
Facebook-
https://www.facebook.com/MorganandJenniferLocklear/

Write Divas
Website- **http://www.writedivasediting.com/**

Proofingstyle, Inc.
Website- **http://www.proofingstyle.com/**

The Blurb Bitch
Website- **http://www.blurbbitch.com/**

Just Write. Creations
Facebook-
https://www.facebook.com/justwrite.creations/?pnref=lhc

Jada D'Lee Designs
Website- **http://www.jadadleedesigns.com/**

Tempting Illustrations
Website-
**http://www.temptingillustrations.com/#sthash.bFewra3c.dp
bs**

Ruffles and Restraints
Website- **http://rufflesandrestraints.com/**

The Hype PR
Website- **http://www.thehypepr.net/**

Other Titles Offered by Enchanted Publications

Canada Square by Carrie Elks
Fireworks by Lindsey Gray
Breathe Again by Sydney Logan
Chasing Castles by Jiffy Kate
The Other One by Jiffy Kate
Compass by Jeanne McDonald
Politically Incorrect by Jeanne McDonald
The Contract by Melanie L. Moreland
All Over You by Ayden K. Morgen
Jackson Stiles, Road to Redemption by Jo Richardson

PUBLICATIONS

http://www.enchantedpublications.com
Not where the storyline ends...